THE WILD GARDEN

Kate Mackenzie is on the brink of success as an artist when she meets Gabriel Erskine, twenty-two years her senior. She's not looking for a relationship, but Gabriel's understanding of her paintings and his outlook captivate her. Six months later, she moves into Allansfield, his beautiful house in Fife. The arrival of Gabriel's son, Hugh, with his young child brings the age difference with her lover sharply into focus for Kate. When she realises too that Gabriel has lied to her about the past, Kate begins to wonder if she can ever be fully part of his life — and if this is in any case what she wants.

Love is
a time of enchantment:
in it all days are fair and all fields
green. Youth is blest by it,
old age made benign:
the eyes of love see
roses blooming in December,
and sunshine through rain. Verily
is the time of true-love
a time of enchantment — and
Oh! how eager is woman
to be bewitched!

HARRIET SMART

THE WILD GARDEN

Complete and Unabridged

ULVERSCROFT
Leicester

First published in Great Britain in 1997 by
Headline Book Publishing
London

First Large Print Edition
published 1997
by arrangement with
Headline Book Publishing Limited
a division of
Hodder Headline Plc
London

The right of Harriet Smart to be identified as
the author of this work has been asserted by
her in accordance with the
Copyright, Designs and Patents Act, 1988

British Library CIP Data

Smart, Harriet
    The wild garden.—Large print ed.—
    Ulverscroft large print series: romance
    1. English fiction—20th century
    2. Large type books
    I. Title
    823.9'14 [F]

    ISBN 0–7089–3728–4

Published by
F. A. Thorpe (Publishing) Ltd.
Anstey, Leicestershire
Set by Words & Graphics Ltd.
Anstey, Leicestershire
Printed and bound in Great Britain by
T. J. Press (Padstow) Ltd., Padstow, Cornwall

This book is printed on acid-free paper

1

MELANCHOLY surprised Kate Mackenzie as she packed up her room in Liz's flat. She felt the prick of tears in her eyes as she emptied the cupboards and drawers, trying to cram the debris of several years into the boxes, shovelling the most worn-out of her old clothes into a plastic bin bag. Then, when she came to gather up her painting equipment, a tear actually had the audacity to run down her nose and land ostentatiously on the cover of one of her sketch books. She stared down at it, trying for a moment to be irritated, then sat down on the paint-spattered bentwood chair and permitted herself to cry.

She would never have cried if she had not been alone. If Gabriel had been there, or Liz, or even her mother (perhaps especially her mother), she would not have given in to sentiment. For that was all it was, wasn't it? An agreeably miserable wallow in the past, a necessary rite of passage. She and Liz had had such good times together in that flat in Barclay Terrace, but things like that did not last for ever. They were both moving on. Martin, Kate guessed, would be moving in pretty shortly, and she was going to Gabriel and to Allansfield.

She sniffed hard and wiped her eyes, laughing at herself now. Gabriel and Allansfield — there was nothing to cry about there. She was not being turned out on her ear into the freezing streets. She was going to live with Gabriel Erskine in his country house in Fife.

She got up and began to throw tubes of oil paint and brushes into a large green shoebox, wondering if she ought to stock up with more paint before she left, and then remembered that Gabriel had assured her there was a good art supply shop in St Andrews. "There is civilisation beyond Edinburgh, you know, Kate," he had said with a smile. He was right, of course, and she needed to be weaned off Edinburgh. She had never lived anywhere else, and she knew this showed a distinct lack of curiosity on her part. Her contemporaries in the Fine Art honours class at Edinburgh College of Art had scattered far and wide in the four years since graduation — some to London, some to New York, but many of them had gone to Glasgow. Kate went to see them sometimes and had been quite tempted by their spacious studios in old warehouses. Being in Glasgow seemed to do great things for their careers. Yet the moment she was back in Edinburgh, she had always known Glasgow would not suit her. Edinburgh, she had found, fed her imagination — and so, with a bit of luck, would Allansfield.

* * *

Falling in love with Gabriel had been a strange business. Kate had not intended it to happen. She had not been in the mood for getting involved with anyone. She had just broken up messily with an abstract expressionist called Simon, whose attitude to commitment had been as sloppy as his brushwork. She had, as a result, adopted a hostile attitude to men. Yet at the private view for the

Manzoni Gallery Winter Show she has been fascinated to see a striking man, looking at the two large pictures that she had persuaded Sandra Manzoni (with some difficulty) to put in the show.

He had been, at first, looking at her *Pandora*, tapping his catalogue gently on his chin as he read every detail of the composition, his lips fixed in a careful line of concentration, his eyes never wavering, one arm folded across his chest. Then he'd rocked slightly and moved on to *Triptych*, glancing back at *Pandora* as he did.

Kate had tried to be inconspicuous. She even pretended to study one of the large abstract spatters that hung nearby, but she kept glancing at this man, who appeared quite rooted to the spot in front of her picture. She moved beside him and pretended to look at *Pandora*. She heard him stir slightly, and took as long a look at him as she dared. She found herself looking longer than she had meant to. His face was interesting. It was not the look of concentration which impressed her most, but the physical quality of his features: they were somewhat craggy,

4

seeming worn by age and experience. Kate wanted at once to paint him, and wished she had the cheek to suggest it — for it was clear he liked what he saw in front of him. She knew she should have had no qualms about jumping for a bit of business. She could see from the cut of his dark, elegant suit and his gold cuff-links that he was well-off, but she held her tongue. She did not wish to break the spell of his looking.

He realised that she was standing beside him. With an elegant gesture of his catalogue he surrendered *Triptych* to her attention, as if he did not like to hog it. He'll move on now, she thought; but he moved back to *Pandora*. I ought to say something; he might want to buy it. I might actually have a customer here. But her throat was dry.

"These really are the best things in the show," he said suddenly. "Why they hang such gems down here, I don't know."

He was speaking to her, and she knew she ought to come up with some appropriate response. All she could manage was a foolish grin, and the odd thought that his voice was as interesting

5

as his face: a little hesitant, a little husky, but very expressive.

"Do you know the painter?" he said, looking at the catalogue. "Kate Mackenzie — is that it?"

"Yes, Kate Mackenzie," she said, managing to speak. "I do know her — well, I mean to say — that's me . . ."

"Ahh . . ." he said, and nodded to her in a fashion which in a more ceremonious age she might have mistaken for a bow. "Then, many congratulations."

He had introduced himself and they had begun to talk about her pictures. He was knowledgeable about painting without being pretentious. She sensed at once he understood what she was trying to do in her work, and she began to bask in the agreeable glow of his intelligent appreciation. Then he had made her jump out of her skin by telling her he was going to buy them both.

"Both?" she said. "Are you sure?"

She wanted to add: Do you know how much they are? But he, as if reading her mind, said, "I think they are bargains at a grand a piece."

Kate grinned, recalling the conversations she had had with Sandra Manzoni over the price. "Your pictures are too large, Kate. People don't have room for such big pieces. You're more likely to sell at a lower price — seven hundred and fifty, perhaps." She was glad she had stuck to her guns over a thousand.

"Well, my bank manager is going to like me," she had said, "for a change."

After the sale had been settled, with Sandra Manzoni fluttering and crowing with delight, he had asked, with a certain amount of diffidence, whether she would like to go for dinner somewhere. She found she could not resist this request. She wanted to celebrate — and it was business after all. Perhaps, she thought, she might get commission from him.

They went to a fish restaurant which Kate had often walked past with envious glances, feeling she would never be rich enough or smart enough to eat there. That night, she had felt quite comfortable amongst the art-deco panelling and glowing lamps. She was wearing her best clothes, and, now she had become used to the idea that she was an artist who actually sold pictures, she felt she had a right to be there. Or was that feeling of confidence due entirely to the lovely cold Chardonnay? They had drunk a bottle down pretty swiftly (hardly very difficult from those vast glasses), and it was settling on her empty stomach with incredible ease. She felt beautifully relaxed and not at all as if she were out with a stranger. Perhaps it was not the wine at all; perhaps it was Gabriel Erskine. He had the knack of making her feel quite at home with him.

They had finished their first course, the bottle of wine and a very good conversation about food, when Gabriel leant back against the banquette, stretching his arm along the back of it, and smiled, most contentedly. "That's the best smoked salmon I've had in ages. It so rarely has any taste these days."

Kate finished her last mouthful of prawns in saffron sauce and smiled. "I wish I had such a long perspective on the matter."

"I am very spoilt in that respect," he said. "We used to have wonderful smoked salmon at Allansfield — that's my house in Fife. It came from my mother's family, up in Argyll. They had their own smokehouse on the estate, but then my cousins had to sell the place in the sixties. A great shame really."

"I wonder if it really tasted that good," said Kate, leaning her elbows on the table and resting her chin on her knotted hands, trying not to be overawed by his casual references to country estates. "Or is that just nostalgia?"

"The young can be very cruel, can't they?" he said, reaching out and refilling her glass. "Well, just you wait — you will have your own sacred notions to be disabused of . . . " He smiled. "Probably, it didn't taste any different. I just associate it with the wonderful holidays we used to have up there when I was a child."

"That is definitely nostalgia," she said.

"All right," he said. "Your turn. What do you remember eating as a child?"

"Oh, sherbert dabs and Refreshers!" she said flippantly, and then grimaced. "But there's nothing interesting to remember really," she went on. "The Mackenzies are such a very dull family."

9

"I can't believe that. How could they have produced you?"

"Oh, I'm dull too," she said airily, with a slight wave of the glass. "It's only my work that's interesting. The rest of me is a mess."

"A mess is not the same as dull," he said.

"You can have a dull mess rather than an interesting mess. I'm a dull mess."

He laughed and said, "If you insist."

She took another great mouthful of wine and considered her family for a moment. "Well, I suppose they're not so dull, my family."

"Tell me about them."

"Well, my mother's a recently retired civil servant and my sister, Fiona, she's a junior doctor, in Manchester."

"And your father?"

"He's dead, died three years ago now."

"I'm sorry," he said.

She glanced up at him, realising he was about the same age as her father when he died. But her father in her recollection seemed a great deal older. She shrugged, and went on, "The worst thing about my family is they're all very

10

public spirited. Dad was a civil servant too. And what am I — a bloody artist!" She grinned. "I used to pretend I was adopted, but unfortunately I look very like my mother."

"Then she must be good looking."

"That's dreadful!" she said, and laughed to cover her surprise. His remark, she felt, had crossed that invisible line from ordinary friendliness into the realms of flirtation.

He laughed too, and nervously. "Yes, that was a little glib, but I couldn't resist it," he said. "Will you forgive me?"

"Of course," she said.

"It's just my inexperience," he went on.

"Inexperience?" she queried.

"Oh God, you don't think I am, do you?" he said. "Oh, but I can imagine how this might appear . . . " He began to laugh, and covered his mouth with his hand to compose himself as the waiter brought the next course. When the waiter had gone, he said, "Please excuse me. It's just I hadn't quite cast myself in that role — the disgusting old divorcé sinking his fangs into an innocent girl."

"Well, I am not an innocent girl. I'm twenty-six," said Kate calmly.

He stared at her. "Goodness, you're the same age as my son." He put down his knife and fork and thought for a moment. "But really, I am sorry, I didn't mean to appear to be . . . how do I put this? Pushy?"

"You're not," said Kate. "I wouldn't be here if I didn't want to be, would I?"

"But I don't like the thought that . . . "

"I wouldn't worry," said Kate, dipping a potato into the buttery juices of the halibut. "I mean, we're having fun aren't we? Isn't that all that matters?" She found she was rather proud of herself for saying this. She felt excited and altogether quite reckless.

"You're absolutely right," he said, smiling broadly. His smile was magnificent. She tried to picture him as he would have been at her age, and realised it was time that had made his face so interesting. Then he would have been just another handsome young man with not half the assurance he had now.

She had recounted the evening the next

day to Liz, who promptly labelled him the Angel Gabriel, because Kate had made him sound so perfect. It did seem almost impossible that anyone could be quite so perfect, and Kate felt apprehensive about their next meeting — they had decided to go and see *The Magic Flute* together. As she got ready to go, she found herself wishing it were possible to hover forever on the brink of expectation, at that impulse of first attraction, the equivalent of that delicious moment before the roller-coaster plunges downwards. She was nervous of going on, although she wanted to. What if she found out something awful about him? What if he had lied, and did in fact still have a wife, as well as a string of mistresses? Perhaps he had some obnoxious sexual habit for her to discover; surely that was not at all impossible for someone of his background? Weren't boarding schools and nannies supposed to do strange things to people?

Her nerves were not helped a great deal when Martin, Liz's boyfriend, informed her that Gabriel Erskine was probably one of the wealthiest men in Scotland. Martin worked for a pukka firm of chartered accountants, and Gabriel turned out to be a client.

"It's steel money of course," said Martin. "And ships. The family made a killing with nationalisation, and the amazing thing is they've held on to it. He's very canny, apparently."

"Well that explains why he could spend two thousand quid without blinking," said Liz.

Kate felt disappointed. It was as if her pictures were trifles to him, which had required him to make no sacrifices. But at the theatre, just before the lights went down and the overture began, Gabriel told her that he had spent two days moving the pictures around at Allansfield so that he could find a good spot for *Pandora*.

"I'm afraid there was no room for *Triptych* though — and anyway it would have been selfish of me to keep them both — so I've sent that off to the Erskine-Lennox trust."

"What's that?"

"It's a rather charming trust my grandfather set up. It sends pictures all over Scotland, to places that don't have collections of their own — schools, hospitals, village halls, that sort of thing. Do you mind?"

"Mind?" said Kate, a little incredulously. "It sounds like the sort of thing painters dream about."

As the performance proceeded, she realised she was sinking fast. She had felt profoundly comfortable, knowing that he was watching the action with the same attention as her. When, almost at the end, Pamina and Tamino sang their duet, with the accompaniment of throbbing strings, she could not resist glancing at him. He had the same thought and turned to her, reached out for her hand, squeezed it gently for a moment and then let go again. It was an instant of pure communication that she had never experienced with a man before.

★ ★ ★

Kate had just finished wrapping up the last of her unfinished paintings when the doorbell rang. She went to answer it, knowing it would be either her mother or Gabriel. It proved to be her mother.

She came into the flat, a little breathless from the three flights of stairs, carrying two large shopping bags.

"I'm not going to miss those stairs, you know," she said. She put down the bags in the hall. "How's the packing going?" Before Kate had a chance to answer, she added, "You've been crying."

It was useless to deny it. "Just nerves, I suppose," Kate said with a shrug.

"Well, I'd be nervous in your shoes," said Mrs Mackenzie, following Kate into the kitchen.

"Well, I think it's a good sign," said Kate. "I mean, you should feel nervous doing something important — and this is important."

Kate appreciated the fact that her mother said nothing at this point. It had taken Mrs Mackenzie a while to get used to the idea of Kate going out with a man who was twenty-two years her senior. The first time Kate had taken him to the house in Craiglockhart Loan, she had almost visibly blenched at the sight of him. It had been ironic really. Gabriel was

16

probably the first respectable-looking male Kate had brought home to her mother, and yet she could see in Mrs Mackenzie's panic-stricken eyes that she would have preferred an unshaven yob with Doc Martens and ripped jeans sprawling on the sofa in the front room to this forty-eight year old.

"What's in the bags?" Kate asked as she made the tea.

"Just some family things I thought you ought to have," said Mrs Mackenzie. "Things your father would have wanted you to have when you left home."

"I left home four years ago," Kate pointed out. "Don't you mean when I got married?"

"Yes, I suppose I do, and since this seems to be the nearest you're going to get to that just now . . . " she said with a sigh.

"Would you prefer it if we were getting married, Mum?" said Kate. "If we were engaged or something?"

"Yes," said her mother. "Frankly, Kate, I would. I wouldn't feel you were rushing into things so. You've only known him six

17

months. You can't really know someone in that time."

"So that's why I'm moving in with him, isn't it?" said Kate. "I can't think of a better way to get to know someone than living with them, properly living with him."

"I suppose that's the way people arrange things these days," said her mother. "But it still surprises me that he should suggest it."

"Gabriel didn't suggest it. We came to a mutual decision."

Kate saw again that her mother was biting her tongue. She was only five years older than Gabriel, but the psychological gap between them seemed far wider sometimes than their own twenty-two-year gap. Besides, Kate never thought of Gabriel as being old — he was merely older than her. He never pulled rank on her in respect of age. That was one of the things she liked about him most of all: he never patronised her, never suggested that he knew any better about anything than she did, except perhaps in the matter of Latin names for plants, which amused her. His pride in his botanical knowledge was endearing.

She went into the hall and looked into the bags. There were some old books that had belonged to her father, and other, less identifiable items, carefully wrapped up in newspaper.

"They're nothing special," said her mother. "But you should have them. And I dare say Gabriel will have more room for them than I do."

Kate wondered if Mrs Mackenzie had quite understood how large Allansfield actually was. The way Gabriel talked about it sometimes made it sound like nothing more than a farmhouse. She was going to get a shock when she first saw the place, just as Kate had done.

Kate lifted out one of the newspaper packages and unwrapped it. Inside she found an old brass candlestick.

"They belonged to your grandparents," said her mother. "Fiona's got the other."

"Thanks, Mum," said Kate, realising that the candlestick meant Mrs Mackenzie would, with time, accept the situation with Gabriel. "I really do appreciate this." Her mother smiled briefly and went into the chaos of Kate's half-packed-up room. Kate, following her, went on, "And I am sure about this, absolutely sure that this is the right thing for me. I'm crazy about Gabriel, and Allansfield is the most fabulous place . . . "

Her mother, who had automatically begun folding a jumper, looked up and said wryly, "Oh, Kate, are you sure that 'crazy' is quite the right word to use to your old disapproving mother?"

2

GABRIEL ERSKINE came out of his meeting, bubbling with nervousness. It was a feeling that took him straight back to Cambridge, to a curiously sultry October day at the beginning of the 1967 academic year. He had been running over from Trinity to Newnham, his stomach crippled with a potent mixture of fear and anticipation at the prospect of seeing Henrietta again for the first time in three months. She had been back to America to spend the summer with her family, and the passionate correspondence they had conducted across the Atlantic took their relationship to new heights. Their future together had seemed so dazzling that he had begun to wonder whether he could actually bear it. He had stood twitching outside her door for several moments before actually daring to knock and go in.

Now Gabriel stopped short in George

Street, mystified that he should remember that. He did not often think about Henrietta — he had schooled himself not to think about her — and the circumstances today were hardly similar.

He distracted himself quickly by going into Liberty's, noticing in the window a display of sweaters knitted in a hundred dazzling colours. He decided to buy one for Kate, in exchange for a jumper she had stolen from him and to which she seemed very attached. The thought of reclaiming it after she had worn it so much was irresistible. He realised it was the sort of sentimental logic better suited to a sixteen year old than a man nearing fifty, but the impulse was strong. He picked out a jumper that glowed with all the colours of autumn, which he hoped would match her extraordinary dark red-gold hair.

"You're going to be popular," said the girl, as he handed over his credit card. "Is this for someone special?"

Someone special. It was a birthday-card commonplace, a phrase so wastefully used it had lost any real meaning. How could he begin to answer such a question? He managed a grin, and he wondered if he had looked slightly guilty, for the girl responded with a smile that seemed to say, "Ah, you're an old dog, aren't you?" Perhaps she was used to helping Edinburgh businessmen buy presents for their mistresses. Well, if that was how it looked, he could do nothing about it.

Further along George Street, looking into the windows of Hamilton & Inches, he saw an art-nouveau pendant that might have been made for Kate, but resisted the temptation to go in. He disliked this urge in himself to heap adornments on her, as if she were some common flirt who demanded to be placated with trinkets. Kate could not be less like that. Besides, it was hardly appropriate to go into Hamilton & Inches. He had too vivid a memory of going there with Jane to choose her engagement ring.

Henrietta, and now Jane. Well, was it really so surprising that he should remember them today, when he stood on the brink of this new life with Kate? He had waited a quarter of a century, after all, to find another woman who roused in him the same strength of feeling as Henrietta. If the world did not find his choice particularly rational or honourable, he was determined not to let that spoil it. He had not meant to fall in love with Kate, after all. He had, at first, actively tried to stop himself from doing so. He had meant only to be a kind, disinterested patron — but the sheer force of her personality, her razor-sharp mind and her determined creativity had overwhelmed him. He had fallen profoundly in love.

Gabriel had been suffering from a mild bout of depression the evening he met Kate. He had been stuck in Edinburgh for a couple of days, tied up in various meetings, and wanted to be back at Allansfield. He'd wondered if this alienation, this sudden attack of childish insecurity, was simply another warning sign of imminent old age. No, not old age, he corrected himself — middle age. He was approaching the half century and was determined that would only be a half-way marker. He fancied himself going for the hundred, standing at life's wicket with all the endurance of a first-class batsman, ploughing on steadily and carefully to get a century.

No, it was not old age that made him feel like that: it was Christmas. That afternoon — or what was left of it after the long trustees' lunch which always followed the morning's meeting — he had decided to amuse himself by doing a little early Christmas shopping. He usually left it until the week before, with a frantic dash about Edinburgh. The shops were already decked up in their relentless Christmas finery (probably they had been for months), and although he managed to solve one or two awkward problems, the laboured jollity of it all began to wear him down. Being unattached at Christmas had a feeling of perversity about it, when large, brightly coloured photographs showed couples exchanging their consumerist orgy of presents. It was like a sharp dig in the ribs demanding to know why he had not conformed. It was a question he could answer easily enough, at least superficially. When people did ask, he had his answer ready: simply that he had not recently met anyone whom he liked enough to get involved with. This was not strictly the truth, of course, but whoever answers such questions truthfully? It was an answer he gave to close the subject rather than to enlighten anyone. How could they begin to understand how comfortable he had become with solitude?

Yet that night he could not manage to be comfortable with himself. Returning to the flat in Drummond Place, he had longed suddenly for companionship, for a burst of idle chatter to break the silence. He sat, wanting someone to emerge from the bathroom, wrapped in a towel, with dripping hair and rosy skin; someone to suggest where they might go for dinner after the private view, or perhaps someone who would give him the perfect excuse for not going to the private view at all.

With a sigh, and annoyed at his self-indulgent mood, he had gone and sorted through the carrier bags of presents he'd dumped in the hall when he came in. He took out a large glossy book on Early Renaissance paintings — intended for Hugh, his son — and flipped through it. The pictures made him remember with a smile the awkwardness of a visit to Italy he had made with his parents when he was about seventeen. They had seemed woefully out of place to him, gawkishly provincial, as if they had never left Scotland before in their lives. All the time they had spent in India seemed quite forgotten. Allansfield had enclosed and protected them to such a degree that they could not see beyond its own peculiar brand of civilisation any more. It was the same with him now, he supposed.

He had closed the book, after a long lingering look at the Giotto painting of St Anne greeting St Joachim at the golden gate with the momentous news of her pregnancy. Yes, he would go to Italy next spring. His grandmother had once told him that his grandfather always used to say: "If I don't get to Italy every few years, my soul might dry up." His grandmother had died the day the Allies liberated Monte Cassino. It was the last piece of news he was told. In fact, this story had been told to Gabriel both by his grandfather and Aunt Chloe. It was part of the Erskines' own Golden Legend. He could hear his aunt's voice still: "I had heard the news on the BBC and went up to tell him. He was in the West Room, and mother was sitting there holding his hand. I took the other and said, 'Daddy dearest, Monte Cassino — we have it back. Isn't that good news?' And I think he smiled, and a few minutes later . . . " Her voice had trembled even then, twenty or more years after the event, as if it had only just happened, as if she had just come down the stairs to the drawing room to tell everyone the great Ralph Erskine was dead.

You live too much in the past, Gabriel, he had told himself. It was like being haunted sometimes, with all those intricate threads of family history wrapped about him. Well, a visit to Sandra Manzoni's gallery would bring him back to the present. The previous show he had been to had featured sculptures made out of barbed wire and sprayed with psychedelic paint. Mrs Manzoni always took a broad view of contemporary art. It was as if she expected her customers to sort out the dross from the genius according to their own terms. She simply provided the spectacle — and a little circus was just what he needed.

When he had first shaken hands with Kate, her palm had felt hot, as hot as her pink cheeks suggested. He had watched her flushing when he praised her pictures. It was a delicious natural pink flush, of the sort that could only settle on young skin. He found he could not switch to the automatic avuncular-cum-paternal feeling that he felt he should extend to a girl of that age. He had corrected himself — she was not a girl. She was well beyond that — she was a young woman, or at least he tried to think of her as that. He felt he was juggling words to justify what were really quite inappropriate feelings. She was young and very attractive to him. Feeling the heat in her palm was like touching at the quick of life, and he had hardly wanted to let go of her hand.

He had managed though, and turned back to the pictures, hoping they would distract him. Of course they did not. They could only amplify that extraordinary feeling of attraction. He stared, hypnotised by the dancing figures who moved across the three panels of *Triptych*, in a composition so fluid and elegant that he seemed to hear the music of it.

"It's a dance of life, this one, really," she had explained. "If you look, all the plants are in season — at least, I think I've got them all right. Snowdrops, then daffodils, then lilies and roses, and then fruit and autumn leaves." She pointed them out to him.

"You must be a gardener," he said. "They're all quite right."

"Oh, I've no garden," she said.

"You should have. I could imagine you would be a great gardener. I've often thought — I'm a gardener myself — that gardening is the closest most of us get to painting."

"Not in my mother's garden," she said with a laugh. "That's all straight lines and raked red chippings. It's so neat I'm surprised anything as unruly as a plant is allowed in there. But I like the way plants just go mad sometimes and just can't stop growing for the life of them."

He had nodded, thinking of the lush, overgrown spaces of the wild garden at Allansfield in the height of summer. He wished suddenly that he could take her hand and lead her into it, on a warm June night, when it was full of scents and insects and gauzy light.

"That's the difference perhaps," he said, "between painting and gardening. With a picture you are always in control, I imagine; but with a garden, it's something of a lottery. You never know quite how something will grow. You must always be more of a master of your materials."

"Oh, I don't think it's so different," she smiled. "No matter how much you plan a thing, it never quite works out the way you wanted it. There is always another element creeping in that won't behave itself. That's the magic again, perhaps."

He had returned to Drummond Place that night feeling a massive surge of adrenalin, although he was thoroughly ashamed of himself. She was the same age as Hugh. He had no business pursuing her, but he wanted to do nothing else. He thought of the other women with whom he had been mildly involved in the past few years. None of them had provoked anything like the feelings that

Kate had woken in him in the course of a single evening. He had not felt such a violent tug of attraction since he had first met Henrietta at that sherry party in Cambridge. That had pulled him up short. He even wondered if he had the strength for something like that. Women like Henrietta only appeared once in a lifetime, surely.

* * *

Now, Gabriel walked from George Street to Bruntsfield, by way of the Old Town and the Meadows. The exercise, on a perfectly crisp April day, was exhilarating, and as he approached Barclay Terrace across the windswept reaches of Bruntsfield Links he felt any last remnants of self-doubt and guilt blow away. In the distance, he could see Kate coming out from the door of the tenement block carrying a large box. He ran to help her.

"I'm not a weakling," she protested as he wrested it out of her arms.

"It's just my guilty conscience," he said, putting it into the back of the

Range Rover where there was already a pile of boxes. "Looks like I've missed all the hard work."

"Yes, this is just about the last of it," she said. "How was your meeting?"

"Dull," he said, kissing her on the forehead. He would have kissed her on the lips but he saw Valerie Mackenzie and Liz coming out into the street. "Hello, there!" he called out. The sight of Kate's mother always unnerved him, although their relations had always been perfectly cordial. Her forbearance had been frankly remarkable. It could not have been an easy situation for her to accept. She was holding a heavy-looking bag and he went to relieve her of it; but she only surrendered it with a certain reluctance, almost as if the bag were Kate herself.

"That's the last of it," said Liz, shoving a plastic bag into the back. Kate slammed the door shut. The two women looked at each other for a moment and then Liz suddenly flung her arms around Kate and exclaimed, "Oh, Katie, I'm going to miss you so much!"

"I'll miss you too," said Kate.

They were almost in tears.

"Come and stay soon then," Gabriel said, "won't you? Both of you," he added, including Valerie Mackenzie in his invitation.

"You bet we will," said Liz, letting go of Kate at last.

"And there is the telephone," Gabriel pointed out.

"Of course!" said Kate. "And I shan't miss cleaning the bathroom after you." She turned to her mother, hugged her briefly and then jumped into the passenger seat. "Let's go, shall we?"

"It seems I have my orders," said Gabriel, and got into the car.

As they pulled into the Lothian Road traffic, Kate said, "I'm determined not to be sentimental."

He laughed. "You can be if you like. I don't mind. Of course you're going to miss them. I feel very selfish taking you away like this."

"You're not taking me away. I'm going of my own volition. It's time I went. I'm ready for an adventure," she said, and laid her hand on his knee for a moment.

"An adventure — is that what this is?" he said.

"Don't you think so?" she said.

He glanced at her. She looked to him suddenly like nothing more than a child, sitting there with her red-gold hair lying loosely over her shoulders, shining magnificently against the dull grey of the jersey she had stolen from him. Adventure was not the word he would have chosen. It did not fit with the idea of the long idyll with Kate at Allansfield that he had been imagining, which he saw as the end to an adventure, rather than the beginning of one. An adventure had an element of uncertainty to it that he could not quite relish. He swallowed for a second and said, "Well, yes. I suppose you might look at it like that," and turned his mind quickly to the matter of negotiating the junction at Tollcross.

3

AFTER a week Kate felt she was beginning to adjust to the facts of life at Allansfield. There was an ordered quality to Gabriel's life there that she had not guessed at during her previous weekend visits. During the week he had a routine from which, although he had not exactly set it in stone, Kate sensed he would not be easily diverted. After breakfast (always at eight o'clock — he woke up around seven, invariably), Kate had noticed, he would refill his coffee cup, pick up his copy of the *Financial Times*, and go from the kitchen into the library to deal with the morning's post, of which there was always a substantial amount. Only when the post was opened and dealt with, and any necessary telephone calls made or letters drafted, did he permit himself the indulgence of reading the *Financial Times*, and then only for half an hour. After that the garden or the nursery or the estate office claimed him until lunchtime.

Kate found it hard to equal this exact self-discipline. She knew she should start painting again, she knew she wanted to, but she could not establish her own routine. Her life in Edinburgh had been very busy and yet disorderly. If she was consumed by an idea for a painting she would do nothing else for days but work on it, and then, when she was satisfied, she would vegetate for a while, exhausted by creative effort, until the next big idea hit her or someone asked her to marble their kitchen cabinets or teach water-colour sketching to old ladies in Morningside. It was strange that now she had exactly what she wanted — the financial freedom to do nothing but pursue her painting — she should be so lacking in motivation. She sat in the library, nursing her own cup of coffee, watching Gabriel at his desk, hoping that some of his self-discipline would rub off on her.

Yet, instead of finding the will to get up from her chair, she found her mind drifting instead. How was Gabriel able to work in that room? It was distractingly beautiful. It was one of the more intimate rooms in the house, with some of the best pictures in it, as well as a tempting glazed door to the terrace. There were low book shelves around the walls, on top of which a mixture of objects was on display, from exquisite little bronzes and ancient Chinese bowls to family photographs and potted spring flowers. Kate found herself focusing on the photograph nearest to her — a recent one, taken at the christening of Gabriel's grandson. It showed Hugh, and his wife Lara, with Gabriel's ex-wife Jane standing between them (a triumphant grandmother if ever Kate had seen one), holding Andrew, who looked red-faced and thoroughly furious in a christening robe that was dripping with antique lace. Kate had been a little surprised, if not disturbed, to see a picture of Gabriel's ex-wife on prominent display, until he had explained to her all about Jane and about their brief and disastrous marriage, which had fallen apart in the early seventies. She squinted at the picture and wondered what Jane must have looked like then. In the photograph she looked exactly like what she was: a successful QC's wife, dressed in a smart but entirely predictable crisp, pink Chanel-style suit, her gold hair neatly styled under her hat. She was still good looking. At twenty or so she would have been very pretty indeed, and she was almost as tall and leggy as Lara Erskine beside her. Yet Kate could not quite imagine Gabriel being drawn to a girl because of good legs and a pretty face. Kate wondered what had attracted him. He had said that he'd married Jane thinking he was in love, and then found he was not, and that they simply did not have enough in common to keep the thing going. Perhaps she had been too conventional for him — and yet Gabriel was extremely conventional in many ways — Kate only had to think of those immaculate, conservative dark suits of his hanging in the wardrobe in the dressing room upstairs to realise that. But there was so much about him that seemed entirely at odds with Allansfield and all its paraphernalia. She smiled, finding herself remembering the first time they had made love.

They had been out to lunch, a long,

self-indulgent, rather alcoholic lunch, and then she had invited him back to Barclay Terrace to show him some sketches she had done. They had walked through the Meadows from the Old Town together, talking quite happily, and yet the moment that they reached the door of the flat nervousness had seized them, as if they both realised what was happening. Standing in the hall, there had been a awful moment of hesitant awkwardness as they took stock of each other.

"So this is where you live," he said, and suddenly he thrust out his hands and grabbed hers.

"Yes, this is it," she said.

He had pulled her to him and kissed her on each cheek and then on the lips. She could not resist flinging her arms around him and holding him very tight, as if afraid he might slip away. She sensed his surprise and then the sudden relief in him as he responded, relaxing also.

"Here we are then," she had managed to say. She found her voice was breathy with excitement.

"Yes, here we are," he said. He'd

looked at her for a moment, stroked her hair, and sighed heavily. She saw him close his eyes as he came to press another kiss, this time on her forehead. They resumed their embrace. It had felt very intense. Their frustration crackled in the air like static electricity. She felt her whole body begin to throb with desire.

He was kissing her neck, and he muttered, "I want you, you know. I shouldn't but I do."

"Then let's do it," she said. "There's no one here." She pulled him towards the door of her room.

"Are you sure?" he asked. "Your flatmate . . ."

"At work. Come on." He was shaking his head, but laughing. "Come on. Are you a coward, Gabriel?" she said, highly amused and yet touched by his sudden diffidence.

"Don't you dare call me that," he said with mock fury.

"Then come on," she said.

By the time they got into her room they were laughing hysterically, drunk with anticipation and their own audacity. In a matter of seconds she had fallen back on to the bed, with him on top of her. The bed springs creaked wonderfully, provoking them into another fit of laughter. It had been quite absurd, and then in a moment the absurdity had vanished, as they had looked suddenly into one another's eyes and realised that there was something serious going on between them.

His lovemaking had been as vigorous and as lustful as she had dreamed — and she had been dreaming of him, she realised — but he had combined it with all the tenderness of his beautiful manners, so that she had never quite forgotten that he was still a fascinating person. It had not just been wonderful sex — there had been more to it than that, a strange fusion of spirit as well as body.

★ ★ ★

"I'm afraid I have to go," Gabriel said now, getting up from his desk. He turned and smiled at her apologetically.

Kate stretched up her arms to him, provoked by her memories, wondering if she could persuade him to abandon his plans and come upstairs and make love instead. She wound her arms around him as he bent to kiss her, and he responded, but after a moment detached himself, saying, "I really must get down to the estate office and catch up on some of that paperwork. Not that I want to, but . . . "

"Of course," said Kate. "It's your job, isn't it? Besides, I've been trying to psych myself up into doing some painting."

"Then get to it," he said, reaching out and pushing his hand through her hair. "I can't persuade you to change your mind about tonight though, can I?"

"Oh, your gardening society thing?" she said with a smile, remembering that Gabriel had been booked months ago to speak at some horticultural society in St Andrews. She feigned a yawn and said, "You'll have to give me some time to get obsessed with a garden."

"I'm not worried — I know it's a highly infectious condition." And he kissed her again, this time only on the forehead. "I'll see you at lunch, then."

After he had gone she continued to

sit for a while, finding herself attacked by exactly the indolence she had feared. At length she decided she must make an effort, or else fall asleep. She would have to go upstairs and attempt to get to work again.

She wandered along the passageway from the library into the large hall. Hearing the sound of vacuuming coming from the drawing room, she went over to see who was in there. More procrastination, she knew, but it did not quite seem right to walk past, ignoring the cleaners, Carol and Betty, as if they did not exist.

It was Carol, the younger of the two, wielding the vacuum cleaner — rather fiercely, Kate could not help thinking — over that faded, rather fragile carpet, while Alison, Gabriel's housekeeper, was polishing the front of a marquetry bureau with considerably more care. There was a basket of dusters and cleaning equipment on the floor, and Kate's instinct was to grab a duster and join in. Not, however, that the room even needed dusting. It was not a room that got used much. The real living room was upstairs, in the old smoking room, which retained, as its name suggested, a good deal of gentlemanly comfort about it.

Carol switched off the vacuum cleaner suddenly and saw Kate standing there. Kate, feeling like a spare part, managed to smile at her.

"Oh, was there something you wanted, Miss Mackenzie?" asked Alison.

"No, no, I was just . . . er . . . " She gave up attempting to explain. "Passing through. I'll be upstairs if anyone needs me. In the day nursery."

"Yes, of course," said Alison, resuming her polishing.

Kate left the room, annoyed that she had not had the guts to call the nursery her studio, because that was what it was going to be. At least, in theory it was. Gabriel had been full of ideas on this matter. He had talked about getting a room in the old stables converted for her, but she had been quite happy, when she had first seen it, to settle for what he had called the day nursery. It was a plain, square room at the end of the passageway, with a large north window overlooking the gardens behind the house. What had appealed to her was that, unlike anywhere else in the house (except possibly the kitchen and the bathrooms), this room had furniture in it that did not look valuable and lino on its floor. When she had first seen it she had been sure she would be able to work very well there. Looking at it now, she did not feel so certain.

The room, he had told her, had not been much used since Hugh was a child. Before that, Gabriel had used it. Thinking of that, she found her mind straying back to the photograph of Hugh and his family in the library, wondering when she would meet them. According to Gabriel they usually came up from London for a few weeks in the summer. She wondered what Hugh felt about his father's new girlfriend, and whether they would get on when they did meet. She decided that since he was a potter he could not be an entirely alien spirit; and his wife, Lara, the Polish dress designer, sounded intriguing.

She decided she was going to get her unfinished picture of Adam out and on to the easel, so that it would dominate the room and focus her mind. Like all the rest of the house, this room, for all its plainness, struck her as distinguished. The soft green of the paintwork might be a little chipped, the sunny yellow-painted plaster walls cracking here and there, and the gingham green and white curtains bleached in places — but she had the same feeling of distraction, as if everything was so perfect already she had no need to add anything to it by her efforts.

She laid the package containing the panels on the table, and began to undo the fastening strings. On top was the black panel for Eve, which she lifted up and put on one side. Beneath it, protected by a gruesome old towel, was *Adam*. Gently, because she felt the moment should have a little ceremony attached to it, she removed the towel.

She looked at it hard, realising it still needed a great deal of work. Her mind flashed back to the James Henderson that she had just passed hanging on the stairs. She would have to work very intensely to get up to that standard, and she did not feel quite capable of it. She was wondering how to start when the door opened behind her. She turned, expecting it to be Gabriel, but to her surprise a man, carrying a small child, strode in confidently, saying, "Let's see if we can find you something to play with here, Andrew."

Kate found to her embarrassment that she had let out a squawk of surprise. He stopped in his tracks when he saw and heard her.

"Oh. I'm so sorry . . . I didn't expect there to be anyone in here."

Kate knew at once from the photograph that this was Hugh, Gabriel's son. In the flesh the resemblance to Gabriel was striking, although he was about a head taller, and he wore his dark hair long and wild. What he was doing there she could not guess, and it felt downright peculiar that he should appear just when she had been thinking about him.

"That's OK," she managed to say. "You just gave me a start, that's all," she said.

"You must be Kate," he said. Andrew, in his arms, was babbling and struggling.

Hugh dumped him down on the floor and he teetered for a few steps before reverting to a crawl. "Dad's told me all about you."

"And vice versa," said Kate, shaking his hand. "And hello, Andrew." Andrew was gripping her legs. She reached down and touched the soft pale hair of his head. "This is quite a surprise."

"Well, yes, I know — we only came up from London yesterday," Hugh said. "I had an I-can't-stand-being-in-London-anymore fit, so I closed the workshop and drove like a madman all the way up the M1. And it was worth it," he added, looking around him with satisfaction. "Though Lara's still lying in bed looking as if I've subjected her to g-forces."

"Are you staying at your cottage?" Kate asked. Gabriel had told her that he had given Hugh and Lara a cottage on the estate as a wedding present. He nodded and she ventured, with a smile, "You're sure you haven't come to check me out?"

He laughed. "It might look like that, I suppose, but it wasn't meant that way. I knew what to expect, you see.

49

I know we're exact contemporaries, both twenty-six."

"You got over the shock, you mean. Actually, you're a month or two younger, I think," said Kate. She found she was vaguely shocked herself. Seeing Hugh and Andrew in the flesh, she realised she had not quite come to terms with the fact that Gabriel was both a father and a grandfather.

"My parents did get married rather young, I suppose," said Hugh, as if reading her thoughts.

You weren't much older yourself, thought Kate, watching him pick up Andrew again. According to Gabriel, Hugh and Lara had only been married a year or two ago. She tried to remember how old Andrew was.

"This is one of yours then?" said Hugh, carrying Andrew over to the easel. "I wish I could paint," he said. "Making pots is very satisfying, but I've always envied painters."

"Gabriel gave me one of your pieces," said Kate. "A dish with a deep crimson lustre glaze. How do you get those amazing colours?"

"Well, it's rather complicated. It depends on the metals in the glaze and how you fire them. That red lustre took a lot of experiments. I like that, though — mucking around, trying to get really good colours."

"Yes, it can be fun, can't it?" said Kate. "I waste a lot of paint doing that. It's because I'm puritanical about it. I won't use modern chemical mixtures. I like to mix everything up for myself, from the basics."

"Are you going to paint now?"

"That was my idea," she said, reaching for the old shoebox in which she kept her oil paints and opening it. She put it down on the table. "But I don't seem to have much concentration this morning."

"Funny to think of this place being turned into a studio," he said.

"Do you mind?" said Kate. "Wasn't it your playroom once?"

"Only intermittently," he said with a sigh. "I only spent my school holidays here really." He sat Andrew down on the table. "Dad used to come and fetch me. I hated it at first — I mean this man dragging me off to Scotland . . . No, keep your paws out of those," he said to Andrew, who was about to dive into Kate's paints. "He gets into everything if you give him half a chance. I came to find him some of my old toys. I think they're still in this cupboard." He put Andrew down on the floor again, and went over to the press.

He looked inside, and laughed. "Goodness, I'd forgotten about these. Look!" He pointed to the back of the press door.

Kate could not help smiling at the dozens of pencil lines marking heights, each labelled with a name and a date. Gabriel, 1953, she picked out at once, and then, almost alongside it, Hugh, 1918, and then, in Gabriel's handwriting, Hugh, 1974.

"You should measure Andrew," said Kate.

"Yes, we should, shouldn't we?" said Hugh, catching Andrew. "Now, have you got a pencil? Silly question, for a painter," he added, as Kate produced her tin of pencils. She offered him the open tin. "No, you mark and I'll hold, because otherwise he'll wriggle all over the place, won't you, varmint?"

"Are you sure?" she said.

"Go on," he said, holding Andrew still. "Make your mark on the place."

Kate picked up her marl stick and used it to rule a line above Andrew's head, and then, in neat capitals, wrote, Andrew, 1995.

"Not bad for eighteen months, eh?" said Hugh, turning Andrew round to show him his mark. "It's all that food you put away."

"Is he very greedy?"

"He's like a combine harvester," said Hugh, and swung Andrew up into the air so he crowed with delight. "Aren't you? Andrew Combine-Harvester Erskine!"

"I suppose I should ask you to stay for lunch."

"You sound rather diffident, if you don't mind me saying so," Hugh said with a grin.

"I am," said Kate. "I only just moved in, remember. It feels a bit funny still."

"Well, I'm glad you decided to move in. I think Dad deserves to be happy. I'm really pleased for you both."

"Thank you," said Kate, wondering

how she could ever have been nervous about meeting Hugh. Of course he would be as charming and civilised as his father.

"I'd better let you carry on," he said. "Do you know where Dad is?"

She still could not quite get used to hearing Gabriel referred to as 'Dad'.

"The estate office, I think."

"Of course," said Hugh. "Come on, Andrew, let's go and find Granddad."

"I'll see you again at lunch then?" Kate asked. "And Lara, of course."

"Yes, Lara of course," he said, and Kate thought, though she could not be sure, she saw him frown.

★ ★ ★

Gabriel came out of the estate office into the Home Farm yard to find Hugh and Andrew admiring a premature lamb which Ted, the farm manager, had successfully resuscitated overnight in the bottom oven of his Aga. The lamb was now teetering around in the pen, looking very picturesque, while Ted's wife, Helen, stood by with a feeding bottle. Andrew

54

seemed to be far more interested in the feeding bottle.

"This is very charming," said Gabriel. "And quite a surprise! You could at least have called, Hugh."

"That would have been no fun," said Hugh, shaking his hand.

Gabriel picked up Andrew to kiss him, but was met with a violent squeal of protest.

"I don't think he likes me any more," said Gabriel.

"He's just awfully hungry," said Helen. "Shall I take him in and find him some milk, Hugh?"

"Yes, would you? But please don't put him in the Aga," said Hugh. "Not unless he's really horrid." Helen carried an instantly pacified Andrew off towards the farm kitchen. "What is it about women and babies?" Hugh went on. "Natural authority. Your Kate has it too. He shut up the moment he saw her."

Gabriel could not help smiling at the phrase 'Your Kate'. "So you've met her, then," he said.

"Yes, I found her in the day nursery — though I suppose it's the studio now."

55

Gabriel nodded and turned to lean against the pen wall, enjoying the spring sunshine on his face. He felt full of contentment, having all the people who mattered in his life gathered about him. "I'm glad you came up, Hugh," he said. "It means a lot."

"You mean as a vote of approval?" said Hugh. "You don't need that from me, Dad."

"You're magnificently reasonable, you know."

"I'm just returning a favour," said Hugh.

Gabriel was pleased to hear that. He felt he always carried a residue of guilt about Hugh. He had missed too much of his growing up. It had been unavoidable, of course, but he regretted it still. Divorce settlements in the early seventies rarely favoured fathers and he had not been granted custody. At first he had not quarrelled with the court's decision that Hugh should be with Jane. It had not mattered then, because he had still been living in London, attempting to be a barrister, and had been able to see Hugh regularly. But then his own father had died and Gabriel had to come back to Allansfield, to look after his mother and run the estate. By that time, Jane was engaged to marry Tony Cherrington and Gabriel had gone back to court, attempting to get complete custody. All he had got for his pains, however, was three months a year, which for the sake of convenience was spread over Hugh's school holidays. The first time he drove Hugh, then five years old, up to Allansfield for the summer, it felt more like kidnapping than access.

They had settled to this arrangement, with various squabbles intervening over the years, mostly over Hugh's education. Jane, ever a creature of convention, had decided that Hugh should be sent away to board at eight, although Gabriel had fiercely opposed this. Hugh, nevertheless, had been packed off to a grim little school in Sussex (which, of course, Tony Cherrington had once attended) at Gabriel's expense. The summer after that, at Allansfield, Gabriel had constantly needed to tell Hugh not to call him 'sir'. By the time Hugh was ready for public school, the system had got to him so thoroughly that he actually wanted to go to Uppingham, just as his stepfather had done.

Yet Uppingham had not been such a bad choice after all. A sympathetic art master had awakened in Hugh his passion for pottery, and by the time Jane and Tony (by now a QC) were talking about Oxbridge entrance and law degrees, Hugh had quite independently decided that he was going to study ceramics at Harrow College of Art. Gabriel had been scarcely able to conceal his triumph when Hugh spent the whole summer at Allansfield before his A-level results arrived, attempting to build himself a wood-fired kiln in a disused steading.

Hugh had gone on to disappoint his mother and stepfather further by making what they described as a reckless marriage. Gabriel had not liked to point out to Jane (when she bombarded him on the telephone on the subject) that Hugh's marrying Lara had not been more reckless than their own foolhardy marriage. Perhaps she imagined that Hugh was repeating their mistake, but Gabriel felt he could not judge his son like that. Hugh had seemed to be deeply in love with Lara, and there really was no comparison between his son's choice and his own.

Marrying Jane MacNab had been the most obvious, conventional thing for Gabriel to have done. They had been invited to the same shooting lodge in the Highlands with exactly that object in mind. He had that on the authority of Jane's grandmother, a venerable dowager who cast around for spouses for her many children and grandchildren with the same dexterity that her husband cast for salmon. In getting engaged on a grouse moor that summer, Jane and Gabriel had done exactly what everyone wanted. Ostensibly, of course, they had married for love, but Gabriel knew that Jane would not have allowed herself to fall in love with anyone who did not meet with certain strict requirements with which the heroine of any eighteenth-century novel would have found herself in complete agreement. Money and family were important to Jane — perhaps too important. If she had allowed her instinct to speak a little more loudly, she might have been able to see that the feelings that they had whipped up between them were as transient as the sunshine in a Highland summer. Yet it was unfair to lay the blame entirely on Jane. Gabriel had been equally at fault. Jane had seemed so safe, so kind, so very sweet. It had seemed ideal, an affirmation of all the principles with which he had been brought up.

By contrast, Gabriel was certain that no one would have picked out Polish fashion student Lara Essen as Hugh's ideal spouse. They had got married for the right reason — love; and if Andrew had appeared with alarming rapidity after the marriage, who really minded? Except Jane, of course.

It had been at Andrew's christening that Gabriel had last seen Jane. Lara, on becoming a mother, had remembered she was a nominal Catholic and insisted on an elaborate ceremony at the Polish church in London. Jane and Tony and Gabriel had been invited, along with Lara's mother and aunts from Krakow, as well as a host of Hugh and Lara's Spitalfields friends. It had been an uproarious occasion, with a party at the

Polish Club afterwards, when everyone had got drunk except Tony and Jane.

Recalling Jane's prim expression on that occasion, Gabriel asked Hugh, "Have you told your mother about Kate?"

Hugh laughed. "Vaguely," he said. "And she was very curious."

"I bet she was," said Gabriel, rubbing his face.

"Oh, my mother could disapprove for England, I think," said Hugh with feeling.

"Have you had a fight?"

"Oh, only over Lara. We were invited to dinner and there was a bit of a scene. Mind you, Lara was being rather impossible," he admitted.

Gabriel was surprised. Hugh did not usually criticise her. "Is everything all right between you?"

"Yes, yes," said Hugh, thrusting his hands into his pockets and strolling away a little. "Well — it's nothing that a few weeks up here won't sort out."

"Are you sure?"

Hugh gave a brief grimace, and then stared at the sky for a minute. "It just all seems to have got very complicated lately," he admitted. "Do you know what I mean?"

"Tell me what happened with your mother," said Gabriel.

"Well, you know what Mum's dinner parties are like," Hugh said.

"God, yes . . . " said Gabriel with feeling. Jane, when they had first been married, and living in that tall, unlovely house in South Kensington, had thrown herself wholeheartedly into the complex machinations of a busy social life. She had been very keen on building herself a reputation as a chic young hostess, and Gabriel, who had still been reading for the bar, had soon found himself glad to have the excuse of eating so many dinners at Lincoln's Inn. The college-like atmosphere had been comfortingly anonymous compared to the social agonies of their own dining room, where Jane, triumphant and pregnant, presided over the large dining table that had come from his grandparents' house in Edinburgh. He had tried so hard to be proud of her, to share her pleasure in these social forays, but time after time he just sat there, feeling bored and ill-tempered. And then, later, as his career at the bar failed to take off, there was shame added to this poisonous cocktail, as Jane carefully invited those counsel and their wives who had witnessed him faltering in court. She had done this, of course, for all the right reasons: to help him along, to plead his cause in the way she knew best — and she was good. They loved Jane, all of them. He was forever being told how lucky he was to have her, but as he grew more alienated from her, the more certain he became that there was malice in it, that she was punishing him for not loving her the way he had loved Henrietta.

"Well," Hugh went on. "It was typical. Seventy-five per cent lawyers. I don't know why she asked us really. Well, I do — it was because the dinner was really for Ellie's boyfriend, Jonathan, because he's looking for a pupillage. '

Gabriel nodded. Ellie was Jane's eldest daughter, who was still at Oxford.

"So I suppose we were there to make him feel more at home — but he hardly needs it. He's one of those naturally confident people, bumptious really, to be frank. Anyway, you could tell it was going to be difficult right from the start."

"And . . . ?"

"I lost it," Hugh said, after a pause. "I had too much to drink and Lara was flirting with this bloody man next to her. She was just being herself, I suppose, but it was driving me mad; and Mum, of course, picked up on it and told her to stop monopolising him . . ."

"And Lara didn't like that, I can imagine."

"No," said Hugh. "She went off like an H-bomb. But what really pissed her off was that I didn't come jumping to her defence. I couldn't. I should have done, I know, but . . . So she went storming home, and I was left with Mum in the kitchen getting the lecture from hell."

"Did your mother cry?" asked Gabriel, remembering Jane berating him with tears over the dirty dishes.

"What do you think?" said Hugh. "So, anyway, things have been somewhat fraught, and I thought a holiday might help us get back on track."

"I do hope so," said Gabriel, disturbed. Hugh and Lara's situation sounded dangerously slippery. There was something in Hugh's tone that was too familiar for comfort. It depressed him profoundly to think that Hugh and Lara should find their marriage collapsing when it had all seemed so promising. Without either meaning or wanting to, they were inflicting upon each other the same nasty emotional scars that he and Jane had suffered. Yet how much worse would it be for Hugh to suffer that slow, painful alienation, because he had seemed to be in love with Lara in just the same way that Gabriel felt he had once loved Henrietta.

4

HUGH, when he got back to the cottage, found Lara wrapped in the duvet and sitting on the settle in the kitchen.

"So bloody cold!" she exclaimed as they came in. "Aren't you cold, darling?" she said to Andrew, stretching out her arms to take him from Hugh. Andrew, who had been getting distinctly grizzly, was all at once in a good mood again, as he snuggled up against his mother. "That's better, isn't it, my love?" she said. "Much better. You shouldn't have taken him out, Hugh."

"He would have screamed the house down," said Hugh, putting the kettle on the Aga. He went to the time switch and flicked on the central heating. "It'll warm up soon. You just needed to switch on the heating."

"Why didn't you switch it on?" she retorted. "You knew I would be cold."

"You were fast asleep. It didn't feel cold to me."

"It never feels cold to you. Bloody freezing Scotland." She put Andrew down on the floor and emerged from her cocoon. She was wearing a skimpy T-shirt and a pair of socks. She scuttled across the kitchen on her long, slender legs, looking for her cigarettes and giving Hugh an inadvertent flash of her bare backside. There was a time when that would have driven him wild. Now he found he was more concerned about whether Andrew was in danger on the floor.

Lara had established herself back in her cocoon and had lit her cigarette. The duvet would smell of smoke now, Hugh thought, sitting down on the floor to help Andrew play with his yellow plastic truck. He was aware of Lara's scrutiny.

"So you saw her?"

"Saw whom?"

"Your father's girl, of course. The Kate person."

"Yes, I met her."

"And?" said Lara. "What's she like?"

"Oh, well . . . " Hugh sat back on his heels, considering for a moment.

Blandly, he settled for, "Very nice, I think," though that hardly did Kate justice.

"You don't like her?"

"No, no, I like her. I only spoke to her briefly, though. She was about to do some painting."

"That's right," said Lara. "She's an artist, isn't she?" She got up from the sofa and went over to the kitchen window. She exhaled a long ostentatious puff of smoke.

"Well, you'll meet her soon," said Hugh. "We're going up there for lunch."

"Oh, are we?" said Lara. "You seem to be making all my decisions for me these days, don't you Hugh? Like whether we come here or not."

"I don't think we should start on that again," Hugh said carefully. "We're here now, and that's it, OK?"

"I don't know how you can say that, I really don't know!" she exclaimed, and stubbed out her cigarette. She bent down and picked up Andrew. "Come on, darling, come and help Mama get dressed, eh? We have to go and have a boring lunch at Allansfield."

The kettle began to boil. Hugh, as

68

politely as he could, asked, "Coffee?"

Lara shrugged and strolled out of the kitchen.

At one time it had seemed to Hugh that Lara lived on nothing but black coffee, cigarettes, alcohol and emotion. The first time they spent any real time together was in a farmhouse in the Dordogne belonging to some mutual friends. Large meals had formed an important part of the holiday, but Hugh noticed that Lara hardly ate anything — she had no time, what with smoking, drinking and talking, or more particularly flirting. After the first week, Hugh, to his delight, found himself on the receiving end of her attentions. She had broken up explosively with Jamie, the man she had arrived with. Jamie had gone off in a huff to his parents' house nearby, effectively abandoning Lara. She had made a great deal of it, picking Hugh as her particular shoulder to cry copiously on. Hugh, who had been admiring her from a distance for a couple of months, could not quite believe his luck. She seemed like the embodiment of all his fantasies, this six-foot Polish girl, with her broken accent and broken heart. When they made love for the first time she had talked all the way through, half in Polish, and Hugh had not been able to decide what had turned him on more: her naked body or her voice.

After three weeks of unbridled hedonism, it had seemed obvious that he should drive Lara back to London. On the journey back they had stopped for the night in a slightly seedy hotel in a tired little French town. In a bedroom with flowery wallpaper on the ceiling, their lovemaking had been so passionate and so energetic that the condom burst. At the time, they had been in such a state of elation it had not seemed to matter, but three weeks later Lara made the announcement that she was pregnant.

By then, she had become a fixture in the tiny flat above Hugh's crumbling workshop in Spitalfields. She had moved in without his asking her, but he would have asked her anyway. She took up residence like a stray cat, immediately appropriating the best corners for herself, but Hugh had loved that. It had been wonderful to come up the cast-iron stairs from the pottery and find her sitting at the kitchen table sketching out her extravagant dress designs and drinking coffee that tasted of tar. She cooked him vast spicy stews of Polish sausages and cabbage and introduced him to the pleasures of chilled vodka. He even came to tolerate the smell of her cigarettes. Living with her was like having a front seat in the stalls for a melodrama. When she announced to him, with so many tears and exclamations, that she was pregnant, he found he was not really that surprised. It felt only like another exciting twist of the plot. It had taken less than five minutes for him to decide how to resolve it. He told her they would get married and she fell on to his chest with a gratifying operatic swoop.

Unkind acquaintances, of course, had hinted that she had married him to stay in London (her visa was about to expire), and others said that it was his trust fund that was the attraction, but Hugh had not cared. He knew how he felt, what he needed, and by then he had convinced himself that what he needed was Lara. Whatever the circumstances, he knew he had fallen in love with her. He could not live without her.

They had set up house together in a grand but only half restored early Georgian house in Spitalfields, around the corner from the pottery. Hugh had fallen for the house in much the same way he had fallen for Lara. He knew that the floorboards all needed replacing, that the roof was an expensive liability and that the cellar was full of creeping dampness, but the place was irresistible. Imperfections did not matter; it was the sweeping romanticism of the thing he liked. The house suited Lara beautifully, and Lara suited the house. They had given lots of huge candlelit parties in the sparsely furnished rooms, with a log fire roaring in every grate. Lara, heavily pregnant, held court by the fireside and enchanted everyone. Hugh had felt he was falling in love with her every time he woke up in the morning and found her in bed beside him.

Then Andrew had been born and everything had changed. They had begun to quarrel. Without wanting to do so, he found himself becoming irritated with Lara. Hugh felt he had woken up suddenly into the real world, a world that did not revolve about his own desires, but around Andrew, for whom they were responsible in every sense. He realised that this stranger in their house, who was helpless, demanding and enchanting by turns, would be with them for the rest of their lives and was their son, the product of their own thoughtless sensuality. He was not a scratchy image on an ultrasound scan but an individual with a strong personality (that Hugh had sensed even when he held him for the first time in the delivery room). Some friends from art college, now on to their second baby, had told him that their children had cemented their relationship and made them realise just how much they had in common. He had only been able to nod politely in response, feeling that Andrew, wriggling, pink and innocent, was in fact about the only real thing he and Lara had in common. Other than Andrew, there was nothing solid to hold them together. If there had been no Andrew, he began to suspect, they would have gone their separate ways months ago. As they could not, their life together had subsided into a series of skirmishes.

Now, he followed Lara up the steep cottage stairs, carrying the duvet. She had gone into the little bedroom on the right, where the old cot from the nursery at Allansfield had been put. She had put Andrew in it and was standing with her hand over his eyes until he fell asleep. Hugh watched for a moment or two, then went back into their bedroom and sat down in the old chintz-covered armchair by the window.

Lara came back into the room and closed the door behind her. She leant against it, regarding him with some hostility.

"Look, I'm sorry," he said. "I just thought it would be a good idea for us to get away for a bit. Things have been so confusing lately . . . haven't they?"

She shrugged and stretched up to pull her T-shirt over her head. Naked, she wandered across the room and began to rummage through their unpacked baggage. Her silence unnerved him as much as the powerful beauty of her naked body. In the spring sunshine, her thick pale-gold hair looked more like a sheep's fleece.

"I just thought," he said, getting up, "that here, without any distractions, we might be able to sort things out, get things back to the way they were. Allansfield can be very therapeutic, you know."

"No, I don't know!" she exclaimed. "I don't know at all. I just know you drag me up here without my say-so, like a bloody tyrant."

"I know, I know, that was wrong — but I had to do something. We had to do something. We need fixing up, Lara, can't you see that?"

"You need fixing up, Hugh," she said. "You're the one who's lost his mind, not me. Now get out of here, I want to get dressed."

Obediently, he went towards the door.

"And don't think I'm coming to lunch," she said.

"Lara . . ."

"No, go on your own. You can complain all you like about me then. The way you do to your mother and Tony."

"I do no such thing."

"Of course you do. They love to hear you complain about me, because they hate me."

"You know that isn't true, Lara. What happened that night was just a bit fraught. Mum didn't mean what she said."

"She meant every word, Hugh. I could see it in her eyes. And you agree with her, don't you? Because you hate me now, don't you?"

"Oh, for God's sake, Lara, if I hated you would we be here now? Would I still be trying to make things work?"

"You never loved me," she said.

"I do love you. How many times do I have to say it?"

She shook her head and turned to the window. She propped herself against the embrasure, the curves of her body outlined by the strong sunlight.

"I don't think you know how to love, Hugh," she said. "Not like a man. You just play at it like a boy, and when it goes wrong you run to your mother or your father. There's no real passion in you. Cold, you are, like bloody Scotland." She wrapped her arms around herself.

76

"What the hell is it you want from me, Lara?" he said.

"Just now, you can leave me alone."

★ ★ ★

After that little run in, Hugh went back to Allansfield and sat in the sitting room, inexpertly playing the piano. He had helped himself to a large whisky, but neither the Scotch nor his mechanical ploughing through a Bach two-part invention, nor even the soothing and familiar comfort of the house, had managed to make him feel any better. He wished he had been able to invent some clever argument to dispel Lara's accusations, but he could not, not even sitting there in detachment.

The sitting room at Allansfield was a pleasant, sunny room, with walnut-panelled walls and clutter and books everywhere. Because it was late April, there were also bowls of narcissi filling the place with their sweet scent, and on the little table by his father's favourite chair, Hugh noticed, someone had put a tumbler full of scarlet and yellow primulas. He wondered if this was a gesture of Kate's. He sat there and nursed down the last of his whisky, remembering without wanting to all the little gestures of affection that he had used to show to Lara.

The door opened and Kate came in. She laughed and said, "Oh, it's you again." She was carrying the larger of the two Allansfield cats, a lazy old black tom called Bingley.

"Sorry," he said, getting up. "Am I getting under your feet?"

"In this house?" She smiled. "Where's Andrew?"

"Snoozing — and I'm afraid Lara won't be coming for lunch. She's still a bit whacked after the journey."

"Oh, I'm sorry. I was looking forward to meeting her," said Kate, sitting down on the sofa with the cat.

"Would you like a drink?" he said, indicating the butler's tray.

"Well, since I don't seem to be getting any work done today, I might as well. A very small whisky with lots of water, please."

He made her the drink and refilled

his own. He sat down and watched her stroking Bingley's head, observing that her own head, with its deep red hair, smoothed down, straight and shining, was a little like that of a cat.

"I hope I didn't ruin your concentration by bursting in," he said.

"No, I didn't have any concentration to ruin today," she said. She glanced around the room. "All these lovely pictures ought to inspire me, but . . . I guess I'm just being lazy."

"I should think they might inhibit me," said Hugh. "Perhaps that's why I didn't take up painting."

"It must be quite something, growing up with Ramsays and Grants and Hendersons on the walls."

"Only during the summer holidays," he pointed out, "and then I spent most of my time outside. We always used to go to the beach at St Andrews if the weather was even passable."

She laughed suddenly and said, "Do you know, we were probably there at the same time. My family used to go to St Andrew quite a lot. Isn't that an odd thought?"

"What is?" Gabriel had just come into the room.

Kate jumped up and went across the room to him. Gabriel threw his arm affectionately around her.

"That we probably used to play on the beach at St Andrews together, years ago. Hugh was just telling me."

"I rather wish you hadn't told me that," said Gabriel. "It makes me feel ancient."

"Did you used to build sandcastles?" Kate asked Hugh. "My sister and I would built the most brilliant ones, with moats and everything."

"I probably used to jump on them, then," said Hugh.

"I wouldn't have allowed you to do that," said Gabriel. "I hope. Or if you did, it was without my knowledge."

"I distinctly remember doing it — and enjoying it," said Hugh. "How shameful. Well, I'm sorry Kate, if I got one of your masterpieces."

"Humph," said Kate, with mock indignation. "I might forgive you."

Hugh found he had a vivid recollection of the pleasure of that destructiveness, of hurling himself on to some carefully constructed sandcastle and feeling the whole edifice crumble and give way underneath his weight. Was that what he was doing to Lara and himself, finding fault and then destroying for the pleasure of destroying? Had he dragged her up here not to make things better but to make them worse? She had told him that he did not love her. Perhaps she was right. Perhaps he needed at last to admit that to himself, instead of continuing to pretend, to insist to himself that he adored her. Lara was no fool after all.

He watched his father kiss Kate briefly on the lips as he crossed the room to fetch himself a drink. He saw his hand pass over her sleek head, and felt he ought to slip away and leave them to their private affection. It was like being a voyeur on a honeymoon and he felt suddenly convinced of the profound and authentic feeling between them. Lara might accuse him of not knowing how to love, but at least he could still recognise it and feel deeply envious when he did.

★ ★ ★

"No food," said Lara, strolling into the kitchen just as they were sitting over the remains of lunch. "Can we beg, Gabriel darling?"

Kate swivelled round at the sound of Lara's distinctively throaty and accent-laden English and Andrew's crying. Andrew was, in fact, bawling vociferously, his face crimson, struggling on his mother's pushed-out hip. Lara seemed implacable, though, dressed in black leather jeans and a tight white T-shirt, a pair of sunglasses pushing back her abundant blond hair. All in all, she was an exotic item for the kitchen at Allansfield.

"Here, let me take him," said Hugh, jumping up and taking Andrew from her. He seemed to wrap his arms about him almost defensively.

"You know you don't need to beg," said Gabriel, going to kiss her. Lara pouted slightly and then clearly surprised him by insisting on kissing him in return on the lips. Then it was Kate's turn. She had been hoping to get away with a handshake, but Lara was determined on one of those nebulous social kisses that women sometimes exchanged, and which Kate had not mastered. They pressed their cheeks together for a moment, and Kate came away with a strong impression of unfiltered cigarettes and forceful perfume. Then Lara took a step back and scrutinised Gabriel and Kate for a long moment.

"Don't they look happy, Hugh?" she said, and reached out and touched Gabriel on the cheek. "You've surprised us, Papa, you know," she added a little slyly.

"Well, I'd hate to be predictable," said Gabriel. "What can we get you?"

"A drink," she said, sitting down. "A real drink."

"Of course."

"There's some white open," said Kate, going to fetch her a glass. In the corner of the kitchen, by the dresser, Hugh was already down on his knees, feeding Andrew the remains of the soup from his bowl.

"What did I tell you? A combine harvester?" Hugh said. Andrew, licking his lips and grinning, looked up at Kate, stretching out his small hand to her.

"I think there's a bit more in the pan," she said. "Do you want some more, Andrew? Do you like lentil soup, then?" Kate wondered suddenly what it would be like to be the mother of such a child, to have made such a delicate and yet lively thing. She had not really thought much about having children before, but seeing Hugh feeding Andrew made the whole idea rather appealing. She was slightly astonished at this attack of broodiness and repressed the thought quickly, reaching for a wine glass for Lara. It was not a practical idea, not with Gabriel being nearly fifty. How on earth could Hugh have a half-brother or sister who was younger than his own son, after all? Besides, she knew how babies played havoc with people's careers. Children, she decided, were perhaps just one of those things that were not going to happen to her.

Lara's hunger seemed sated by drinking the rest of the bottle of white wine and a token piece of cheese, while Andrew, after a second helping of lentil soup and some stewed apple and yoghurt, was soon nicely drowsy in Hugh's arms. Andrew,

Kate decided, was the only one of them at his ease. The conservation had been difficult, to say the least.

"We'd better get him back to the cottage," said Hugh, getting up carefully so as not to disturb Andrew.

Lara shrugged and got up languidly. "It's so quiet here, everyone falls asleep," she said, yawning. She followed Hugh out of the kitchen, her hips swaying. Kate glanced back at Gabriel to see his reaction. He was sitting with his elbows on the table, his hands pressed over his mouth. He gave a slight grimace.

"Something wrong?" she asked.

"With them, yes," he said, and then pushed his hand through his hair. "Hugh said that they were going through a rocky patch, but . . . "

"I have to say they didn't exactly seem comfortable with each other," Kate said.

"No," he said. "Oh dear, that's very depressing. Especially for Andrew. I wonder what one can do to help. I have a horrible feeling they may be beyond help. It seemed all too familiar. Isn't that odd, that two people whom you think are so different can behave in the same way? I mean Lara and Jane. One couldn't imagine two women less alike, but her expression just then . . . that look . . . " He gave a slight shudder and then stretched out his hand, laid it over Kate's and squeezed it. "And here I am, feeling so smug and lucky to have you. I wish they could be as happy as we are."

"Perhaps it's not a lost cause yet," said Kate.

"Perhaps not," he said, smiling, and then he released her hand. He glanced up at the kitchen clock. "Well. I have umpteen trays of seedlings clamouring to be pricked out," he said, getting up from the table. "My reward for doing all that paperwork this morning. I'll be in the potting shed if you need me." And having kissed her on the forehead, he was gone.

5

"WELL, that's everything, I think, Dr Winthrop," said the estate agent, when they had finished going through the inventory. "If you'd just like to sign at the bottom . . . here."

"Great," said Henrietta. She signed cheerfully, and condemned herself to six months of attending diligently to the welfare of the fixtures and fittings of Mon Abris, 25 Lade Braes, St Andrews, in order to preserve the vast deposit she had been required to put down.

As the estate agent left, Henrietta followed her out into her newly rented front garden and the spring sunshine. As she listened to the young woman's modest heels tap-tapping away up the lane back towards the town, she made a systematic tour of the borders. Even taking into account the fact that the ground and the shrubs seemed only just to be recovering from the onslaught of winter, it was not an impressive sight. The border edges were ruler straight, and the shrubs ordinary and unprepossessing. There were roses for later in the year, but she feared they were hybrid teas, and there was altogether too much privet. The clumps of large, rather butch-looking daffodils were slender compensation. It was not quite the garden that she had had in mind. She walked around its limited compass once more, deciding what might be done about it, then turned back towards the house. She looked up at the grey stone façade, wondering whether the clematis skeleton that crawled up the green-painted drainpipe would come to anything. She was about to go in again when she heard a woman's voice behind her calling her name. She turned and saw a grey-haired woman, a few years older than herself, coming up the garden path.

"Dr Winthrop?" she said, her hand outstretched. "Eleanor McCleod."

"Oh, Professor McCleod!" exclaimed Henrietta. "At last."

"Yes, doesn't it seem odd?" said Professor McCleod. "After all those e-mails and faxes — and now, at last we meet!" They shook hands. "Call me Eleanor, please, by the way. How's the house?" She peered up at the engraved name in the glass over the door. "Mon Abris — goodness, what a name! Is it a shelter?"

"I'm not sure about that yet," said Henrietta. "I've just finished the inventory."

"Ah, those things are such a bother," said Eleanor. "Now, what can I help you with?"

"Oh, nothing, though thank you," she said as they went into the hall together.

"Actually, this is very thoughtless of me," said Eleanor. "Calling before you're properly sorted out."

"Of course it isn't," said Henrietta. "It's very nice to be welcomed."

"Well, to tell you the truth I couldn't resist it. You are such a feather in my cap, so to speak, that I had to see you as soon as possible, just to tell you how delighted I am that you've decided to come and join us for a while."

"It was an honour to be asked," said

Henrietta, as they went into the sitting room. "And everyone should have a sabbatical every now and then, shouldn't they? A complete change of scene. Now, what can I get you? I do have some duty free — a bottle of Glenlivet, no less. Is it too early for that for you?"

Eleanor McCleod smiled. "Too early for a dram, with a name like McCleod?" she said.

Henrietta dug out the bottle and a couple of glasses from the kitchen.

"I'm supposed to be cutting down on this stuff, actually," she said, as she poured out two measures. "After my operation."

"Oh yes, your hysterectomy," said Eleanor, sitting down. "Do you think you're over all that now?"

"Yes, I think so," said Henrietta, swilling her whisky around slightly in the glass. "Physically, anyway, But psychologically . . . "

"Yes, it's an emotional wrench, isn't it? Even when you've never had children. When I had mine, I knew it wasn't logical, because I was way past the age when I could have had a child, but I still

90

felt robbed. De-sexed a little, even."

Henrietta nodded, and said, "It's crazy, isn't it? We spend all our lives proving that we don't need to function as women have always functioned, as baby factories, but when they finally decommission us, we feel cheated. Crazy." She took a long drink of whisky.

"Decommissioned," said Eleanor. "I like that. It's genes, though, they're the trouble."

"Ah yes, bloody nature," said Henrietta. "No matter how you try and civilise, it always gets the upper hand." She laughed slightly, thinking of the garden outside. "Spoken like a gardener."

"Oh, are you keen?" enquired Eleanor.

"Keen, but not entirely successful. Suitably obsessive, though. You'll find Christopher Lloyd as well as *Ms* on my bedside table these days."

"He does write so well," said Eleanor. "Well, if you're interested, there's a meeting of our local horticultural club tonight at the Town Hall. They usually have quite good speakers. It would give you a chance to see a little of the town. I think it's a question-and-answer session tonight. I'm not sure who is on the panel, though."

"I take it you're an obsessive too," said Henrietta.

"Yes, although my gardening has become a little theoretical since we set up the Centre. Ah, wait until you get a chair — you'll never guess how much administration there is."

"I'm not sure I'm in the running for a head of department," said Henrietta. "Besides, I'm egoist enough to think I'm a maverick."

"Well, we need mavericks as well as administrators. And you will have a better garden than I. That I envy you."

"After all you've achieved?" said Henrietta, thinking of the string of impeccable scholarly books that Eleanor had published.

"A garden is the closest to immortality most of us get," she said. "My works may crumble into dust, but the fruit trees I plant . . . "

"If they're like mine, they pack up the first winter," said Henrietta, laughing. "What did you do to yours?"

"You had better come along tonight,"

said Eleanor, getting up. "Though I'm not sure anyone will be particularly well versed in North American conditions. It kicks off at seven-thirty — at the Town Hall. I'll meet you outside, shall I?"

When Eleanor had gone, Henrietta resisted the temptation of the whisky bottle and set about making a start on the unpacking. Her doctor had told her not to carry large weights for a while, so she opened the suitcases in the hall and ferried her clothes upstairs in batches. Seeing them hanging in the large Edwardian wardrobe she began to feel she had a stake in the place. She was glad she had spent a week in London before she came north. It would have been grim doing this with jet-lag. She closed the wardrobe door, studied herself in the mirror for a moment, and decided she was in dire need of fresh air. Besides, she needed to buy some basic provisions. The rest of the unpacking could wait.

St Andrews, as she walked around it armed with a map, proved to be an agreeable little town, with a great deal packed into it. It struck her as quite an achievement for a small place to have so much crammed in: a ruined Cathedral, a harbour, a castle, several beaches and umpteen golf courses, as well as a flourishing university. Its scale and its architecture were manageable, though. It did not appear to brag of itself, not as Cambridge had seemed to when she had first seen it all those years ago. Her first impressions of Cambridge had been overwhelming, but at twenty-one she had wanted to be overwhelmed by all that extravagant golden stone. Now, at fifty, she preferred the effect of St Andrews. She liked the puritanical solidity of all those grey stone churches, the ever present prospect of the sea, that slap of the salty cold wind. She could appreciate austerity better now.

How time changed one's view of things, she found herself thinking, settling down at a marble-topped table in the little Italian café in Market Street. She ordered a pot of camomile tea and watched with amusement the two student lovers at the next table, pledging themselves over cappuccino and extravagant ice creams. She wondered if, presented with her own self at that stage, in such a situation, she would actually recognise herself. The Henrietta of nineteen had been an earnest young student at Smith College, mildly radical in the fashion of the time, but with her head and heart full of literary dreams. Nourished on Henry James, Jane Austen and E. M. Forster, she had wanted nothing more than to come to Europe. Going to Cambridge became her own particular quest, and when she had got there and fallen in love and drunk wine and breathed the poetic air, she had thought she had grasped her own Holy Grail. Yet almost as soon as she had it, she had realised, it had not really been what she wanted. The dazzle of the place had worn off, to be replaced by a terrifying sort of suffocation. The Old World had suddenly seemed very old, and constricting. She had gone back when she had finished her degree and thrown herself into a busy, constructive, entirely American life.

It had been 1969, and women's liberation had ignited her mind and her soul. She had not burnt her bra, but she had written a couple of polemic tracts which had caused a minor sensation at the time, and she had been a leading light in the reassessment of nineteenth-century women writers. After graduate school, at Radcliffe-Harvard, she had spent an agreeable few years as a junior professor at a conservative women's college in Virginia, stirring up the rest of the faculty with her progressive ideas and complicated love life. She had also discovered a real pleasure in teaching, and more constant happiness in her own solitude than with any man. She had nearly given in once or twice, though. There had been David, the crusading civil-rights lawyer she had met in Washington at an Anti-Vietnam demo. He had had his eye on a seat in Congress, but she could not quite stomach the thought of being a political wife. Then there had been a ragged-round-the-edges visiting Irish professor, Colm, who had made her laugh and with whom she had had an intense and stormy affair, until she discovered there was a wife back in Ireland, and several children. After that she had been very cautious. She had got a professorship in the English department at Harvard and come back to her native Massachusetts, although she chose to live on the Boston side of the Charles River, away from the worst excesses of University politics. Her mother had been diagnosed with cancer, and Henrietta had nursed her till she died. Then, with her inheritance, she had bought an old farmhouse in Vermont, her mother's native state, and discovered the pleasures of gardening. When the offer had come from Eleanor McCleod to teach at St Andrews for a year, Henrietta had decided that she was finally old and wise enough to cope with going back to Europe. She had acquired, she told herself, finishing her tea and watching the young couple kiss over the ice-cream wafers, enough detachment.

She made her way back to the house and prepared to go to the meeting at the Town Hall. First, she tested the mettle of the bathroom at Mon Abris by having a bath. She decided, once the heating was running and there was enough steam going, that the place was not so bad after all. Afterwards, she wandered downstairs in her towelling bath-robe to the kitchen, to pick out a meal from the oddments of food she had assembled. She had bought a bunch of crimson tulips and arranged them in an old jug she found under the sink. Sitting on the counter top, they made the room look quite cheerful. Henrietta ate some bread and cheese, and drank a glass of Beaujolais, and went upstairs again to dress, confident that the decision to come had been the right one.

It had not always felt like that. When she had been packing up, and subletting the apartment in Boston and her house in Vermont, it had seemed little short of lunacy at times to undertake such a journey so soon after the operation. She had been constantly dogged by exhaustion, by panic, by a hundred old-womanly fears which she had despised in herself as being unworthy of someone who was only fifty, but which she was powerless to prevent. Yet now she was here, and in possession of this odd little house, she felt herself relax for the first time in months. In time, she would be able to resume, she hoped, the serenity and productivity of her normal life — except it would be more stimulating because it was a new place, with new people, and she had always loved meeting new people.

She smiled to herself as she selected her clothes from the wardrobe. She put on a black jacket and trousers, with a flowing white silk shirt underneath, the collar of which she turned up. She hung a string of amber beads at her neck and put on her favourite jade and silver ring on her wedding-ring finger. With deft fingers she twisted and pinned up her hair into its usual loose chignon, and then she sprayed a little Miss Dior on herself.

She strolled down the Lade Braes towards the town in this pleasantly hedonistic state, glancing at her neighbours' gardens as dusk fell gently on them. She even stole a sprig from a particularly vigorous rosemary bush that seemed bent on colonising the lane, and decided she would plant a mass of herbs back at number 25. The house was supposed to be south-facing, and she wondered whether she would be able to manage to keep alive a pot of basil on the step.

On her earlier walk she had located

the Town Hall, a stupendous piece of Victorian baronial architecture. Eleanor was now waiting outside for her.

"I'm glad I made you come," said Eleanor. "Gabriel Erskine's on the panel tonight. He's quite a plantsman and always terribly interesting."

"Gabriel Erskine?" said Henrietta. She felt something jump in her stomach and nip at her nerve ends. "You did just say Gabriel Erskine?"

"Yes, do you know him?"

"Well," said Henrietta, surprised at how calm she managed to sound. "It's such an unusual name. I knew someone with that name at Cambridge. It's probably not the same man at all . . . "

"He'd be your generation," said Eleanor, going towards the Town Hall door. "It could be the same person."

"He was Scottish, I know that," Henrietta said, and then shook her head. "This must be a coincidence. It couldn't be my Gabriel." *My Gabriel* — heavens, what did that sound like? she thought. She decided to be more emphatic and dismissive. "He couldn't have turned into a plantsman. He was a rowdy Trinity boatie, the Gabriel Erskine I knew."

"Stranger things have happened," said Eleanor.

"No," said Henrietta, as they climbed the stairs. "No, it can't be."

"You sound, if you don't mind me saying, as if you don't want it to be the same man."

"No, I don't," said Henrietta, "to be honest."

"Ah, well, I won't enquire further," said Eleanor with admirable tact.

The hall was quite crowded, and there was a mass of people to whom Eleanor introduced Henrietta. She shook a clutch of hands and smiled at many faces to which she did not think she would later be able to fix names. Her mind was plummeting into the past. That the possibility of his being there should make her feel so nervous was utterly irrational. It had all happened so long ago. It ought to be like all her memories of Cambridge, well composted and rotted down.

"Shall we sit down?" said Eleanor. "Before all the seats go."

"Yes, please . . . " said Henrietta. She sat down in the red plastic chair with some relief, and closed her eyes for a second, trying to regain some composure. She opened them again and permitted them to focus on the platform; indeed, she went to the extent of extracting her glasses from her pocket and resting them on her nose. She felt safe to do so, having guessed at first glance that none of the men on the platform could possibly be Gabriel Erskine. There was a small, thin man with a wonderfully bushy black moustache, who looked as if he were the chairman, and then a venerable white-haired man, in equally venerable mud-coloured tweeds, who Henrietta felt sure was going to be the vegetable expert. There was a token woman as well, of about her own age, but dressed more as Henrietta remembered her own mother dressing, her hair in a careful set and her collar decorated by a large chiffon pussy bow, pearls clipped to her ears. A very conservative-looking group, all in all, and none of them bearing any faint shadow of the Gabriel she knew. She decided to be relieved, although there was still an ominous empty chair on the platform. Then, as the bushy moustache appeared to be getting up to call the meeting to order, she saw him from the corner of her eye.

He was coming up the side aisle, half running actually, and his gait was unmistakable. He had run alongside her once, while she cycled, breathlessly bombarding her with questions: "So, you will have dinner at the Blue Boar? About seven? You promise?" She had promised. There had been something irresistible about Gabriel Erskine, as he ran along with her, through that thicket of other bikes, a cricket sweater tied about his shoulders, his easy athleticism, his ridiculous lack of caution, his eyes shining at her.

Yes, it was Gabriel, there was no doubt about it when she saw him turn and stride up the steps to the platform, taking, of course, two at a time. Oh yes, it was Gabriel Erskine all right.

She felt Eleanor glancing at her, and she nodded slowly, watching him stand there, exhibiting all that agreeable poise again. He stood with his hand in his pocket, the other on his head for a moment, while he spoke with the chairman. Clearly they were discussing how they all should sit, for the hand came off the head and pointed to the empty chair. He nodded, gave a brief, charming smile, and went and sat down with the others. He said something to them and they all laughed. It struck her, as he sat down, that he looked happy.

She watched him fold one arm across himself, and rest his chin on his other hand, covering his mouth and crumpling his brow as he listened to the first question.

It had been a question about unusual vegetables and the old man, just as Henrietta had expected, was answering at some length. She declined to listen and found herself studying the details of Gabriel's appearance. He was wearing blue jeans, a dark blue denim shirt, with an exotic, floral tie and a discreetly checked tweed jacket with large leather patches on the elbows — clothes that were simple, but clearly well looked after. There were creases, she fancied, down the front of those jeans. His hair was thinner, and shorter, receding slightly, but it was still soft and looked attractive to the touch. In all, he had aged quite well. The slight wrinkles were distinguished, and the grey which was just touching his eyebrows made those unforgettable hazel eyes even more distinctive. She watched them flit across the audience just before he was about to speak. Could he see her, she wondered?

Gabriel had taken over from the other speaker and was describing how to grow an exotic-sounding vegetable, the cardoon, but Henrietta found she was not listening to the substance of what he said, but how he said it. His voice had changed, she thought. There was a hesitancy about it. It was deeper and drier, like a wine that had been in the bottle for a few years.

For the rest of the evening she found she did not listen properly to anyone else. She was no wiser on the subject of propagating strawberries, or good perennials for a shady bed, or the way to prepare the ground to plant a Japanese Maple. She found she was constantly assessing Gabriel for style rather than content, like a judge at a beauty pageant. Normally, she knew, what he was saying would have fascinated her — or rather, if anyone else had been saying it she would have been fascinated. There was no doubt he knew his stuff: Latin names slipped effortlessly from his tongue; he had anecdotes to make them all laugh and pieces of arcane information which suggested that he was not just a gardener but a person of considerable general culture. All in all, it was an impressive performance, but she could not detach it from her own emotional turmoil. Damn it, why could she not have any perspective on this? Why could she only sit there and think how attractive he still was, and remember too many of the good things which had happened between them?

★ ★ ★

It had been at a Cambridge sherry party that she'd first met him, in the autumn of 1966. It had been her first term, and she seemed to have done nothing but go to sherry parties and stand in corners having fruitless but earnest conversations. On this occasion, at Trinity, she had got stuck with some hearty vicar-to-be, who had seemed only to be interested in talking about rowing and religion.

"I suppose, as a New England puritan, you'll probably think me rather high," he said, "but I do find that Our Lady is becoming a more and more important part of my devotional life."

Henrietta had smiled politely, swallowing down her glass of sticky sweet sherry and wishing she could have a martini, the sort that her aunt in New York mixed.

"You should try it, you know," he went on. "A prayer to Her now and then works wonders. I couldn't find my cuff-links yesterday, so . . . " He stopped, noticing her empty glass. "I say, would you like another sherry?"

"Thanks," said Henrietta, glad to see him go.

"I wouldn't have said yes if I were you," said the voice of a young man behind her. "This sherry's awful."

"Isn't it?" she admitted, turning to him. He was about a head shorter than her, and most definitely younger. He was wearing the usual shabby tweed jacket and battered cord trousers, except that his clothes looked more shabby than most. He had a couple of days' growth of stubble on his chin and Henrietta wondered if he was postponing shaving simply so he would have enough to make it worth the effort. He also had striking hazel-coloured eyes.

"I expect Godfrey's been boring you to death," he went on.

"Well . . . " she began.

"Or are you high and pi too? You don't look as though you are."

"I may get high, but not on religion," she smiled. "Who are you?"

They introduced each other, and then Gabriel said, "Look, here's bloody St Godfrey coming over again. Shall we make a run for it? I've a bottle of claret which will taste far better."

"OK," said Henrietta, realising she had nothing to lose. She liked his eyes anyway.

His rooms were startlingly untidy, with books and newspapers and discarded clothes everywhere. He shoved a shilling in the gas meter and they sat in front of the fire drinking claret. A quick examination of his bookshelves revealed that he was reading law, but his passion was for eighteenth- and nineteenth-century novels, a passion which she shared.

"So, which is your favourite Jane Austen?" he asked, when he refilled her glass.

"I can't answer that."

"You have to," he said. "It's a deliberate test question. Don't think you'll get any more wine unless you answer correctly."

"You mean unless I say your favourite?"

"Exactly."

"Why should I? What would we have to argue about if I said the same?"

"You like arguing?"

"Of course I do. It's the best discipline for the mind."

"So, which is your favourite Jane Austen?"

She thought for a moment, took a long drink of wine, and said, "Well, at the moment . . . *Mansfield Park*." She was sure that would not be his favourite.

"I'm sorry, we've nothing to argue about," he said, pouring yet more wine.

The bottle was empty now.

"I don't believe you. I can't believe that *Mansfield Park* should be your favourite."

"Why not?"

"Because you're too young. What are you, Gabriel, a second year?" He nodded. "Nineteen years old — it's too young really to appreciate the subtleties of *Mansfield Park*."

"Sweeping statement!" he said. "And how old are you? Fifty?"

"You seem to forget I've already done my first degree," she said.

"Oh, a Yank degree," he said dismissively. "We all know they're not worth tuppence. That's why the university makes you foreigners start from scratch again."

"What a charmingly obnoxious little shit you are," she said with a smile.

"Aren't I?" he said. "Shall I open another bottle?"

"Why not? It's raining outside and I don't fancy walking back to Newnham just now."

"Good," he said. "Now, where were we? Ah yes, *Mansfield Park*."

110

* * *

At last the meeting was over, and a woman from the floor, a member of the committee, presumably, got up and gave a vote of thanks, the wording of which struck Henrietta as needlessly baroque.

"There's tea and biscuits now," said Eleanor as the audience began to move out of their seats.

"I think I'll pass," said Henrietta, watching Gabriel squatting down on the edge of the stage to listen to some additional question. "I could do with some fresh air."

"Ah, you need a pier walk," said Eleanor. "It's just the night for it."

"So, is Gabriel Erskine still a . . . What was it you said? A rowdy Trinity boatie?" Eleanor enquired with a smile as they walked down the steep path towards the harbour.

"No, he appears to have grown up quite successfully," said Henrietta. "He always did have his civilised moments actually."

"Were you very close?" said Eleanor.

"We were engaged," said Henrietta,

111

"but I broke it off."

"I'm sure you had very good reasons," said Eleanor.

"I did," said Henrietta.

Eleanor did not answer but strolled forward on to the broad stone pier that jutted out into the sea. They walked down it together in companionable silence. When they reached the end, they climbed the iron ladder to the viewing platform.

"There, that's the best view of the town, I always think," said Eleanor. "Especially at night."

The lights of the town shone out through the lattice work of the Cathedral ruins.

"This is just how I always imagined the Cobb at Lyme Regis," Henrietta remarked. "You know, in *Persuasion*?"

"Well, I don't know about that," said Eleanor, "but I always find it's a wonderful spot to clear the mind. I don't do the undergraduate thing of walking back along the top there, though. That's the tradition, you see, on Sunday mornings and after balls."

"I can't say I fancy it," said Henrietta.

The sea wall was only about two feet wide and there was a sheer drop down to the rocks below. "Though I suppose at that age I would have been along there like a shot. You have strong nerves at that age, don't you?"

"You need them," said Eleanor. Henrietta silently agreed. It had taken all the will-power she had to break off that engagement; and standing there now, with the calm sea lapping over the rocks beneath them, she still felt ashamed of what she had done.

6

"MAY I look?" enquired a woman's voice, an American woman. Kate looked up from her sketch pad.

This was a hazard of working outdoors, especially in such a picturesque and tourist-filled spot as the Cathedral ruins in St Andrews. She had become part of the entertainment of the place, with people peering over her shoulder. She had already had a pair of enormously tall German boys chatting her up and a very polite Japanese man who had asked, most respectfully, if he might take a photo of her. Now it was this American. Kate did not really mind. All in all, it had been a good morning, and she had done a really satisfactory ink and watercolour sketch. It was a medium she was getting to like. Ink was much less predictable than pencil. Working in pencil, she had felt her line was too smooth, too accomplished, too relaxed. A scratchy steel nib gave tension and vigour to the line, not to mention some wonderfully fortuitous blots. Now she was starting another sketch, this time from a low viewpoint, with a thicket of graves directly in front of her, while in the distance St Rules Tower shot up in a breathtakingly vertical line that seemed to defy its very square, very stumpy shape. The satisfaction she was getting from this was almost enough to obliterate the memory of the business over the car.

Almost, she found herself thinking, cross hatching with particular virulence. It was the first time she and Gabriel had had a row, although she supposed by other people's standards it hardly merited that name. It had not been an out and out disagreement, after all, but there had been an unaccustomed tension between them, coming down over them like one of those heavy, damp fogs from the sea, blurring communications.

It had happened the afternoon before, when Gabriel had come back from Cupar driving a brand new, metallic green Range Rover. Kate had expressed her surprise, and he had handed her the keys, telling her it was for her. She had said nothing

115

about wanting or needing a car, let alone a new Range Rover with plastic still covering the seats. The extravagance of this gift had rattled her. She had begun to protest at it, but Gabriel had seemed not to hear her. He had all his arguments rehearsed for her, seemingly sensible ones: that it was impossible to manage in the country without a car; that although it might seem extravagant, it was not really — he had driven them for years and found them very reliable; the only cars that could cope with the back roads on the estate; and that she needed something capacious after all, something into the back of which she could easily fit a six-foot canvas. Et cetera, et cetera. They had all been perfectly good arguments and she had found herself nodding in mute agreement with them, while something inside her felt uneasy. It had been as if he were trying to prove something to her, to prove his love by this magnificent piece of generosity and also to prove (and this was what had really disturbed her) that he knew exactly what she wanted and required without his having to ask her opinion on the matter. Yet what annoyed her most of all about the whole thing was that she had not said, quite straightforwardly, "Well, you might at least have asked me what I thought about it before you spent all that money." He had been so childishly excited about his present to her that she had not had the heart to puncture that and to disappoint him. She should have said it though, she knew.

She had taken it out that morning with guilty pleasure, when Gabriel had, as usual, gone to the estate office. She had felt, as she drove away from Allansfield, that he had been right to think she had needed a car. Perhaps he was just saying in his own peculiar way that he understood the slightly oppressive atmosphere in the house and that he understood she needed to feel independent still and not subject to his routine.

She studied the American woman who was now standing slightly in front of her. She was a striking person altogether, with fair, slightly greying hair, caught up in a beautifully composed loose chignon. She wore elegant gold half-glasses on her nose, and she stood with a basket in one hand and a book in the other, her finger folded into it to mark her place.

"I've been watching you for the last half hour," she confessed, "and I couldn't prevent myself being a nosy Yankee any longer. Although to break your concentration seems a little sinful."

"Oh, I think I need a break, actually," said Kate, finding she was stiff suddenly from sitting cross-legged, her back against a gravestone. She staggered inelegantly to her feet and displayed the sketch to the American woman. "There . . . " Yet the moment she showed it, she found it annoyed her.

"It's delightful," said the woman. "What's your name — would I know it?"

"Probably not. I'm not that established yet. It's Kate, though, Kate Mackenzie."

"You should be," she said, putting out her hand. "Henrietta Winthrop."

They shook hands and Henrietta Winthrop continued to look at the drawing.

"It's a bit John Piperish, I'm afraid," said Kate.

118

"Please don't apologise," said the woman, calmly but almost sternly. She was scrutinising the sketch with care. "It is always a fatal mistake women make, apologising for their creativity. I've done it myself and always regretted it. It seems all wrong to me that you should apologise when you are so clearly a professional."

"Thanks," said Kate. There had been something in the woman's smile so graceful and intelligent that she had felt warmed by it. She reached into her portfolio for the sketch she had done earlier in the old nave of the Cathedral. "Here, this is what I did first. I can't resist a ruin. I think I shall be back here in all weathers — there are so many good bits of crumbling masonry, and the light today, although it's clear, isn't what you'd call exciting."

"This is really very gothick — with a k, you know."

"Oh, yes, there are supposed to be masses of ghosts, or so I'm told," said Kate. "Not that I've seen any yet. I've only just moved here."

"Me too," Henrietta said. "This is wonderful, you know," she said, tapping her finger on the sketch. "I know dealers in New York who would give their eye teeth for stuff like this."

"I don't usually try and sell this sort of thing. This is just preparatory work as far as I'm concerned, practice. Are you from New York?"

"No, but I know it quite well," said Henrietta. "You must be a perfectionist if this is only practice."

"Probably, I'm over pernickety," said Kate.

"Oh, that feels like rain," said Henrietta. A large drop spattered on to the sketch.

"Shit!" exclaimed Kate with feeling, and blotted it hastily with the cuff of her shirt. Quickly she slid the sketch back into her portfolio and zipped it shut. She began to gather up her painting things.

"The life of a *plein-air* painter is never an easy one," said Henrietta. Kate glanced up and saw that she had turned her face up to the rain, as if she were standing in the shower. She seemed to be relishing it, her book pressed to her chest, still with her finger marking her place, her eyes slightly closed. She had the most astonishing profile. As if she were aware of Kate's scrutiny she opened her eyes again and looked back at her. "You can come and shelter from the rain in my office, if you like. Don't worry, that isn't a proposition, I'm perfectly straight."

Kate burst out laughing and said, "OK, thanks — that'd be great."

★ ★ ★

The room Henrietta had been given at the Centre for Women's Studies in North Street was a great deal more satisfactory than Mon Abris. The centre had taken over two elegant eighteenth-century houses, painted pale green, and had managed to achieve, in this small space, the atmosphere of civilised tranquillity that Henrietta had frequently noticed in institutions run by women for women. From nunneries to girls' schools she had observed this same orderly sweetness that did not attempt to crush individuals with any sense of architectural pomposity.

Her room was in an attic, at the back, up three flights of an elegant curving staircase, and had from its deep-set dormer window a tantalising view over the sea. There were bookshelves covering one wall, fitting in neatly under the sloping ceiling, and she had soon filled them up. The departmental secretary, Molly, had kindly provided some geraniums for the window-sill, and Henrietta had bought a bunch of daffodils for her desk.

"I love your view," Kate said, standing by the window with her hands in her pockets. "It must be good to be able to see the sea as you work. It lets you put things in perspective."

"That sounded like it came from the heart," Henrietta observed, as she made them peppermint tea. "Have you got problems?"

Kate turned back and smiled. "Only very small problems," she said. "Problems of adjustment, like getting a new coat to fit properly. Moving to a new place is hard, isn't it? I'm sure you're finding that."

"And it's affecting your work?"

"I'm just looking for a direction, I suppose. Something new to grip my imagination."

"You need a short-term goal in mind,"

said Henrietta. "If you were one of my graduate students having problems with her thesis, I should know exactly what to say to you: 'Write a paper for so and so journal.' But I suspect it is not so easy for an artist."

"In theory," said Kate, sitting down, having accepted her mug of tea, "it should be. I should just carry on painting. I've a half-finished picture on the easel at home but I can't get excited about it. I'm not sure why I'm doing it. I need a reason."

"Would that be a show, or a commission, or what?"

Kate shrugged and sipped her tea. "I usually work for internal reasons," she said. "I've shown at quite a good gallery in Edinburgh, and other places once or twice, but that doesn't drive me. I paint because I have to, because of something in me, not because I need to sell anything." She smiled apologetically. "I'm lucky. I don't need to worry any more about money though. I can paint exactly what I want, but . . . oh, I'm finding it so difficult."

Henrietta sighed slightly and nodded.

She thought again of the easy brilliance of that sketch in the Cathedral, that mere practice piece, and wondered of what Kate might be capable. "Could I see that sketch again, do you think?" she asked.

"Of course," said Kate, reaching for the portfolio. She laid the sketch in front of Henrietta on the desk.

"I would love to see your real work," Henrietta said.

Kate shrugged and drank some more mint tea, cradling the mug in her hands. Henrietta lolled back in her chair, impressed again by the accomplishment of the drawing in front of her. The different colours in the sandstone walls were perfectly done, and the ink lines delineating the architecture had a life entirely of their own, crackling like lightning across the page.

She smiled suddenly, and said, "Do you know, I've just had the most wonderful idea. I can't promise you anything on this, but I know there is a marvellous exhibition space downstairs — that room on the right as you come through the door. Why don't I put it to the head of the Centre, Professor McCleod, that you have a one-woman show there, in a few months or so, in the fall, perhaps? That would really give you something to work towards, and it would get me some brownie points. I am supposed to be contributing something creative to this place while I'm here, after all. You'd be just the sort of person she likes, I know, and she's got some very good contacts. We would make quite a puff of it all, publicity wise. It would be quite helpful to your career."

"A one-woman show?" said Kate. "Are you quite serious? I mean, you've only seen two sketches by me, and — "

"Yes, I know, but I like taking risks," said Henrietta. "And I can tell you are good, just from this. Besides, you are exactly the sort of person that a Centre for Women's Studies in a Scottish university should be helping out, aren't you? You're Scottish, you're a woman — and I suspect you're rather outstanding in your field."

Kate looked dazed.

"Of course, you may be worrying about being ghettoised and not competing openly," said Henrietta. "Does it bother you to be thought of as a woman artist?"

"Well, I am a woman, aren't I?" said Kate. "But I've never thought consciously about it. I don't think that I'm . . . politicised. Is that the word?"

"Perhaps you should be," said Henrietta, and then held up her hands apologetically. "I'm sorry. I'm preaching."

"No, no, I should think about these things."

"Be careful what you say," laughed Henrietta. "Or I'll make you read my books."

"I think I'd like to," said Kate. "Will I find them in the book shop here?"

"Well, *Masters and Slaves* was reprinted by a British publisher last year, so it may be around still. Some people have been kind enough to call it a classic, although I think it's mostly polemic. I was very angry when I wrote it. I was about your age. It's a good time to achieve things, mid- to late-twenties. I found my time was very focused."

"I wish mine was," said Kate.

"It will be," said Henrietta. "I'm going to fix this show up for you and you are going to confound us all."

"All right," Kate said, and then grinned. "If you dare."

"That's much better," said Henrietta. "You'd better give me your phone number. I'll call you as soon as I get a response."

They exchanged phone numbers, and Kate gathered up her things. Just as her hand was on the door handle, she said, "You really must come and have dinner with us sometime."

"Yes, I'd like that," smiled Henrietta.

When Kate had left, Henrietta contentedly opened up her lap-top PC. It had turned out to be a rewarding morning. There was nothing she enjoyed more than gently propelling a young woman in the direction of success. Two years before, she had been thrilled when one of her students had picked up a major poetry award in a competition that Henrietta had encouraged her to enter. It was hardly an official part of her duties, but it was one that she enjoyed most of all.

★ ★ ★

Gabriel went looking for Kate in the old nursery. She was not there, although the room now showed real evidence of her occupation. It had made the transition from being a nursery into a studio. Her painting things had been set out on the table, the easel was up with a shrouded picture on it, her painting apron was thrown over a chair-back, and along the chimney piece she had propped some coloured postcards. On the table was Hugh's red lustre dish, full of apples, and on the press door she had pinned up several large sketches. One, he particularly admired: it was a pen and watercolour sketch of the south front of the house from the terrace, with the sky behind a spectacular inky blue-black, shot through with spring sunlight. He had seen that sort of light often enough, and relished the extraordinary drama of it, but he did not think he had ever seen it captured so well in paint.

He moved to the easel, and could not resist removing the dust sheet from it. The image that presented itself startled him. A young, extremely virile man stared out at him with arrogant, predatory, intensely charged eyes. The figure was modelled with extraordinary detail. The veins seemed almost three dimensional, the muscles and tendons taut as if supporting real bodily weight, the pale hair so crisply defined in every long curl that he felt he might touch it and feel it yield beneath his fingers. The figure alone was a *tour de force*, but around it, painted with the same dazzling precision, were the most intricate and elaborate patterns of foliage, flowers and fruit, some not yet finished but already drawn out in Kate's elegant sparing line. Why had she not shown him this before? he wondered. It had been sitting in her room, presumably, under its cover, every time he had visited her in Edinburgh. But even as he admired, he felt disturbed. This was not a picture about Kate's painterly bravura. It was a painting about the destructiveness of passion itself. This was Adam, after all, about to be exiled from paradise itself because of his indulgence in human love.

The door opened and Kate came in, carrying her portfolio and her bag of painting equipment.

"Oh," she said, "I didn't want you to see that yet."

"I'm sorry, should I not have looked?" he said. "I couldn't resist it."

"It doesn't matter now," she said, putting down her things.

She came and stood in front of the picture, her arms crossed, one shoulder tilted up, one hip thrust slightly out, carefully looking it over, absorbed, concentrating, pursuing her own independent and professional line of thought, her face both grave and intelligent.

"I had an amazing piece of luck today," she said, smiling slightly and turning to him. "Which, if you hadn't been so damned extravagant with that car, wouldn't have happened at all."

"Are you still cross with me about that?" he said.

"Oh, so you saw I was cross?" she said.

"It was horribly obvious," he said, rubbing his chin. "And I just went on and on, didn't I, assuming it was what you needed? I'm sorry, Kate, I should have asked you first. It was just that I wanted to surprise you, that's all."

"Well, you shouldn't always just assume what I want, should you?" she said, and then added, in a slightly more mollifying tone, "Please?"

"Point taken," he said. "I'm too used to running my own show, aren't I?"

"But it is a great car," she admitted. "And just what I need. Thanks."

"So," he said, sitting down, "What was your piece of luck with it?"

"Well, I went to St Andrews, and I found that lovely art shop you told me about, and then I went down to the Cathedral ruins and spent the morning sketching. While I was there, this amazing American woman came up to have a look at what I was doing, and we got chatting . . . " As she spoke she began to comb her fingers through her hair. Gabriel was so distracted by the beauty of this simple action that he hardly heard what she was saying. "She was so interesting, Gabriel. And such a fascinating face, like a classical statue or something, but with beautiful eyes. Here, I did a little sketch of her from memory to show you." She dived into her painting bag, brought out a little ring-bound sketch pad and, flipping it open, handed it to him. "Just a doodle really, but I think I got something of her in it."

Gabriel knew Kate's talent for catching a likeness with a few strokes of a soft pencil, and this likeness was so strong that he found himself squinting at it, mentally constructing and then deconstructing the lines as if it were one of those brain-teasers he recalled from the comics he had read as a boy. Surely it could not be . . .

"Isn't that an interesting face?" Kate said.

"Did you find out her name?" Gabriel asked carefully. Kate's answer would settle the matter. After all, there was no way that this woman could actually be Henrietta. It was just his brain playing a trick; and yet that fact alone was disturbing enough, for it begged the question: Why should he want to see a resemblance?

"Oh, yes," said Kate, sitting down opposite him. "Her name is even better than her face. When she told it to me I thought of you. I knew it would amuse you — it's like something out of a novel: Henrietta Winthrop. Isn't that amazing?"

Slowly her words reached his consciousness. He found he was sitting with his hand pressed over his mouth. He gave a nod in answer to her question, and then a slight wave of his hand to suggest she continue with her artlessly painful narrative.

"Anyway, when it started raining, she asked me if I wanted to shelter from the rain in her office — it turns out she's a visiting lecturer at the university. So I went back with her and we talked some more, about pictures, about feminism, about . . . oh, all sorts of things. Anyway, she really liked the sketch I'd done, and she suggested that I do a show there, in the Centre for Women's Studies. Isn't that a great idea? It's just what I need, isn't it, for my career? Manna from heaven, really!" she finished, triumphantly tossing back her hair. She stared at him, still sitting there. "Well, isn't it great?"

"It's . . . marvellous," he managed to say.

"Bloody marvellous," she said. "And I was feeling so purposeless, so unsure about my work, and then this comes along. She's a really inspiring person. I bought one of her books." Again she plunged into her painting bag and came out with a paperback. "Here we are."

Gabriel found himself staring at the book's title: *Masters and Slaves*.

Kate began to read aloud from the flyleaf: "'Henrietta Winthrop was educated at Smith College in the United States before coming to study at Cambridge in 1966.' Isn't that when you were at Cambridge?" He nodded heavily. "She must be a contemporary of yours, Gabriel. Do you remember her?"

"It's a large university," said Gabriel.

"But with a name like that — and those looks. I'm sure she was the sort of person everyone knew about. There are always people like that in any institution."

"Perhaps, I vaguely remember the name," he said, lamely. What a tiny, pathetic admission that was, when he really should have sat Kate down in front of him and told her everything, there and then. But he found he could not, and when she spoke next it felt like a punishment for his own cowardice.

"Well, perhaps you'll remember more when you meet her. I thought we could have her to dinner when Liz and Martin come through next week. Liz will be really impressed by her, I know. It'd be perfect — didn't you say you were going to ask Bob? He was at Cambridge with you, wasn't he? He might remember her too, mightn't he?" She was looking at him. "You did say I was to invite people, Gabriel," she went on. "That is all right, isn't it?"

"Of course it's all right," he said, getting up. He was aware how sharp his tone was, but he could not prevent the anxiety that gripped at his throat. "This is your house now, Kate, as much as mine. You may ask whoever you like. You don't need my permission, for God's sake. I'm not an ogre."

"OK," she said, clearly taken aback. "OK. I know that, Gabriel."

"Sorry," he said, and put his arms around her, pulling her close to him, wishing he could drown all recollection and all apprehension in this simple act.

Yet, even with Kate in his arms, he could not stop himself thinking of the first time he had kissed Henrietta. It had been on a frosty November night, and they had been to hear a concert of Bach cantatas in King's College Chapel. She had only been wearing a thin jacket, and as he had walked her back to Newnham she had started shivering in the bitter East Anglian wind.

"It's almost as cold as New England," she'd said. "I never thought it would be this cold . . . "

Irresistibly moved by her chattering teeth, he had pulled off his own sturdy tweed overcoat and put it round her shoulders. The gesture had turned naturally enough into an embrace, and he had felt he could have stood there all night with her in his arms. Yet suddenly she had broken away and laughed with giddy delight, throwing back her head to look at the bright starry specks in the sky above them. He had tried to kiss her again but she had resisted, pressing her icy cold palms to his cheeks and saying, "Wait until tomorrow. Come and see me tomorrow afternoon."

And she had run away from him, his coat flapping from her shoulders like a cape.

So he had gone back the following afternoon, ostensibly to retrieve his coat, but drunk with excitement at realising that her words had implied she would be offering him more than the usual cup of coffee. He had been right. She had slowly and deliberately seduced him over Earl Grey tea, walnut cake and cigarettes. He could still remember the taste of her kisses and that extraordinary feeling of losing himself completely in her presence. He felt he had not just given up his virginity to her then but his soul.

7

GABRIEL found Bob Kavanagh, as usual, in his subterranean laboratory. It had once been a car park under one of the university science buildings, but Bob had commandeered it for his research team, and it was now filled with his strange robot creations. As Gabriel came in, Bob was almost obscured by a shower of sparks as he welded together the leg joint of what looked like a tin-plated pantomime horse.

He caught sight of Gabriel and switched off the welding iron. He pushed back his goggles and waved for Gabriel to come over.

"How's Kate?" he asked.

"Settling in, I think," said Gabriel.

"I'm surprised you can tear yourself away."

"Well, I've had to. I need to talk to you."

"About what?" said Bob. "Sounds serious."

"Maybe, maybe not."

"Let's go into my office," said Bob.

Bob, having offered Gabriel a can of Irn Bru (which he declined), straddled his chair, and said, "OK, spit it out. You look distinctly rattled."

Bob had left Sydney for good when he came to Cambridge on a Commonwealth scholarship, but he had scrupulously preserved his Australian accent.

"It's Henrietta. She's here," said Gabriel, and related Kate's encounter with her.

Bob swallowed down the last of his Irn Bru and shook his head. "Who'd have thought it, after all this time?" he said. "Now, where is that thing?" He began to search the piles of paper on his desk. "Here we are — this should give us the full gen." He held up a copy of the St Andrews' University Bulletin. "I never read this. I haven't really the least idea of what goes on in this place." He flipped through it. "Aha, this is our girl: 'Dr Henrietta Winthrop, of Harvard . . . '" Bob raised an eyebrow. "No less, ' . . . joins the Centre for Women's Studies this term for a year's sabbatical as a Lennox Visiting Fellow.

Dr Winthrop's research has centred on women novelists of the eighteenth and nineteenth centuries, and she is the editor of the quarterly . . . ' Blah de blah . . . Ah yes, and a picture too. Look at that." He thrust the magazine over to Gabriel.

Gabriel studied the picture for a moment and then threw down the magazine. In black and white Henrietta stared out at him, looking levelly and dispassionately through half-glasses. Kate's doodle from memory had been phenomenally accurate.

"Well preserved, eh?" said Bob.

"You always were jealous, weren't you?" said Gabriel. "Even when you had half the girls in Cambridge queuing up to sleep with you."

"That was just sex," laughed Bob. "What you and Henrietta had was the great big love affair. When you two were around, it was like there was a bloody great symphony orchestra scraping away in the background, just like the movies. Romeo and Juliet, Anthony and Cleopatra, Ingrid Bergman and Humphrey Bogart. It was bloody romantic."

"Complete with the obligatory unhappy ending," said Gabriel, picking up the magazine and looking at Henrietta again.

"What did Kate say?"

"I said I didn't know her."

"Why?"

Gabriel shrugged. "It wasn't quite the right moment to explain."

"I would have thought you'd told her ages ago. You told her about Jane, didn't you?"

"Of course. That's different. That was easy. But this, it's peculiar. I don't want to tell her. The whole thing's so . . . " He got up. "I know I should tell Kate, and I will, but . . . "

"What are you afraid of?" said Bob. "We're talking ancient history, remember."

"Of course."

Yet, as he walked down from the North Haugh into St Andrews, it did not feel like ancient history. The sight of her photograph had triggered a hundred vivid memories. He could see her sitting drinking tea in her blue silk dressing gown after they had been making love; lying on her stomach in Grantchester Meadows, deep in a book; or gesturing

141

with her wine glass in the full flight of some passionate argument: "No, no, I don't accept that at all. That's sloppy logic and you know it, Gabriel!"

He was in North Street now, outside a pretty little eighteenth-century house which labelled itself 'The Centre for Women's Studies'. He could not resist the impulse any longer and went straight up the path to the front door.

He was not entirely sure though, as the departmental secretary showed him to Henrietta's office door, exactly why he was allowing himself to give in to this impulse. He had a few minutes to consider why. The secretary had explained that Dr Winthrop was taking a tutorial just then, but would be free on the hour, and Gabriel waited on the landing outside her door and pretended to study the cluttered notice-board while he turned the problem over in his mind. He decided he was there to make certain that the ghost in his mind, labelled Henrietta, was nothing more than that, and that the Henrietta Winthrop in St Andrews, whom Kate had met, bore nothing but a superficial resemblance to the woman with whom he had been so desperately in love. He had seen her photograph and Kate's vivid little drawing; all he needed now was to see her in the flesh as the final evidence to convince his dim-witted senses that his feelings were in no danger from her. He found it irritating in the extreme that he should still feel this vulnerable, as if nothing had happened between then and now. He had Kate now, didn't he? Taking into account that fact alone, this was extraordinarily irrational of him. He took his mind on another, more practical tack. He was going to see her out of common courtesy. Kate had announced at breakfast she was going to call Henrietta that morning, and Henrietta had probably already accepted her invitation to dinner, without realising quite what she had accepted. It was only fair to explain the situation to her in person.

He continued to stare at the notice-board, not the least bit convinced by his arguments. It was curiosity, that was the unpalatable truth. He distracted himself by reading one of the posters in front of him. It was a call for papers for the Fifth Annual Conference on Feminism and the Arts, to be held at the University of Montana in 1997 — but this was no distraction at all. It sent his mind shooting back to the day he least wished to remember, the morning two days before his twenty-first birthday, in March 1968.

★ ★ ★

He had been given rooms in Trinity Street in his final year at Cambridge, and he had enjoyed the privacy of being out of college. Those two large irregularly-shaped attic rooms, with steps up into the bedroom from the living room, had struck him as the perfect lovers' retreat. Henrietta could come and go when she liked without having to pass the officious and old-fashioned college porters. He wished she might move some of her stuff from Newnham in there, beyond her toothbrush, for she spent two or three nights a week there, and he felt he would like the comfort of her things about him when she was not around. She was being very conscientious about

144

work that year, far more conscientious than he was, and he had his finals next term. Sternly, he reminded himself of this fact, as he lay on his stomach on the floor of his sitting room, attempting to study — his mind was failing to get to grips with Williamson on Tort. It was far more enjoyable to think about Henrietta and the little plan he was hatching. He would tell her all about it on his birthday, at the same time he gave her the engagement ring that he had finally persuaded his father to let him take from the family collection. At Christmas, when he had told his parents that he and Henrietta had decided to get married, Hugh Erskine, assuming his best Indian Army officer manner, had pointed out that it was not at all good form to get engaged to a girl unless you were in a position to marry her within three months. "And you're hardly in a position to get married until you finish at Cambridge, are you?" he had said. "And then, I really don't think you should think of it until you've at least established yourself at the bar."

Gabriel had held his ground, though

at times he almost wished he had never raised the subject, until his mother had pointed out, "At least Gabriel is intending to get married, which is something we should be grateful for, considering that the fashion these days seems to be all for 'living together'." This phrase had fallen so awkwardly from his mother's lips that Gabriel had had to repress a smile, thinking how horrified she would be to know that he had slept with Henrietta. "And a long engagement is not such a bad idea," she had gone on. "It gives them a chance to get to know each other properly. You must invite her to stay at Easter, Gabriel — we're looking forward to meeting her very much, aren't we, Hugh?"

Gabriel had no intention of abiding by his parents' suggestions, however. He had not yet discussed with Henrietta when they would get married. When she finished at Cambridge seemed the obvious time, but he was no longer sure he could wait that long. The thought of next year, when he would be in London and she still in Cambridge, had been frankly frightening until he had realised that, if they got married after he graduated, those times which they must spend apart would seem only like temporary interruptions. They would be able to set up house together in London, and she could get married quarters in college, so that he could go down to Cambridge every weekend to be with her. His long-cherished plan of travelling round Italy with her that summer had been transformed deliciously in his mind into a wedding journey. He rolled on to his back, abandoning the dreary Tort textbook entirely to the intoxicating thought of Henrietta in Venice.

He had closed his eyes and was dreaming when there was a gentle knock at the door. He opened his eyes to see Henrietta coming in. He jumped to his feet, feeling he had conjured her up by thinking so intensely of her.

"Henry!" he said, putting his arms around her. "What a wonderful surprise. I thought you were keeping away from me until you'd finished that essay . . . but you couldn't keep away, could you?"

"I've a bit of news," she said, gently detaching herself. She walked over to the window and dug into the pocket of her leather coat to produce her cigarettes. She gestured with the pack towards him. He nodded, although he was trying, somewhat feebly, to give up smoking. There was something in her manner that made him want the easy comfort of a cigarette.

"What's up?" he said, lighting their cigarettes. "Are you OK? This news, is it bad news?" He reached out and laid his hand on her arm. "Your family or something?"

"Depends how you look at it," she said, her elbows on the window-sill and looking out at the rooftops. "You know that article I wrote on Maria Edgeworth?"

"Oh yes . . . "

"Well, the journal has accepted it."

"That's good news, isn't it?"

"Yes, very, it's quite a coup actually, since I'm still a student," she said.

"I knew you were a genius," said Gabriel, attempting to kiss her — but again she slipped out of his arms.

"The thing is," she went on, "the editor, Dr Landesman, in his letter asked me whether I wanted to teach at his summer school in Connecticut this year."

"Ah, well," said Gabriel cheerfully, "it's nice to be asked, isn't it?"

"It's more than nice, it's a small miracle."

"Still, it won't be as much of a miracle as Italy, will it?"

"It is not the sort of invitation I can refuse," she said, after a slight pause.

"What do you mean?"

"What I say. You don't spit in the face of Dr Theodore Landesman, not if you want to get anywhere in my field."

"Oh sod Dr Landesman, Henry. We're going to Italy, remember. You do remember, don't you?" he added, teasingly.

"Yes, yes, but that is not exactly set in stone."

"What the hell do you mean? Of course it is." He stared at her. "Have I got this straight? You'd rather go and teach at some summer school than go to Italy? I thought you were desperate to go to Italy . . . "

"Italy is going to have to wait. Dr Landesman won't. He wants my answer soon and I can't really afford not to accept. Opportunities like this don't come round twice, you know. I have to get my feet in that door."

"Why?"

"Oh, you know why, Gabriel. Don't be obtuse! Because it's what I want to do."

"But I honestly can't see what good teaching at this Hickville American summer school is going to do you, when you're going to be living over here for the rest of your life. I mean, who the hell is Theodore Landesman, Henry? He isn't exactly Q. D. Leavis, is he?"

She did not respond at once, but took a long drag on her cigarette and then said quietly, "Well, actually I think that's something we need to discuss as well, Gabriel."

"What?"

"I'm not being straight with you, am I?" she said. "Landesman, that's just a symptom rather than a cause. I'm being a coward, I guess, because I don't really want to say this, but I have to, because it has to be said. It isn't very pleasant, but . . ."

"What are you talking about?"

"Our future," she said bluntly. "Or rather our lack of it."

"I'm sorry?"

"Sit down, Gabriel," she said. "Sit down and listen." Mutely he obeyed. "Now, I know this is going to be tough for you, but I can't think of any way round it. Please just listen and try to understand. I haven't come to this decision lightly at all. It's been bothering me all term, and the letter from Dr Landesman, it just confirmed everything I've been thinking . . ."

"Oh, for Christ's sake, Henrietta," he burst out. "If you're going to say something terrible, just say it, OK?"

"OK," she said. "I think we should split up."

He found himself staring hard at her, noticing as she stood by the window how the sun was lighting up the stray strands of pale gold hair which had escaped the bandeau she had tied round her head. Then he leant back in his chair and pushed his fingers through his own hair and said, almost laughing as he spoke, "I simply don't believe you just said that."

"I did," she said.

"Well, then you didn't mean it." He waited for her to deny it. "Did you?" he said, looking at her, She nodded, and took another drag on her cigarette.

"You did ask me to come to the point," she said. "And so I have. I think we should split up."

"Jesus . . . Jesus! Henrietta, you are not actually . . . " He broke off and stared at her again. She was looking levelly at him, and seemed so calm that he could not believe she was actually saying what she meant. "This is a joke. You'd never be so calm if you meant that."

"I'm quite capable of self-control," she said, walking over to the desk and stubbing her cigarette out in the ash tray. "In fact, this is really what all this is about: self-control. A matter of cold, hard, logic, over . . . " She hesitated for a moment. "Over transitory feelings."

"Transitory feelings?" he said, jumping up. "What sort of shit is that? We're engaged, for God's sake."

"Not any more we're not," she said. "It's over, Gabriel, all over."

"OK, OK, what have I done? What?" he said, marshalling his thoughts quickly.

"Let me try to put it right, at least."

"It's nothing you've done," she said. "Nothing in particular anyway."

"What do you mean by that?"

"I mean that I've been thinking, and the more I think the less I can see it. I just can't see how it's going to be for us in ten, fifteen years' time. I can't even see next year, to be frank. We've been living a dream, Gabriel. This isn't the sort of thing that lasts. It's like a bottle of good wine, or a garden in high summer, or a night at the opera — it's all intense and beautiful, but then the bottle's empty or autumn comes or the curtain comes down and the house lights come up, and what are you left with? Reality, cold reality. And if I stayed here, with you, I'd feel I was running away from what I really am and what I really want from life."

"This is just nerves," he said, putting his hands on her shoulders. "Silly nerves. Of course you're frightened. I mean, who wouldn't be? I dare say I shall be terrified on the day. It's a big thing, I know that, but — "

"This is not nerves," she said. "This is

not cold feet. This is deadly serious."

"*We* are serious," he said.

"No," she said, shaking her head. "No we're not. I can't see it any more. I can see another sort of life for myself, but not your idea. It feels all wrong. I can't see myself fitting in, settling down."

"It'll hardly be that . . . "

"Yes it will. For me it will. You'll be just fine. You'll go off and play your lawyer games — because they will be just games for you, because you don't actually have to do it, do you? You've all the money you need. You'd have studied a damn sight harder if you actually had to make your own way, or even if it meant something to you. But really, for you, the law, it's just something respectable to do, isn't it?"

"I don't see what that has got to do with anything."

"It has everything to do with it," she said. "You and I are so different, so fundamentally different. You see, what I do, what I want to do, matters more than anything . . . "

"More than me, obviously."

"Yes, I'm afraid so. I am going back

home when I'm done here, and I am going to make my reputation as a scholar. That's what I've always wanted, and I don't see that happening if we stick together. I'll just get side-tracked, and I don't want that to happen. Perhaps I'm being selfish, but then again, perhaps it's time for women to be selfish. You ought to understand this, Gabriel — didn't you tell me all about that great-aunt of yours who went to gaol for the right to vote?"

"I can understand a kick in the teeth," he said. "That's what this amounts to."

He walked to the window and stood with his palms pressed on the sill, trying to deal with the mixture of pain and anger that seemed to be taking hold of him. He felt close to tears, in fact, but he was damned if he was going to give into that, at least not in front of her.

"I think you're actually enjoying this," he said after a moment. "First you catch the little fly in your web, let him dangle a while, and then you rip out his heart and let him bleed to death in front of you! Is that what you're trying to do to me, Henrietta?"

"I am not enjoying this, I assure you," she said.

"Then why the hell are you doing it, Henry?" he said, turning and marching over to her. "Why?" He grabbed her by the shoulders and shook her.

"Let go of me," she said.

"Not until you tell me why you are so determined to make us both utterly miserable. None of your reasons make any sense, do they? Do they?" He shook her again, looking hard into her eyes.

She pushed him back with considerable force. "Don't get heavy with me!" she said sharply.

"You've told me so many times that you love me. Were you lying?"

"We are all capable of self-deception," she said, taking a deep breath. "Wouldn't you say?"

"No," he said, looking back at her for a moment. "No, I can't accept that. You love me, Henrietta. I know that as clearly as I know my own name. What I don't know is why you're saying all this ridiculous stuff."

"It is not ridiculous stuff, Gabriel," she said. "This is the honest truth. I think

I've made a mistake and I want out."

"A mistake," he said, shaking his head. "A bloody mistake! Is that the best you can come up with? A mistake — is that all this has been? Is that why you seduced me in the first place, by mistake? No, I don't think so. I don't think you've ever been mistaken, Henrietta. In fact, I think you've known exactly what you were doing. You've been playing all along. It's like some lovely literary game for you, this. It wasn't that you've ever wanted me, it was that you've wanted the idea of me, the innocent Scotsman of good family — is that it? The American goddess chalks up a European conquest! It's like something out of bloody Henry James."

"If it helps you to accept the situation, then think what you like," she said.

"Do you really want me to hate you?" he said, stretching out his hand towards her, hoping desperately she would take it suddenly and end the nightmare.

There was a long silence and then she said, "If that is what it takes, then . . . "

★ ★ ★

Henrietta's tutorial had gone well. It would have been hard for it not to go well with three very bright young women, full of enthusiasm for their subject. It had been very interesting to hear them outlining their dissertation topics, and she was looking forward to seeing them again in the autumn, hopefully laden down with the fruits of their research.

As they left, she switched on her lap-top, intending to get on with a less agreeable part of the job — revising a paper for a journal — but there was a rap at the door. Before she answered, she glanced at the appointment list Molly had typed out for her. She had wanted to see all the students she would be supervising next year, but there was no one she was expecting just then.

"Come in!" she called out. The door opened and she saw that it was Gabriel. She sank back in her chair and tried to form a polite, non-committal smile, hoping she did not look stupidly surprised. "Well, Gabriel . . . ah . . . " She pressed the palms of her hands together. "I suppose I was half expecting to run into you at some time or another. I saw you the other night, at the Horticultural Society, you see."

"Oh . . . " he said. Now he looked surprised. "Oh, did you? Well that's Fife for you. A very small place. You know that Bob Kavanagh's here as well?" he added.

"Goodness, no," she said. In her mind she could see Bob and Gabriel sitting on the floor of Gabriel's sitting room, rolling joints, Bob always with a great deal more dexterity than Gabriel. "Why — does he teach here?"

"Artificial Intelligence. He'll be descending on you at some point, I imagine. Another shock?"

"Somewhat, yes. But it must have been quite a shock for you too, I imagine, hearing about me. How did you know I was here?" she asked.

"Kate told me."

"Kate. Yes . . . " she said. "Of course — you know Kate. You always were interested in painting." She smiled suddenly. "You know, when you just said that I thought suddenly, goodness, she could be your daughter or something.

That would have been ironic, wouldn't it?"

"Yes, very," he said, carefully. "The thing is . . ."

"Yes?"

"I gather Kate has asked you to dinner this Saturday."

"She called this morning. Why, are you going too? Can I catch a lift? It's out in the country somewhere, isn't it? She said she'd send me a map . . ."

"I think I ought to explain about Kate and me. You see, she's invited you to my . . . our house," he corrected himself.

"Your house?"

"Yes, to Allansfield," he said. "Surely you remember Allansfield."

"Yes, I do. I wrote to you at Allansfield, didn't I?"

"You certainly did. All that summer."

She could see herself, sitting in the family room of her parents' summer house in Maine, addressing an airmail envelope to Gabriel Erskine, Allansfield, By Cupar, Fife, Scotland. "So you and Kate are . . . ?" Henrietta found she did not want to put the question too

160

bluntly, in case she had drawn the wrong conclusion.

"Ah, you have me there. I still haven't quite hit on the right terminology," he said. "Kate tells me the current expression is 'partners'."

Henrietta walked slowly across the room to the window, breathing deeply, staying consciously calm as she digested this revelation. It seemed incredible that Kate should be Gabriel's partner. Henrietta had imagined, after seeing him the other night, that he would have been long and solidly married to a woman, like the English girls she remembered at Newnham. Gabriel's wife, she had decided, would no doubt be a passionate gardener and an obedient, quiet wife, who was intellectual without being in any way astringent. She had not for a moment thought he would be living with someone as young as Kate. No wonder, she thought with a touch of disgust, he had seemed so happy.

"Well, I think I need a drink now," she said. "Perhaps you might like one?"

"Coffee?" he asked.

161

"I'm afraid I don't drink coffee any more," she said.

"You don't?" he said. "How do you get by without it?"

"Scotch," she said, getting up. "Do you want one?"

He looked at her, considering the question for a moment. "A very small whisky?" he suggested.

As she poured out the drinks, she watched as he walked to the window and looked out, standing exactly as Kate had done, with his hands in his pockets.

"Splendid view," he said. She came over beside him and handed him the drink. As she drew this close, she remembered how he had been shorter than her and how she had always teased him about it. He had never been riled, though. He had said, "I like to have someone to look up to." Now he said, "That's the one thing wrong with Allansfield, you can't see the sea from there."

Henrietta took her seat at the desk again. "Won't you sit down?" she asked.

"This is where your students sit, I suppose," he said, taking the chair opposite the desk.

"You sound as though you pity them."

"Well, I shouldn't like to have my essays ripped apart by you," he said.

"Oh, I'm most humane these days," she smiled.

"Would you have come here if you'd known we'd be neighbours?" he asked after a moment.

"Probably," she said. "After all, we are civilised grown-ups now, aren't we?"

"So," he said at length, getting up again and walking to the window, his hands thrust into his pockets. "Did you ever get married?"

"No, I never did ensnare myself in that particular trap."

"Surely," he said, turning slightly to her, and looking at her with narrowed eyes, "one can never tell if it's a trap until one is in it?"

"There's plenty of evidence to prove otherwise. It is not necessary to experiment on oneself." She smiled slightly, resting her chin on her folded hands.

He snorted with amusement, his eyes still fixed on the sea. "I did, with disastrous consequences," he said.

"Whom did you marry? Was it anyone from Cambridge?"

"No, no, she was an old family friend. Jane MacNab. A huge mistake."

"I'm sorry it didn't work out."

"I was on the rebound, I suspect," he said.

She shrugged as best she could, though she had the strangest feeling of time telescoping itself, as if it had been only a day or two ago they had been arguing over the points. She needed to fortify herself and so she poured out another drink.

"But you and Kate, now that's . . . er . . . "

"Yes, I know it must seem a little odd," he said. "But these things happen sometimes." He smiled. "It's very extraordinary and very wonderful."

The sincerity in his voice awakened some ancient ache in her. At Cambridge she had both loved and hated his declarations. They had been an impossible torture, but like some masochist she had not been able to resist hearing them. It had fed her like a drug, that love of his, and hearing it now, again, but expressed

164

for some other woman, she felt, with some shock, the grip of jealousy about her throat. He had pledged his life to her a thousand times and now he felt nothing.

"Good," she managed to say. "Good. That's exactly how it should be." She stuffed down all that irrational emotion. Kate had stolen nothing from her. Henrietta had thrown Gabriel away. Looking at him now, his eyes ignited with the thought of his darling Kate, Henrietta wondered, as she had often wondered, why she had broken off their engagement. The reasons had seemed so compelling at the time — the chance of a teaching post at a good college when she had finished at Cambridge; the chance of academic glory, of an independent life, made on her own terms — but so often, as time passed, they had not seemed like good reasons at all.

"So, about this dinner," she said at length. "Perhaps you'd rather I didn't come. It's not really fair on Kate, is it?"

"Well, I'm sure she won't mind, when I've explained it all to her. Besides, dinner is the least we can do, after your marvellous suggestion about the exhibition. Kate is cock-a-hoop about the idea. And as you said, we are civilised adults now, aren't we?"

"Yes, yes, of course we are," said Henrietta, and swallowed down the rest of her whisky.

When he had gone she sat back in her chair, her mind painfully alive with memories: lying on the sofa in Gabriel's sitting room in Trinity, her head in his lap, his hand gently and patiently stroking away her headache; Gabriel standing on a table, breathlessly reciting T. S. Eliot; but most of all she remembered the arguments, those wonderful furious arguments over trifles which sometimes turned into explosions, and usually ended with a bout of furious lovemaking. How intense, how frighteningly intense it had all been, she thought, staring down into her empty glass. Sometimes she had felt certain she would drown and never find her real self again. That was why she had felt the need to pull herself away so violently. Yet could she honestly say she had ever been as happy since?

8

"NO," said Lara, holding up her hand to Hugh, as the train began to draw into Cupar station. "Not another word. I've had enough talking. We're going back to London and that's it. If you want to come, you come. If you don't . . . " She shrugged and turned to look at the creeping train. "Ah, darling," she said to Andrew, who was sitting on her hip. "Look, it's our train. Are you excited?"

The train drew to a halt and Hugh, to stop himself thinking about what was actually happening, busied himself with gathering up Lara's and Andrew's luggage and stowing it on to a carriage. There was no time to talk any more anyway — the train would be leaving in a moment, and he only just had time to get out on to the platform again before the doors were slammed shut. Lara held Andrew up to wave at him from the window.

Hugh did not know whether to feel angry or relieved as the train pulled away and he watched Andrew press his small hands against the window. He walked alongside for a few moments until it got up speed, and suddenly he could no longer see either Lara or Andrew. He stopped at the far end of the platform and felt a stab of anguish, realising that history was repeating itself. His mother had taken him back to London a couple of times from that very station. He had been six or seven at most — and he could see his father waving at him as he stood at the train window. He remembered vividly his own childish sense of loss, but now he felt what Gabriel must have felt and how it hurt, to see his own son carried away like that.

The worst of it was that it was his fault. If he had not been so convinced that the best thing for them was to come to Allansfield, if he hadn't forced the issue so, then Lara and Andrew would not now be whizzing away from him towards Edinburgh. Lara had absolutely refused to stay a moment longer, and he had absolutely refused to leave. Stalemate.

They had argued until their throats were sore and Andrew was wailing with distress. *That* had silenced them. Then Hugh had swallowed hard and said as calmly and as rationally as he could, "I really can't go back to London just yet. But if you must, you must, I suppose . . . "

"Good!" Lara had said, and marched off triumphantly to pack. He had stood there cuddling Andrew, attempting to soothe him, knowing that he had taken a step which above all things he had not wanted to take. In letting them go and staying there himself he was being actively destructive. He was ripping the thing apart with his own hands, when that was the last thing he had intended. He thought he wanted to preserve his marriage — then why on earth was he meekly letting Lara go like this? Because, he told himself sternly, he needed a little time apart from her, to sort out what he felt. They both did. Breathing space — isn't that what people called it?

It might have seemed a perfectly sensible thing to do if Andrew had not been involved. That was what was so frightening about the whole business. Of course he knew that the parents of small children could and did split up, but he had been absolutely determined that it would not happen to them. That was why he had insisted on their all going to Allansfield, in an attempt to sort things out. If it had been just Lara he could probably have scuttled away without much thinking about it.

Perhaps he should have done that in the first place. Then Andrew would have been spared hearing them quarrel — and he had already heard enough of their quarrels. It was impossible to know, of course, what was better for a child — two parents living together in a state of active war (which, being frank about it, was exactly what it had been between him and Lara over the last six months), or two separated parents who were at least calm and hopefully happier. Hugh had always longed for his mother and father to be together again (especially when Tony was laying down the law about something), but at the same time he had known this was his fantasy. There had always been a discreet bitterness in his mother's voice when she had spoken of Gabriel. Later she had explained to Hugh why their marriage had fallen apart. "Because," Jane Cherrington had said, "his heart wasn't in it. He simply did not know how to love." Hugh gave a slight shudder when he recalled that. It was exactly what Lara had accused him of.

Cupar station was deserted now, and the train was not even visible in the distance. Hugh shoved his hands into his pockets and walked out to the car park. They were gone and he was alone now, left to cool his heels and wonder what on earth to do next.

★ ★ ★

Kate was in the kitchen making a chocolate cake for the dinner party that evening. Even though Alison had cooked everything else — watercress soup, and a cold dressed salmon with new potatoes and asparagus from the kitchen garden — Kate had decided she must do something towards the feast. It was not that she particularly missed cooking. Having meals appear on the table at regular intervals without any effort on her part was perhaps one of the most luxurious things about living at Allansfield. It was like staying at a very pleasant, extremely private hotel. It was a miracle really that Gabriel was as self-sufficient and as thin as he was, having had Alison tending to him for all these years. Kate felt certain she would get very fat if she did not watch out, and extravagances like this chocolate cake were not going to help. When she had made it before, for the rather haphazard supper parties she and Liz had sometimes thrown at Barclay Terrace, it had always been a huge success. There had never been any left over to gorge on in the morning.

The tiny kitchen at Barclay Terrace was a world away from the kitchen at Allansfield, which had not been substantially altered since the house was rebuilt at the turn of the century. The range had been replaced by a large cream-coloured Aga, and a dishwasher and a huge American-style fridge freezer had been added, but the cupboards and shelves were still painted green, and were getting a little battered round the edges. Half the kitchen implements were equally antique; even the radio was an old valve Ferguson that took three minutes to warm up. Gabriel referred to it as the wireless when he wasn't thinking, which amused Kate.

She had separated six eggs and tipped the whites into the large copper bowl with a dent. There was an electric mixer, but Kate had decided to do the thing properly and beat the egg whites by hand with a whisk, as if the extra effort would improve the taste.

She had just got them frothing nicely when the back door from the scullery swung open. She glanced over her shoulder to see Hugh. He gave a brief but rather half-hearted smile, propped himself up against the Aga and said, "I'm afraid your dinner table's going to be messed up tonight."

"Oh?" she said.

"I've just put Lara and Andrew on the London train," he said, and rubbed his hand across his face, a gesture Kate was sure he had caught from Gabriel.

Kate put down the bowl of egg whites, wondering if this meant they had just had some major disagreement. Hugh looked distinctly bruised. Lara had made very few appearances at the house, which had fuelled Gabriel's gloomy speculations about the state of Hugh's marriage, and to discover they had departed so abruptly only seemed to confirm his theories.

"I'm sorry," Kate said. "It'll be quiet without Andrew."

"You mean nice and quiet," he said. "He was a bit boisterous yesterday."

Hugh had left Andrew with Kate and Gabriel for a couple of hours the afternoon before. Gabriel had been called away reluctantly to deal with some crisis at the estate office, and Kate had been left in sole charge. Initially terrified, she had found herself surprisingly resourceful in entertaining him.

"No, I enjoyed playing with him, honestly," she said. "It was fun — if a bit exhausting — and I did manage to get him to sit still long enough to do a sketch of him."

"You did?"

"It was only a lightning sketch," said

Kate. "But I might work it up into a little portrait. Gabriel would like that, I know. Actually, I think he'll be annoyed to have missed saying goodbye to them."

Hugh sighed and said, "Yes, I know, but it can't be helped. What are you making there?"

"Chocolate cake."

"My favourite," he said. "Is it a good one?"

"I think so. It usually gets eaten up fairly quickly, though it's a bit fiddly. These egg whites are quite hard to work."

"May I?" he said, gesturing towards the copper bowl.

"Do the egg whites?" she said.

"I need something to do," he said.

"OK," she said, bemused. "Shall I make some coffee?"

"Coffee sounds a very good idea," he said. He picked up the bowl and gripped it to his chest and begin to whisk the eggs briskly and competently. The sleeves of his checked shirt were rolled up and Kate noticed the hardness of the muscle in his forearms. Pottery, she supposed, made for strong arms. The pattern of the musculature and tendons interested her. It would make a good pencil study.

She put the kettle on the hob and turned back to watch him finish the job. He had soon turned the pale froth into dry white snow.

"That's very impressive," she said.

"It's therapy," he said.

"Do you want to talk about it?" she ventured, but Hugh did not answer. "I'm sorry," she went on. "I didn't mean to be so direct. It's just that Gabriel's been worried, and — "

"I want to," he said, putting down the bowl. "But that doesn't mean I should. And I don't want to bore you to death. People do go on interminably about relationships sometimes."

"Perhaps, but maybe you need to talk."

"No, it would only be self-indulgent whining," he said. "And hardly fair to you." He lifted the whisk and shook it to test the stiffness of the egg white. "Is that about right for you?"

"Perfect."

"It's an extraordinary texture isn't it?" he said.

"And such a brilliant white too," said Kate, peering into the bowl. "Almost a chemical white. You know — well, I'm sure you do — that they used to use egg yolks as a mix for paint. I wonder why they couldn't find a use for the whites . . . "

"Meringues," he said.

Kate continued to study the egg whites. "They look great against the copper too," she said. "That would make a really interesting still life."

"Go and get your paints then," he said.

"What about the cake?"

"I'll make the cake. You paint."

"But then I won't get the credit for it tonight," she pointed out with a smile. "My ego needs that."

"And what about my therapy?" Hugh said.

"You can tell me if you like," Kate found herself saying. She wondered whether she was motivated by genuine sympathy or curiosity. "I really don't mind."

"I wouldn't know where to start," he said. "It's all such a bloody mess." He pulled the open cookery book towards him across the table. "Now, what do we do next?"

"You melt the chocolate, I think," said Kate. "And I'll get my sketch book, shall I?"

He looked up from the book and smiled broadly at her. How like his father he was when he smiled, Kate could not help thinking.

She returned to find Hugh meticulously assembling and measuring out the other ingredients. He had also made a pot of coffee. She sat down and did a very impressionistic pastel of the egg white while he heated the chocolate and egg yolks together in the double boiler, stirring them with determined patience. Kate wondered what exactly had gone wrong. Gabriel had told her that Lara and Hugh had been wildly in love. Perhaps they were the sort of couple who enjoyed having volcanic tiffs, but she could not imagine Hugh being quite that type.

"How's that?" she said, showing him her sketch. "I don't think I've really got the copper quite right. Oil or gouache would be better, don't you think?"

He studied the sketch for a moment. "Don't you think," he said, "it needs something else, some more colour? Perhaps the background should be . . . " He squinted slightly at it. "Blue? Yes, blue would look good."

"Yes, but what sort of blue?"

"Robin's egg?"

"Too pale."

"Bluebell blue?"

"Too purply."

"Something with a touch of green. I could mix you it in glaze in a moment," he said. "But I don't know what you'd call it. Run some more names past me."

Kate complied with delight. It was exactly the sort of puzzle she loved to solve and clearly he did too. Turquoise they rejected, and deep sea green. Eventually they settled for peacock.

"Well, it isn't often you meet another colour freak," said Kate, laughing.

"I don't think I've ever met one — at least not such a pedantic one," said Hugh.

"It is not pedantry," Kate protested. "It's scrupulous accuracy."

Hugh laughed and then broke off suddenly, as if laughter was an indulgence he could not quite permit himself. Once again, as she filled the background of her sketch with peacock green, and he went back to making the chocolate cake, Kate found herself trying to work out what was going on with Hugh and Lara. She thought of all the disastrous relationships she had been through and how painful the unmeshing of just two people could be. What could it be like to break up when there was a child involved, especially a child as small as Andrew? Hugh so obviously doted on Andrew that letting him leave with Lara must have been agony, and things between them must have got to a dire state for him to have allowed that to happen. Moved, she flipped back a few pages in her sketch book to her drawing of Andrew, and ripped it out.

"Here," she said, handing him the sketch. "I know it's hardly a substitute, but . . . "

He stared across the table at her for a moment, and then, having wiped his hands, took the sketch. He gave a lop-sided smile as he looked at it, and then looked back at her.

"Thanks," he said. "That's great, really . . . "

She felt self-conscious, suddenly; his gaze felt a little intense. She shrugged and moved away, saying, quickly, "How are you doing with the mixture? The one thing that bothers me is which oven to put it into. I've never used one of these Aga things before, you see. What on earth do you do with four ovens anyway?"

★ ★ ★

Later that day, Kate stood naked in their dressing room, rubbing rose and lavender scented oil into her skin. The large sash window was pushed right up and the curtains were open, but there was no fear of her being seen from outside. The view from the window was empty of prying humanity — there was only the tranquil pattern of varied coloured fields and bands of trees and hedges, fresh with new greenery. The day had been mild, and the breeze that came through the window was not strong enough to be an annoyance. All in all, it had been a very satisfactory day. She had spent the afternoon working intensely on *Adam*, and as she had worked she had found herself planning *Eve* again. It was all a question of finding a suitable model; and now, catching sight of her naked self in the long cheval glass, she wondered if she ought not to use herself. She stood in front of the mirror for some minutes, striking various poses, amused by her own narcissism, but also pleased at the idea. Surely she made an appropriate Eve — she found sex all too tempting.

She turned away, rubbing the oil into her neck, wondering what Liz and Martin were saying to each other in their room. They had arrived about an hour ago and had been distinctly overwhelmed by Allansfield. It had been a good thing only she had been there to meet them — Gabriel was still deep in the garden somewhere. Liz would not have liked him to see her incredulous giggles as Kate had taken them round the house.

The door behind her opened and she

glanced round to see Gabriel coming in. She quickly straightened up and moved away from the mirror.

"You caught me admiring myself," she said, laughing.

"Plenty to admire," he said. He was standing with his hands behind his back. "I've got a present for you."

"Oh, but . . . " she began to protest, but he put his finger to his lips.

"A proper present," he said. "Not a vulgar present," and he produced from behind his back a circlet of clematis, honeysuckle and ivy leaves, wound carefully together. "I've spent hours making this." He laid it with gentle ceremony into her hands.

"It's . . . oh, Gabriel," she said, entirely taken aback. She stared across at him. "It's lovely."

"Put it on," he said, with a smile.

She turned to the mirror and crowned herself. Eve definitely, she thought. It rested heavily across her forehead, the scent of the honeysuckle almost unbearably sweet. What an extraordinarily beautiful thing! She turned back to him. He stood there with his arms folded, looking hot and earthy in his gardening clothes, looking hopelessly desirable, with that slight smile turning up his craggy mouth.

"You'd better get dressed," he said, "before I get tempted. It wouldn't be fair to leave our guests floundering."

"Quite right," she said, rummaging in a drawer for some fresh underwear. "Later?"

"Definitely later," he said, unbuttoning his shirt. "I must get into the shower."

She went into the bedroom, where she had laid on the bed the dress she intended to wear. It was a real piece of extravagance, the sort of thing she would never have dared to buy until she met Gabriel, high waisted and full skirted in almond green silk. The flowers would finish it off perfectly.

"You're a genius," she called out to Gabriel, as she slipped it over her head.

He came through in his dressing gown.

"You see?" she said.

"You look almost too good to be true," he said, shaking his head.

"Well, I am true," she laughed, flouncing the skirts slightly.

He smiled and sat down in the armchair.

"Aren't you supposed to be in the shower by now?"

"There's something I've got to tell you first," he said. There was a quiet gravity in his voice. "A little confession."

"Oh yes?" she said lightly. Knowing Gabriel, this was probably some trivial scruple. She continued to put on her shoes.

"It's about Henrietta Winthrop," he said, leaning back.

"What about her?"

"Well, the other day, when I said I vaguely remembered the name, I was not being strictly truthful."

"So you do know her?"

"Yes."

"Then why didn't you say?"

"I had a sort of mental block," he said. "I don't quite know why — well I do, I was embarrassed."

"What about?"

"Well, I did know her — reasonably well, as a matter of fact. For a couple of terms we were friends, but we had a bit of a row and after that we didn't see

185

anything more of each other."

"What?" she said. "Why didn't you tell me? I wouldn't have invited her if I'd known that. Gabriel, this is — "

"I know, I know. It does seem perverse of me. I should have said, there and then, but her name came as a shock. I hadn't thought about her for years and years, and suddenly you're talking about her, showing me her book . . . and then I thought, I can't be so childish as to say, 'No, don't invite her,' because we had a fight over something nearly thirty years ago."

"What was the fight about?"

"I can't even remember, that's what's really stupid," he said, getting up. "So that's why things might appear awkward at times tonight. I'm sorry, I really should have said something, shouldn't I?"

"Yes," she said, with astonishment. "Yes, you should."

"But when you said she was going to organise an exhibition for you, well, what could I say? I didn't want to spoil that for you with unnecessary baggage. I thought it was a dog that was best left sleeping."

"Letting me invite her to dinner is hardly leaving it sleeping," said Kate. "Gabriel, you are so bloody odd sometimes! Why didn't you stop me?"

"Because . . . because I felt I ought to be able to deal with this like a mature adult. It's been a long time."

"I just wish you had said something earlier!" she exclaimed.

"I know, I know," he said, coming over to her. "Do you forgive me?" He looked thoroughly and endearingly repentant.

"Of course," she said. "At least you did tell me, if rather late in the day. But it was stupid of you, Gabriel. She'll be embarrassed, won't she, I imagine, when she realises?"

"She already does," he said.

"Oh," said Kate, now almost bereft of words.

"You see, I called in to see her the other day, to explain. I thought I had better."

"Oh, you did?" Kate managed to say.

"Yes, and we decided it was all ancient history," he added, going towards the bathroom.

Gabriel locked the bathroom door, appalled at his bravura performance. He had not intended to be such a thorough liar. He had intended to be honest. All the time he had been weaving that crown for her, he had been working out exactly how he would put it, but the moment he had found her standing naked and desirable in the dressing room any good resolutions deserted him. And so, all at once, he found he was dismissing Henrietta as a mere friend with whom he had quarrelled over something he could not even recall. It reminded him uncomfortably of his performances with Jane, all those over-strenuous denials: "No, of course I don't love her any more, Jane. How could I? I married you, didn't I?" He remembered one particular scene they had had at Allansfield — Lara and Andrew leaving so abruptly and Hugh's painfully comprehensible and defeated demeanour had called it vividly to mind. His parents had had some friends to dinner, and the talk had turned to the circumstances of some neighbour's scandalous divorce.

Gabriel's mother had given him a long peroration on the subject. "I think people give up far too easily on their marriages these days. Marriage is not like a coat; you can't just take it back to the shop if it doesn't suit you." Afterwards, in their room, Jane had said in a tone of abject misery, "Your mother's right. I wish she wasn't, but she is. Do you know I felt like taking Hugh and walking out of this house this morning? I nearly did, but I decided that, unlike you, I would attempt to do the right thing. I would try and put some effort into this marriage. One of us at least should make an effort, I thought."

He ran a very hot, deep bath and lowered himself into it, trying to distract himself with thoughts of the garden. There was the new south border to think of. He had planned it all out last November before he had met Kate, and since then he had almost forgotten about it. He rested his head on the rolled edge of the bath and closed his eyes, trying to think of textures and colours and scents, but his subconscious would not accept such calm rationality. He found he was drifting deeper still into his past, to the afternoon he had spent locked in a bathroom in Newnham with Henrietta. They had made love on the floor and then sat together in the bath tub, their bodies slippery with soapy water, intertwined. They had smoked a joint and he had fallen asleep, his head resting against her naked breasts.

He sat up sharply, the water cascading off him, disgusted at himself for remembering that. He had been so convinced that Henrietta meant nothing any more, he had even managed to say it to her face. Yet, he felt a great burning residue of unresolved feeling, not just anger but something far stronger. If she had meant nothing still, he would have been able to explain it all to Kate. He would not have been so afraid of being misunderstood in his explanation — or rather, so afraid of making it all too plain that there was still feeling left in him for her, despite all that time, despite all that he felt for Kate. He had felt certain his love for Kate was so powerful that he might block out those old feelings, and yet they were with him still, more insidious, more invasive than ever.

He rubbed himself furiously with a towel, angry at himself for insisting to Henrietta that she accept the invitation, and yet finding a sort of guilty anticipation at the prospect of seeing her. Not even the sight of Kate standing there naked with his crown of flowers in her hair could stop him feeling that.

9

HENRIETTA had not anticipated that Allansfield would be quite so beautiful. She had spent weekends in impressive old houses in New England and elsewhere before, some of them a great deal larger and more luxurious than this (even though their owners called them cottages), but there had been nothing like the peculiar charm of this house. Everything in it seemed to be just right, chosen with careful attention to belong there without seeming at all contrived. There were things everywhere of surpassing beauty, but their setting was so simple that one hardly noticed them. There was a patina of age on everything that made it seem deliciously comfortable and even occasionally shabby.

Gabriel, in this context, seemed as much a part of the fabric of the place as one of the pictures hanging on the walls, or one of those shapely Chinese bowls she had seen lying almost carelessly on a side table when Gabriel had taken them all into that incomparable little library to show them one of Kate's paintings. Oh, that room, that heart-stopping little room, with its wall of books, the deep chairs by the fireside, the friendly old desk, with the clutter of real work on it, the glazed door to the garden . . . How she had instantly craved that room! She should have been looking at Kate's remarkable *Pandora*, she knew, but she had found her eyes stealing to the draftsman's table in one corner, where a half-finished garden design was laid out. She wondered, if she had known of all this, if she had seen this place, whether she would have resisted him then. Would Henrietta at twenty-two have been so moved, so spoken to by all these quiet, lovely things? Would the scent of the borders drifting into a dusk-filled house have broken her will?

It had also been a shock to see Bob Kavanagh again, his thick blond hair thinned now to an inelegant straggle; but more of a shock was the sight of Hugh Erskine, looking so very like the Gabriel she remembered. When Gabriel had said he had been married it had not crossed her mind that he might have had children as well, let alone grandchildren. It was really rather silly of her to be so surprised — reproduction was the normal course of things. Almost all her friends had had children, after all. Perhaps it was because Gabriel was fixed in her memory as a young man. She had not yet reconciled the Gabriel from Cambridge with the Gabriel of Allansfield, with a grown-up son and a girlfriend, who in this context looked disturbingly young.

And so they sat at dinner, with the candles burning, eating salmon with asparagus from the kitchen garden. Henrietta felt a hopeless sort of understanding of why Kate loved him, why she sat there with that ridiculous but extraordinary crown of flowers in her hair, looking more pre-Raphaelite than her painting, her eyes full of ardour for him. That could so easily have been my place, she found herself thinking, as she looked at Kate at the head of the table.

Gabriel had got up to refill the wine glasses, while Bob was talking about his robots. When he filled Kate's glass, he paused to kiss her on the lips, swiftly enough for it not to be ostentatious, but with enough passion in it to make Henrietta remember the force of his kisses on her own lips. Seeing it was like opening an old, well-stoppered bottle of perfume and smelling a sweet, heady, forgotten scent, made intense by long captivity. He had once kissed her like that, pressed his hand against the back of her head and pressed his lips to hers, and she, like Kate, had stretched up her neck, anxiously, to make the moment last. Hastily, anxious for a distraction, Henrietta took up her wine glass and swallowed a large mouthful of white wine in a manner that hardly respected its quality.

"Drop more?" Gabriel said. He was hovering at her shoulder. She found she could hardly bear to look at him, but she forced herself, the required polite smile on her lips.

"Thanks, it's delicious," she said, and held up her glass.

As he poured, their eyes met for a moment, and it seemed to her that there was a flash of odd communication between them. She was certain she saw something in his eyes: a troubled, haunted look that mirrored her own confusion. Was he remembering too, despite himself? She saw the muscles of his face twitch into an involuntarily spasm, and he turned, it seemed, all his concentration to the simple business of pouring out the wine. She was glad when he moved away.

"So," Liz, Kate's sassy young lawyer friend, was saying, "when do you think it'll be possible to have those wonderful robots that do everything round the house?"

"Yes, Jeeves Mark One," said Martin, her boyfriend, who was sitting at Henrietta's right. "We could do with one of those for our place, pronto."

"I don't think," said Bob, "that'll happen for years. The problem has been to integrate all the functions. You have a robot that can see, and another that can manipulate objects, and another that can move, but the logic required to combine all that, and then get them dextrous enough to make the bed, is still fairly awesome."

"Damn," said Liz with a smile. "Back to tussles about who does the Hoovering then, Martin."

"Martin's a dab hand with the Hoover," explained Kate. "I've seen him."

"Oh well, I'm a New Man," said Martin. "Brilliant young chartered accountant who can also wield an iron, if necessary."

"Is that a five iron or an electric iron?" said Hugh.

"Both," said Martin.

"Smug git," said Liz, affectionately. "That's the ridiculous thing though, isn't it? When men finally do some housework, they expect to get gold stars for doing it, as if they were doing something really exceptional. I think to some men doing a pile of ironing is like climbing Mount Everest, whereas to women it's just another thing on the list of chores."

"Well, that is because men are perpetual romanticists," said Henrietta, plunging in. "Their egos are such that they cannot approach any task without turning it into an heroic endeavour. The male psyche requires to be constantly assured that it is both heroic and powerful. If men had always done household chores, there would be Greek epics on the noble art of sewing, and Latin elegiacs about scrubbing floors."

"Bullshit," said Bob calmly. "Absolute bullshit. God, I'd forgotten how good she was at that."

"Now, how did we get here from domestic robots?" said Martin suddenly.

"I was going to get back to them, actually," said Henrietta.

"God help us," said Bob. "More wine, Gabriel, more wine please!"

"What about them?" said Kate, encouragingly.

"I'll leave this bottle with you," said Gabriel, getting up and putting it down in front of Henrietta. "Our orator will need lubrication."

"So will the audience," said Bob, refilling his glass and emptying the bottle. "Open another one. I remember how she used to go on."

"I'm not as bad as I used to be," said Henrietta, smiling. "Wine doesn't make me as rhetorically minded as the demon weed used to."

"You lot should be very thankful that we are now all law-abiding, respectable adults." said Bob to the others. He began to wheeze with laughter.

"Bob only intermittently," said Gabriel, pulling the cork from the bottle, "I believe."

"I smoke it occasionally for old times' sake, yes," said Bob. "But it never seems to have the clout it used to."

"Because we were stoned on life then, not just on cannabis," said Henrietta. "Anything one does at that age is bound to seem more intense, especially at this distance."

"Do you remember that time?" said Bob, suddenly. "That amazing afternoon — you were there, and that girl from Girton, the funny one . . . What was her name?"

"Bob never remembers the name of any woman he slept with at Cambridge," said Gabriel. "I don't think you even made a point of finding out, did you?"

"Well, it seemed easier to call them 'Sheila'. A good few of them were probably called Sheila anyway, and the others were so captivated by this authentic piece of Australiania that they didn't mind."

"Bullshit!" said Gabriel and Henrietta almost in unison. "Total bullshit."

"I think her name was Vanessa," said Henrietta.

"That's right," said Gabriel, crouching down at the corner of the table between Kate and Henrietta. "Vanessa. Her father was a High Court judge, wasn't he?"

"That's right," said Bob, "and she said that's why she wouldn't smoke pot. Because if she got caught she thought her father's career would be ruined. So I rolled these joints that looked just like ordinary cigarettes, and she sat there drinking tea, and smoking and eating cakes from Fitzbillie's . . . " He broke off, incapacitated with laughter.

"We shouldn't have done that," said Henrietta, covering her mouth with her hand, trying not to laugh. "We really shouldn't. It was shameful."

"Ah, she was a prig," said Bob. "And she loosened up wonderfully after that. And that was the afternoon that you got so high, Gabriel, do you remember, you were so high that you decided to go and have a bath in the fountain in Trinity Great Court?" Bob looked around at the others. "It was an amazing sight. He just walked down the stairs, stripping off his clothes as he went, and climbed straight into it, absolutely stark bollock naked. It was February, would you believe? February! There was even a thin layer of ice on it! But you got into that fountain like it was a hot bath. The bravest thing I ever saw a man do."

And afterwards, thought Henrietta, afterwards. He had sat hunched up against her, wrapped in all the blankets they could find, the gas fire eating up shillings, his teeth chattering, his limbs jerking with the cold, his skin blue and white, and unpleasantly pallid. She had rubbed and rubbed his body, rubbed it until the life came back to it. Then they had made love with desperate ferocity, as if he really had been on the brink of death.

"I thought you were going to die of cold then," she said, finding she was looking at him as he crouched there still, at the corner of the table.

"I think you saved my life," he said quietly, looking back at her, his eyes grave. Then suddenly he jumped up

201

again, and went on. "This is really appallingly bad manners of us, I think," he said. "There is nothing so boring as other people's university anecdotes."

★ ★ ★

Kate found it was a relief to bustle away into the kitchen with a pile of dirty plates. She was glad she had told Alison to go off duty. She needed to have something to do, something to make her feel some semblance of control over this situation. Bob Kavanagh's anecdote had been too vivid. The three of them had suddenly formed themselves into an intimate, self-referential circle, almost as if there was no one else in the room. For those few minutes they had seemed to be back there again, in their own private, golden world that no one else was allowed to understand simply because they had not experienced it. Kate felt that a door had been slammed in her face. Gabriel had never talked to her about Cambridge like that. In fact he had hardly said anything about it, she realised as she rather aggressively scraped remains off the dinner plates, and although she had burbled enough to him about her time at art college, he had never responded in kind. When there was so much about his past that he had told her this struck her as extraordinary, and now to have it all come out so casually, so spontaneously . . .

"There's no need to do that. Where's Alison?" said Gabriel, coming into the kitchen.

Kate continued to stack the dishwasher. "I told her we wouldn't need her after the fish was served."

"Oh," said Gabriel, mildly surprised. "It's what she's paid for."

"Well, we don't have to exploit her," said Kate, "do we? Anyway, I know she likes to watch *Casualty* . . . "

"She does?" said Gabriel. "Good grief . . . "

"And we are not incapable of clearing a few dishes and making coffee," Kate went on. "Well, I'm not, at least not yet."

"Fine," said Gabriel. "Well, I'll open the Sauternes then."

As she took the covers off the puddings

Alison had left on the kitchen table, and Gabriel opened the bottles, Kate had a sudden and horrible sense of being an utter stranger there. She felt like the hired help for the evening. The man in the kitchen seemed so apart from her that for a moment it seemed impossible that they had any common life between them. She felt she knew nothing about him. All the things he had told her about himself seemed like so much small talk. She felt no nearer to the essence of this man than she had on the night when she had first seen him standing looking at her pictures.

That was ridiculous, she told herself. At that moment Martin came in with the rest of the dirty plates. Kate found she was relieved to see him.

"You see, I am a New Man," he said, putting them down on the draining board. "Oh look at all this," he said, throwing his hand carelessly but affectionately on her shoulder. "You should have warned me, Kate, that you were going to be making your demon chocolate cake. I would have skipped lunch."

"You can work it off with a long country walk tomorrow," said Kate.

"This cake is simply . . . Well, I'm sure you've had this before," said Martin to Gabriel. "Actually, I'm glad to get you alone for a minute, Kate. What do you think of this? Do you think Liz will like this?" He dug into his pocket, produced a ring box and flicked it open. "What do you reckon? You know her taste as well as mine."

It was an elegant, modern-style ring with square-cut diamonds and sapphires.

"I take it this is an engagement ring," said Kate, laughing.

"Well, I decided: What the devil am I hanging around for? Do you think she'll like it?"

"She'll love it," said Kate. She handed it to Gabriel. "Don't you think?"

"Definitely," he said, taking it out and holding it up to the light. "Very pretty indeed." He replaced it in the box and handed it back to Martin. He picked up the bottle of Sauternes he had opened, and began to go back towards the dining room. "But I would get a move on if I were you. If you leave her talking to

Henrietta too long, she'll put her off the whole business."

"Oh, that doesn't bother me," said Martin, picking up the chocolate cake. "Liz has read her book. She reckons it's a bit out of date now. I mean, all that master and slave stuff, it's irrelevant when we both earn exactly the same amount of money, isn't it? There's no inequality there. It's more like a business partnership. Now is there anything else you want me to take through?"

The rest of the evening went well enough, superficially. Over the cheese, Martin and Bob got a good discussion going about the relationship of industry with academia, to which the others contributed only intermittently. Kate, who felt she had nothing to say on the subject, found herself sitting back in her chair at the far end of the table, feeling, despite herself, the same sense of isolation she had felt in the kitchen. She sipped her claret and watched Henrietta, wondering whether she had really heard Gabriel say to her, "I think you saved my life." How could she have saved his life? She found herself going over the scene that Bob had recounted, attempting to stage it in her mind. She looked down at Gabriel sitting at the other end of the table, so utterly composed, nodding in agreement to something Martin was saying, and tried to picture him at nineteen, or twenty, with a boy's body, being entirely reckless, stoned out of his mind, in some ancient university quadrangle, climbing naked into a gothic fountain, his bare, unfeeling hands heedlessly cracking through sheets of ice.

She looked at Henrietta, drinking her wine, apparently listening to the conversation, and she had a sense that the image of that afternoon hung with perfect clarity in *her* mind's eye too. She possessed something of Gabriel that Kate could never have, no matter how hard she tried. There would always be those great swathes of time in his life of which she could have no understanding. She thought of Martin and Liz, who had been going out together since about the age of eighteen when they had met as first-year students at Edinburgh University. Kate, Liz's best friend from school, had seen it all, been part of it herself, watched them quarrel and patch it up, often envying them profoundly for the steadiness of their love, while she had gone from affair to affair never finding anyone with whom she felt she could settle. Together they had formed a triangle of friendship, just as Bob and Gabriel and Henrietta had at Cambridge.

She put down her wine glass, astonished, understanding now why their sudden plunge into the past had disturbed her. For the first time she had witnessed from the outside the pattern that Liz, Martin and she had formed: the two lovers and the friend. "I thought you were going to die of cold then," Henrietta had said, and Gabriel had replied, with such quiet significance, "I think you saved my life."

Gabriel, she realised, had lied to her.

10

KATE sat on the end of the bed in their room, watching Gabriel undress.

"Well, that all went quite well, I think," Gabriel said. "And your chocolate cake, Kate . . . Martin was right, it's incomparable."

"Hugh made most of it," she said banally.

It had taken hours for everyone to get up to bed, for Kate to be alone with Gabriel again, and now that she was she could not think how to begin. Instead, she took off the crown of flowers he had given her and laid it on her lap. It had lasted well, with the flowers wilting only here and there. It still appeared much as it had done when he presented it to her earlier, when he had enchanted her with it. Then it had seemed such a simple thing, a beautiful expression of his love, but now it felt like a trick, a sweetener to soften her up. For moments later he had been telling her that he did know Henrietta after all, and that she had been a close friend with whom he had quarrelled. It had all sounded so convincing. Why would it not have? She did not associate anything about him with deception. Gabriel and lying were not concepts she would have bracketed together — until tonight.

She hooked the flowers over the brass knob at the foot of the bed, and lay down on her back, her eyes fixed on the ceiling above her, trying to concentrate on the airy, pale space as if it might empty her mind, and dissolve that feeling of alienation which she could not shake off.

"You're very quiet," she heard him say.

She propped herself up slightly on one elbow and looked at him. He was standing at her feet. She raised one eyebrow, hoping to suggest that indeed she was, and he was responsible for it. Silently she found herself praying: "Come clean with me, Gabriel. Tell me, prove me wrong!"

"You're tired," he said, and gently

lifted her foot and began to stroke her ankle, just as he had done before after a particularly long walk in Edinburgh. He did it with such tenderness that it was agony to her. It was an action heavy with affection. How could it be deceitful? How could anything about him be underhand? He was not capable of such a thing. Gabriel could not lie; at least, he could not lie to her.

She began to wonder if she had not had too much to drink. They had got through quite a lot, with all that Pimms before dinner, and then the wine. Perhaps that was what was inducing these unkind suspicions. She had probably imagined the whole thing, and even if it was true, did it honestly matter that he had been Henrietta's lover? It was nearly thirty years ago, a world away from Gabriel and her. Then, he would probably have seemed a different Gabriel altogether. Of course he had a past — she had one herself, for goodness' sake; and did it really matter that he had not been entirely straight about it? He was probably embarrassed to admit the truth, and embarrassment was easy enough to forgive. What was the point of agonising over such a tiny thing? Student flings never meant anything much.

She was pleased to see the stranger had disappeared, and she was looking again at the Gabriel who was familiar to her. She stretched out her hands to him and pulled him gently on to the bed beside her.

"You know, you needn't have been embarrassed," she said. "About Henrietta. You should have said."

"About what?" he said.

"That you had a thing going with her at Cambridge. I guessed."

"Oh, you did?"

"Of course I did," she said, laughing, amused by the nervousness in his voice. "Did you think I wouldn't? You should have just said so in the first place."

"I know, I'm sorry," he said, picking up her hand and kissing it.

"I should be very cross with you. But since I haven't told you about every man I ever slept with . . ."

"You're very generous, Kate."

"Not really," she said. He wrapped his arms around her and she remembered the rush of desire that she had felt earlier that evening. "As you said yourself, it's ancient history, isn't it? Quite funny, really. And she's great company — I'm glad we invited her."

He kissed her then, and gave a deep sigh of relief. Kate felt rather proud that she had broached the subject in such a civilised fashion.

"You know, I think we agreed earlier . . . " she began.

"We did," he said, slipping his hand up her leg, under the crumpled folds of her skirt. She pressed herself close to him, feeling triumphant that she had banished their demons. The past did not matter, only their future together. She kissed him on the lips and felt his arms lock about her. Then, suddenly, he released her and got up from the bed. He walked a little distance across the room. She saw him bite his lip.

"What is it?" she said, sitting up.

"Oh dear . . . I don't quite know how to put this."

"To put what?"

"Well, you see . . . " He was rubbing his forehead with his hand, and was

213

still not looking at her. "I want to ask you something, but . . . I had this idea this evening, you see . . . " He poured himself a glass of mineral water, took a large mouthful, and said, "But I find I am having the most extraordinary attack of nerves." He said each word with great deliberation and precision, as if he were enunciating to make a foreigner understand. She noticed he was staring at the ceiling now.

"What is there to be nervous about?" she asked, getting up and placing her hand on his shoulder.

He covered her hand with his own and, laughing slightly, said, "You might well ask."

"I might," she said, laughing a little herself now. "You've mystified me."

With a slightly solemn gesture, he put a hand on each of her shoulders. He looked at her gravely, took a deep breath, and said, very simply and rather quietly, "Kate, will you think about marrying me?"

She felt her mouth drop open and her eyes widen slightly. His reaction was instantaneous — his face twitched as if he had experienced a sudden spasm of pain.

Quickly she pressed her hands to his cheeks and tried to find her voice. "Oh Gabriel . . . " was all she could manage to say. It came out sounding very bewildered.

Slowly, he detached her hands from his face. "You don't have to say anything just yet," he said, "but you will think about it? Please," he said earnestly.

"Of course," she said.

They made love then, fiercely and satisfyingly, and Kate, instead of falling asleep, found herself lying in his arms, wondering why he had suddenly come out with a proposal. She had made it clear enough times that marriage was not an idea she was particularly interested in. It had always struck her as an unnecessary piece of red tape, a mere public rubber stamping of a private contract, an excuse for a big party. She had thought that in asking her to move in with him he had cared as little for it as an idea as she had. His experience with Jane would certainly be enough to make him cautious. They had had, he had told her with certain disgust in his voice, a society wedding in St Giles' in Edinburgh, with all the showy trimmings. It was so disappointingly conventional of Gabriel to be suddenly thinking that they ought to do the same. Puzzling over it still, she gradually fell asleep.

★ ★ ★

Henrietta was exhausted, but she knew she was not in a state that would allow her to sleep. Her mind was too restless, too full of distracting, conflicting emotions to permit herself simply to switch off into oblivion. She propped up the generous pile of pillows against the imposing mahogany bedstead, and settled to investigate the books which had been left on the bedside table. She had bought two books with her, but the prospect of others was, as ever, too tempting. They were an interesting mixture: a couple of very glossy gardening books that looked as if they had not been much read (Christmas presents, Henrietta thought); a copy of an elegantly produced gardening journal called *Hortus*; Housman's *A*

Shropshire Lad (a first edition, but very battered); *Mansfield Park*; two very dilapidated detective novels; and Richard Dawkin's *The Selfish Gene*. After some deliberation she settled on *Mansfield Park*, which she opened entirely at random and found herself in the midst of Fanny Price's agonies of disapproval over the amateur theatricals. Perhaps Jane Austen was not the right choice. Her clear-sighted morality, her absolute sense of standards, was sometimes too painful. What she would have made of that evening's little charade, Henrietta did not like to think. She closed the book and gazed at the painting over the fireplace, a misty grey-green landscape of trees. Was that a Corot?

She got out of bed and went to look properly at it. It was indeed a Corot, and she found herself a little stupefied at the thought of being in a house where there was a Corot in the spare bedroom. She wished she could enjoy this experience, enjoy all the rarefied grandeur of this room in an uncomplicated, appreciative way, without all this deadly weight of significance pressing down on her.

She heard someone knocking softly on the door.

"Yes?" she said, a little suspiciously.

"It's me — Bob."

He came in and closed the door behind him.

"I thought you might want some company," he said, gesturing with the whisky bottle he was carrying.

"I could use the company better than the Scotch," said Henrietta with a smile.

He climbed on to the bed and stretched out his legs. "I'm fulfilling a lifelong ambition, you know," he said, "getting into your bed."

"Getting *on* to my bed," she pointed out.

"At our age who's bothered?" he said. He poured himself a small glass of whisky. "What I want to know is, what *is* he on?"

"Gabriel, you mean?" Henrietta said.

"He always did have very good taste," said Bob, looking at her. "Even the ex-wife was a stunner."

"Ah, yes," said Henrietta, sitting down beside him on the bed. "What was she like?"

"A pain, but a stunner. God, you should have been at the wedding — there again, perhaps not . . . "

"Tell me about it," said Henrietta with a smile.

"You would have been very amused," he said. "The full society whack, it was — St Giles' Cathedral in Edinburgh, no less, with most of the bloody Scots aristocracy there as far as I could work out. I was the best man, would you credit it . . . " For a moment Bob was incapacitated by laughter. "Worst man, more like. Gabriel's father — did you ever meet him?" Henrietta shook her head. "Well, he was quite a character, very much the retired Colonel type, you know. On the morning of the wedding he actually sent for his barber — I can't believe this happened now, really — and insisted we both had a haircut. So there we are in this damn great church looking like a pair of army privates . . . Really, you wouldn't have thought the sixties had happened. Gabriel didn't care. He was absolutely crazy about her. He would have done anything for her then, I think."

"So what went wrong?"

"Who knows?" said Bob, and then looked at her for a moment. "But I wasn't surprised when it fell to pieces. It would have been more fun if you had married him."

"Oh, I don't know . . . " said Henrietta dismissively.

"Come off it, of course it would. I bet you've been thinking that all night, looking at this place. This place suits you, Henry."

"I think it suits Kate," said Henrietta carefully. "My instincts, I'm sure, were right."

"Maybe, maybe not," said Bob, putting down his whisky glass and settling more deeply on to his pile of pillows, his hands tucked behind his head. "But I bet you're a bit jealous of her all the same."

"Rather, aren't you a bit of jealous of him?" said Henrietta, determined not to answer his question.

"Of course I bloody am," said Bob. "Kate's something else. And he's not going to give you a second glance now, is he?"

"And why should I want him to?" said

Henrietta as coolly as she could.

"What are you doing here, then?" said Bob.

"Curiosity, I suppose," said Henrietta.

"That covers a multitude of sins," said Bob. "Are you sure you don't want a drink, Henry?" Henrietta resolutely said nothing. "Or perhaps," he went on, laying his hand gently on her arm. "We should find another way of distracting ourselves."

"No, Bob, I don't think that would be such a good idea."

"Pity," he said. "But it does prove my point, doesn't it? You're not interested in me like that, you never were. Gabriel was the one you chose to seduce."

"I think he seduced me," said Henrietta quietly.

"Well, now you know how I felt," said Bob. "You know you're not going to get a look in again, not while the celestial Kate is in his firmament."

"Do you honestly think that I would want 'a look in', as you so elegantly put it?" said Henrietta. "Credit me with a few principles, please."

"Oh, I'm sure you've got principles,"

said Bob. "We've all got principles. But that doesn't allow for feelings, does it? You can't do anything about those."

★ ★ ★

Hugh decided to spend the night in the old night nursery when he found he had drunk rather too much to drive safely back to the cottage. He could probably have managed to walk, but it seemed easier to grab a pair of sheets from the linen cupboard and make up a bed for himself at Allansfield. He instinctively went to the night nursery as well, rather than one of the grander guest rooms; the slightly Spartan familiarity of it was comforting. He had not actually slept in the house since they had got the cottage, and certainly not in this room since he was a child, although nothing much had changed in there. With the light out, the view was the same he had seen at the age of six. He remembered the sense of security he had felt then — in being put into the very bed that his father and grandfather had slept in — and wished he could find it again now — and sleep.

But he had drunk too much wine and then too much black coffee, and there was far too much going on in his mind for anything as simple as sleep.

He switched on the light again and sat drinking water, his bare shoulders pressed against the cold brass uprights of the bedstead. He tried to organise his thoughts. What did people do when their marriages collapsed? It was not an eventuality for which he had prepared himself — and who, in all honesty, ever did? Marriage was something you went into with all the optimism cylinders firing, especially with a baby on the way. Anything else would have been cynical. But now he had to face reality. Things had gone badly wrong. He had only to think of the couples he had watched at dinner that evening to know that his relationship with Lara had become untenable. Martin and Liz, for example, had actually seemed to be communicating in a way Hugh could not remember adopting with Lara for at least a year. And then, of course, there was his father and Kate.

He gulped down some more water,

ashamed at the sudden rush of envy he found himself feeling. He wanted simply to be generous and wish that they might always be as happy as they had appeared that night, the perfect couple, hosting dinner at Allansfield. But the sight of Kate had disturbed him. Seeing her there, at the head of the table, with those flowers in her hair, and in that clinging silk dress, her arms bare, he had felt an embarrassing and highly inappropriate rush of sexual desire. He felt it again now, and tried to put this down to nothing but his sexual frustration, but he could not dismiss her image. It merged with the recollection of that long and satisfying conversation he had with her about colour in the kitchen that morning. They had been exactly on each other's wavelength. She had seemed to understand just how he had been feeling about Andrew when she had given him that wonderfully vivid little sketch of him. He realised, with deep shame, that it was not his father's happiness of which he was jealous, but more specifically, more painfully, it was Kate he coveted.

He switched off the light and buried himself in the bedclothes, determined to sleep and not to think any more. He did not like any of the conclusions he had reached.

11

GABRIEL had woken up at about five in the morning, annoyed again to find himself sweating as if in a high fever. His pyjamas were soaked through and he had had to get up and take a shower. He contemplated going back to bed, but found that Kate, who was still very much asleep, had completely conquered the bed by lying rather extravagantly in the middle, her arms flung out one way and her legs the other. Neither of them, he realised, had quite got used to sharing a bed, and he decided that to get back in would only disturb her. It would be far better to go and work for a couple of hours in the garden and productively shake off the remains of his hangover. He was surprised that the wine had affected him so much. He had not been aware of drinking that much the previous night. Perhaps it was a sign of his age, this increasing lack of tolerance. He smiled at that thought. It was of course the received wisdom that being in love with someone younger was supposed to make one feel young oneself — but looking at Kate, sublimely and solidly asleep, he realised it actually made him more aware of his age.

He wondered whether it would have helped if he had been more aware of that fact last night, when he had asked Kate to marry him. He had not thought it through at all. It had been an impulse, triggered for the most part by her charming forgiveness about Henrietta. To have her understand and dismiss that had made him euphoric. It had made him realise how bloody lucky he was to have her — and if she were to agree to marry him, then what could be more perfect? Yet looking at her now, asleep, and somehow very separate still from him, he wondered if he had blundered. That had been his great mistake with Henrietta, after all — to ask her to marry him.

He was glad to distract himself in the garden. May was always a favourite time, with everything a flurry of activity and new growth, the first roses accompanied by an explosion of lilacs, peonies and pale flag irises. Even the legions of rhododendrons (which Gabriel did not greatly care for) planted by Gabriel's father, were obliged to make themselves interesting by flowering in May. He took his tools to the long, south-facing mixed border to work over the soil for the summer bedding, which would soon be ready to plant out.

It was cool, but perfectly light, and he had soon worked up another sweat with some furious digging. He stopped, a little breathless suddenly, wishing he did not feel so tired. He stepped back on to the lawn, and turned to see Henrietta, coming from the house. She was dressed in a long blue skirt and shirt, with a sweater thrown over her shoulders, and as she came towards him he saw that she was carrying her shoes and walking barefoot through the long damp grass. The dew was already staining her hem as she approached him. She loved to walk barefoot; he remembered that. She had once walked barefoot through Grantchester Meadows with him.

"Henry!" he called out to her. The old name had come as spontaneously as the memory of her in Grantchester Meadows, wearing one of those flower-sprigged milkmaid smocks that all Newnham girls had seemed to wear then. She stopped for a moment, as if she were deliberating whether to respond to him, and then walked over.

"Someone else couldn't sleep, I see," she said.

"No, and perhaps we'd feel better about it if we'd never gone to bed at all."

"Those nights are long gone," she said, "I fear." She glanced at his half-dug patch of earth. "Very industrious."

"There's a lot to do this time of year."

"Then I won't distract you. Point me in the direction of your best prospect, Mr Erskine," she said.

"Do you seriously think I'm going to give up the chance to show off my garden to you?" he said.

"Oh, swanking are we?" she said.

"Of course. But it would be a pleasure," he said. "If you went so far as to go to the Horticultural Society, then you must have a bent . . . "

"I admit I do," she said. "But no success. I don't go for such wonders as the cardoon."

"Ah, *Cynara cardunculus*," he said. "I can show you that if you like."

"Show me what's through there," she said, pointing to the gates to the wild garden. "That intrigues me."

"Ah, well, that's my wild garden."

"You made a wild garden — oh, Gabriel!" she said, with a naive delight in her voice that surprised him.

"Come and see it, then."

The lilac trees on either side of the urn-topped gate posts were just coming into flower, and Gabriel pulled down a branch to catch a breath of scent. As he did so, Henrietta leant across and buried her face in the double plumes of white flowers. Her hair, which was loose, swung with her and brushed his face. He stepped back, disturbed by her sudden closeness.

"It's called 'Jeanne d'Arc', that variety," he managed to remark.

"What a terrible name for a lilac," said

Henrietta. "A virgin, soldier nun. Lilacs should be named after sensualists, don't you think?"

He wanted to say, "Like Henrietta Winthrop?" It would be a splendid name for a lilac. Instead, he thrust his hands in his pockets and began to walk along the path to the first clearing, talking rather deliberately about how he had constructed the garden. But it was soon clear that Henrietta was not listening. She had gone on ahead, her skirts swinging through the grass and the bluebells towards the large granite sculpture of a recumbent goddess in the centre of the clearing.

"Who is she?" she said, turning back to him.

"Athena — well, it's called *Fallen Athena* — it's by a rather famous Irish sculptor . . . " He broke off, watching as she pressed her hands against the face of the statue, which faced downwards, as if it had been deliberately toppled.

"Athena?" she said. "Did you say Athena, Gabriel?"

"Yes."

"You bought a statue called *Fallen*

Athena?" she said. "Don't you remember that — "

"Yes, yes, of course I remember. But that hasn't anything to do with it. What are you thinking, Henrietta?"

"I'm just thinking it's a little odd you should buy something called that, when that was what you always called me."

"Only when you were angry and I was being pretentious."

"That seemed to be pretty much all the time," she said. She was leaning against the statue, her arms folded, and looking acutely at him.

"It's just a coincidence. The sculptor chose the name. Hugh introduced me to him." Gabriel valiantly tried to change the subject. "Hugh's been very good about getting me interested in contemporary art, actually. If he hadn't, I might not have met Kate."

"But *Fallen Athena*, Gabriel?" said Henrietta.

"What do you want me to say?" he said. "That it was wishful thinking? That all these years I've wanted to see you laid low, and that I subconsciously bought a piece of sculpture to embody that?

232

How utterly ridiculous! Well, if that's the sort of critical twaddle you've made your reputation on, then — "

"OK, OK!" she exclaimed. "Forget I said anything. It's just you do seem a mite sensitive about it."

"Well, wouldn't you be, in my shoes?"

"Why? Am I so dangerous, Gabriel? What about Kate?"

"What about her?"

"Well, if everything is so secure with Kate, why are you standing there looking like you want to shoot me? Actually, I think it's nothing to do with what happened to us in the past. No. It's that you can't cope with your own irresponsible behaviour. You must be disgusted with yourself — a woman of twenty-six, Gabriel, for God's sake. That is not something to be proud of!"

★ ★ ★

I must be going off my head, thought Henrietta, when she had concluded this speech. What the hell did I say all that for?

Gabriel had started to walk away across the clearing.

"I'm sorry, I really shouldn't have said that," she called out.

He turned and looked quizzically at her. "You never used to apologise," he said.

"I hope I'm less arrogant than I was," she said, resting her back against the statue again. Oh God, what is going on here? she thought. I shouldn't have come, I know, but . . . She covered her face with her hands, anxious to stop the tears that seemed to be leaking from her eyes.

He was standing over her now, and she looked up at him, at that slightly battered face, at the dark stubble on his cheek, at those magical hazel eyes that had first entranced her. She felt then that she had never known such love as she felt for this man, and never such loss either. It was far stronger, far worse than what she had felt then.

"Oh, don't cry, for God's sake," he said. "I can't bear it. You never cry, remember."

She nodded, her own bravado echoing

234

in her mind. She swallowed hard, and tried to speak. "No, I never cry. I never cry, do I? It's a weakness, an admission of weakness . . . " Her throat was so contorted she could hardly utter the words. "But Gabriel, oh Gabriel, I cry all the time now . . . " She pressed her face into the crook of her folded arm, looking away from him, not wanting him to hear this terrible admission.

"No, don't, don't," she heard him say in a desperate voice. She felt his arm round her shoulder, his hand on her hair, stroking it, not calmly but with anxiety. "Henry, no . . . "

She turned to look at him, and saw a look of pain in his eyes. She was struggling to control herself, but she was annihilated at the touch of his hand on her hair. With heroic effort she disentangled herself, knowing that if she had left it a moment longer she would have kissed him.

"I'm OK now," she said, reaching for her handkerchief. "Nothing that a good cup of coffee won't solve anyway," she added, as she began to walk away from him across the clearing. The sunlight was pouring through the trees now, dappling the new growth of leaves, and she deliberately wiped her eyes so she would see it.

"I thought you said you didn't drink coffee any more," he said.

"There are always exceptional circumstances," she said. "If you'll excuse me, I really ought to get my feet dry. I am obviously past the age of adolescent fancy."

"Henrietta . . . " he said.

She stopped and looked back at him. He was standing with his hands in his pockets, his head slightly bent. He did not meet her gaze.

"Yes?" She found herself prickling with expectation for a moment.

"Nothing."

She decided she had been spared a platitude. After all, what else could she expect from him? Bob was right, and she had been very silly, not to say downright wicked, to think otherwise. How could he still be remotely interested in her when he had Kate; and while he was involved with Kate how could she, Henrietta, permit herself to feel anything towards him?

She hoped she was at least a decent enough person to be able to resist doing something as despicable as making a play for another woman's partner. The beauty of the wild garden and that strange statue had led her into a state of self-delusion. She had seen things as she wanted to see them, not as they really were. The touch of his hand on her hair had merely been compassionate.

12

"THE really weird thing," Liz said to Kate the following morning, "is that I'm filled with a wild urge to go out and buy a pile of those revolting glossy wedding magazines. It's daft, isn't it? Martin gives me this ring and I want to turn myself into a Cindy doll. All my feminist credentials go out of the window. All I can think about is wild silk and chiffon!"

Kate had wanted to discuss more than wedding dresses with Liz. She had wanted to tell her about Gabriel's proposal last night; in fact she was rather desperate to ask her opinion about it. But it had not seemed quite fair to steal her limelight by saying, "Oh, by the way, Gabriel asked me to marry him last night too!" Liz was in such a flush of engaged enthusiasm and so besotted with the idea of marriage that Kate was not sure she would be able to give her the rational advice that she wanted. Kate had decided she would say nothing just then. She needed a few days to order her own thoughts on the subject, let alone give Gabriel an answer. She had decided to focus on Liz's happiness.

So, while Bob and Gabriel peaceably immured themselves with the Sunday papers in the library, Liz and Kate spent an hour or so lingering over the breakfast table and Alison's home-made brioche, getting into the pleasant nitty gritty, such as whether the groom should be asked to wear a kilt or whether they could manage to go through a church service without feeling hypocritical. By the time Martin came in from his run, there were only a few more details to settle.

Liz and Martin did not stay for lunch as they wanted to call in on Martin's parents in Dunfermline and surprise them. Bob left at the same time. Henrietta had gone immediately after breakfast, saying she had a conference paper that had to be finished. Of Hugh, there had been no sign all morning, and at lunch Gabriel and Kate were alone again.

It was odd that, having been perfectly happy to be alone with him before, that lunchtime she felt distinctly uncomfortable.

They were both unusually quiet, as if all their fund of conversation had been used up the night before. This was something that happened to all couples from time to time, she knew, but it was hardly a comfortable silence for her, at least. Gabriel struck her again as he had done last night, as almost a stranger. She watched him as he drank his spinach soup, finding she was watching him rather too objectively for someone who was supposed to be wildly in love. She felt ashamed of herself, but she could not help it. She found herself wondering whether she really knew what was going on in his mind.

He looked very self-contained, and she realised he must have sat there at the kitchen table eating so many solitary meals that he was probably not even aware that the quietness was making her uncomfortable. Gabriel, in fact, seemed so perfectly comfortable that she asked herself why he had bothered to pick her out of the crowd and put her down there. She felt she had been collected by him, acquired, like all the other objects in the house. She was not expected to do a great deal except amuse him occasionally, like one of the cats with their antics. His asking her to marry him, she decided, was merely paying the balance on the deposit. He was securing her in perpetuity to sit still and be available for occasional consultation.

She hated this line of thought, but it was irresistible. She felt stiff with inhibition. She wanted to jump up and switch on the radio to break the silence. The radio was tuned to Radio 3, of course, which usually she did not mind, but today she wanted to hear something vulgar, self-indulgent and entirely transient. She wanted to remind herself there was a world beyond Allansfield. She wanted Liz and Martin back, and the chatter of guests, not Gabriel's civilised silence. It left far too much time to think.

She found she was thinking about what he must have been like at Cambridge, attempting to make sense of the details she had gleaned last night. If Hugh was anything to judge by, he would have been very good-looking. She wondered how serious he had been about Henrietta. If they had been very close it would explain his reticence. Or perhaps it was simply family tradition, this aristocratic tight-lippedness, this damned self-containedness.

But that was rubbish, she knew. Gabriel was not coolly self-contained — or at least he had not been when they met. She would not have fallen in love with him if he was really like that, and he certainly would not have let himself fall in love with her if he was that repressed. He would not have dreamt of bringing her here without a nicely correct wedding ring on her finger. That was what had appealed to her, that he had not been obvious and formal and correct. He had asked her to come and live with him, without caring that she was the same age as his son.

So why was he asking her to marry him now? She put down her soup spoon and enquired, "How long have you been thinking about marriage, Gabriel?"

He looked a little startled — her voice had sounded rather aggressive. "Have I put my foot in it with this?" he said after a slight pause. "Well, as I said yesterday, I thought of it last night. Martin seemed to have a very good idea there."

"It must have crossed your mind before."

"Once or twice," he admitted. "But I didn't want to force the issue, until last night, when it seemed the blindingly obvious thing to do."

"Blindingly obvious?"

"Well, to me, but perhaps not to you . . . " She did not reply. "You did look very surprised, Kate. Perhaps it seems a very grotesque idea to you, but I did ask in good faith."

"What does that mean?"

"It means, I suppose, that I should have done it long ago. My conscience — "

"What are you going on about?" she exclaimed. "You're not going to tell me you feel guilty about things as they are?"

"Yes. To be frank, I do."

She did not know what to say to this.

"I've shocked you, haven't I?" he said, getting up from his seat. "I'm sorry. I did ask with the best intentions."

She felt she should get angry with him, but she was still too astonished. She felt he had slapped her in the face with this unexpected admission; but she sat there staring at her half-finished soup while he kissed her briefly on the forehead.

"I must get back into the garden," he said. "Weather like this never lasts."

You're running away, Gabriel, she thought. But from what?

She let him go, and went up to the day nursery where for a couple of hours she fiddled around with various painting jobs, without losing herself in her work. Her mind was still grappling with what Gabriel had said, or rather with what he had not said. She was not at all satisfied, and decided she would have another go.

A little while later, then, she carried afternoon tea out to the walled garden. Alison had insisted on arranging everything with her customary care on a large mahogany tray, so Kate's spontaneous thought of grabbing two mugs of tea and taking them out to Gabriel in the garden was rather spoilt. It was difficult to do anything at Allansfield without a certain degree of ceremony.

The walled garden was already looking

voluptuous in its first flush of late spring growth. There were tresses of budding roses hanging from the walls, and green- and grey-leafed plants of all sorts springing up underneath them, occasionally punctuated by fascinating irises, their petals displaying strange combinations of colours. She put the tray down on the grass by the central fountain and turned about, trying to spot Gabriel in the complicated maze it all formed. She spotted him in the far corner and called out, "Tea!"

He straightened up and turned to her. He was standing deep in a border, and he picked his way through it carefully to come and meet her as she came forward. She saw his face was red and shining with sweat. She noticed too that there were sweat patches sticking his shirt to him.

"You look as though you've been hard at it," she said.

"Yes," he said, wiping his hand across his face. "I suppose I have." He smiled at her. "Tea — wonderful idea."

"All here," she said, pointing at the tray.

She sat down and poured out some

elderflower cordial while he splashed his face and hands vigorously in the water that sprouted from the bronze fish in the centre of the fountain.

"That's better," he said, flopping down on the grass beside her. "Is it very hot today, or is it just me?"

"It's pretty hot," she said, handing him a glass. He drained it at once and lay down on his back, closing his eyes.

"I'm exhausted," he said, yawning. "I'm getting past it. All I've been doing is planting out a few bedding plants."

"Not too exhausted to talk, I hope."

He sat up. "Oh?"

"Mm," she went on, her mouth full of scone. "I'm not satisfied with what you said earlier. I don't believe you."

"Why shouldn't you believe me?" he said.

"Because I simply don't. Why on earth should you suddenly start feeling guilty?"

"It's the way I'm made, the way I was brought up," he said with a shrug. "Perhaps what in Edinburgh seemed perfectly all right seems wrong here."

"Amongst the shades of your ancestors?" she said tartly.

"Well, yes. And I want you to feel you belong, Kate — properly. I want you to be a part of all this."

"You want me to be an Erskine."

"And why not? Is it so dreadful? Are we so impossible? Besides, I want you to belong because I love you, Kate. I want to give you something permanent."

"Isn't this permanent enough for you?" she said. "This is a big commitment for me, Gabriel. I don't take it lightly; and I don't feel that I have to stand up in front of a minister and say I'm committed. I know what I feel, and I know what you feel. Why on earth do we have to make a public show of it? It would be like saying we didn't trust each other, that we need legal sanctions to stop us misbehaving."

"That's not what marriage is for," he said.

"What is it for, then?" she said. He did not answer. "My game, I think," she said.

"Marriage is a legal contract, yes," he said after a pause. "But there is a great deal to be said for legalising such contracts as ours. What if something were to happen to me? I have altered my will already, actually, but I should like you to have legal rights to my estate, Kate."

"Oh, for God's sake, don't talk like that!" she said.

"One has to be practical."

"It's revolting. I don't want your money, Gabriel."

"You'll get it whether you want it or not," he said. "So don't be stupid."

"You sound like my bloody mother!" she said.

"Well, I know she'd agree with me on this one."

"Yes, I know, but I don't think my mother or your warped conscience is a good enough reason for getting married." She lay down on her back and stared up at the empty blue sky. "You know, what I really need is not a wedding ring, Gabriel, but my own space."

"We can easily have something fixed up with a skylight. There's a marvellous room in the steadings, remember. I told you about it . . . "

"My own space," she said emphatically. "Not Erskine space. It's all so inhibiting!"

"I beg your pardon?" he said.

"Well, it is," she said. "All of it. You can't see it, I suppose. You're so used to it. It's all perfectly normal to you."

"But I thought you liked it here," he said.

"I do. But . . . Well, look at this, Gabriel," she said, sitting up. "We can't even have tea in the garden without all this fuss," she said with a gesture at Alison's immaculately laid tray. "It took some effort to stop her coming out with a table."

"She's just doing her job," said Gabriel.

"Yes, yes, I know, and it's very nice, really it is, but . . . all the time, it gets at me. I feel . . . " She broke off.

"What do you feel?" he said. She decided she would not answer. "What do you feel?" he repeated sharply.

"I feel," she said, intensely needled by his tone of voice, "I feel like another thing in the house that you've collected. I just sit in there like an antique chair and do nothing. I feel I don't have any control over anything, not over anything that matters!"

For a long moment he said nothing, then he got up and began to walk away.

"Gabriel . . . I'm sorry. I didn't mean to be so frank, but . . . "

He stopped and looked at her, and pushed his hand through his hair. "But you meant it, didn't you?"

She nodded and he sighed.

"Of course I do understand how you feel," he said. "But it's just that I want you to be happy. I want you to feel this is your home. That's why I want you to marry me."

"I am happy. This way, my way. Trust me, please," she said, and reached out to touch his cheek. "Besides, I'm sure I will get used to it, that I will love it just as much as you do. You just have to give me some time."

"Of course," he said, and took her hand and kissed it.

"So you won't mind if I look for a studio somewhere else?" she said carefully.

"I suppose it would be unreasonable if I did," he said. "But I wish you would look at the steading."

"I promise I will, but I can't promise anything else," she said. She sat down again on the grass, feeling rather triumphant. "Come and have some of these scones."

"I'm not really very hungry just now," he said. "Look at that spiraea — what an utter mess it is. I really ought to do something about it now, or it won't flower properly next year." And he walked away and began to attack the recalcitrant plant with a pair of secateurs.

13

ON Monday morning, Hugh was on the telephone in the library at Allansfield, waiting for Lara to answer. He knew he had to be patient. She never saw any need for urgency in answering the telephone. At least today the phone was ringing. For the last few times he had tried, he had only got his own voice on the answering machine. He had not bothered to leave a message, knowing that Lara habitually ignored them.

At last the phone was picked up.

"Hello!" said a sunny New Zealand female voice.

"Hello — is that double seven, two, nine?" Hugh enquired, sure he had a wrong number.

"Yes, yes, it is."

"Right . . . " said Hugh, trying to place a New Zealander amongst Lara's friends. "Is Lara there?"

"No, I'm afraid she's still asleep," she

said. "Can I give her a message?"

"Yes. Could you tell her Hugh called, please?"

"Sure. Hugh . . . got it. Oh, are you Andrew's dad?"

"Yes, yes, that's right."

"I'm Terry," she said. "The new nanny."

"Oh . . . " said Hugh.

"He's a lovely kid," Terry went on. "And I should know, I've worked with some monsters."

"Glad to hear he's behaving himself," Hugh managed to say. "Well, you will give Lara my message, when she wakes up?"

"Yeah, of course — though I don't know when she will. She was out pretty late last night," she added cheerfully.

"I see," said Hugh, trying to sound calm. "So, how's Andrew?"

"Fine, just fine," said Terry. "I'll give him a kiss from his Dad, shall I?"

"Thanks," said Hugh. "I'll ring later. Goodbye . . . Terry."

"Bye!" said Terry.

Hugh made an effort not to slam down the receiver, although he was incensed.

253

He stood twitching with annoyance for a few moments, unable to decide what he ought to do about this astonishing revelation. They had been apart for only a week, and Lara had already hired a nanny without consulting him.

The door opened and he turned to see Kate come into the room. She was dressed in black jeans and an oversize white shirt that looked as though it was one of his father's. Her hair was pulled back from her face by a rolled-up red and white spotted handkerchief. He was disturbed by how acutely these trivial details registered with him.

"I've lost my car keys," she said. "Are they on the desk there?" She glanced at the desk and then at him. "Hey, are you OK?"

"No," he admitted, walking over to the window and running his fingers through his hair in his agitation. "No, actually I'm not."

"Do you want to talk about it?"

"You're going out," he said, knowing he wanted to talk to her. It would be easy to talk to her, but not strictly fair.

"Not for anything urgent," she said,

coming up behind him. He turned and looked down at her. She rested her hand lightly on his arm for a moment. "I think you should."

"Would it do any good?"

She sat down at the desk and rested her chin on her knotted hands. "I don't know," she said. "I just don't think it's a good idea to bottle things up."

"How the hell do I start?" he said, shaking his head. "Oh God, I'm so bloody confused. I don't know whether I'm right to feel what I feel. I just feel it. Or rather I don't feel it — feel what I should, I mean. Hell, that makes no sense, does it?" He saw her bite her lip, and there was something in her demeanour so gravely sympathetic that he felt he ought not to take advantage of her. There would be too much pleasure in unburdening himself to her. "Sorry," he went on. "This is just self-indulgence."

"Tell me what's the matter," she said.

"What is the matter . . . All right," he said, unable to resist any longer. "The matter, to be blunt, is that I don't love Lara any more. That's what it boils down to, I suppose. It's as simple and as complicated as that."

"Oh . . . " Kate said, with a slight wince.

"I didn't mean to stop loving her. I didn't think I could, but things just heaped up — no, not heaping up, that's not right. It was more like the thing wore away. Suddenly what I had felt just wasn't there any more. There was nothing, nothing where it mattered. Do you know what I mean?"

Kate nodded.

"Everything she does now sets my nerves on edge. I feel so angry, really frighteningly angry — like just now. I found out she's hired a nanny for Andrew without asking me about it. Now I know that's probably quite responsible — in fact it's very responsible — but all I feel is . . . " He broke off and shook his head vehemently. "I shouldn't have let her go on Saturday, should I? But I couldn't help myself. I wanted her to go. I wanted her to go so much that I didn't mind that she was taking Andrew. Well I did, I bloody did, but what else could I do?" He stopped and looked at her for a moment. "Am I being wilfully destructive, Kate?"

"I don't know," she said, "to be honest. I know lots of people would say you should stick it out, because of Andrew — but what is the best thing for him, to see you two miserable for his sake, or something else?" She hesitated for a second and then said, "Do you know what Lara feels about you?"

"Rank contempt," he said. "It's true. She says I don't know how to love properly. She's probably right, as well. I mean, God, Lara is the sort of woman that every man dreams of. She's beautiful, she's sexy, she's talented, and yet I can throw her away. And that's what I'm doing, aren't I? I can throw her away because . . . Oh, I don't know why. Because I'm a whining, spoiled brat, probably, who doesn't know what's good for him."

"No, you're not, Hugh," she said. "You don't have to loathe yourself like this just because of what you feel . . . ."

"No, Andrew will do the loathing for me," Hugh said bitterly. "And he will hate me, I'm sure, for breaking up on a whim."

257

"Do you hate your father?" Kate said.

"No," he admitted after a pause. "No, I never hated him for it. I was angry, though." Exhausted by his own anger, he threw himself into the armchair. "You know I always used to wonder why they split up. I mean they seemed to have everything going for them, just like Lara and me, I suppose. Perhaps there doesn't always have to be a specific reason, just a combination of annoyances. But it is depressing, isn't it, that history should repeat itself like this?"

At length she said, "You shouldn't be so fatalistic. History doesn't always repeat itself."

"You're right," he said, getting up from his chair. He went and stood by the French window, looking out on to the terrace.

"So what will you do?" she said behind him.

"I'm going to call a friend and ask them to check out the nanny for me."

"Good idea," she said. He turned to look at her. She was standing with her arms folded across her chest, stroking her jaw with her finger. "You should,

258

I suppose go down and try to talk again. What about marriage guidance or something?"

"I need some more time to think," he said. "Andrew apart, it's good for me to have a break, to calm down a bit."

"OK," she said. "Well, good luck with it."

"Thanks," he said, and was unable to resist patting her on the forearm. "You've been great."

* * *

Later, Kate drove to St Andrews to start hunting for a studio. She had very little luck. The estate agents had nothing suitable, and although she scoured every notice-board she could find, there was hardly anything on offer. In desperation, she bought a ham and pickle bap and a can of lemonade and went to have a picnic on the West Sands. It was a beautiful day of blazing sunshine and she was sitting on a steep bank of soft dry sand leading up to the dunes, giving her a perfect view of the beach.

She scanned the glittering horizon

where the sea met the sky. The sun on the sea almost dazzled her, and she looked back up towards the town, at the cheerful jumble of eccentric buildings that crept up the Scores, at the dipping and soaring of the roof lines, at the red stone and grey stone and white stucco, at ruins and villas, and at the tremendous exclamatory punctuation of St Rules Tower, rising above it all.

She looked back towards the sea, at the promenade of figures who were walking along at the water's edge, some in pairs, some solitary like herself, or with a dog or two always outstripping them and then returning to them. She thought of Gabriel then. He had gone off early that morning in a dark suit to a dreary meeting in Dundee, and she knew how he would hate being confined inside on such a day. She tried to focus on that, seeing him sitting in some oak-panelled board room, growing politely impatient, running his finger around his collar; but her mind kept flashing back to that long conversation she had had with Hugh. His misery seemed extraordinarily tangible to her.

Nearby a group of children were digging in the sand, just as she and Hugh had once done. She wondered if she had ever spoken to him then, or seen him. How strange it would be if they had spoken. She found she could not dislodge the feeling that it was somehow significant that they might have done. It was just a trivial coincidence after all.

Driving back from St Andrews she decided to go and look at the steading. It was on the back road off the estate, remote from the house but across the lane from Hugh's cottage. She was glad to have the chance to look at it alone. She did not want Gabriel confusing the issue with clever arguments.

She parked in the lane and went into the yard. The yard was depressingly full of old bits of farm machinery, and looked very unpromising. She scowled at it and then, to her surprise, Hugh emerged from an open doorway, pushing a wheelbarrow. He had obviously been working hard, as he had stripped off his shirt and tied it round his waist.

"Oh," she said, annoyed. "Has he got you in on this too?"

"Sorry?" he said.

"Gabriel — did he ask you to clear this out?"

"No," he said. "Why would he?"

"Because . . . " she began, and then decided against an explanation. "Then why are you clearing it out?"

"I'm excavating the kiln I built," he said. "I needed something to do, to take my mind off things. I'm going to try firing it up again. What's this about my father?"

"Oh, just a silly thing," she said, shoving her hands in her pockets and looking round at the interesting jumble of shapes that the machinery made. "This looks like modern sculpture in progress."

"Needs more rust," said Hugh with a grin. "Have you ever made sculpture?"

"I've thought about it once or twice, but really, two dimensions are hard enough to keep a grip on. You? Well, I suppose pots are sculptures, really."

"Sort of," he said.

"You've set yourself quite a job here," she said.

"All help gratefully received," he said. "Yes, it's got into a fair old state. Saves

Ted and the boys going to the tip, dumping everything here. I suppose."

"I should stop you really. You are ruining one of my arguments," she said. He gave her an enquiring look as he unfolded a fertiliser bag and began to transfer the bits and pieces from the barrow into it.

"Your father thinks I should have my studio here," she said.

"Good idea — the old tack room would be ideal for that," he said. Kate frowned and he saw her. "But you don't like the idea? There's a stove there, if you're worried about the cold."

"I think I should have a studio in St Andrews," she said, "but Gabriel doesn't quite understand that. Perhaps you don't."

"No, I think I understand. Allansfield takes some getting used to, I suppose. My mother never liked it you know; and Lara, well . . . "

"Oh, no, I don't dislike it," she said quickly. "It's not that at all. It's just . . . " She decided to change the subject. "I can't believe you built a kiln. That sounds amazing."

"Come and have a look, then," he said.

She followed him through the open door into a large whitewashed room, lit by a row of high windows and divided up into stalls. In one stall was a large igloo shape built out of bricks, with a chimney pipe sticking out of the top and snaking its way out of the nearest window.

"These used to be loose boxes, of course," said Hugh, "but we haven't had horses since just after the war. We've never been a horsy family really. I had this place really well set up, though you wouldn't know it now."

"That's the kiln, I take it," she said, pointing at the igloo.

"That's my baby," he said. "Primitive but effective. And I had the wheel in this stall, and did all the glazes here. Better than my workroom now. More space. I wonder where the wheel's got to. I never took it down with me to London, I know that . . . " He went to the door at the far end. "Should be in here somewhere . . . This is the old tack room, by the way. What do you reckon?"

"Damn," she said, looking at it. "It's

264

a very good space."

"Isn't it?" he said.

It was a square, airy room, with two big windows with arched tops, and a fireplace with a wood-burning stove between them. The floor was brick and there was an old table, heaped with old paint cans, as well as a settle by the fire. It was exactly the sort of space she had been hoping to find in St Andrews.

"You could pretend it's not Allansfield," he said. "And if I'm going to be working next door . . . "

"You are?" she said.

"Yes. Here's my wheel!" he said with delight, unfurling it from several layers of polythene sheeting. "So, we could keep each other at it, couldn't we? Much less distracting than being up at the house. It would be like coming to work properly for you."

"How come you understand?" she said.

"I know my father, and I know what Allansfield's like."

"But I would have thought that you — "

"Felt the same as Dad? Yes, perhaps I do, but I'm not in an advanced case of obsession, at least not yet." He swept the dust off the settle and sat down. "That will come with time, no doubt."

"He did make you clear this out, didn't he?"

"Honestly, he didn't. I'm doing it entirely for myself."

"So, you are intending to stay for a while then?" she said, leaning against the table.

"Yes, I think I need to sort myself out properly before I go back," he said with a sigh. "A sort of retreat, really." He got up from the settle, untied his shirt from round his waist, and put it back on. "Yes, a retreat, that's it," he said again. He looked up from buttoning the shirt and regarded her for a moment. Suddenly he looked away and began to gather up the old paint cans from the table. "Now, shall I take this rubbish to the tip for you?"

"I'll give you a hand."

They worked for the rest of the day on the steading, taking several large loads to the tip at Cupar in the back of Hugh's Volvo estate. While Hugh was away with the last load, Kate picked up an old broom and swept the brick floors. She was tired but oddly exhilarated. Making this space for herself had been therapeutic. She no longer felt the least bit cross with Gabriel. In fact she realised she had hardly thought about him at all. She had forgotten where she was and why. The act of doing had obliterated everything.

"Time to stop!"

She turned and saw Hugh standing in the doorway from the courtyard. The late afternoon sun was flooding through the windows, catching him like a stage light. In each hand he held a bottle of Budweiser.

"Beer!" she said. "You read my mind."

They sat down on the settle and drank from the bottles, gulping it down.

"Don't worry, there's more in the fridge," he said when she finished her bottle before him.

She wiped her mouth with the back of her dusty sleeve and laughed.

"I'm filthy!" she exclaimed. "But it was worth it, wasn't it? This is going to be a great studio. I'll feel like an idiot, though. I shall have to admit to Gabriel that he was right after all." She gave a mock growl.

"I'm sure he'll be very gracious."

"Of course he will," she said. "That's what will be even more annoying!" She got up and paced round the tack room with a proprietary air. "But what does it matter? What really matters is I've found this wonderful studio." She spun round and smiled at him. "Thanks for persuading me."

"You didn't need much persuading," he said, getting up. "Now, can you bear to go back to the house yet? I'm going up there to scrounge some food from Alison."

"No, come and stay for dinner," she said. "Please."

★ ★ ★

After dinner, in the library, Gabriel suggested they play Scrabble. Hugh agreed but Kate declined. The two men sat, therefore, on either side of a little pie-crust table, Hugh astride his chair, his arms folded on the top rail, while Gabriel was more elegant, in a carver, his chin resting on his hand. From where Kate sat, in the armchair by the fireplace, she had them both in profile as they bent their heads over the table. She could not resist slipping out of her chair and fetching a piece of paper to do a sketch.

She found she was concentrating on Hugh. She told herself that it was because his pose was more interesting, and it was the first time she had ever sketched him. A fresh subject was always a challenge. Yet she was aware, as she did it, that there was admiration in her line. She was looking at him not as a group of lines to be turned into a composition, but as a man, a very real and very attractive man, whose cheeks were a little red with wine and whose long hair was so disordered that she wanted to rake her fingers through it and set it straight. Shocked at this thought, she turned quickly to Gabriel again, trying to lose herself in sketching the complicated drapery of his shirtsleeves.

"We've hemmed ourselves in here," said Hugh. "I'm completely stuck."

"Me too," said Gabriel. "Someone's

being productive though." Kate looked up. "May we see?"

"Of course," she said, handing over the sketch.

"That's wonderful!" said Hugh.

"Yes, yes, it is," said Gabriel. "Definitely one for the family archive."

"You have a family archive?" said Kate. "Though should I be surprised? You never throw anything away do you, Gabriel?"

"I just call it an archive. It's not as grand as that. Though some houses, you know, have muniment-rooms — "

"No, Dad, no . . . " said Hugh.

"I'm only thinking of future historians," he said.

"And who do you think will be interested?" said Hugh. "Only the family."

"That's a good reason for keeping them."

"How much stuff is there?" asked Kate.

"Just a few cupboards full. The photographs are wonderful. You must see them."

"Actually, they are rather good," said Hugh.

270

In a moment, Gabriel had pulled out several boxes from the deep press in the wall, and the past of Allansfield was soon spread out for Kate on the rug on the floor. There were land girls in 1943, reaping corn, wearing turbans and lipstick; there was the family playing in the garden in the 1930s; Gabriel's father, throwing a ball at a West Highland terrier who appeared as nothing but a white blur; and then older, more formal pictures — Ralph, Gabriel's grandfather, clearly uneasy in his officer's uniform, outside the portico, about to go off to the First World War, his wife's face and emotions hidden by her broad-brimmed hat. Kate felt she was undergoing an initiation ceremony in being shown these intensely personal and vivid fragments of the past.

"All the ghosts of Allansfield," said Hugh.

The phrase stuck in her mind, as she sank back on her heels and looked over the pictures he had laid out on the rug.

"Is the house haunted?" she said. She addressed Gabriel. He had retreated to his chair, and was staring at a photograph in his hand. "Gabriel?"

"What?" He looked up.

"Kate wants to know if the house is haunted," said Hugh.

"No, no," he said. "I'm going to make some coffee." He put the photograph down on the table as he passed. When he had left the room, Kate reached up and took it. She turned it over and saw Henrietta, standing next to Gabriel, in a washed-out colour photograph. She was wearing a silky white evening dress, her hair brightly blonde and piled high on her head. On the back was written: 'Trinity May Ball, 1967.'

14

"COFFEE time," said Hugh, coming into Kate's studio. She had been working at the steading for over a week, and this morning coffee break had quickly become a ritual with them. "And fudge doughnuts. I've been into Cupar, and of course Fisher and Donaldson . . ."

"Of course," laughed Kate, putting down her pencil. She was ready for a rest. She had been sketching hard all morning, wrestling with the composition for her new picture. She propped the drawing board up on the table, against the wall, so that it was surrounded by all the preparatory sketches she had taped to the wall, along with the photocopies she had taken of the photographs in Gabriel's family archive. She looked again at her morning's work, wondering if she had the balance right.

"Where are the doughnuts, then?" she said, as Hugh handed her a mug of coffee.

"In the bag there," he said, holding out a paper bag. He too was looking at the drawing on the panel. She pulled out a doughnut and bit into it absentmindedly.

"What do you reckon?" she said.

"What is it going to be?" he said.

"A hotch-potch if I'm not careful. I've got this idea, but I'm not sure I can get it out on paper. It's very clear in my head, but . . . " She sighed. "Perhaps I'm being over-ambitious."

"That doesn't answer my question," he said. "Why have you done all these photocopies?"

"Gabriel thought I'd gone mad too," she said, laughing. "It's going to be a sort of fancy picture, a fantasy really. You gave me the idea actually. What you said last week when we were looking at the photos. The ghosts of Allansfield, you said. So I'm trying to paint them all, in the gardens, drifting about, as I'm sure they do."

"What a wonderful idea," he said. "Oh yes, I see it now. There's my grandmother — that hat could only be one of hers!"

"And there you are, and Gabriel," she

274

said, pointing at the bottom left hand corner. "And the cats." She had put Hugh in at the age of six or so, and, looking now, she found that her sketch of Gabriel looked more like Hugh as he was now.

"Where are you, though?" he said.

"Oh, I'm the painter. I don't need to put myself in," she said.

"I do like the idea of *Fallen Athena* coming to life," he said.

"You think that's OK?" she said. "I think it needs another figure. Something here. Another mythical figure. Pan perhaps."

"Pan?"

"Well, he should definitely be there. A real garden God. I do need to get some more models, though. If this is to work, it has to be from life." She glanced at him, remembering how he had looked without his shirt. "You'd make a good Pan, you know."

He looked vaguely embarrassed for a moment, and then smiled and said, "Don't I need horns and goat's legs?"

"I'll improvise those," she said. "What about it?"

"Me, model for you?"

"Would it be a bother?"

"No, I'm just . . . " He rubbed his face and then grinned. "Amused. And flattered. Pan, eh?" He laughed. "Fine, why not?" he finished, striking a flamboyant pose for her.

"That's no good," she said. "And you'd have to take your clothes off."

"All of them?" he queried.

"All of them," she said. "It's no use to me otherwise."

"Oh Gawd," he said. "Are you sure?"

"You'll forget about it soon enough," she said. "I promise. I've sat for a life class before — twenty evening-class students, imagine that. Your mind goes blank after a while."

"It does?"

She nodded, hoping she could convince him. He would make the most marvellous Pan with that wild dark hair of his.

"All right," he said. "When?"

"Well, are you busy now?"

"Are you serious?"

"Well, if you get used to the idea quickly, it won't seem so bad. You might change your mind by tomorrow and then

I'd be short of a wonderful Pan."

"You're too persuasive."

"Right then," she said with a grin. "Let's get on with it, shall we?"

"You are brutal," he said, and started to unbutton his shirt.

She went to pick up her sketch pad and a piece of charcoal, and tried not to watch as he stripped off his clothes. But she could not help herself. His body was well made and strong looking, the flesh on his shoulders and arms taut with muscle, his belly flat, his waist narrow. He was down to his boxer shorts now, with his back to her, and she found she was not thinking how she should pose him, but thinking how attractive he was. She was appalled that the sight of him could produce such a fierce spasm of erotic desire in her, especially as she saw him pull down his shorts to disclose a very handsome backside. She stared down quickly at the blank page of her sketch book.

"OK," he said. "What do you want me to do?"

She looked at him. He was standing there, trying to look nonchalant, but she could tell he was not from the tension in his musculature. She, affecting the same false nonchalance, said, "Oh, well . . . er . . . " and tried to think of a suitable pose. "Try some poses out for me," she said. She waved her arms helplessly, trying to make a suggestion with them. "Something, anything . . . Yes, hold that — that's perfect." He had turned away from her, but twisted his torso back to look over his shoulder. She would paint him looking directly out at the spectator, with a sharp gaze that would draw them into the rest of the composition. "Just stretch out your left arm," she said, "with your palm upwards."

It was an extremely difficult posture to draw, and she was glad it was. She needed to fix all her concentration on abstract line and form, to forget that this was a handsome man standing naked in front of her, or rather to reduce that merely to charcoal marks on a page.

She worked at it for ten minutes or so. He held the pose well, without wavering, and stayed quiet too. It was as if he knew she needed to concentrate.

"That's great!" she said when she had at last an approximation that satisfied her. "You must be in agony. I'm sorry . . . "

"A bit, yes," he said, stretching up, still with his back to her. With a lazy hand he rubbed his neck. Suddenly he was a man again, and not merely an object. She felt disturbed again and looked quickly down at the sketch. "God!" he exclaimed. "And I need the loo too."

She heard him scrabbling round to fetch his clothes, and then go dashing out of the steading. She did not look up until he had gone.

★ ★ ★

Hugh, in the bathroom of the cottage, washed his face with cold water and wondered what the hell he was playing at. That he had just been extremely stupid he was certain.

He thanked God that Kate was a professional artist, completely used to dealing with live models. The fact that she had asked him to sit would have meant about as much to her as her

279

asking him to make a cup of coffee
— and if he had said no, there would
have been no more said about it. But
the invitation had been irresistible to
him. His pathetically jumbled brain had
found himself interpreting her request as
something more than aesthetic need. He
had wanted to expose himself to her, as
if by taking off his clothes and standing
naked in front of her, he was in fact
ripping himself open and showing her
his soul and his heart.

He rubbed his face dry and tried to
keep a grip on the facts. What he was
feeling about her was totally ridiculous.
It was only because his marriage had
just collapsed, and because she was
around the place, and intelligent and
sympathetic. They just happened to have
a lot in common, to be on the same
wavelength. At any other time, he tried to
convince himself, he would not have been
blundering around like this, having all
these inappropriate feelings towards her.
She had done nothing at all to encourage
him. His mind had just careered off the
rails. This was not real feeling — it was
just unfocused, sloppy emotion. It was

after-shock. How could he possibly feel so strongly for her? She was his father's girlfriend, for God's sake!

He was behaving like a spoilt child. It was jealousy, nothing more. He was jealous of his father's happiness. He wanted a simple, tranquil life again; he wanted a relationship like his father had with her, not Kate herself. He told himself this sternly as he walked up to the house to look for his father.

He found Gabriel in the walled garden, where the borders were just beginning to start their spectacular summer show. He was deep in the border, distinctive in his battered panama hat. He was examining a large and distinctly languorous frilly white peony.

"Ah, I could just do with a hand," he said as Hugh approached. "Grab a couple of those stakes will you? She's a beauty, this one, but somewhat lacking in backbone." Hugh waded into the bed and set out a triangle of stakes round the peony. Gabriel produced a roll of twine and his penknife and turned the stakes into a green string barrier. "Much better." He smiled and straightened up.

"You're not experimenting with that kiln then?"

"No, it's too hot to be building fires," said Hugh.

"This weather is amazing," said Gabriel, looking up into the sky. "The best summer we've had for years — though I don't suppose it feels much like the best summer for years to you . . . "

"No, not exactly," said Hugh.

"I'm sorry, Hugh, it must be . . . " He began to deadhead a riotous clump of small-flowered blue geraniums. "Well, what do I say? I know exactly what you're going through."

Hugh, crouching down beside him, began deadheading too. "I've talked to Kate."

"Oh?"

"Yes, yes. She's been a great help."

"Good," Gabriel said, stepping back and eyeing the geranium bush. "This is a rather vulgar colour isn't it? Too strong for here, anyway. Shan't do this again next year. Too much blue altogether."

"Yes, it needs something silvery, or very dark green. To offset those big white thistles."

"The 'Miss Wilmot's Ghost', you mean?" said Gabriel.

"Oh, is that what they're called?" said Hugh. "I must remember that. Very appropriate actually. You know Kate's painting this ghost picture — the Ghosts of Allansfield."

"She did mention it briefly," said Gabriel, walking on along the border. "So, about you and Lara, have you made any definite plans yet? Will you have another go?"

"No, no, I don't think so. It's all adrift. I'm not in love with her any more. I'm just making her miserable instead. She says I don't know how to love her, and I think she's right. I'm not good for her. She would be better off with someone else."

"Goodness," said Gabriel softly, "this all sounds so familiar."

"I ought to be able to love her, but I don't. I don't feel committed. God knows I should be, with Andrew, and I don't want to split — but I honestly can't see that I can go on living with her. It would be a sham, and that's no good for Andrew is it?"

After a pause, Gabriel asked, "If we'd given you the choice, what would you have chosen?"

"I wanted you back together. Every child does. But at the same time I can still hear those arguments you used to have."

"You heard us?"

"Oh yes, I did." His father looked stricken. "I'm sorry, I don't suppose you wanted to know that."

"I should never have married her," Gabriel said, wandering away slightly. "It was an utterly indefensible thing to have done. I was in such a mess and I could get no grip on myself, and then suddenly there she was, your mother, at Auchintrae, being so kind and sympathetic and understanding. She picked me up, she sorted me out, and I asked her to marry me. I should never have done it." He shook his head and then looked across at Hugh. "But then we should never have had you," he added very simply. "For all those rows, that fact remains. I don't regret that part of it. That's the only defence I can offer." He gave a slight laugh.

"You can see why I never made it as a barrister."

Hugh turned away and looked at the just-flowering rose that was clambering up the grey stone wall. It was festooned with clusters of pale pink buds that in a week or two would burst open.

"So I suppose you'll be heading up to town again," said Gabriel. "To start clearing things up a bit?"

"Actually, I'm going to stay here a while longer," Hugh said. "If I may?"

"Of course," said Gabriel. "But what about Andrew? Aren't you missing him terribly?"

But Hugh was not thinking of Andrew. He knew why he wanted to stay and it was for all the wrong reasons. He knew the danger he was in, but he could not stop himself. For all that his father had just said about his mother, he could not convince himself that what he was feeling about Kate was the same misguided, recently damaged emotion. He could not, simply could not, convince himself.

★ ★ ★

Kate went upstairs to bed that night later than Gabriel. She had stayed up to watch the end of an exciting but gruesome American thriller on the black and white set that was the only television at Allansfield. Gabriel never watched television much, and she felt a little ashamed sometimes of her need to lounge in front of it from time to time, watching whatever terrible rubbish happened to be on. It was her way of relaxing, and she found she was very tired. She had been working so intensively since she had moved her studio to the steading. In a week she had achieved a great deal.

She went upstairs, the images of the film still lingering in her mind. There had been rather a graphic sex sequence and she had found herself being rather turned on by it. She realised she was quite frustrated. It had been at least a week since she and Gabriel had made love. She decided, as she pushed open the door, that she would remedy that.

Yet she found that Gabriel had fallen asleep, although all the lights were on. He was propped up on a pile of pillows, with a book open on his lap. His head had fallen back at rather a ghastly angle and his mouth was slightly open. His face looked purply red and sweaty against the white pillow, and his neck muscles stood out as if under excessive strain. For the first time she found herself thinking that he looked old.

She detached the book from his hands and glanced at it. It was *Emma* — a book which he had told her he sometimes found almost too painful to read. She closed it and put it down on the bedside table.

He stirred and woke up.

"I was trying not to wake you," she said.

"How was your film?"

"Excellently relaxing twaddle," she said.

"Good," he said with a smile, and touched her forehead with the knuckle of his index finger. "You've been working so hard, you need to relax."

"Yes, I do, I do," she said suggestively, and ran her fingers through his hair. She climbed on to the bed and straddled him. "And there is nothing that relaxes me more than . . . " She bent and kissed him on the lips. "Well, you know me, Gabriel."

"I'd love to, Kate, but . . . " He gave an apologetic smile. "To be frank I am quite whacked. It's this heat."

"Excuses, excuses," she said, pressing herself against him. "You only need a little encouragement."

"No, honestly, my love," he said, and very gently pushed her away. "Go and get ready for bed, eh?"

She got off the bed and wondered, as she went across the room to brush her hair, whether a slow strip-tease would put him more in the mood. But, sitting down at the mirror, she saw that he was already lying down with his eyes closed, and in a moment or two he appeared to have fallen asleep again.

15

THE heat had become unbearable. Gabriel could not remember heat like it at Allansfield in June. It hung in the air around him, cloying and thick, making every movement an effort. It was not as if he was doing anything particularly strenuous — deadheading a camellia required care but not any physical effort — and yet here he was, dripping. He was not even, he realised, concentrating properly, noticing how many dead flowers he had missed. His mind like his body seemed to be demanding rest.

He abandoned the camellia, frightful though it still looked with so many half-rotten flowers hanging lamely from it. It looked as bedraggled as he felt. He rubbed his face and decided he must get out of the sun. He would go up to the wild garden, undoubtedly the coolest and shadiest part of the gardens. Perhaps there he would feel a little more active.

He wandered about there for a while, noting various jobs that needed to be done, and the satisfactory progress of the alpine strawberries which he had planted out under the trees, but eventually his lassitude overcame him and he lay down in a swathe of long grass by the stone temple, which promised a cool, damp embrace. He meant to sleep, but the moment he closed his eyes his mind seemed to jump to life, filled with aggravating little worries that he could not suppress. He found himself thinking of how last night he had for the fourth night running woken up in the small hours, sweating feverishly, his skin prickling viciously with some unknown irritation. That, combined with the lack of stamina that he felt during the day, his lack of appetite for sex or food, seemed to suggest that something was wrong, but he was loath to admit it to himself. It was probably something that would pass, a strange bug.

He drifted off to sleep then, but for how long he was not sure. When he woke he found the sun had moved round and he was no longer lying in the shade. He felt it burning down on him, and he opened his eyes to find himself staring fully into its brilliance. He turned aside quickly, only to see Henrietta sitting a little distance away from him on the temple steps. She was reading a book. He blinked for a moment, checking whether she was real.

Gabriel propped himself up on his elbows and said, "What on earth are you doing here?" He found his throat was dry and hoarse.

She turned and smiled at him. "Trespassing probably," she said. "Do you mind? I found you here, and it seemed a shame to wake you."

"What are you reading?" he asked.

"*Emma*," she said, and he staggered to his feet, laughing.

"How appropriate!" he said. "Have you seen my strawberries then? 'Hautboy — infinitely superior — no comparison,'" he quoted. "Except they're not Hautboy. I can't find that variety anywhere."

"Is that Mrs Elton?" she said, flipping through the pages of the book. "Oh yes, here we are: 'Cultivation — beds, when to be renewed — gardeners thinking exactly different — no general rule — gardeners never to be put out of their way — delicious fruit — only too rich to be eaten much of'." She laughed. "Is that why you planted them? A literary conceit?"

"Possibly," he said. "And the birds don't get them; and the taste, of course."

She closed the book and got to her feet. "I came looking for Kate," she said. "But there seemed to be no one about at the house. I rang the bell."

"It's Alison's day off. Kate's in her studio. What did you want her for?" he asked.

"I've some good news for her. About the exhibition. Eleanor McCleod's given us the go-ahead and a date."

"Good," said Gabriel. "That's excellent. Look, I'm dying for some tea. Come up to the house and wait for her. She won't be long, I'm sure. There must be things you need to discuss."

"Yes, there are a few things," she said. "Thank you."

They walked back to the house and went into the kitchen, which was stiff with the roaring heat of the Aga, and he felt suddenly utterly exhausted, to the point of faintness. He went to fill the kettle but found himself staggering slightly at the sink, and sweating violently again. His hands were shaking as he attempted to turn on the tap.

"Are you OK?" said Henrietta behind him.

"I . . . I . . . " He gave up trying to fill the kettle and left it on the draining board. "I think I've got some sort of a virus at the moment."

"Come and sit down," she said, and steered him into a chair. She pressed a cool hand on his forehead. "You are running a dreadful temperature."

He propped his elbows on the table and rested his head in his hands, finding he was gasping slightly for breath. He could feel his heart pounding. With effort he looked up to see that she was setting the kettle on the range.

"Do you want a glass of water?" she asked.

"A large glass of water."

He watched her systematically searching the cupboards. There was something calming about the sight of her doing it.

"Oh, you have a proper American ice box," she said. "With an ice maker!"

"My vulgar fridge," he said, wearily leaning back.

"You always did have doubts about American culture," said Henrietta with a smile, putting down a glass of water that jingled with ice in front of him. "But you gave in to an ice box. I must have had some good effect on you," she added, as she sat down opposite him.

"One fridge would hardly show up on the US trade figures," Gabriel said, and drank most of his water. She smiled again and once more he felt calmed by her presence in a way he hardly expected to be. She looked comfortable there, at the other end of the table, as if this had been her kitchen for years. One of the cats even came and jumped into her lap without a qualm.

Well, it would have been her kitchen if she had married him. To be sitting there alone with her, waiting for the kettle to boil, felt like a sudden interruption by a parallel universe, in which they had been married. They would have had over twenty-five years together, a good many of those here at Allansfield. The vision seemed so strong, so credible as they sat there, that he half expected some child of theirs to come in. He wondered if the same thought was crossing her mind as she got up to make the tea.

"Can you find everything?" he said, dismissing this nonsense as a by-product of his temperature.

"I think so," she said. "How are you feeling now?"

"A little better," he said. "I think I should go and have a shower."

"And go to bed," she said. "You should take it easy for a few days."

"I find it very boring being ill. I don't usually allow myself to be ill."

"I know what you mean," she said. "But you should pay attention to these things. You don't want to make yourself really ill. I am speaking from experience here."

"What happened to you?"

"Well, I had all these silly symptoms which I thought were nothing in particular, until a physician friend of mine insisted I have an exam and I found I needed a hysterectomy."

"Oh . . . "

"Sounds worse than it was," she said. "And I don't suppose that's your problem. Men aren't supposed to get menopausal, although there are some schools of thought — "

"No, definitely not," he said.

"Black, no sugar, isn't it?" she said, pouring out the tea. "If memory serves me?" He nodded and she put the cup in front of him. "You should get yourself checked out."

"Perhaps," he said.

"Definitely," she said.

"I never respond well to orders," he said. "You should know that."

"Yes," she said. "You never would do what I wanted."

"You mean go away?" he said, managing a slight smile.

"Possibly," she said, tracing a pattern with her finger on the table top. "Well, talking of going away — I shall be going away myself for the next few weeks. I have to go to Edinburgh and work on some papers in the National Library."

"What are you working on?"

"Susan Ferrier, and a couple of other

less known Scottish women writers. Have you read Ferrier?" He nodded. "Of course you have," she said. "You got me on to Maria Edgeworth, after all."

"So I did," he said.

"I can remember your bookcase at Trinity, you know. I never saw such an odd mixture of books," she said. "*Wind in the Willows*, Proust, Jane Austen, Maria Edgeworth, T. S. Eliot, and Surtees — and those awful hunting novels. You made me read one but I never finished it. Why were you so mad about them?"

"We all have our vices," he said. "Where will you stay in Edinburgh?"

"Oh, I haven't found anything yet. Some B and B, I guess. I shall be coming and going a bit to begin with."

"Why don't you use my flat in Drummond Place?" he said. "It would save you a lot of bother."

"I couldn't," she said quickly.

"Why on earth not?" he said. "We're not using it. You might as well. It only sits empty otherwise."

"Well, if you're sure . . . ."

"Of course I'm sure," he said. "I insist

you use it. I'll go and get you the keys. They're just in the library." He got up from his chair.

"You're sure you're not going to collapse?"

"I don't think so."

"I'll come with you, just in case. Besides, I'd like to look at some of the pictures in there again, if I may."

"Of course. We'll take our tea through."

The library was a great deal cooler than the kitchen, and he opened the door to the terrace to catch the breeze while Henrietta made a careful study of the pictures. He sat down in the armchair to watch her, tired still, but more relaxed in her presence than he had expected to be. There was a comfortable silence between them. Then after a long examination of *Pandora*, Henrietta said, "We shall have to borrow this one for the show."

"Naturally," he said.

"How can you bear to part with it?" she said. "I should love to have something like it hanging in my office."

"Why don't you commission her? She could do your portrait, perhaps."

"I'm not that vain," said Henrietta.

"She told me she thought you had the face of a classical statue," he said. "She'd be interested to do it."

"You used to say that too, and I thought it was just silly flattery."

"It's more true now than it was then," he said, studying her. "War-like Athena."

"Except I am not war-like today, am I?" she said.

"No, you've been very kind," he said.

"You sound surprised that I can be," she said, sitting down opposite him.

"Well, I'm glad. We shouldn't waste energy digging up old quarrels. Which is why you should have these," he said, and held out the keys of the flat to her.

"I'm not sure . . . " she began, but he reached out and took her hand and folded it round the keys.

"Take them," he said, his hands still resting over hers. Her hand was cool and he found he did not want to release it. But he forced himself and sat back in the chair. He watched as she looked down at the keys in the palm of her hand. She did not, he noticed, look him in the eyes.

"Thank you," she said.

It had been utterly stupid to agree to that much, but perhaps no more stupid than going there in the first place. She had thought she had things under control, but there was something about Gabriel at Allansfield that made her utterly helpless. She had wandered about those heavenly gardens, drowning in the scent, luxuriating in the colour, hoping ostensibly to find Kate but really wanting all the time to find Gabriel. It had been a little like getting drunk, and when she had found him, lying there like the helpless Tamino in *The Magic Flute*, like an answer to her uncomfortable desire, she had wanted to touch him and see if he was real. It had taken a great deal of will-power not to kiss him on the lips. She had been glad to have a book in her bag, and had settled to concentrate fiercely on it until he woke up. She had taken a sort of perverse pleasure in sitting there as he slept, enjoying the false intimacy of it, as if they were together again as they had been at Cambridge.

It was very pleasant as well to be sitting

there in the library with him, drinking tea. She knew she should go away but it was too enjoyable.

"I found something that might amuse you," he said, getting up and going to his desk again. He pulled open a little drawer and took out a photograph, which he handed to her.

"My God!" she exclaimed, bursting out with laughter when she saw it. "Oh that dress — and my hair . . . Oh, how horrible of you to have kept this, Gabriel, to taunt me."

"It wasn't deliberate," he said. "If anyone looks ridiculous in that picture it's me."

"I think we look rather sweet actually," she said, studying it for a few moments. "That was quite a night, wasn't it?"

Gabriel took back the photograph, and had just returned it to the drawer when Kate came in to the room.

"Ah, here you are," she said. "Oh, and Henrietta! I wondered whose car that was."

"She's got some good news for you," said Gabriel, getting up.

"The exhibition? We're on?" said

Kate. Henrietta nodded. "Wonderful! Brilliant!" She threw back her head and punched the air. "You don't know what this means to me." She threw her arms about Gabriel and kissed him, and then she kissed Henrietta. "Thank you, thank you so much!"

"My pleasure," said Henrietta.

"Do you want some tea?" said Gabriel. "I'll go and get you a cup, shall I?"

"I'd rather have a beer," said Kate, "if there is any."

"I'll go and see," he said.

Kate sat down at the desk. She was positively jigging with delight. "Oh, this is just so good. I think we should do something wild to celebrate," she said.

"Perhaps you should go out to dinner," said Henrietta.

"Hardly wild," said Kate. "I shall have to think a little about this . . . " She glanced at the papers that littered the desk. "God, what a mess this is," she said absently. "What is all this stuff anyway? This looks intriguing." She picked up a fat envelope. "Probably a seed catalogue."

Gabriel returned with a bottle of beer

and a glass. Kate took the bottle and not the glass.

"Can I open this?" she said. "You haven't."

"Yes, of course," he said, a little bemused.

"Look at this," said Kate, who was clearly in a slightly skittish mood. "A paper knife." She waved it in the air. "Gabriel uses a paper knife, you see."

"Very sensible," said Henrietta.

"Letters should be ripped open," said Kate. Gabriel laughed as she tore open the envelope. "Ooh," she said. "Gold-edged cards, no less."

"Oh, I know what that is," said Gabriel. "Very dull. It's that blasted charity ball. They asked me to subscribe for a table months ago."

"Eight tickets for a ball!" exclaimed Kate, staring at the tickets. "A ball at the Old Course Hotel."

"I don't think — " began Gabriel.

"This sounds great," said Kate, who was studying a leaflet. "Listen to this — champagne reception, four-course dinner, jazz band, Scottish country dance band and all-night disco with laser show.

Breakfast, four a.m. It's next Saturday. Well, I said we should celebrate."

"Actually I hadn't imagined we would want to go," said Gabriel. "These things are pretty grim. I took the tickets out of habit. I usually give them away."

"What do you mean, not go?" said Kate. "Of course we'll go. It'll be a huge laugh. We'll make up a party. You'll come, Henrietta, won't you?"

"I was going to Edinburgh next week . . ." she began.

"But not on Saturday night," said Kate. "I insist. I absolutely insist. How could we not go, Gabriel? Are you mad?" Gabriel looked as though he were about to reply but Kate was not going to let him. "We'll ask Liz and Martin — and Bob, yes? And Hugh of course. That makes seven . . . We need someone else — another woman, I suppose."

"Kate, are you sure you want to go?"

"What an utterly daft question," said Kate, going to the door. "I'm going to have a shower and then I'll call Liz. You make sure you convince Henrietta, OK?" And with that instruction she left.

"Damn," said Gabriel. "I detest charity

balls. I haven't really enjoyed any large party since Cambridge, you know. Jane used to drag me to some appalling things in London . . . " He groaned. "And it's the last thing I feel like doing at the moment."

"Would you have told her about it?" said Henrietta.

"To be frank, no," he said. "I know that's dreadful, but I really do hate these things."

"But she doesn't, clearly."

"No."

"So you can't let her down," said Henrietta.

"Neither can you," he said, looking across at her.

"I think I've forgotten how to dance," she said.

"We can tread on each other's toes if necessary," he said. "Just like the last time."

16

"WELL?" said Kate, coming out of the fitting booth in the designer room at Jenners. "What about this one?"

"Oh, yes, yes. That's it, definitely it!" said Liz.

Kate laughed. "You're just saying that because you're bored to death."

"No, of course not," said Liz. "That is absolutely the best dress so far — not that they didn't all look pretty good, but that one . . . it's got it all."

"Yes," said Kate, looking at herself in the long mirror. The dress was made of inky-black crêpe de Chine, and clung suggestively though not vulgarly in all the right places. It had a high halter neck, an open back, criss-crossed with straps, and was cut away deeply and dramatically at the shoulders. She swung her hips slightly, watching the way the drapery rippled. "Yes, this is the one."

"It's going to melt your credit card,

though," said Liz, glancing at the price on the label. "Though that isn't a consideration with you these days, really, is it?"

The remark was casual enough, but Kate could not help feeling there was a note of criticism in it. There was, after all, a heap of expensive carrier bags on the floor beside Liz's chair, all of them belonging to Kate.

"You make it sound as though I do nothing but spend Gabriel's money," said Kate. "And I don't. I've had my head down for weeks."

"I know, I know," said Liz. "And God knows, I enjoy shopping — but doesn't it feel a bit funny spending money you haven't earned?"

"Well, Gabriel hasn't earned it either," said Kate, going back towards the changing room. "Strictly speaking."

Kate could see from Liz's expression that this argument had not convinced her, and as she went back into the chintz-hung cubicle she knew she was not entirely convinced herself. She slipped off the dress, handed it back to the assistant and, as she put her own clothes back on — a pair of baggy white linen trousers and one of Gabriel's blue poplin shirts, the double-folded cuffs fixed with a pair of handsome antique cuff-links — she totted up the amount of money she had already spent that morning. She had been spending impulsively, she realised, shamelessly even, buying things she scarcely needed. She had never spent money so quickly in her life before. No wonder Liz had been shocked when she arrived at Jenners to find her with that pile of carrier bags. And now she was proposing to spend six hundred pounds on a little black dress. She hesitated for a moment and then decided she would not be a puritan. Of all the things she had bought that morning, it was the one that had a definite use. She needed a dress for the ball in St Andrews, and a black dress was in some respects quite a sensible purchase. She was bound to wear it quite a few times — and besides it was a delicious, sexy dress. It was irresistible.

She came out and went to pay for it. Liz had drifted off into the bridal section, and was standing with all the carrier bags looking wistfully at a cream brocade dress on the mannequin.

"That would be perfect on you," Kate said as she approached.

"Yes, except for the price," said Liz. "We started doing some sums the other night and we nearly fainted." She smiled and said, "Wouldn't be a problem for you two, though. Have you ever talked about it?"

"Getting married?"

"Mm," said Liz, her eyes still on the dress. "I was quite surprised that he was prepared for you to just live together. I wouldn't have thought — "

"Why not? He's that sixties generation, free love and all that," said Kate. "But as a matter of fact, we have talked about it and decided not to."

"Or *you've* decided not to," said Liz, glancing at her. "Yes?"

"Yes," said Kate. "What's right for you and Martin — well, perhaps it isn't right for us." She glanced at her watch. "We'd better get going. The table for lunch is booked for one."

They went to the same fish restaurant where Gabriel had first taken her to dinner. It was cool and quiet, despite the heatwave that had struck the city.

"I still can't believe you've bought all this stuff," said Liz, looking into each of the bags on the banquette between them. Kate sipped her wine and shrugged. "Wow . . . " Liz went on, lifting out a corner of a caramel silk and lace bra. "Someone's going to like that, aren't they?"

"Well, all my other underwear has fallen to pieces."

"I thought you didn't approve of this stuff," said Liz. "You were always telling me that . . . "

"I am allowed to change my mind," said Kate. "Aren't I?"

"Yes, yes, of course, but . . . " Liz put down the bag and said, "Everything is OK, isn't it?"

"Why shouldn't it be?" said Kate.

"I don't know," said Liz. "Perhaps I'm just being an interfering old flatmate, but I can't help thinking this isn't you at all."

"You think it's air-headed, don't you?"

"No, but it's just not what I expect from you. Usually you're so unbothered by things like clothes. I always used to feel so materialistic compared to you. I was the one always lusting after things and there you were surviving on a quarter of what I was earning, doing those grotty jobs just so that you could paint as you pleased. I sort of envied that. It was so principled."

"Perhaps you should have fallen in love with Gabriel instead of me then," said Kate, refilling her glass. "Then I wouldn't have had to compromise my principles, would I?" she added a touch bitterly, and then, regretting it, went on, "I didn't mean it like that. I wish he didn't have the money sometimes. It is odd, bloody odd, that he should be so well-off. It's like he's never been in the real world sometimes — but then, I suppose he wouldn't be like he is if he had been. Does that make sense?"

Liz frowned and tore apart her bread roll. "Isn't that his age, as much as the money?" she said after a pause.

"I don't know," said Kate.

She took another large mouthful of wine, keenly aware of just how little she had actually said to Gabriel recently.

At times they seemed to be living on different planets. They talked, of course, but without seeming to say anything really significant to each other. She had been aware of how distant he seemed, even when they were lying in bed. He still kissed her, warmly enough, but it was without passion, and she could not quite remember when they had last made love. Certainly they had not since the really hot weather had started. It could not matter really, for she felt scarcely bothered about that herself. They had both, she told herself, been too absorbed in their work to take much notice in the other. That was all it was. She had been painting like a demon and Gabriel had told her that high summer was the busiest time in the garden and the estate.

"But," she said decidedly, "there's nothing to worry about, Liz, really."

"If you're sure," she said.

"Of course," said Kate.

"It's just all this," said Liz. "It looks like comfort shopping. It's what I'd do if I was pissed off. I'd go and spend lots of money — if I had the money to spend. But that's just me, of course, isn't it?"

★ ★ ★

Kate went on and had supper with her mother, and only left Edinburgh just after nine. By the time she reached Cupar it was still only just getting dark. The night was perfectly calm, the hedges voluptuous with brambles and wild roses and the sky violet above her. The quiet perfection of it all seemed to increase as she rolled carefully down the long driveway that led through the estate to the house and through the embracing belt of trees that circled the house and its gardens, making it perceptibly warmer than the world outside. She saw that the sitting-room light was on, and that the windows were wide open. She pulled up and let the engine die, sitting there in darkness for a moment, staring blankly at the rampant spectacle of the clematis which had covered the entire entrance façade with flowers. Gabriel would have heard the engine, surely, and she wondered if he might come to the window to greet her. She rather hoped he would.

She stood for a moment in the warm

scented air, feeling she was nothing but an insubstantial shadow which would soon be obliterated by the last veil of the evening dropping down. Through the open window she could hear music playing — Mozart's *Marriage of Figaro*, Gabriel's favourite opera. He would not be coming to the window. He would be totally lost in the music.

She collected up her shopping, let herself into the house and went quickly upstairs.

At first, coming into the room, she could not see Gabriel. He was not in his usual chair; and then she saw he was sitting on the floor, between the two windows, his back to the panelled wall. The bottom drawer of the large bookcase bureau was open and there were various piles of paper spread out on the rug around him. He was reading a piece of paper and did not even look up as she came in.

"Hello?" she said.

He looked up, startled. "Hello," he said, and staggered to his feet. He went across and switched off the stereo. As he did it, she noticed he rubbed his eyes, as if he was wiping away a tear.

"Are you OK?"

"Fine," he said. "How was your shopping trip?"

"Horribly extravagant," she said, "I'm afraid."

"How much?" he said.

She wondered if she ought to say. Would he get angry with her?"

"Nearly eight hundred quid," she said. "I know it's awful, but I need the stuff . . . "

"Well if you need it, you need it," he said simply, and looked down again at the paper he had been looking at so intently when she came in. She found she was disappointed. She realised she would have quite liked him to get cross with her about the money.

"Would you like to see what I got?" she said.

"Uh?" he said, looking up again from the piece of paper.

"What is that?" she said.

"A letter. My grandfather wrote it to my grandmother, when he was in France during the Somme. It's a most astonishing thing . . . "

"Oh . . . " said Kate, putting down her bags.

"Listen to this," he said, and began to read aloud. "'I think of you all constantly, and of course of Allansfield. This world about me here is not my reality at all. It is an endless nightmare, from which I am always trying to wake, and if I try hard enough I know I will wake up again and be there, and find you lying in my arms, in our room, in our bed together, lying there late on a Saturday morning in June, with the sound of the girls' piano practice filling the house. We waited so long to find each other, my darling Jessie, and when I am at my most pig-headed and gloomy here, I find myself regretting all that wasted time. However, that is pure stupidity, for the time we have had together, although so very brief, is not to be measured by usual standards. Our minutes are other people's hours, and I count myself the most fortunate man in the world to have the recollection of so many minutes spent in your company. Each fragment of that time seems set in my mind, like so many pieces of a glittering mosaic — like the mosaics at Ravenna that have lasted throughout the centuries and yet are still glorious. That is how indestructible and how precious our time together has been.'" His voice cracked slightly as he read this last passage, and he walked towards the window, turning his back on Kate, clearly embarrassed by his emotions. "Well, perhaps it isn't the greatest piece of prose," he said, more lightly. "But one can't doubt the sincerity of it."

"No," said Kate. "I wasn't . . . " He seemed not to have heard her. He was reading the rest of the letter, still standing by the window. She felt annoyed. He had had all evening to read these old letters. Why could he not stop now and pay her a little attention instead? "Gabriel," she said, "Gabriel, are you here tonight at all?"

"Here?" he said, turning back to her with a smile. "What do you mean 'here'?"

"I mean, are you here in June, 1995 — or at least a substantial percentage of you? I feel you are about to dematerialise."

He laughed and said, "I suppose I am a little preoccupied. It's been ages since I've looked through these letters. Forgive me."

"I might," she said, going over to her shopping. "If you promise to pay attention now. I want to show you what I've bought. I need your approval to stop me feeling so guilty about being an extravagant hussy."

"There's no need to feel that," he said. "I'm glad to see you've finally decided you don't need to stint yourself. We did open that joint account for a reason."

As he spoke he began to gather up the papers on the floor. Kate produced her black dress with a flourish and held it against her. He did not look up.

"Gabriel," she said. "What do you think of this?"

"Very nice," he smiled, and returned to the papers.

"That isn't good enough," she said, deciding it was best to make a joke of it. "I expect a full-blown flowery compliment."

"All right," he said. "I'm sure it will look splendid on you."

"Pathetic!" she exclaimed.

"What exactly do you want me to say?" he said, putting the papers back into the bureau drawer.

"Oh, I don't know, I . . . " Kate gave up, and let the dress fall over the arm of the sofa. Suddenly it looked very ordinary. "Mum thought it was great, and you know how fussy she is," she added, sitting down on the sofa, a nasty curdling feeling of sick disappointment growing in her stomach. It was not his lack of reaction to the dress that bothered her. It was her own discontent. She had not expected to feel so annoyed with him, especially over something so trivial. She had been certain that what she felt for him had been different from what she had felt for other men, that they would easily be able to dismiss the petty irritations of everyday life. She had not expected perfection — she was not as naive as that — but she had not expected to feel this awful disappointment with Gabriel. But now she realised she had felt it, felt it for weeks now. She remembered what she had so bravely said to her mother on the day she moved out of Liz's flat: "I can't think of a better way to get to know someone than living with them, properly living with him." Well, she knew Gabriel better now — and she was beginning to wonder whether he was really the sort of man she wanted at all.

17

"**H**ENRY, what do you look like?" said Bob Kavanagh as she opened the door of Mon Abris to him.

"Mutton dressed as lamb?" Henrietta suggested. She had bought herself an extravagant white satin dress, and Bob's face was suddenly making her nervous about it.

"No, no, not at all," said Bob, following her into the house. "I know what it is you look like — and it's really against my republican principles to say this as a compliment — but you look like one of those minor royals. You need a tiara."

"And wings and a magic wand," said Henrietta, going into the kitchen.

"You also sound like you need a drink," said Bob. "Good job I bought this." And with a flourish he produced a bottle of Cordon Rouge from behind his back. It was ice cold and the neck had been decorated with curling gold ribbons.

"That is far better than an old-fashioned gardenia," said Henrietta as Bob popped the cork.

They sat in the meagre back garden, in the warm dusk, and drank the champagne, Bob down to his shirtsleeves already. It was too hot a night for their elaborate clothes, and Henrietta at that moment would quite happily have passed up the prospect of the ball. It would have been preferable to spend the evening in the garden drinking quietly with Bob, although she knew she wanted to see Gabriel. That was why after all she had been weak enough to agree to go in the first place. She had this foolish desire to gorge herself on his company, as if that alone would assuage that simple-minded, sentimental craving for him which she did not seem to be able to cast off. It did no good to tell herself, as she had told herself a hundred times, that he was in the first place unavailable and in the second place quite uninterested. She could not help persisting in her delusion. Why else would she have bought that ridiculous white dress?

"I think I'm going senile, Bob," she said, getting up to refill her champagne glass.

"Well, you don't look it," he said as he lolled back in his deck chair. "You look magnificent." She shook her head. "Yes — you do, believe me." She raised an eyebrow at him and he smiled. "Come on, we're going to have a bloody good time," he said, heaving himself from his deck chair.

"I think I'm going to go and change," she said. "This dress, it's too . . . "

"The dress is wonderful," said Bob, catching her in his arms and kissing her on each cheek in turn. "You'll turn every head in the place."

"That isn't what I want," said Henrietta.

"Are you so sure?" he said, stroking her cheek for a moment.

"Bob, please . . . " she said, leaning back a little, attempting to evade him.

"I can't," he said, pressing his forehead to hers. "You're an even more beautiful, devastating woman than you ever were, Henry. You're like claret that's been in the bottle a few years. I'd rather have you now than ever before."

"You're very kind, but — "

"I think we should get out of here, you know," Bob went on cheerfully. "What are you doing all summer?"

"My research, of course."

"Well me too, but damn it, why should we? These friends of mine have a farmhouse in Provence which I can borrow. When term ends, let's just pile into my car and get away for a month or two together. How about it?"

"Bob, that's a lovely, sensible, generous idea, but I really don't think that . . . "

Bob was now shaking his head and waving his hands for her to stop talking. "Well, at least you can be decent enough to let me dance with you a few times tonight," he said.

"I might," she said, and leant forward and gave him a kiss on the cheek.

They walked down to the Old Course Hotel with increasing briskness, aware that they were going to be a little late. Bob and the champagne had lifted her spirits, and by the time they were strolling along the long driveway to the hotel Henrietta decided she was quite in control again, and was almost seriously contemplating Bob's idea of going to France. Her research could wait — it would be a much better idea to sort herself out.

They went into the lobby of the hotel, where they found a crowd of other people whose clothes reassured Henrietta that she was not overdressed. These people, both young and old, were turned out with sleek flamboyance — the men in their kilts, or dark dinner suits, the women in shimmery long dresses of every conceivable style. Looking at them, she was reminded of a Republican fund-raising dinner she had once, in a moment of weakness, gone to with a desperate colleague. She could understand at once Gabriel's unwillingness to go. Gabriel did not belong in such crowds of hearty, solidly sociable people. Even as an undergraduate, when heartiness had been virtually compulsory, she had observed in him a tendency towards detachment. It had been one of the things that had appealed to her about him. He had never quite been one of the crowd, though he was hardly a social misfit. His mantelpiece at Trinity had always been loaded with engraved cards, she remembered, but he had chosen to ignore them, and when they had gone to parties together, he had often suggested they leave early.

"There he is!" said Bob, waving.

She looked and saw that Gabriel was sitting alone on a leather-covered sofa, his elbow propped up on the arm, his face half covered with his hand, gazing rather absently ahead of him, while around him the glittering crowd of acquaintances greeted each other and laughed as they prepared to have a good time for a good cause. At last Gabriel saw them, jumped up and began to thread his way through the crowds towards them. His progress was stopped by an elderly woman in yards of frilled sea-green chiffon who seemed to have a great deal to say to him, and Henrietta instinctively knew rescue was required. She hustled her own way through the last few people and, smiling, burst into the tête-à-tête.

Gabriel blinked at her for a moment, and then, smiling, took her hand, the hand that was nearest to him, and quickly folded his fingers around it. Henrietta was so startled by this unexpected greeting that she did not have the presence of mind to prevent it. The old woman in chiffon stared at them both, her flow interrupted, and then said, delightedly, "Oh, you must be Kate! We've all been wondering when we were going to be allowed to meet you." Gabriel very quickly let go of Henrietta's hand. "Oh, look there, Mary wants me . . . I must go now. We'll have a proper chatter later. Better still, you must come to dinner, both of you . . . " And she trotted away.

"Well," said Gabriel, glancing at the retreating tide of green chiffon, frowning slightly. "I'm surprised at that. I would have thought Jane had told her. That was Jane's godmother, Veronica Nisbett, by the way."

"Perhaps I do look younger than you tonight," said Henrietta. "It's this dress. And the way you just took my hand would be easily misinterpreted, I imagine."

"Yes, I suppose it would," he said, with a touch of embarrassment. "I didn't think . . . "

I guessed that, Henrietta thought. The

gesture, so tiny, had been absolutely unconscious, and despite herself she wanted to ascribe something significant to it. She looked back at Bob, who had followed in her wake, and tried to focus on him. He looked almost distinguished in his dinner jacket, the long greying hair tied back neatly. Two months in a French farmhouse with Bob would certainly be amusing, and there would not have to be anything sexual about it. He might want that, but she knew it could never happen. She would never feel anything more for Bob than warm affection. There was too much of an obstacle for that, an obstacle of her own construction which she had to try and demolish. Seeing Gabriel dancing with Kate, she decided, might do the trick.

"Let's go and find the others," she said quickly.

★ ★ ★

"These are lethal," said Liz, "but delicious."

"We'll catch you if you keel over," said Martin.

Hugh, Kate, Liz and Martin were sitting in a conservatory, drinking their second round of champagne cocktails, and were bolstering themselves against the effects with a heaped plate of hors d'oeuvres that Martin, with unconcerned ruthlessness, had culled from the buffet table in the middle of the room.

"It's a sacrilege to do this to champagne really," said Liz, taking another sip.

"If it is champagne," said Martin.

"Of course is it," said Liz. "I saw the bottles."

Hugh watched as Kate delicately peered into a tiny puff-pastry horn.

"What is in these things?" she said.

"Who cares?" said Martin, popping a whole one into his mouth. Liz and Kate were laughing at his greed. Hugh wished he could fix his attention so wholeheartedly on the canapés. He found he was aching with an entirely different sort of hunger. The sight of Kate, laughing in her svelte black dress, her hair piled up on her head in a new style, her lips glowing with crimson lipstick and her arms sheathed in long black satin gloves, was enough to make any man look twice at her. Hugh had noticed one or two admiring glances even as they stood there, but he could not manage to feel that ordinary, meaningless male admiration, that detached and idle lust towards a stranger that can be dismissed in a moment. He could not manage to disentangle his emotions. He wanted to make love to her. If he had just wanted to screw her and gratify his senses it might have been easier to bear, but he wanted more than that.

He remembered how he had found her in the studio that morning. She had put a huge board down on the floor and was on her knees, painting with a broad brush in a very free and fierce way, using vivid, scarcely mixed colours. In her intense concentration she had not noticed that he had come in, and she gave off little unconscious noises as she struggled with what she was doing. He had known exactly what she was doing — she was giving herself up to the danger of an experiment. He did it himself sometimes with a lump of clay, kneading and pushing the material as well as his mind to the limits, to see what new form might emerge. He had stood in the doorway, equally compelled by the constantly evolving shapes and patterns that she was creating as by the sight of her, lost entirely in the passionate fury of her creativity. He had known then that he had fallen in love; and then suddenly she had stopped, turned and looked up at him.

He had not been able to read that look, just as he could not read her now, as they sat there all dressed up in their party clothes, drinking champagne cocktails. He knew how he wanted to interpret it, but he knew he could not. He would not allow himself to project his own feelings on to her. If he did, he might do something very stupid.

He swallowed down his drink quickly, and tasted the bittersweet remains of the sugar cube soaked in Angostura bitters dissolving in his mouth. He could see his father coming across the room with Bob and Henrietta. Henrietta was dressed rather unexpectedly in a spectacular white satin dress and looked coolly formal and elegant, rather as one might imagine an ambassador's wife would look. An ambassadress, he corrected himself, as they approached.

"What are you drinking?" asked Gabriel, looking at all the empty glasses on the table in front of them.

"Champagne cocktails," said Hugh, getting up to give Henrietta his chair. He saw his father grimace. "I didn't think you'd approve."

"Let's hope they haven't adulterated all the champagne," Gabriel said. "Shall we go and find some, Bob?"

"The only cocktail worth drinking," said Henrietta when they had gone, "is a proper New York martini, fixed by my aunt Louise."

"How do you make a proper martini?" asked Martin. "I've always wondered."

"Well . . . " Henrietta began.

Hugh looked for another chair and pulled it up so he was sitting between Henrietta and Kate. He found that he was not listening to Henrietta, but watching Kate from the corner of his eye. She was holding her glass in her black-gloved fingers, resting it on her thigh, and it seemed to him that she was not listening either. He wished he knew what was going on in her mind, wished he knew what it had meant when she had looked at him that morning with that long searching look.

He realised suddenly he was close enough to her to smell her scent. It was a dizzying, warm scent of vanilla and roses, and he leant back quickly, staring up at the lights and the ceiling. He prayed silently for self-control.

★ ★ ★

"Quite a sight, eh?" Bob said to Gabriel as they stood at the bar together. "You know, I think she's improved with age."

Gabriel turned back to look at their party. Henrietta and Kate were sitting on either side of Hugh, but he found he was looking only at Henrietta.

"Vintage claret, that's what she is. I've asked her to come to France with me."

"Well, good luck," said Gabriel, turning back to the bar.

"That was sincere," said Bob.

"Of course it was."

"Bullshit," said Bob.

"Why do you think I should be

bothered? I am not in a position to be bothered," Gabriel said. "Am I?"

Bob gave him a searching look, and then said, with a sigh, "But you bloody are, aren't you? God, Gabriel — "

"God, Gabriel what?" Gabriel cut in defensively. "What the hell do you think I'm up to?"

"I don't think you're up to anything," said Bob. "But I reckon you haven't stopped feeling what you felt back then."

"I never had you down as a sentimentalist. You surprise me."

"And I know when you resort to sarcasm you're covering your tracks," said Bob. "I've known you long enough for that. You should front up to yourself. For Kate's sake."

"There is nothing to front up to myself about, as you so poetically put it," said Gabriel with careful emphasis. "Take Henrietta to France if you like, do what you like with her — you hardly need my permission. But stop making these crass assumptions, please. It doesn't suit you, Bob."

"And lying doesn't suit you."

"Look, what the hell do I have to say

to convince you?" said Gabriel. "I know — I've asked Kate to marry me. Isn't that evidence enough for you?"

"You have?" said Bob.

"Yes, and I am very optimistic about her answer," Gabriel went on. "So, is that enough for you? Now let's get back, shall we?"

Bob shrugged slightly and picked up the large ice bucket with the two bottles of champagne in it. Gabriel wondered if he had convinced him, or whether Bob had simply given up. It had been risky to bend the truth about Kate's reaction to his proposal, but he did not suppose that Bob, even at his most irritatingly indiscreet, would mention the subject to Kate. The risk had been necessary — not just to convince Bob, but also to convince himself. He had needed to assert that he was in a committed relationship, to remind himself that Kate was as good as his wife. He thought with shame how he had impulsively taken Henrietta's hand on seeing her in the lobby, how he had been unable to prevent himself from doing so. He had been so very pleased to see her.

18

AFTER dinner, as Kate washed her hands surrounded by women chattering, repairing their lipstick and powdering their noses, she looked at her reflection in the mirror. She was glad to see she did not look as nervous as she felt — if nervous was the right word for the peculiar mood she could not shake off. Perhaps these nerves were like those of an actor testing out a new part. She had been aware that there was a certain amount of play-acting going on with most of them at dinner. Only Liz and Martin had seemed quite genuine to her. It was as if the others, herself included, had put on disguises rather than smart evening clothes.

She reached for her scarlet lipstick and told herself that she was being silly. They had all come here to enjoy themselves, after all; and ritual, display and play-acting were all part of a ball, part of the enjoyment of the thing. She must not expect normality on an occasion dedicated to spectacle.

"Oh, what an absolutely super colour," said the woman next to her at the mirror. She was outlining her own lips with a pale coral pink. "I wish I could wear that colour."

Kate grinned. Lipstick was not something she usually wore at all, but this was another product of her expensive foray into Edinburgh. The sight of the cosmetics counters, with their displays of rich colours, had intoxicated her. Tonight it felt like war-paint. She needed to feel brave and confident and utterly untroubled.

She went to find the others in the dining room, but found they had moved on. They would have gravitated, she supposed, like everyone else, towards the dancing. A Scottish country dance band was already playing, and there was quite a crowd round the edges of the room watching the first set of an eightsome reel. Kate watched too. Martin and Liz were dancing, but she could not see the others. She stood and watched for some minutes, envying their perfect coupledom. That ought not to bother me now, she tried to tell herself, but she could not push aside the creeping doubts about having made a mistake about Gabriel. She turned away, determined to go and find him, to set her own mind at rest with the sight of him, and found she had walked straight into Hugh.

"Sorry!" they said simultaneously, and then they both laughed. As they did, the eightsome reel ended and Hugh said, "Do you fancy dancing this next one?"

"I was going to look for the others . . ." Kate began, and then the band leader announced it would be the Gay Gordons. "Oh, but I can't resist that. OK, let's do it."

"Great," said Hugh, and grabbing her hand he led her on to the floor.

* * *

Five dances later they stopped for a rest and a drink. Kate, utterly breathless and quite exhilarated, flopped down on a chair beside Liz, while Martin and Hugh went off to fetch the drinks.

338

"Well, you look as though you're enjoying yourself," said Liz.

"He's a brilliant dancer, isn't he?" said Kate. "Amazing. I've never danced like that with anyone before. It's like . . . " She exhaled sharply.

"Like what?" said Liz.

The phrase that had sprung to Kate's mind had been 'like good foreplay' — which was quite ridiculous — and she was not going to say that, even to Liz. "Like being on *Come Dancing*. I feel we should be up for a gold medal or something."

"You were both too natural for that," observed Liz.

"What do you mean?"

"I don't know quite how to put this," she said after a moment, "but — well, it looked a bit as if you were flirting . . . well, that he was flirting with you. I'm sure you weren't."

"No, of course I wasn't," said Kate. "And I don't think he was. His marriage has only just bust up, for goodness' sake."

"Which makes him extra vulnerable."

"Rubbish," said Kate dismissively. She

looked over at Hugh and Martin, who were standing in the queue by the bar. Hugh, she thought, looked more relaxed than she had ever seen him. His face had gone quite ruddy and he had abandoned his dinner jacket. He was wearing braces and a most beautiful tuck-fronted and rather baggy evening shirt with a wing collar. One hand was in his pocket, the other was engaged alternately in pushing back his hair (which seemed to have got wilder and curlier than ever) and making expressive gestures to back up whatever it was he was saying to Martin. Suddenly, they were both laughing uproariously about something.

"They're getting on well," said Liz, "aren't they? He's a real charmer."

"Hugh or Martin?" said Kate.

"Hugh, of course."

"He takes after his father," Kate said carefully. She was still looking at Hugh, remembering how he had looked when he had posed for her. Oddly, she found the sight of him tonight, in that crisp white shirt, more disturbing, more magnetic. She found she was imagining how it would be to press her cheek against his

340

chest and feel his hand caress her hair, the way he caressed his own.

"You like him, don't you?" Liz asked.

"Of course. He's family, sort of."

"No, not like that," said Liz.

"Liz, this is silly . . . " Kate protested.

"I know you," said Liz, undeterred. "I know what you're like on the rampage. I've seen you before."

"And why on earth should I need to be on the rampage?"

"OK," said Liz. "You're not — but you ought to be careful. Gabriel might get jealous."

"We were only dancing," said Kate. "Not screwing. Haven't you and Martin developed the concept of trust?" And in her mind she added the rejoinder, "And where the hell is Gabriel to mind, anyway?"

Martin and Hugh returned with a bottle of champagne and two bottles of Guinness.

"Black Velvet," said Hugh, setting them down on the table. He squatted down and began to pour out the champagne, grinning across at Kate as he did. "For stamina." He topped up a glass with Guinness and handed it to Kate. "It goes with your dress, too." Their eyes met and she found herself smiling.

"I've never tried this before."

"There's a first time for everything," he said.

She took a deep gulp, closing her eyes for a moment to savour the bitter, bubbly, aromatic taste. When she opened her eyes again, she found that Hugh was still gazing at her, the way he had stared at her that morning in the studio, when she had looked up from her painting and found him standing in the doorway. She blinked, licked her lips and took another large mouthful. If she drank enough she might stop thinking how bloody attractive he was.

The band had started up again, with a slow sentimental waltz.

"Come on," Hugh said, reaching out and taking the glass from her. "That'll wait. A waltz won't."

* * *

Gabriel had got himself stuck in an uninspiring conversation about roses with

Veronica Nisbett and another woman to whom he was introduced but whose name he had instantly forgotten. He swallowed down yet another glass of wine as they chattered on, not listening at all. From the corner of his eye he could see Bob and Henrietta sitting together, laughing over something, and it irritated him profoundly.

"What do you think for a north-facing wall then?" asked the woman. "Up here?"

He realised he was being addressed. He found his mind swimming. If he had ever known any rose names they escaped him now. He was feeling faint and somewhat nauseous, and was sweating again. He searched frantically for a name.

"Something like 'Zépherine Drouhin', perhaps?" he managed to say. He heard how slurred his voice was.

"How do I spell that?"

He started to spell it and then realised he was going to be sick imminently. He muttered an excuse and bolted from the room, desperate to find the lavatory.

He found it and vomited violently for some minutes, then rested back on his heels, deeply ashamed at this undergraduate behaviour. He realised how little he had eaten and how much he had drunk, as he stooped forward again for a bout of painful retching that brought tears to his eyes. He had not eaten much at all lately. He sat on the lavatory floor, his back pressed against the cold tiled wall, gasping for breath, the taste of bile poisoning his mouth. He found he was shaking from cold suddenly, and pulled his arms around him for comfort. He wished desperately for Henrietta to be there, taking control, just as she had done in the kitchen, calming him with her presence. This bloody virus — he did not seem to be able to cast it off. He would have to go and see someone about it. Henrietta was right.

He staggered to his feet, flushed the lavatory and went to wash his face. His face in the mirror looked haggard and tired, and he realised he could not face the dance again. He had a strong urge simply to walk out of the hotel. The others could all look after themselves. Kate was with her friends, and Bob and Henrietta were clearly having a splendid time. He was superfluous to requirements.

He emerged from the lavatory and found Henrietta standing a discreet distance away. She seemed to be waiting for him.

"Henry?"

"How are you?" she said. "I couldn't help noticing that was a pretty speedy exit."

"Oh, I'm fine now, I think," he said.

"I don't think you look it," she said. "I would have asked how you were earlier, but I didn't quite dare to."

"Thank you for your forbearance," he said. They began to walk together. "Where's Bob?"

"I've sent him off to join the others. I'm supposed to be fetching you."

"You sent him away?"

She smiled and said, "He was coming on a little strong. Making up for lost time, perhaps."

"Well, don't let me stand in your way."

"I wouldn't," she said lightly, "if that was what I wanted."

Gabriel ran his finger round his collar,

feeling it was half throttling him. He pulled off his jacket. "Look, shall we get some fresh air?" he asked.

"Good idea," she said.

They went through a pair of French doors out on to a terrace, but the temperature was not noticeably different. The air was still warm, but at least it was real air, touched a little with the smell of sea, which lay not so very far beyond them and was almost visible in the perpetual dusk of Scottish summer evening. Henrietta swept on ahead of him towards the edge of the terrace, her white satin skirt billowing, and she stood resting her hands on the parapet wall. Gabriel dragged over a chair and sat down beside her.

"Feeling any better?" she said.

"Yes, thanks," he said, and leant back in the chair. "You know, this is the moment in our past lives," he said, "when we'd be lighting up cigarettes . . . "

"Or a joint," said Henrietta, and then she laughed. "Instead I feel I ought to nag you about seeing a doctor."

"I've already decided to," he said.

"Good," she said. "For Kate's sake,

you should look after yourself."

"Yes. In fact, I should probably call it a night altogether," he said, getting up from his chair. He was strongly conscious though that he wanted to stay there with her, looking out to sea, talking calmly. But he suspected that this inclination, however innocent it might appear, was not permissible. He was aware that things could never be that simple between Henrietta and himself, that any calmness was illusory, that if he lingered there the moment would become significant even if they said nothing. He felt like an archaeologist uncovering a piece of ancient glass that would usually have been broken into many fragments but which by some strange chance had survived intact. He had the appalling and entirely unacceptable thought that he still loved Henrietta, exactly as he had loved her all those years ago, that he felt the same towards her as he had done that morning two days before his twenty-first birthday. The only way he could think to deal with this was to retreat. He could not spend any more time in her company than was absolutely necessary.

"Good-night then," he said.

She turned from her study of the sea and looked at him. For a moment she looked as though she was going to speak. He was nervous that she had come to the same dangerous conclusion and she was going to say something reckless, something that would pull them into a place where they ought not to go. In the past, he knew, neither of them would have hesitated. But she said nothing, just gave a slight half-smile and raised her hand to make a gentle gesture of dismissal. Relieved, he quickly told himself he was mistaken.

19

KATE and Hugh were jiving energetically to 'Rock Around the Clock' when she noticed Gabriel standing at the edge of the dance floor. She felt immediately embarrassed, as if she had been caught doing something slightly shameful, and she realised that Hugh felt it too, for the uninhibited enthusiasm with which he had been dancing suddenly dried up. They both stopped dancing and made their way across the floor towards him.

"Why did you stop?" said Gabriel. "That was very impressive."

"I think I ought to give you a turn," said Hugh, shoving his hands into his pockets.

"Goodness, no," said Gabriel. "You know I couldn't compete with that."

Kate felt a prickle of disappointment. She wanted Gabriel to sweep her on to the floor and dance magnificently — but dancing, she realised then, was not at all

Gabriel's style. It was not, of course, the sort of thing that ought to matter in a relationship — if one person liked to dance and the other did not — but she had forgotten until then, until she had danced so much with Hugh, just how much she did enjoy it. She loved it, in fact.

Gabriel went on, "I've just come in to tell you I'm heading home now . . . No, don't look like that, Kate — you don't have to come with me. This is the point in the evening when people my age give up gracefully. I don't think I can see it through till dawn, but you must."

"Are you sure?" said Kate. "I can come home if you like . . ."

"But you want to stay, don't you? So stay. Hugh will look after you," Gabriel said, and kissed her on the cheek. "Enjoy yourself. I must go and see if my cab's here."

"But . . . " Kate said, as he began to move away.

"Shush," he said, pressing his finger to his lips. "And please don't feel guilty. I may be a selfish old fool most of the time, but at least occasionally I know what the right thing to do is."

When he had gone Kate turned back to Hugh, who looked as bemused as she felt. He was still standing with his hands in his pockets. 'Rock Around the Clock' had finished playing and had been replaced by 'Twist and Shout'.

"There's no arguing with Dad," he said.

"Should I go?" she asked, glancing back at the door.

"Do you want to go now?" he said.

"To be honest — no."

"Then why worry?" he said, putting out his hand to her. "This is a great song; we can't miss this one now, can we?"

Kate and Hugh, along with Liz and Martin, saw the ball through till the four o'clock breakfast, when they drank yet more champagne, this time accompanied with a great deal of orange juice and black coffee. They posed for the survivors photograph, after which the party atmosphere began to disintegrate as reality caught up with people.

"We should get out of here quick," said Hugh, as they sat at the breakfast table. "Who's for the beach? The sun will be up soon."

And so, with a paper napkin full of purloined croissants, they bundled into Hugh's antiquated Volvo estate and rolled along the narrow road that ran parallel to the West Sands, until it ceased to be anything more than a track. The darkness of the night, which had never really been more than a soft black veil, was lifting swiftly, and they got out of the car into a pale, pearly light that the sun had not yet warmed through with yellow. Yet the air itself was extraordinarily warm and calm.

"This is not Scotland," Martin was saying incredulously.

"Freak conditions," said Liz, as she rolled down her stockings.

Liz and Martin, now barefoot, ran like children down the steep dune path to the beach, while Kate and Hugh collected various rugs and coats from out of the boot of the car. By the time Kate and Hugh got down the path, Martin and Liz had reached the water's edge and were embracing passionately.

"That," remarked Hugh, spreading a

352

tartan rug out on the dry sand at the foot of the dunes, "makes me bloody jealous."

"Yes," said Kate. She almost said, 'me too'. Instead she sat down on the rug and found she was still watching them as they kissed.

"It isn't often you see a perfect relationship."

"I don't think they'd say it was perfect," said Kate.

"That makes it even better, surely," said Hugh. He stretched himself out on the rug beside her and stared up at the sky. "Oh God, what a strange night it's been."

"Yes," Kate said. "I don't think I've ever danced with anyone as much as I danced with you tonight."

"Sorry," he said.

"For what?" she asked.

"For giving in to an irresistible impulse."

"Well, isn't that what dancing is?" she said, turning to him. "An irresistible impulse? It's something physical and emotional. You don't rationalise when you dance."

"That's why I'm apologising," he said.

"I shouldn't have danced so much with you. I was indulging myself."

"Well, so was I," she said.

"I bet you're disappointed that my father doesn't dance," he said after a little silence.

"Perhaps," Kate said, and glanced at him. She could see his chest rising and falling gently under that thick, white and now crumpled shirt. "But we're different people; we do different things."

"Yes, yes of course you do," he said. "I just wish . . . " he added almost inaudibly.

"What?"

"Don't ask," he said.

"I have to ask now," she said. "Now you've said that."

Slowly he sat up. She watched him dig his hand into the sand and bring up a handful in his cupped palm. He let it run through his fingers, then took a deep breath. "Well . . . I don't know about you, but I'm . . . Oh, God . . . " He began to rock back and forth slightly as he sat there. Suddenly he looked directly at her and said, "Tell me there's nothing going on here. Tell me I'm just being stupid. Please. And do it quickly."

"I can't," she found herself saying. She wanted to deny it, but she could not. "Tonight was so . . . "

"I've been trying all week to decide what to do, and trying not to think about you, or at least to think about you rationally, but . . . but . . . "

She nodded but could not look at him any longer. She found she was staring at her black skirt, at the way the cloth was stretched over her tucked-up knees.

"You're driving me crazy, Kate. Absolutely crazy."

She felt his hand on her bare arm and looked at him now. He reached out and with a trembling finger touched her cheek, and then moved closer to her. He pressed his forehead to hers, and she felt his breath on her face, as his hands rested on her shoulders, heavy and hot. Then suddenly he began to kiss her, so that they fell back on to the rug in a disordered heap. There was nothing tender in his kissing. It was aggressive and bruising, and yet the desperation woke something in her, roused the heat in her own blood. She clung to him with the same vehemence, finding her mind could only think how much she wanted him, with atavistic, animal greed, as she dragged her fingers through his tangled hair and pressed her palm on to the bare, sweating skin of his back.

Suddenly she heard Liz laughing in the distance. He must have heard it too, and they froze and then broke apart.

"Oh, shit. Shit," he exclaimed, staggering to his feet. "I'm sorry, I really am sorry."

"No, no, it's OK. My fault as much as yours," said Kate, her face crimson. She found her dress had been half yanked up round her waist, and frantically adjusted it. "Adolescent post-party stuff, OK?"

"OK," he said. "Yes, yes. Too much champagne."

Their voices were brittle and jaunty.

"Definitely."

"Do you think they saw us?" he said, looking towards Liz and Martin.

"I don't think so," said Kate, praying they had not.

"I'm sorry," he said. "I really am very sorry."

"Please, let's just forget it. It didn't

happen," said Kate, getting to her feet.

"The tape is already erased," he said, shoving his hands into his pockets and walking away a few steps. She saw him stare up at the sky. "It's going to be a lovely hot day again," he said after a few minutes.

★ ★ ★

It was about six o'clock when they got back to Allansfield. Liz and Martin were half asleep in the back of the car, while Hugh and Kate were painfully awake. Hugh dropped them at the door of the house and drove on to the cottage. Kate climbed the stairs behind Liz and Martin and watched them go off to their room, their arms about each other's waists. They would probably soon be making love, she found herself thinking.

She stood, her shoes and stockings in her hands, for a few minutes in the passageway, not wanting to go into their bedroom and find Gabriel asleep. She went into the dressing room instead and dumped herself down on the Empire day bed on which, Gabriel had told her, his mother had used to make his father sleep after a quarrel. It was hard, rather narrow and suitably penitential, even with its cream and primrose striped silk cover. She propped her feet up on the bolster cushion at the far end, closed her eyes and tried to empty her mind.

However hard she tried, she could not do it. Hugh's kiss haunted her, although she tried to dismiss it as a trivial mistake on his part. She could not help feeling that for Hugh it had not been at all trivial. There was something in the force of that kiss that was profoundly unsettling. It was impulsive, yes, but it was not casual opportunism. It had not been like the usual drunken grope at the end of a party. She had seen his eyes just before he turned away, and wondered what she had done to make him feel like that — because she was certain he was feeling something about her, something deep and complicated. She found herself thinking of all the long satisfying conversations they had had. Had there been something flirtatious about them?

She turned the problem over and over

in her mind, asking herself whether she had been provocative. She thought of the way they had danced together that night. They had been dancing as if they were already lovers. She scourged herself with that thought, as she lay there, the birdsong in the gardens outside growing in a tremendous, insistent crescendo, and again and again she reached the same terrible conclusion: that she had wanted him to kiss her like that.

Hadn't she felt, when he had undressed to model for her, a great raw attraction to him — as if in stripping off his clothes he had also stripped away the obscuring layers in her mind to leave only the simple, basic fact of her desire for him? It was not, however, she realised, just a simple rush of physical desire. That would be excusable; that would not make her lie there squirming. It was more than that. There was something about Hugh that had set some deep low note resonating in her. There were times when they had seemed to be thinking exactly the same thought. Even the first time she met him, she had noticed that. It was such a quiet thing, this understanding of theirs, but suddenly it seemed so significant.

She rolled on to her side and curled herself up like a child, wishing suddenly she had not come to this appalling conclusion. How could she feel anything for anyone else when there was Gabriel? But she found herself thinking of Hugh, still, unable to stop her imagining what might have happened between them if he had not stopped kissing her.

★ ★ ★

Gabriel went into his dressing room at midday and found Kate asleep on the little day bed. She was lying on her back; the skirt of her black dress had ridden up almost to her waist and her legs were spread, as if she was waiting for a seducer. One hand lay across the tight (and now wrinkled) bodice of the dress, as if to draw attention to the place where the cloth clung across her breast. He felt like a voyeur, finding her there like that. He knew he ought to feel a great rush of lover-like desire, but he found himself looking at her objectively, rather as if she were a figure study for one of her own paintings. He frowned, and was on the verge of leaving her there to sleep when she stirred suddenly and woke up.

She sat up quickly and stared at him, looking startled, as if he had actually invaded her private space. He found himself apologising.

She shuddered and wrinkled up her face, drawing her knees under her chin.

"Are you all right?" he asked.

"I think I've got a hangover," she said with a slight groan. "God . . . you must think I'm really stupid. I should have come home with you."

"No," he said. "You were having far too much fun for that. What time did you get back?"

"About six, I think," she said.

"Oh. That's why I didn't hear you. I was in the kitchen garden by then."

"You didn't sleep much."

"No," he said, watching as she got up rather stiffly from the day bed. "You needn't have slept in here, you know. I know you probably did it so you wouldn't disturb me, but that bed must have been murder . . . "

"It was OK," she said, stretching. She

began to pull the pins that had held up her hair, combing it through with her fingers as it fell down. Gabriel remembered when the sight of her playing with her hair had driven him mad with desire. Now he only felt a sort of confused numbness, and found himself making for the door, anxious to leave her in peace.

"Well, thank you anyway," he said. "I'll go and see about some lunch, shall I?"

20

THREE days later, on Midsummer's Day, Gabriel went to Edinburgh on business, leaving Kate alone at Allansfield. She had wanted to do some painting but she found herself dawdling about the house finding excuses not to go down to the studio, just as she had been making excuses for the last two days. She did not know whether Hugh was at the cottage or not. She was not surprised that he had not put in an appearance. She imagined he would be as reluctant to come up to the house as she was to go down to the studio. The embarrassment factor was too high. Yet, she knew she wanted to see him as much as she knew she should not. It was more than embarrassment that was keeping them away from one another.

She went and sketched in the wild garden all morning, doing studies of foliage for the *Ghosts of Allansfield*, but by half-past eleven it was really too hot to stay out any longer, even in the shade, and she went back up to the house.

Alison (whose day off it was) had diligently drawn down all the old holland blinds before she went out, to keep the sun from the house, and the rooms were cool and welcoming, suffused by the creamy gold light the blinds let through. Kate collected a beer and some cold chicken from the fridge and went into the library. There was a message on the answering machine, and she was surprised to find it was for her.

It was from a woman whom Kate did not know, with a double-barrelled name and accent, and a London telephone number. "Sandra Manzoni gave me your number," she announced. "Please do get in touch."

Kate dialled back at once, smelling a commission. Mrs Serafini-Brown answered promptly and seemed delighted to hear from her.

"Sandra told me you've some teaching experience," she explained. "I need an art tutor quickly, you see. I run a painting course in a castello in Tuscany, and one of my regular tutors has had to drop out.

I think you'd be just the sort of person we need. I love your work. It would be for most of July, August and September. Is that any good for you?" Before Kate had a chance to answer, she went on, "Of course, there'd be plenty of time for your own painting too — the duties are quite light. The students are on holiday. It's a super place, so inspiring."

Kate found herself silently swearing as Mrs Serafini-Brown rattled on. Last summer she would have killed for such a chance. To go off to Italy, at someone else's expense, to teach and paint!

"Can I get back to you about this?" she said. "When would you need to know?"

"Early next week, if that's possible," said Mrs Serafini-Brown. "I know it's a big time commitment, and the money isn't all that wonderful, but the clients are such good contacts. Some of my tutors have done really well out of it. You're bound to sell a few things."

"Well, let me think and I'll let you know as soon as I can," said Kate.

She wondered, when she had put the phone down, why she had not said no at once. There could be no possibility of her going away for three months. She was not single any more. Why was she even thinking about it? She drank down the rest of her beer and finished her chicken. She felt hot and tired and vaguely irritated. She decided she would go upstairs and have a siesta. If she slept, she knew she would not have to think.

She did not sleep though, even though the bed with its linen sheets was deliciously cool and inviting. She lay, dressed in only her T-shirt, her mind churning over a confused jumble of thoughts. The only thing she found she could think of with any clarity was Hugh, and how much she wanted him. Her desire was almost as tangible as the heat in the room, and she wrestled to shake it off, but she could not. Her body seemed to be twitching with frustration.

She heard someone running up the stairs. Could Gabriel be back from Edinburgh already? Feeling guilty, feeling she had been mentally unfaithful, she got out of bed and went out to greet him.

But as she opened the door, she saw it was not Gabriel at all. It was Hugh.

He stared at her as she hovered in

the bedroom doorway. She realised how skimpy her T-shirt was, how her nipples, which were erect, would be clearly visible. She folded her arms around herself, finding she was going crimson, and leant diffidently against the door frame.

"You startled me," she managed to say.

He was gripping the carved dolphin on the newel post of the stairs, his large white hand strained over it, the veins tense.

He did not look directly at her. "I came to say goodbye," he said. "I'm going back to London tomorrow — early. Is Dad around?"

She shook her head. "There's no one here except me," she said, and ran a finger over her lips, feeling how dry they were.

He released the newel post and took a step forward. "That's a pity," he said, and then looked at her. "But you're here. I can say goodbye to you."

"Yes. Yes, you can," she said, venturing a lop-sided smile.

"The trouble is," he said, pushing his hand through his hair and looking about him. "I don't want to say goodbye to you."

Kate closed her eyes and leant back against the door frame. She swallowed hard but found she could not help giving a slight, involuntary sigh.

"Difficult, isn't it?" she heard him say.

She breathed in hard, smelling as she did the peculiar smell of Allansfield, a scent of wax polish, pot pourri and old wood. She could hear the clocks ticking and she could hear Hugh breathing, rather loudly and irregularly. She opened her eyes and looked at him again, gripping her bare arms more tightly round herself.

"Yes," she said, and put out her hand to him.

She knew when she stretched out her hand that she had not intended him just to shake it. It had been a gesture of invitation. She gave up struggling with her conscience. She could only put out her hand and wait for him to take it, wait to see what he would do. He took it lightly in his fingers and then bent his head and kissed her palm.

Then he kissed each finger in turn, gripping at her hand now with sudden agitation. He looked up at her, staring at her with questioning eyes, as if asking her permission. She stretched out and cupped her hand around his cheek. It was rough with stubble and his skin was hot. She felt she could sense the blood throbbing in his veins just under his skin.

"I want . . . " he began.

"I know," she said. "I want it too."

"I haven't been able to think about anything else," he said.

"Neither have I."

He let go of her hand and straightened up. He was looking down at her now, and gently resting his hands on her shoulders.

"Then may I?"

She answered by stretching up and kissing him gently on the lips. She could no longer resist the impulse — in fact, it had ceased to be an impulse, which she might have been able to dismiss. She needed him. Her nerves were now aching for him.

Nothing more needed to be said as

they went into the bedroom together, Hugh pulling off his clothes. They fell embracing on to the bed, their limbs entangled. He pushed up her T-shirt and began to kiss her bare stomach. His every touch seemed electric to her. It felt as if they were the only two souls in existence, discovering passion for the first time. She shuddered as his tongue touched her flesh, as his hands stroked the insides of her thighs, and she closed her eyes. She was lost in the onslaught, her cheek pressed against the thick linen of the sheets, the faint smell of dried lavender filling her nostrils. She stretched out her hands and clutched at the cloth in her ecstasy, wondering if she might die from such an excess of sensuality.

She lifted her knees to let him come into her, meeting his lips with hers as he pressed down on to her, breathless already, his eyes haunted with the intensity of it. He lay with all his weight on her, driving his hips so that he forced into her with exquisite precision, with extraordinary depth, touching her very guts, destroying and yet renewing her with every powerful thrust. They twisted their hands together and she felt his hand might crack the bones in her fingers as he pushed and pushed into her, his cheek squashed against hers, while she felt more and more dizzy, more and more unable to bear it. She cried out, feeling every muscle in her contract and then release, like so many buds in a garden exploding from the tension of spring into the full-blown ease of summer sweetness. Then he came too, and collapsed on top of her, panting with his own private ecstasy.

They lay there for some minutes, stupefied and breathless, and then Hugh rolled off her and on to his back. He stretched out and gathered her into his arms, gently kissing the back of her neck and her hair. The air in the room was still and warm; and in a moment, locked in his secure embrace, Kate had fallen asleep.

★ ★ ★

She stirred, woke up, and remembered. His arms were still around her and he was deeply asleep, breathing in and out so heavily that he was almost grunting. Carefully, so as not to disturb him, she detached herself and sat up. She gazed at him, at his naked body in its lust-sated languor, at the gleam of his skin in the pale and glowing light of the shrouded bedroom. His bare right shoulder, hard with muscle, was gleaming faintly in the cool light, and through the sheet which covered the rest of him she could read each contour of his well-made body. She resisted the temptation to run her hand along the ridge of his side before it fell into the dip of his hips. It was a moment for detachment. She sat there for some minutes, her knees drawn up under her chin, looking at him.

Yet she found she did not really see him. Another image of a man, physically similar, but very different, superimposed itself. She found she was remembering how Gabriel had looked as he lay under the rumpled covers of her bed in Barclay Terrace, last December. It had been too cold to sit up for long looking at his craggy face, and in a moment she had dived back into the warm nest of his body and the bedclothes.

She found she had a throbbing headache and was thirsty. She got up from the bed and put on her dressing gown, feeling suddenly the immense stuffiness of the room. She felt desperate for air and water. She went down to the kitchen where she drank half a glass of water, and then found she could resist the onslaught of her emotions no longer. She grasped the edge of the draining board with her hands, bent her head and wept bitterly. She loathed herself for doing it — she always hated to cry, she regarded it as a weakness — but she could do nothing else but stand there, sobbing relentlessly.

The kitchen door swung open on its creaky hinge, and she turned to see Hugh come in. He stood there, dressed only in his shorts, his thick hair disordered, with a horrified look on his pale face. She swallowed hard and managed to say, "Don't worry, I'm OK." She turned away slightly from him, reaching out for the kettle. "Shall we have some tea?" she asked with all the normality she could muster. Yet she could still feel his eyes boring into her, and she felt his hand on her shoulder. She reached up and patted it, with what she hoped was a dismissive gesture, but he would not be dismissed. Gently he turned her to face him, and with a careful finger swept away the accumulation of tears on her cheek. Then he cupped her chin in his hand and bent his head towards her for a kiss.

"No . . . " she managed to say, retreating from him. "No. Don't, don't, please."

"But . . . " he said, putting his hands back on her shoulders.

That one pitiful 'but' was enough. "No," she said.

His hands fell from her shoulders and he looked away from her, his hair falling in a shock to cover his eyes from her. He gripped his own shoulders with his hands, his arms crossed on his chest, and turned away.

"I know I sound brutal," she said. "I know, but you must see that we really mustn't let this mean anything."

"I know," he said, flinging up his hands. "Of course I bloody know!"

She sat down at the kitchen table, and sniffed and wiped away the rest of her tears. She saw him wince.

"Then," he said after a long silence,

"what the hell did we do that for?"

"For a fuck, of course," Kate said bitterly. "That's our nature," she went on, trying to detach herself from her feelings. "We're animals, aren't we?"

"Well, that makes me feel a lot better," he said. "Yes, much bloody better. I'll remember that the next time I do something unspeakable . . . "

"Oh don't get melodramatic!" she exclaimed. "That wasn't murder, you know. It was just sex. Stupid sex perhaps, but — "

"Just sex," he said, and began to pace around the room. "Just sex? Oh, I just screwed my father's girlfricnd — well, more than that — you're as good as his wife, aren't you? Effectively then, I just screwed my stepmother in my father's bed — "

"You screwed me, Hugh!" she said, incensed. "Me! I'm not your bloody stepmother. There's no need to turn this into incest. It's complicated enough as it is."

"You are my father's girlfriend," he said. "And that, in my book, makes things worse."

"Don't you think I'm feeling guilty?" said Kate. "Or do you think I make a habit of this sort of thing?"

"No," he said, "I don't suppose you do. *I* certainly don't." He stopped pacing and pressed his hands to his face for an instant. "Oh, God, I'm sorry . . . "

"No, I'm sorry," said Kate. "I . . . I . . . "

He looked across at her with a hang-dog expression.

"What do we do now?" she asked. "Write it off as midsummer madness?"

He stood, gripping the top rail of one of the Windsor chairs, curling and uncurling his hands in spasms. "I don't want to do that," he said softly after a moment. "The truth is I want to remember it. It was good, wasn't it?"

"Is that why we feel so bad?" Kate said. "Because it was so good, because . . . " She was going to add, "because it felt like it meant something?" but he pressed his finger to his lips to silence her.

"I'll leave today instead," he said, going towards the door. "I think that's for the best, don't you?"

21

"WELL," said Harry MacBryde, "there are one or two possibilities, but I don't want to commit myself to a specific diagnosis until we've done some more tests."

Gabriel, as cheerfully as he could manage, got dressed. He was feeling mentally and physically bruised from MacBryde's vigorous examination, smarting as much from the humiliation of having to submit to various undignified procedures as from the discomfort they had caused him.

MacBryde went on consulting his notes. "You've lost weight too," he commented.

"I thought we were all supposed to lose weight," said Gabriel.

"Your weight was fine," said MacBryde.

"Well, I haven't had much of an appetite lately, certainly," admitted Gabriel. With his tie half knotted he sat down in front of MacBryde, feeling too exhausted to stand any longer. "One or two possibilities, you say?"

"We'll wait until you've had the other tests," said MacBryde. "Now, I suggest you get them done as soon as possible. Tomorrow morning, ideally."

"Tomorrow?" said Gabriel, his throat going dry.

"I'll see if the clinic can fit you in," said MacBryde, reaching for the telephone. "In fact, we could put you in tonight. They'll take all day, and it might be a good idea for you to have a night's rest before. You are pretty run down."

"I'd rather go home."

"All the way to Fife? Is that wise?"

"No, here — my flat in Drummond Place."

"Oh, well, if you prefer that. It'll be an early start tomorrow, though."

"Well, I'm more likely to rest there than in a hospital, I think," said Gabriel.

"Just try and be calm," said MacBryde. "I'll get things sorted out." He spoke to his receptionist on the telephone. "Could you get me Anna Frazer at the Nuffield, please, Heather?"

Gabriel got up with effort and finished tying his tie. He pulled on his jacket and said, "Why don't you call me at Drummond Place and let me know the wheres and whens? I need some fresh air. You've got the number, I think?"

"Yes, right. Well, whatever you want," said MacBryde, getting up. "Just one caveat."

"What?"

"No alcohol tonight, please — and if you feel up to eating, keep it light. Oh, and you'd better take one of these." He reached into a desk drawer and produced a sample bottle. "Bring that in tomorrow — full, please."

Outside the air-conditioned discretion of MacBryde's consulting rooms the New Town seemed exceptionally humid. It felt more like the American South than Edinburgh as he walked slowly down the hill to Drummond Place, shedding his jacket and feeling his shirt sticking again to his back. MacBryde's caginess was infuriating. He had expected to come out of there with a simple solution and perhaps a prescription for a bottle or two of pills. But a whole day of being prodded by doctors and pricked by needles at a clinic! Half an hour of MacBryde had been humiliation enough. He wondered whether it would be a better idea to cancel the whole thing. The man was probably only being thorough, and at the end of it all he would be told was that it was just a virus after all.

He let himself into the entrance hall at Drummond Place, remembering as he did so that Henrietta might be there. It made him hesitate for a moment, and then he decided he did not have the energy to drag himself away merely to avoid her.

He unlocked the door to the flat and called out for her. There was no answer and he realised with some relief she was out, but her occupation of the place was at once apparent to him. It felt oddly different in there. There were vases of flowers about the place, and a pair of her shoes sitting in the hall, alongside a wicker shopping basket. In the drawing room her papers and books were all over the place. He wandered about, looking with shameless curiosity at all the details of her residence. He found the fridge full of salad and fizzy mineral water (for the latter he was profoundly grateful as he gulped down an inordinate amount), while the bathroom contained a mass of unfamiliar potions and bottles. He even strayed into her bedroom, finding she had chosen the room at the back which he never used. The bed was half made, the curtains not drawn, and the door of the wardrobe had been left open, with all her clothes hanging up neatly in it, filling the place with her particular scent.

He sat down on the bed and finished his glass of water, but he hardly felt comfortable. He felt like an intruder, trampling on her privacy like this, drinking her water. It was as if he had given her the deeds rather than the key to the flat. Irresistibly though, he could not help reaching out to see what the open book on the bedside table was. He smiled at the sight of it — *Perennial Plants* by Graham Stuart Thomas. He had been looking for it at Allansfield and had not realised he had left it here. Yet what struck him more was the piece of paper she had tucked inside the cover — a pencilled list of plants, such as he was in the habit of making as he read a gardening book. It was a habit they shared, it seemed. He stared at it for a long time, at the crabby, determined look of her handwriting (which he remembered well), noticing what a good selection of interesting plants it was. What could her garden be like?

An awful melancholy seized him then, faced with this quiet evidence of their compatibility. He closed the list in the book again and tried to dismiss it, but he could not. His mind kept imagining what their life together might have been like. They would have made a garden together, and children, and experienced together all the ordinary trials and tribulations of ordinary married couples. All too easily he could picture her working away deep in one of the borders at Allansfield, wearing the same straw hat that was lying on the table in the hall.

He realised he was sweating violently again, and decided it was his fever that was making him think so stupidly. He struggled to his feet and decided he would have a shower. Then he would telephone Kate and explain why

382

he could not get back to Allansfield that night.

* * *

Henrietta unlocked the front door of the flat to hear the sound of Gabriel's voice answering the telephone. She went quickly into the drawing room, wondering whether the call might be for her. Gabriel was sitting in the armchair by the fireplace, a bath towel wrapped around his waist, his hair dripping wet.

"Hello, Gabriel Erskine speaking," he was saying. "Aah . . . yes, nine o'clock tomorrow is fine. Do I need to bring anything? Fine, fine . . . Goodbye." He put down the receiver and rubbed his face, grimacing. He looked up and only then seemed to see her. He got up slowly from his seat. "Sorry, I've trespassed on you this time."

"Don't worry," she said. "It is your apartment." She put down her briefcase, unable to take her eyes off him. He looked terrible, his face livid red, the rest of his skin deathly pale. The white bath towel clinging about his hips looked like a winding sheet.

"And drunk most of your mineral water," he said, attacking the glass on the table.

"That's all right," she said. "The thing is, are you?"

"I wish I bloody knew," he said simply. He sat down again. "I took your advice though. I've been to the doctor this afternoon."

"And . . . ?"

"I've got to go for more tests," he said. "Tomorrow morning," he added.

"Probably just precautionary," she said carefully.

"I hope so," he said. She sat down opposite him. "You look nice and cool."

"Libraries are always cold," she said.

"I envy you," he said. "Something as civilised as a library. What did you uncover today?"

"Some nice late-eighteenth-century letters actually," she said. "You would like them. I must show them to you."

"I should like that," he said. "Anything for a distraction. I'm afraid I'm staying here tonight — if you don't mind. If you do, I could always go to an hotel . . . "

"No, no, you must stay here," she said, getting up. "You're hardly in a fit state to go anywhere."

"Unfortunately not," he said wearily.

"I'm going to make you some tea," she said.

"I ought to offer you a proper drink," he said. "There's a cache of bottles in the kitchen, which I'm sure you've been too scrupulous to touch. I'm afraid though I can't join you."

"Then I won't," she said. "Herb tea?"

"Whatever you like," he said. "I shall have to get used to submitting to what other people think is good for me, won't I?"

"And that's the hardest thing, isn't it?" she said.

"Well it's so damn humiliating, the whole process. I feel as if I'm being punished for something when I go into a doctor's surgery. It's too much like the headmaster's study at school. The power is all one side."

"You have had it bad today," she smiled.

"And after all that he wouldn't even give me a straight answer. I have to go back for more punishment."

"You're not being punished. You just happen to be ill."

"I know, but it doesn't feel like that. I feel I deserve this somehow, for taking what I shouldn't take and wanting what I can't have . . . Oh God, will you listen to me? I'm raving, Henrietta!" He reached out for his glass of water and found it was empty. "I don't want water. I want a real drink, but I can't, can I?" He slammed the glass down on the table and pressed his hands to his face, hunching up his shoulders.

"I know what you need," she said.

"Herb tea?" he said with slight bitterness.

"That, and a massage. It never fails. It will send you to sleep like a baby."

"A massage?" he said, staring at her.

"Oil of lavender, sweet orange and ylang-ylang," she said. "A friend put me on to it when I was ill."

"Do you think that's wise?" he said.

"Do you think it's wise to let you sit here tying yourself up in knots?" she retorted. "I'm not talking about foreplay, Gabriel, this is a simple massage — complimentary therapy, if you like."

386

"You'll be sticking needles in my feet next," he said.

"Can be very effective," she said. "Better than half a bottle of whisky."

"All right," he said with a sigh. "I can't say that it doesn't sound like a very pleasant idea."

"Go and lie down, then. I'll get the oil."

In the bathroom, as she collected the oil, she wondered if she was being as disinterested as she sounded. It was not at all disinterested, after all, to want to help him — and that was what had moved her to suggest it. His evident stress terrified her. It was more than pity.

She went into the bedroom — the room she had deliberately chosen not to sleep in. It had seemed so obviously to belong to him even before she had discovered his spare clothes in the cupboard. She knew she had rejected the room with a false sense of delicacy. If she had really wanted to be restrained about Gabriel she would have refused to borrow the apartment in the first place.

He had stretched out on the bed, on

his back, his eyes closed.

"You haven't fallen asleep, have you?"

"No," he said, "just thinking."

"Don't think," she said. "Roll over and empty your mind of everything."

She measured a few drops of oil into her palm and tried to obey her own command. She sniffed the oil, trying to soothe herself with its sweet smell, and then began to rub it gently into his back. His muscles felt stiff as a board, and he flinched slightly when she first touched him, as if he were afraid of her, but after a moment or two he began to relax. She stroked her fingers down his neck, which seemed thick and swollen, and heard him sigh slightly. She remembered how she had touched him before, how running a finger down his spine had intoxicated him, how lascivious and giddy they had been. How odd they would have found this moment, that was so unsexual. The desire she felt for him now, as her fingers circled his shoulder blades, had nothing to do with her body. It was a desire to be with him always, on this intimate, domestic level, when his soul was as naked to her as his body.

His breathing had become deep and regular. "That really is very good," he said. "Where did you learn this?"

"Would you believe it was from a lesbian friend?"

He laughed, and said, "I suspect you've led a far more interesting life than me."

"Maybe," she said, applying a little more oil and massaging him more vigorously.

"I think I'm one of life's cowards," he said. "I shouldn't be so bloody frightened now if I weren't."

"Fear is natural," she said. "Especially of the unknown."

"Of death, you mean," he said.

"They say, though as you get older, *that* gets a lot less frightening."

"I hope that's true," he said.

"Yes," she said, "so do I. Roll over now."

He complied, and she sat on the edge of the bed, stretching over him to rub the oil into his shoulders. She reached out for the bottle and dribbled a little more on to her finger tips. She swept her hands in broad motions across his chest and he closed his eyes, his head sinking more deeply into the pillow. She nodded, and began to rub the rest of the oil into his chest, but suddenly he caught her hand in his own and kissed her palm. She knew she should draw her hand away, but could not bring herself to do it. He pressed it to his face, and she could feel the stubble prickling her skin. "I'm sorry," he said. "I can't help myself."

"I think you should try," she said. She saw him grimace as he looked away. "In fact, we both should . . . " she added, withdrawing her hand. She found herself retreating towards the window, rubbing her hands together, in anxiety as much as to get rid of the excess oil. "I'm sorry, this was a very stupid idea. I don't know what got into me . . . I . . . " She turned quickly and looked out into Drummond Place, at the dense, lush undergrowth in the private gardens behind their railings. Its secretiveness reminded her a little of the wild garden at Allansfield.

"I mean," she said, "there's quite a difference between thinking about what we want and actually doing it, isn't there?"

She heard him sigh, and the bed creaking as he got up. She wanted to look back at him but did not quite dare to.

"Yes, but . . . " he began wearily.

"I mean," she went on as steadily as she could, "it's not as if we have only to decide whether to indulge our whims or not. Kate is . . . . "

"Far too good a person to be treated so shabbily," he cut in. "I know. We both know that. But perhaps the damage is already done. It's what we feel that matters, not what we do. I could never see you again, Henrietta, and I'd still be betraying Kate."

"Is that some specious lawyer's argument to justify our doing something unacceptable?"

"No," he said, "it's the simple truth. I still love you, Henry. I realised that the other night at that wretched dance. I always have. I never got over you, and I don't suppose I ever will."

"Gabriel, please . . . " she protested.

"Are you afraid of my love?" he said. "It was fear before, wasn't it? Are you still afraid? What are you afraid of?"

"I'm afraid of doing something I can't forgive myself for," Henrietta said. "I don't want to hurt Kate. She thinks so much of you. I cannot have what I want. We cannot. You know that, Gabriel."

"But I will still want you."

"Then try not to."

"Do you think I haven't? Do you think I would even be saying this if I hadn't tried a hundred times? You know, it's as if all my adult life I've been trying not to love you, Henry, but I can't stop. It's an unavoidable truth. You know, when I asked you that day whether you wanted me to hate you, you said — "

"I said, 'If that is what it takes . . . ' Yes, I remember. Of course I do."

"Well, you didn't mean it, did you?" he said, coming up behind her now and resting his hands on her shoulders. "You didn't really want me to hate you."

"I did," she said, attempting to shake herself free of him. But he had her quite firmly, and he turned her to face him.

"Did you really?"

"Yes, I had to make you hate me. I couldn't have survived otherwise. If I thought for one minute that I hadn't,

I wouldn't have been able to go on."

"Why?"

"What is this?" she said, detaching herself from him now. "Cross-examination?"

"I just want to hear you say it."

"Say what?"

"You know."

"All right," she said. "All right. I'll say it, but it doesn't solve anything, does it? I had to make you hate me because if I had felt for one minute you still loved me I could never have done without you. All the things I've done, all the things I've achieved, would have seemed pointless if I'd known that. I was not going to let you undermine the rest of my life. Your love was a sort of drug for me, Gabriel, which I didn't need, and I don't need it now, not really. I'm just being weak again."

"Oh for God's sake, Henry, this isn't about weakness, this isn't about too many glasses of sherry at a bloody Cambridge cocktail party. You should be honest with yourself. I'm being honest."

"You are in no position to be honest," she said.

"That's very skewed logic for you, Henrietta."

"You know what I mean. Look, whatever you feel here is irrelevant. I don't know what mad scheme you have in mind here, but — "

"A mad scheme?" he said contemptuously. "I am not suggesting we have some sordid little affair on the side. Do you think I would have said all this if all I wanted from you was the dubious excitement of an illicit fuck? I've told you all this not just because I need to say it, but because you need to hear it. If I can own up to my feelings, you can. You should stop lying to yourself. I know what you feel. I can tell. You wouldn't be here with me if you didn't feel something still; you wouldn't have let yourself give me that damn massage. If you felt nothing, what the hell would we be arguing like this for?"

"I've had enough of this; this is quite pointless," said Henrietta, pushing past him towards the door. "I think I had better get out of here and go back to St Andrews."

Gabriel followed her and caught her arm, pulling her round to face him. Suddenly he laid his hand on her cheek.

"I don't want to think of you as a hypocrite," he said gently.

"I'm not a hypocrite. I'm just trying to do the right thing."

"And what *is* that?" he said. "Think about it, Henrietta."

22

"SINCE you insist," said Valerie Mackenzie, as Gabriel offered her more strawberries. "They are so terribly good. I don't think I've ever tasted such lovely strawberries. They're so unusual, these little ones, aren't they?"

"Well, you had better take some back with you tomorrow," said Gabriel. "We've something of a glut this year. We're getting quite bored with them actually, aren't we, Kate?"

"Yes, a little," said Kate, eyeing the dish. It was one of Hugh's — a large, octagonal ashet, glazed in spectacular swirls of deep ultramarine and jade green, against which the deep red woodland strawberries looked particularly enticing.

"Oh, I don't believe you, Katie," said her mother with a giggle. She turned to Gabriel. "Kate — well, I'm sure you've noticed — loves strawberries. I remember my parents being absolutely amazed by it once. They'd given her some money for some sweeties and she came back with a punnet of strawberries. Do you remember that, Kate?"

"No," said Kate. The wine, she decided, had gone a little to her mother's head. She was not a great drinker and she was being unusually voluble. Or perhaps it was Allansfield that had intoxicated her. For a first visit, the house was looking particularly beguiling, as if the bright July sunlight was in fact artful stage lighting designed to make everything look its best, to dazzle the spectator. Kate glanced around the dining room and felt the odd unreality of all that beauty, as if they were sitting on a film set, waiting for the cameras to roll. She imagined the camera focusing on each telling detail: the silvery patterns of laurel leaves woven into the white linen table cloth; the Chinese bowl of papery, faded pink roses in the centre of the table; the half-filled glasses, luminous with rosé wine; and, lastly, Gabriel's right hand lying on the table, his fingers spread as if to display the slightly battered solidity of his signet ring. There was something a little contrived about his whole posture, she decided, though she had seen him sit like that many times before, with one hand on the table top and the other arm resting on the back rail of the chair. In a moment, she knew, he would lift his hand from the table and rest his chin on it. It was as if he was elaborately demonstrating how entirely relaxed he was.

Kate decided he was making a better job of pretending to be relaxed than she was, but then he had less to be awkward about. For he was merely entertaining his girlfriend's mother for the first time. It was a small domestic-social hump to be got over. He had always been a little nervous of her mother. "I can see her point of view rather too clearly," he had said to Kate, and ever since she had arrived he had been treating her with more than his usual courtliness. In other circumstances Kate might have been amused to watch this delicate ritual of give and take between her mother and Gabriel, but instead it filled her with misgiving. She wished she had been able to put her mother's visit off, but they had arranged it ages ago.

"Fortunately this variety makes very

good jam as well," remarked Gabriel.

"Oh, I bet it does," said Valerie, spooning a little more cream on to her plate. "You know I'd love to have the time to do all that sort of thing. My mother always made everything herself — jam, cakes . . . everything — and they had a wonderful garden. I feel quite ashamed sometimes when I think of it, but you know I'm not much of a gardener, Gabriel. I don't seem to have the right sort of mind for it, probably not enough imagination. I think Katie got all the imagination in our family."

"Perhaps you'd like to see the gardens when we're finished here?" said Gabriel, and then smiled. "Sorry, I always inflict them on our visitors. I'm very immodest about them. You must say if you'd prefer a siesta. This heat is — "

"I'd love to see them," said Valerie. "I'll need a good brisk walk to work off this huge lunch. And the heat's no problem. This summer's been wonderful, hasn't it? I'm a sun worshipper, you see — it comes from being stuck in an office all day, I think."

So a little later they wandered out

into the gardens. Gabriel, distinguished in his old panama hat, was confidently affable, doing what Kate knew he loved best, talking about gardening; and her mother, for someone who was not supposed to be remotely interested, was apparently fascinated. Perhaps, Kate thought, his enthusiasm was infectious. It was certainly easier to understand his passion for the subject standing in the centre of the walled garden, surrounded by the dazzling spectacle of so many luxuriant flowers and leaves. In fact, it was so overwhelming that afternoon, everything so highly scented and brilliantly lit, that Kate began to long to be somewhere cool and private, alone with her thoughts. The garden was too intense. The air was as absolutely still as inside a room, and the walls trapped not only the heat but the scents of the flowers, making them as strong as burning incense. She had the curious sense that time itself was standing still in this place.

She retreated to a bench under an arch of climbing roses and watched as Gabriel and her mother vanished into the far corner of the garden. She stretched out on the bench, closed her eyes, and found herself imagining a succession of these summery Saturday afternoons, showing the garden to visitors. She saw herself standing there, dressed as she was today in an expensive, rather too classic summer dress, an elegant adjunct to Gabriel as he explained the garden. It was such an easy game to play. "Ah yes, we've had quite a success with it this year, haven't we, darling?" she could hear him saying, and she would give a bland, quiet smile. Was that what he thought the rest of their life would be like?

She thought suddenly of all the places in the world she had not seen. How timid she had been, clinging to Edinburgh for so long, thinking that was all she wanted from life. And then Gabriel had come along and suggested Allansfield. But was this really a life? It felt more like a dead-end. Allansfield might have looked like an adventure, but she realised then that it was not enough. She needed something more in her life, an edge that she could not find here. It was not just a question of her work — that had been going well — it was that she wanted to sense the very possibilities of existence. She was not ready to settle anywhere yet. That had been her mistake. Why on earth would she have done something as patently stupid as jumping into bed with Hugh if it hadn't been an attempt to inject a little danger into this safe, orderly, ultimately constricting world? Was that what had been going on? She found she was disgusted at herself, surprised she was capable of playing such games.

She also found she was angry with Hugh. It was fine for him, running off to London like that as if nothing had happened. He did not have to see Gabriel all the time, to feel guilty every time he smiled at her; but then she realised she was not being entirely fair. Hugh was probably torturing himself quite adequately in London, wondering how he was ever going to look his father in the eye again. How on earth had they managed to be so stupid? How had they let that happen? All the time her mind had been slipping back to that day, analysing every moment that led up to it, trying to find the moment at which she could have resisted. She always failed. She had not been able to resist. She had wanted him too much for that.

No, she told herself sternly, it wasn't Hugh you wanted, it was danger, the thought of doing something as taboo as sleeping with your partner's son. That, combined with a healthy dose of sexual frustration, was all it had been about. It was symptomatic of the creeping malaise she had felt about Allansfield. That was the problem that needed to be addressed. Her desire for Hugh was a misleading phantom.

She sighed hard, gripping mentally to this conclusion, and opened her eyes again.

"Oh, you're not asleep," said her mother, who was strolling towards her. "You looked languid there, like the Sleeping Beauty in her bower. I thought you must have dozed off."

"I was just thinking," said Kate, sitting up again. "Where's Gabriel?"

"Gone to fetch his secateurs. He saw something that needed pruning." Her mother sat down beside her and reached out to hold an overhanging spray of roses. She sniffed them delicately. "Ooh, goodness . . . Turkish delight!" She smiled. "You're very lucky, you know, Kate. This place is wonderful. And to think I had doubts about you two." She shrugged. "You were right. You should trust your instincts occasionally."

★ ★ ★

Gabriel walked back to the house, exhausted by his performance. Playing the dutiful spouse to Kate's mother was not a role he could relish in the circumstances, but he was hard pressed to think what else he could do. He had demanded that Henrietta should think about what the right thing to do might be, being at the time arrogantly certain that he knew what it was. When Henrietta had left the flat that afternoon, her puritanical insistence on restraint, her stealing of the moral high ground, had incensed him. He had felt abandoned. He was furious that she should have decided to stick so vigorously to her own agenda, martyring her own feelings again to some principle or other, just as she had done all those years ago. How could she so blithely ignore the real strength of feeling between them again?

Yet coming back to Allansfield the following evening, after an arduous day of tests at the clinic, and finding himself alone with Kate, he had begun to see her point. Lying to Kate, he had been certain, was entirely unacceptable; but finding her, as he had done, reading in the fading light, lying on a rug in the garden, her long hair falling over the pages of her book, he had wondered how he could ever begin to explain to her what had happened. He could not willingly hurt her, and yet he knew he had hurt her already, and that the pain he was inflicting on her by his deceit would grow the more he concealed it. She had looked up from the book she was reading and greeted him with a lop-sided clumsy smile that had made him feel worse.

"What are you reading?" he had asked.

"*The Wings of the Dove*," she'd said. "Henrietta suggested I give it a try."

He had winced a little at that revelation. Kate, if she knew, could easily identify with Milly Theale, duped by a pair of old lovers.

"Nasty scheming people in that," he had remarked.

"I know," she'd said. "It's very well done, isn't it? How was your day? Did your meetings go well? Did anything interesting happen?"

"Oh, no, not really," he'd said, only just remembering that he had told her he would be at a trustees' meeting rather than at the clinic. How had he managed to tangle himself up in this net of lies?

Now, coming back to the house on the trumped-up excuse of fetching his secateurs, Gabriel was tempted to go into the library and call Henrietta, as if that might vent his feelings a little. But he resisted the urge — it would only make the situation worse. There was only one way out of this one, and that was to be scrupulously honest with Kate, and as soon as possible. But how on earth did he begin to do such a thing?

★ ★ ★

For Kate, the rest of the day was a slow, humid torture, with the temperature creeping up in step, it felt, with her own discomfort. By the time they sat down to dinner, with all the paraphernalia that entailed, only one thing was clear to her: that she had to get out of there, no matter how much that might hurt Gabriel. There was no future for her there. She had to finish this ridiculous game they were playing.

Yet, later, when her mother had gone to bed, she was still not quite ready to tell Gabriel of her momentous decision. What had seemed perfectly simple at the dinner table felt much more difficult when she was alone with him. While she distracted herself getting ready for bed, he was standing by the open doorway to the little balcony. She felt him watching her as she brushed out her hair. His looking, in fact, was so intense that it made her profoundly uncomfortable.

A sudden violet-black gloom filled the room, and Gabriel, turning towards the window, said, "Oh, there's definitely going to be a storm." And almost as he said it, a flash of lightning crackled somewhere in the distance, illuminating the room for a split second with ghastly light. A second later it was raining fiercely, and Kate silently counted the seconds before the rumble of thunder came. It came, and it shook the house.

"Goodness!" she exclaimed.

"That's a good, old-fashioned, retributive storm," said Gabriel. Lightning exploded again on the horizon, a jagged lilac electric formation in the sky, and Kate glanced at him, nervous that he might know already, that he might have guessed. "Just the sort to smite heinous sinners on the head and bring them to repentance," he went on.

"What?" said Kate.

"A literary convention," he said mildly, but he looked at her with piercing eyes. She felt a little sick, wishing she could manage to feel again that simple, straightforward affection she had once felt for him. Yet all she could do was smile awkwardly.

"I need some air," she said, moving past him and out on to the little balcony. She plunged out into the darkness and found it was still raining heavily. In a moment she was soaked to the skin, her short nightdress sticking to her.

"This rain is irresistible, isn't it?" Gabriel said, following her out. She wondered what she must look like to him, the cotton of her nightdress clinging across her breasts. Desirable, she imagined, and she felt embarrassed suddenly, as if he had never seen her naked before.

He came and stood beside her, his hands resting on the stone parapet.

"I read somewhere that when it rains, there's a positive charge in the earth's atmosphere," he said, "or something like that. That's why it feels so intense . . . "

She turned and studied him as he gazed out into the darkness of the landscape, remembering all the things that had first drawn her to him: that fascinating face, his talk, his very presence, quietly confident. In her mind's eye, he was standing in the gallery again, looking at her pictures, looking at them as no one, she was certain, had ever looked at them before.

Impulsively, she reached out and put her hand over his. Somehow their fingers twisted together affectionately for a moment and then a second later, gently, he removed his hand.

"Gabriel . . . " she said, wondering how to start, but he shook his head, returning to stand as he had done before, leaning with his hands on the parapet. It was the most delicate of rejections, yet she felt as if he had slammed his palm across her face. She wondered again if he had somehow guessed that she had betrayed him. If he had, he would not reproach her with it. He was too civilised to have a scene.

"We are going to catch cold if we stand here much longer," he said, and went to open the door to their bedroom for her. "Run along and get dry, Kate."

She hardly needed an excuse to bolt into the bathroom.

410

23

DRIVING back to Fife, stuck in the traffic on the Queensferry Road, Gabriel remembered with painful clarity the interview he had just had with Dr MacBryde.

"I know this doesn't sound like much comfort," Dr MacBryde had said, "but you're actually very lucky — very lucky indeed. This is one of the few cancers in which one can be quite optimistic about making a full recovery."

Gabriel had shifted a little in his chair. As Dr MacBryde had carefully explained his diagnosis, he had been filled with mounting incredulity. There surely had to be some mistake. Yet there was nothing about MacBryde's expression or credentials to suggest that could be the case.

He had swallowed hard, and asked, "What exactly does 'quite optimistic' mean?"

"The survival rate is eighty per cent."

"Eighty per cent?"

"Eighty per cent."

"That's good, is it?" he asked.

"Compared to other cancers, yes," said MacBryde. "Lymphadenoma is very rare, but happily it is one of the few in which we can say that, after comprehensive treatment, the chances of survival are extremely good for the patient."

Gabriel had sighed involuntarily and sank back in his chair, feeling the sweat pouring off him. The chair was covered in black leather and he felt he might stick to it, sitting there as he was in his shirtsleeves. He'd reached out and taken a gulp of the tea that MacBryde had insisted was brought in. He saw why now.

"And the treatment?" he managed to say, putting the cup clumsily back in the saucer, aware that his hands were shaking.

"Exploratory surgery in the abdominal region to start with. We may have to do a splenectomy and then combination chemotherapy."

Gabriel grimaced. Chemotherapy was one of those things that happened to other people. When the subject came up in conversation, he had noticed how people assumed a grave and sympathetic demeanour, caught for a moment in collective terror of a dimly perceived torture.

"It's very effective treatment, with no remission in eighty per cent of patients after five years," went on MacBryde. "But as I'm sure you are aware the side effects are — "

"Grim," put in Gabriel. He heaved his thoughts into order with some difficulty. "Look, we can postpone this discussion? I mean, I don't really want to — "

"You probably want to discuss it with your family. Of course. I should have phoned and told you to bring someone with you. We don't usually like to give this sort of news without a relative or a friend present, but you . . . "

"Were very insistent. Yes, I know," said Gabriel. He thought of the optimism with which he had arrived at the surgery. He had been convinced that there was nothing really wrong with him. The real thing worrying him then had been his failure to tell Kate about what he felt for Henrietta. He had been desperately trying to think of some fair way to solve what seemed an almost impossible situation. He remembered how he had seen her that morning, reflected in his rear-view mirror as he drove off towards Edinburgh. She had been leaning against one of the portico arches, half entangled in the clematis; distinctive, though, and slender in her stark black clothes. In that moment, he had felt she absolutely belonged there and it was almost inconceivable that he should have to tell her how his feelings had changed. She was going to hate him, he felt sure.

"Perhaps tomorrow morning might be better?" Dr MacBryde suggested. "I can arrange for John Hepburn to be here, I think." Hepburn was the consultant who had made the diagnosis. "He'll be able to go into the fine points better than I. He's a very good man."

"Fine, fine," said Gabriel, anxious to get out now. "Tomorrow will be fine. We'll talk all the details through then."

Gabriel had made an appointment with the receptionist, who treated him with that cheerful, anodyne manner common to all medical people. He would have to get used to the subtle patronising kindness of nurses and learn to bear the humiliation of being ill with grace. What grace could he find, though, when all he felt was fear?

As he drove across the Forth Road Bridge, he found he could still think of nothing except that ominous margin of twenty per cent. He tried to picture twenty per cent in his mind, tried to imagine two tenths of a loaf of bread, one of Alison's soda farls cut into ten. It seemed too large a piece for comfort — though God knows there had to be some comfort in it, if that was considered a good failure rate. What about those other poor souls, all over the country, their bodies riddled with far more venomous cancers, who had been given a fifty per cent chance or less of survival? He was lucky. God, yes, he had to grip on to that fact. The odds were good, damn good considering what it was, considering it was cancer.

Gabriel found he was already exhausted. He had thought he was fit; but how could he have been for this to have crept over him, this invasion of his lymph glands? He was not even sure precisely what his lymph glands were. He remembered the lymphatic system dimly from school biology, recalling it only, he was sure, because it sounded faintly absurd.

As he drove on up the motorway in the busy summer traffic, he thought of how diseases of various sorts seemed from time to time to attack the garden, taking dozens of healthy plants in their wake, for no obviously discernible reason. At times these plagues had struck him as positively Biblical, and more like straight old-fashioned heavenly wrath rather than any horticultural mismanagement on his part. Was this what it was — a straightforward punishment from a God he did not believe in, or rather from a God that he did not usually believe in? Today God seemed extraordinarily real, a hoary-faced old gentleman who cracked out retribution like a sadistic schoolmaster. It was chance, mere bad luck, he knew, but the idea of the heavenly schoolmaster was hard to dispel.

As he pulled into Cupar, he knew he

needed his demons banished and quickly. He had to see Henrietta. Instead of taking the turning for Allansfield, he drove straight through the town and towards St Andrews.

★ ★ ★

Henrietta had not been concentrating. She had been trying very hard to do so, but all morning she had been lacerating herself about what they were doing to Kate. Her mind kept returning to that evening in Drummond Place, when she had been so stupid and indulgent. If she had never suggested giving Gabriel that massage then she was certain he would not have been provoked into declaring his feelings in such uncertain terms. It was not what she had wanted to happen. She had only wanted to help him a little, but instead she had unleashed the old monster of his love, a monster she could never deal adequately with. And the worst of it was that she knew she had not been as innocent as all that. When he had said it, she had wanted to hear it as much as she had wanted him to be quiet. There was a deep gratification in knowing that he still loved her.

She worked as best she could, sifting through the photocopied family letters of her forgotten Scottish novelist, trying to take her usual pleasure in their gossip: 'Twenty yards of the crimson damask ought to be more than enough for the drawing room. Perhaps this might persuade my husband that I do occasionally study economy. Would you be good enough to send me dear Carswell's excellent receipt for barley water? Poor Willy has the croup and it is the only thing I can think of to soothe him. DV, I will be able to send you better news soon.' A few letters later and poor Willy was dead.

She laid down the letter announcing it. It was full of rather desperate affirmations that the baby would be happier in heaven. She wondered how much of that his mother had actually believed, wondered if she could see old tear stains on this sad little letter and detect grief in the jagged handwriting. It would be a terrible thing to lose a child, even in an age where it happened with sickening regularity. One did not need to have given birth to understand that.

What would it have been like, she found herself wondering, to have children, to have had Gabriel's children? A great wave of regret hit her, far stronger than those other attacks of frustrated broodiness she had experienced in the past. Previously her maternal instinct had annoyed her. It had been something to battle against, to repress sternly; but now it was too late she felt a deep, cold bitterness inside her, which she knew perfectly well was irrational. She had made her choice and could not let herself bemoan the consequences of that choice as if she were some pathetic victim of circumstances.

Yet the idea, the fantasy of it, would not let go, and as she stared down at the intimate records of a family she found herself constructing a mental album of purely fictional scenes, modelled on all the pictures she had seen in the photograph albums of her friends and relations: she and Gabriel crouched together on a plaid rug with a triumphant toddler stealing the foreground; an inevitable, and grossly sentimental, yet irresistible tableau round the Christmas tree; the family holiday on the beach, the children's legs bare and brown from the sunshine; the shots with the pony and the kittens; the college graduation photographs, the weddings . . . With phantom power, this pernicious, retrospective daydreaming caught her and shook her to the core.

She got up from the desk and opened the door to her office, convinced that it was the stifling heat trapped underneath the eaves which was making her think so hysterically. She was an idiot to indulge like this, when her efforts should have been squarely fixed on learning again to do without Gabriel. She could not have him, for all that she might want him, no matter what he might say. If her reasons for breaking with him in Cambridge had been enough to convince her then, how much more convincing were the reasons now? They could not simply trample on Kate's feelings. It was impossible.

"I don't want to think of you as a hypocrite," Gabriel had said. Had he been right? she asked herself. Was it hypocritical to try and act for the sake of someone else's feelings? She thought of him going on with Kate, pretending to love her when he did not, and she realised from his point of view he was right. It was hypocritical. They had to be honest and admit what was going on, but she found herself squirming at the thought. There were no anaesthetics for such revelations. Kate would be hurt, so terribly hurt, and it would be entirely the fault of their own ungovernable, ultimately self-indulgent feelings.

Damn you, Gabriel, she thought bitterly. Damn you. But she knew she did not have the power in her to hate him. She had not managed to hate him then, and she could not do it now, even though it would make things so much easier. She knew she had always loved him with a violent need that frightened her — and she knew then that, whatever it cost, she could not manage to give him up a second time.

★ ★ ★

As Gabriel climbed the stairs to her office, he remembered once going to find Henrietta in the University Library at Cambridge, where she had often been ensconced. It was after a morning on the river, and he had been pleasantly tired from the exercise. He was never much of an oarsman, but he had loved the feeling of being in an eight, pushing the boat along with muscle power, rushing through the water, feeling his body working like a machine. How vivid his memory was today. It was like looking through the pages of a photograph album.

He could see Henrietta as she was, sitting at her desk, that day in Cambridge, looking diligent and beautiful, her hair piled up high and catching the sunlight. He had stood looking at her for a moment, he recalled, with all the unheeding cockiness of his youth, his arms folded on his chest, congratulating himself that this was his girl, that she loved him and that he loved her more than anything he could ever have imagined. He had not been able to stand there for more than a minute before creeping up to kiss her.

Now, from the landing, he could see her sitting at her desk. Her office door had been propped open, presumably to catch the through draught. She had conquered the whole of the large desk with her work. There were books piled up like fortifications around her and documents spread out in front of her. Henrietta was scowling at the piece of paper she held, her sleeves industriously rolled up and a pencil tucked behind her ear. She put down the paper, scratched her temple, and then plucked out the pencil and made a note of something. Gabriel stood and watched as she picked up the next piece of paper, and realised that the love he had felt for her in Cambridge was nothing compared to what he felt now. He felt so strongly for her that he shook inwardly with it, at the sudden agony of it in his twisting gut. He could not leave her, could not let go of life now, when he knew this wonderful, terrible truth.

Yet he was half inclined to walk straight out and attempt never to see her again, simply to go somewhere quiet and lie down and die. Because he *would* die, sooner rather than later, if he did not go for treatment. Perhaps he should die — should willingly embrace the odds against him and free them both, Henrietta and Kate — rather than inflict this awful burden on them.

So he stood there and waited until she looked up and saw him.

★ ★ ★

Henrietta looked up and saw Gabriel standing on the threshold, looking dazed and diffident. He was in his shirtsleeves, holding a crumpled linen jacket against him, almost as if he were a child with a comfort blanket.

"Gabriel, I thought I said — "

"To stay away, yes, I know," he said. His voice was almost inaudible. "But . . . you see . . . the test results . . . " He screwed up his face for a moment.

Henrietta rose from her seat, finding herself dizzy with fear as she made her way across the room to him.

"Gabriel . . . Gabriel, what is it?" she said. He took her hand and wrapped both his around it, and pressed hard, but he would not look her in the face. He did not speak, only bit his lip. "Gabriel?" He was shaking.

"I . . . I think you should sit down," he said hoarsely. "We should both sit down."

She pulled her chair from behind the desk and sat down next to him. "What has happened?" she asked. "You went to the doctor and . . . ?" How thin her voice sounded, how very weak and high. "Tell me."

He grabbed her hand again and, with the other, stroked the side of her face rather feverishly. "I can't . . . I . . . "

"Tell me," she said again.

"It's a sort of . . . " She saw him take a deep breath and took one herself. "C . . . c . . . cancer," he stuttered helplessly. The word was almost indistinct, but the effect was as if he had shouted it. She heard it without needing to hear it, as if she had already known.

She stared down at his hand that lay in her lap and tried to steady herself, but could not. She bent over and pressed her cheek to his hand, her eyes closed, trying not to see the images in her mind of her mother and those two dear friends . . . and now Gabriel . . .

"No," she said, shaking her head,

pressing his hand more firmly against her face.

Gently, he lifted her face to look at him.

"I stand a good chance," he said. "Apparently, a very good chance. Eighty per cent. Eighty per cent's not so bad, is it?" She heard the note of hysteria in his voice, for all that he was trying to reassure her.

"No," she said. "Not so bad." They both struggled to smile, and then they wrapped their arms about each other and clung for dear life.

24

KATE packed up her studio, leaving the half-finished panel of *The Ghosts of Allansfield* until last. That morning its phantoms looked a little less benign than she had intended. She wondered for a moment if she would be able to finish it when she had gone, but then, after studying it for a while, she decided she could not abandon this picture. Even now it had something about it that her creative instinct told her was worthwhile. If she could not think clearly about anything else, she could, she was relieved to find, think clearly about the picture.

She wished she could work on it then. More than anything, she loved to work in oil, loved the smell of the linseed oil and the sight of the unmixed raw colours on the palette. She had trained herself to use the smallest range of unmixed colours: flake white, lamp black, cobalt blue and ultramarine, yellow ochre and madder carmine. If that was enough for Velázquez and for James Henderson, it should be enough for her. When she worked in oil, she felt as if she were stepping into another time, as if she were connecting herself, with the mere touch of a hog's-bristle brush, with the old tradition of painting, that wordless, sensual tradition that required a fierce eye and a bold hand, that required all the best of her and all the concentration of her soul.

With a sigh, Kate lifted the picture off the easel and wrapped it up. It would have to wait. There were more important things to be sorted out. She loaded it into the back of the Range Rover with the rest of her things, and resisted the temptation to take one last look at the studio. It had been the best work-space she had ever had. Gabriel had been right about that.

She drove away from the steadings, towards the north gate to the estate, stamping down the bizarre tide of sentiment that was threatening to overcome her. She knew she was doing the right thing by getting out now, the right thing for both of them — but now, as she

428

drove along under the shade of the oak and chestnut trees that lined the road, dripping with their sumptuous burden of leaves, she felt a sharp sense of loss. Deciding that she had to leave and actually leaving were quite different matters. She was surprised at how much it hurt to leave Allansfield. She had adjusted to the place, despite herself. When she reached the main road, she found her instinct was to shove her foot down on the accelerator and get going as quickly as possible, concentrating only on her driving.

★ ★ ★

"Will you ever be able to forgive me?" Henrietta said, as they sat together on the lawn of the garden of Mon Abris under the shade of the ornamental cherry.

"How many times do I have to tell you that there is nothing to forgive?" said Gabriel.

"Oh, but there is," said Henrietta. "I've wasted our lives. I've wilfully thrown away the best part of our lives."

"That's still to come," he said, stroking her forehead.

"How can you be so brave?"

"Because you won't leave me again. I know. I feel safe. Anything could happen now and it wouldn't matter, because I have you again." He closed his eyes for a moment and then kissed her on the lips. "The person you should forgive," he went on, "is yourself. You did what you had to do. At the time for you it was the right thing."

"But it was the wrong thing," she said.

"Shush," he said, pressing his finger to her lips. "The past doesn't matter any more. What matters is now and tomorrow — more especially now," he said.

"How are you going to tell her?"

"With great difficulty, I suspect."

"Shall I come with you?"

"No. This is something I have to do on my own," he said, staggering to his feet. "Don't get up, you look so comfortable there."

"I don't feel comfortable. I don't suppose I shall for a while."

"It can't be helped," he said, looking up at the sky, screwing up his eyes to the sun. "I'll come over first thing tomorrow, before I go down to Edinburgh, and tell you how it went. Then we can go from there."

"OK," Henrietta said, getting up and folding her arms around him. "Good luck."

"Thank you," he said. "And don't sit here fretting, please. Distract yourself. I know — read *Emma* again."

"I will read *Persuasion*."

"Yes, most appropriate," he said. "Till tomorrow then."

She nodded and watched him walk towards the house. At the kitchen doorstep he stopped to look back at her. She waved to dismiss him and wondered how she was going to get through until the morning.

She sat in the garden for some time, until dusk came on with a sudden, unexpected coolness that made her shiver. She wrapped her arms about herself and thought of what might be going on at Allansfield, remembering all the time the morning when she had told

Gabriel she would not marry him. The pain she had caused him had been so visible in his face. He had been near to tears. She thought of Kate — first plainly incredulous, then angry, and then in flat despair — and yet her despair, her anger, would be far worse because she had been deceived and betrayed by them.

She got up from the rug with stiff limbs and went back into the house. In the kitchen she began, somewhat listlessly, to put together some supper for herself, without feeling very hungry at all. She began to wonder if Gabriel would want her to go with him to Edinburgh for his appointment with the specialist. She hoped he would. She could not bear to idle there waiting for more news.

She had just uncorked a bottle of wine when someone rang the doorbell. She went to the door, hoping it was not Bob, and opened it.

"Gabriel, what happened?" she said. "Did you not manage to . . . ?"

"You'd better read this," he said, handing her several folded sheets of paper. "I found it waiting for me when I got back."

They went into the sitting room, and Henrietta sat down and unfolded it. It was a letter, written in the sort of elegant italic script that could only belong to an artist.

Dear Gabriel, I know that a letter is cowardly and impersonal, but it's the only way I can think to say what I have to say to you. I have tried several times to find the courage to tell you to your face, but I just couldn't find the right words. I suppose there are no right words, no kind words at least.

The thing is, I've come to the conclusion that we have no real future together. It isn't your fault — it's me. I want something else. I thought it was you I wanted, and Allansfield, but it isn't. I can't settle yet — perhaps I'll never settle — and to have stayed and pretended I was happy would only have hurt you far more in the long run. It's best to go now, and quickly, before there's too much history between us to make for more regrets. Please don't think that I haven't been happy with you, and that you are not a dear person to me — you were a great friend, and perhaps that was our mistake. If we'd kept it as friendship, perhaps I wouldn't have to write this horrible letter to you. We lost our heads and thought we were in love, but now I know I'm not. That sounds so harsh, but the truth must be better than a lie.

I'm going to Italy now. I've been offered a job for the rest of the summer, teaching at a painting school in a castello in Tuscany. I can't resist such an offer. You always were amazed that I hadn't been to Italy. You told me you'd take me there next year, I know, and God, this must seem so ungrateful, but it is better that I go under my own steam. I need to make my own way. I've been a coward too long. I just need to see what life will throw at me for a while, and concentrate on making my reputation as a painter.

I'll be back in October with my pictures for the exhibition, and I'll be in touch with Professor McCleod about the arrangements. Perhaps I'll see you at the private view, if you're not still angry with me. I don't think you will be. I'm sure you'll see that what I have done is for the best, for both of us, and I know you're not an intolerant, grudge-bearing sort of person. In fact, I think you're one of the kindest, most generous people I know, so I ask for that generosity now, and hope you can understand a little of my reasoning.

I've taken the car, I'm afraid — I know I shouldn't have, but I need it. Sorry.

Kate.

Henrietta laid the letter in her lap and stared across at Gabriel, who was sitting opposite her, perched on his seat edge, his chin resting on his knitted fingers.

"Well?" he said.

"It's hard to know what to say," Henrietta said. She got up and moved to his side, laying her hand on his shoulder.

"It's certainly damned convenient," said Gabriel, sinking back in the armchair. "I should be glad, shouldn't I? But all I feel is — "

"Guilty?" said Henrietta. "Yes, I know what you mean. Her leaving like that does not exactly absolve us."

He took her hand from his shoulder and kissed it. "It does mean one thing," he said. "You can come back to Allansfield with me tonight."

"Yes, I can, can't I?" she said, bending to kiss him on the forehead. "Let us just hope that she finds whatever it is she's looking for."

25

"WELL," said Jane Cherrington. "It's very sad, Hugh darling, but I can't say that I'm terribly surprised."

"No," said Tony a little gruffly. He heaved his solid body out of the chair and strolled over to the drinks tray. "Another gin, anybody?" Hugh was glad to be of an age when difficult scenes with his mother and stepfather could be eased by the addition of alcohol. Telling them that it was over with Lara without the benefit of one of Tony's powerful gin and tonics would have been even more awkward. In fact, it had been harder telling them than talking to Lara. That had been surprisingly easy, as if now they had finally acknowledged that they had no common future together, they could be civilised again.

"So what will you do now?" his mother asked.

"Well, Lara's been offered this job in

a design studio, and a friend has asked her to share a house in Putney." He saw a slight frown wrinkle his mother's forehead. "A female friend," he pointed out. "She's got a baby too. They're going to share the nanny, you see. It's a very good arrangement, I think."

"Sounds a bit odd to me," said Tony, handing him his drink.

"Lara likes to have lots of people around," said Hugh. "And she says you're to go and see Andrew whenever you like."

"Well, Putney is much easier to get to than Spitalfields," said Jane. "Has the house got a garden?"

"I think so."

"Well, that does sound much more suitable for Andrew," said Jane. "I never did quite know why you bought that house. And you? How much will she let you see him?" The question seemed loaded with suspicion and Hugh was tempted to say, "More than you allowed Dad to see me," but he resisted and said, "When I want."

"And you'll stay in Spitalfields?"

"Yes, of course," said Hugh. "I thought

I might have a few lodgers. It might be fun."

"Thank goodness for that," said Jane. "I had an awful feeling we were going to lose you to Allansfield."

"It's not the black hole of Calcutta," said Hugh.

"No, but . . . well, your real family are all here, darling, you know that."

"Dad is still family," said Hugh.

"You're very loyal," said Jane. "But your father's beyond redemption, I suspect. That girlfriend of his, well, I dare say he'll marry her and start another family. That seems to be the fashion with men these days, doesn't it? They get to fifty and then they do something stupid."

"I can't say it occurred to me," said Tony.

"You're my honourable exception, darling," she said, kicking off her court shoes and drawing her feet up under her. She sat curled up in her favourite armchair, cradling the crystal tumbler of gin and tonic in both hands. Hugh recognised she was settling down to gossip. Tony had clearly recognised it too, and made for the door saying, "I've got a few phone calls to make. I'll leave you two to it."

When he had gone, Jane said, "So what is she like, Hugh? You haven't said a word about her."

"I don't think I should indulge you," said Hugh, who above all things did not wish to discuss Kate.

"Oh rubbish. You see, I had the most curious phone call from dear Auntie Ronnie Nisbett," his mother went on. "She said she saw Gabriel at a dance in St Andrews. Can you believe that? Your father at a dance . . ."

"Well, yes, I was there too actually. It was Kate's idea we all went."

"Good grief," said Jane. "Well, I know Auntie Ronnie's getting a little frayed round the edges these days, but she might have recognised you . . . and why didn't you go and say hello to her, Hugh? You're so boorish sometimes. But that isn't the point. Auntie Ronnie said the woman she saw your father with was his age, wearing the most extraordinary white satin dress. She said they were obviously together."

"Definitely frayed round the edges,"

said Hugh, after a large mouthful of gin. "That was just one of our party — Henrietta Winthrop."

His mother gave a screech of amazement. "Henrietta Winthrop? You're not serious, Hugh, surely?"

"Why shouldn't I be?"

"Goodness," said Jane, shaking her head. "Henrietta. Well, I hardly know what to say."

"That's not like you, Mum," said Hugh.

"But Henrietta . . . " she said. "That was the woman who ruined our marriage."

"What?"

"The great love of his life," said Jane with glib contempt. "Wretched woman. They were at Cambridge together. She broke off their engagement . . . " She stopped and stared at him. "Do you mean to say you didn't know that?"

"Well," said Hugh, collecting his thoughts. "I gathered they'd been at Cambridge together and were great friends, but . . . " He thought for a moment. "He's never mentioned her to me before."

"How typical!" said Jane, shaking her

441

head. "How absolutely typical. So what on earth was she doing there?"

"She's a visiting lecturer at the university," said Hugh.

Jane made a small contemptuous noise and put her glass down on the table beside her. After a moment's thought she said, "If they were involved again, I shouldn't be at all surprised. The way he used to talk about her . . ."

"No," said Hugh, cutting in.

"But it makes such sense. More sense than his being involved with this bimbo person."

"Kate is not a bimbo," said Hugh with rather more passion than he had intended.

"Whatever — all I'm saying is that what Auntie Ronnie thought she saw might be perfectly true. He might be involved with her."

"Dad is crazy about Kate," said Hugh, getting up and going to the window. He found himself nervously tweaking the coral pink ruffles that trimmed the curtains. "She's not the sort of person you could throw over, anyway. She's . . ."

"Very pretty?" said his mother behind him.

"Yes, as a matter of fact she is, but that's not the point."

"No, with your father I suppose not," she said. "He has such peculiar ideas. Henrietta . . . Good God. I used to be so jealous of her. He used to say that he hated her, but he said it with such passion — I suppose that's the word — that I knew he still cared desperately about her. I don't think he could resist her, even now, even after all this time. If she was around then . . . "

"Well, you haven't met Kate, have you?" said Hugh, turning back to her. "She's a pretty remarkable person."

His mother stared at him and shook her head. "Goodness, how like him you sound sometimes," she said. She reached out and took her empty glass. "Top me up, won't you, darling?" She held it out to him.

Hugh was shovelling ice into her glass when Tony came back into the room.

"Telephone for you, Hugh," he said. "Your father."

Jane giggled "His ears must be

burning," she said.

Hugh took the call in Tony's study, a small, graceless and messy room, lined with law books and smelling of pipe-smoke and dogs. On the floor in the centre of the room lay Kiki, Tony's old and lazy golden retriever, wheezing noisily in her sleep.

"Sorry to interrupt you," said Gabriel. "I tried to get you at home but Lara said you were here."

"That's fine. I was ready for an interruption," said Hugh, sitting down at Tony's desk, which was piled with old copies of the *Daily Telegraph*.

"How are things going?"

"OK."

"I'm sorry to have missed you when you left."

"Me too — but I had to get going and start sorting things out. I was just prevaricating."

"And that's going all right?"

"Yes, I think so. We're being very civilised," said Hugh.

"Good. I'm sorry — I haven't been much use to you about it, have I?"

"It was my problem," he said, "not

yours. How are things with you?"

"Well, that's why I'm ringing. I need a favour."

"Sure."

"The thing is . . . " Hugh heard him sigh and hesitate. "It's like this, er . . . " His voice had almost cracked with apprehension. "I don't quite know how to put this, except very bluntly. The thing is, I've got to go into hospital, and — "

"Hospital?"

"Yes — but don't worry, it's all under control," Gabriel said with such haste that Hugh suspected it was not.

"What's wrong with you?"

"Various things — too complicated for the telephone — but it will all be fine. It's just that we need to sort the admin out, you and I. I need your signature on a few things . . . "

"Oh God . . . "

"No, no, it's purely precautionary, Hugh. I promise you. But one has to be prudent."

"Yes, of course," said Hugh. "So I'll come straight up then, shall I?"

"If you feel you can," he said.

"Of course I can," said Hugh. "Andrew's fine. That's all sorted out — as much as it can be, anyway."

"Good," said his father. "Well, thank you."

"You don't need to thank me," Hugh said. "I'll be there tomorrow afternoon. Where are you? When do you go in?"

"At Allansfield, of course, and I go in on Thursday — into the Nuffield in Edinburgh."

"Right," said Hugh. "I'll see you soon."

★ ★ ★

Hugh reached Allansfield at lunchtime the next day. He had left London shortly after Gabriel's phone call, and had stopped for the night at about eleven at a pub in County Durham. He had not slept much, even though he was exhausted. The thought of his father being seriously ill, of having to face Kate, and memories of what he had done, almost paralysed him with anxiety. He had lain on an uncomfortable single bed under an oppressive sloping roof, the windows wide open, listening to the strange and disturbing creaks of an unfamiliar place, trying so hard to sleep that he seemed to become more and more awake the harder he tried. He had wanted more than sleep; he had wanted oblivion. But he knew he was being a coward. This was a situation he had to face up to. He would have to learn to master his feelings for Kate. He could not run away from her. Perhaps a few hospital-bed vigils would be enough to cure both of them.

As he drove the last few hundred yards up the long driveway to the front of the house, he was working hard to compose himself into a semblance of cheerfulness, despite the tiredness which was making him internally more anxious. He parked, jumped out of the car and ran into the house, determined to present a brave, brisk face. He found Alison putting a large bowl of roses on the table in the living hall.

"You're early!" she said with a smile.

If Alison was smiling, he decided, things had to be all right. "You know how fast I drive," he said.

"Too fast," she said. "Your father's in the wild garden."

He ran up through the gardens, enjoying pushing his body with exercise after being sedentary so long. As he ran, he found he could not remember the gardens ever looking quite so beautiful. It was as if all his father's working and planning over the years had now paid off in this glorious spectacle of flashing colour and texture and scent, which he was running past without taking in any of the details, only the overwhelming effect. He stopped when he got to the gate to the wild garden, wondering if he was being morbid in seeing perfection in it, as if it was in some terrible way a final flowering. That, he knew, was stupid.

The shade of the wild garden trees embraced him and he took the winding path towards the temple glade that was lined with sprawling bushes of brambles and wild roses. He shoved his hands into his pockets and wondered if he would be able to look his father in the eye, let alone Kate.

The clearing with the stone temple opened up before him after a sharp twist in the path, a sudden view that never failed to impress him, even though he knew to expect it. Gabriel had designed the thing so well. The temple — which was in effect an overgrown stone summer house, made elegant with a portico of five slender Ionic columns — lay on the far side of the clearing, cresting a slight hill. In front the turf had been left to grow into a wild flower meadow, and today, in the bright sunshine, it was knee deep with crimson poppies, ox-eye daisies and the pale, silvery green and slender ears of many grasses. It seemed criminal to walk through that, so he kept to the dappled shade in the edge of the clearing, watching with equal care that he did not tread on the little clusters of fraise de bois or the purple heartsease.

As he approached the temple he could see his father, sitting in a deck chair in the honeysuckle-draped portico, his hat tipped over his eyes, almost, it seemed, on the verge of sleep. An abandoned *Financial Times* lay at his feet, and in a basket chair nearby, reading aloud, was none other than Henrietta. Hugh stopped, aware that he had not yet been spotted by them, suddenly wanting just to watch and listen. He could not help remembering what his mother had said.

Henrietta's clear voice drifted over to him: "'Henry Crawford had quite made up his mind by the next morning to give another fortnight to Mansfield, and having sent for his hunters and written a few lines of explanation to the Admiral, he looked round at his sister as he sealed and threw the letter from him, and seeing the coast clear of the rest of the family, said . . . '" Henrietta glanced up and, seeing him, stopped reading. "Oh, but we're not clear of the rest of the family. Hello, Hugh! Why are you skulking there?"

"Hugh?" said Gabriel, sitting up. Hugh emerged from the shadows and came out into the sun and up to the temple. He glanced around, at the remains of the lunch on the table. Only two plates and two glasses, he realised.

"Where's Kate?" he asked.

"Ah," said Gabriel.

"It's time for some horrid explanations, I'm afraid," said Henrietta, pulling a bottle of wine out of the cooler box.

"But I think you need a drink first, Hugh." She handed him the bottle. "I think I should absent myself as well."

Five minutes later, Hugh was sitting on a camp stool with a plate of salad Niçoise on his knees, but he was in such a state of shock that he could not manage to eat, although his stomach was grumbling with hunger.

"This is just all too much for me to take in," he said lamely, putting down the plate.

"Of course it is," said Gabriel, "but I don't know how else we could tell you. The thing you have to remember, to grab on to, which I'm constantly trying to grab on to, is that the prognosis is extremely good."

"But not a hundred per cent?" said Hugh.

"No," said Gabriel, "but I think an eighty per cent chance is pretty good. It takes time to start thinking that is good, I know."

"Does Kate know this?" Hugh found himself asking.

"No, thank goodness," said Gabriel. He looked away from Hugh, towards the meadow full of flowers. "I imagine you must think we're pretty cheap."

"No, no . . . I'm just very surprised," said Hugh. Who was he to say they had behaved cheaply? "Do you know where she is?"

"She's gone to Italy to teach," said Gabriel. "I talked to Liz on the phone the other night. Apparently I'm not to bother her. At least I can do that much for her."

"You shouldn't reproach yourself too much. If she wanted to go, then . . . "

"I don't think I can reproach myself enough, but the circumstances were exceptional," Gabriel said. "I can't excuse what I did, but Henry and I . . . well, it's something very odd, very deep that we could not ignore."

Hugh picked up his plate of salad again and stabbed a few beans with his fork, but he had no inclination to eat. He was thinking suddenly of Lara's accusations about not knowing how to love. How wrong she had been. Now Kate was gone, and it was too bloody late, he knew exactly what it meant to love. His father had just summed up entirely what he felt:

something very odd, very deep, that he could not ignore. The awful thing was that Kate clearly did not feel the same — or if she did, she was determined not to let it get in her way.

As you must not, he told himself. There were far more important things to think about now. His father was going into hospital tomorrow for surgery and chemotherapy. That was the important thing to remember.

"So," he said. "Exactly how much admin are you going to let me take off your hands, Dad? Most of it, I hope."

26

"ND this one ... What's this
one called?" asked Lionel Plantin,
pointing at *The Ghosts of
Allansfield*.

"*Myth*," said Kate. "At least, I think
so."

Lionel Plantin squatted down in front
of the painting to get a better view, his
fingers tucked into the pockets of his
crimson waistcoat.

"This is just terrific," he said.
"Absolutely terrific. You know, Kate,
I could sell this three times over." He
glanced up at her and grinned. "We are
going to do you some deals."

"I don't think," said Kate, "I actually
want to sell that one."

"Kate, Kate ... " Lionel began.

"No. You see, I owe someone a picture
and I think it should be this one. For
various reasons." She was intending to
give it to Gabriel.

"But it's outstanding," said Lionel

Plantin. "You are going to put it in your show in St Andrews, aren't you?"

"Yes, yes, but I won't be taking it to New York."

"Think about it," said Lionel. "I know the perfect couple for this picture. I know a couple with a fabulous house on Long Island who buy only very rarely, but I know this is their sort of picture. You can't be sentimental."

"I promise I won't be," said Kate. "But this one is different, OK?"

"OK," said Lionel, shaking his head and then returning to study the picture. "The figure painting on this . . . your Pan at the front here — well, he's as good as Titian."

"I wouldn't say that," said Kate, amused. She had not yet quite got used to Lionel's extravagant flattery.

"He's so very alive. Very sexy, very beautiful."

"Well, I'm afraid the model's not gay, Lionel," said Kate.

"Shame," said Lionel. "I was going to ask for an intro. Let's have some more coffee."

Kate followed Lionel into the kitchen

area and watched as he showed off with the espresso machine. The large, white minimalist-style flat, in a converted warehouse by the Thames, belonged to an English friend of Lionel's who gave him the use of it and its vital fax machine when he was in London scouring for talent. Kate had met him in Italy, at the castello, where he had been a guest of Rosa Serafini-Brown, and they had got on immediately. He had insisted she come to London on her way back to Scotland to talk about the possibility of going to New York. Rosa had counselled her over a bottle of Chianti one evening that she should not sniff at such an invitation. "Lionel is a power in New York. He knows everyone. All the nouveaus come to him when they want to buy good art. They trust him. If Lionel takes to you, you are made." So, she had decided it was an opportunity she could not ignore, and she had turned up, as instructed, fresh from the Dover ferry that morning, the dust of a European summer still caking the Range Rover. It had been a business getting out all the pictures from the car and into the warehouse lift. She had accumulated quite a few canvases since she left Allansfield. The summer had been more productive than she could have guessed.

"You took your time getting here, you know," he said, handing her a tiny cup of coffee.

"Sorry," said Kate. "I rambled back through France. I couldn't resist it — I've never really travelled alone like that. It was great. I think I've got some good material in my sketch books though, but I'm not quite sure what I'll do with it yet."

"You've got that stuff up here?" he said.

"Of course," she said, and retrieved her latest sketch book from a nest of crumpled shirts in her overnight bag.

"Hey, do you want to do some laundry?" said Lionel. Kate laughed. "Lionel Plantin offers the complete service to the young artist," he said, taking the sketch book. "Espresso and laundry." He flipped open the book. "Oh my God, Kate . . . " He whistled. "Where is this?"

"Oh, that was near Chartres," said

Kate, glancing over his shoulder.

Lionel sat down at the glass-topped table and began slowly to turn the pages of her sketch book. Kate wandered out on to the balcony and gazed at the Thames.

It was the first week in October and the light was soft and grey, the air cool with the suspicion of rain to come. Kate wrapped her arms about her and leant on the metal rails edging the balcony, fascinated by the jumble of new and old buildings in front of her and the turbid steel-and-ochre colour of the great river. Soon it would be three months since she had left Allansfield, but it felt like years. So much had happened. Tuscany had been such an experience. To be thrown like that into the cradle of so many great painters, into a landscape that seemed to have been made for painters. She had gone quite crazy over it, she knew — but how could she be insensible to her first sight of those slender cypresses growing on a hillside? It was as if her northern soul had been dreaming for years of such a landscape. The job had not been arduous, and she felt she had given the students the best of herself, because she was so in love with the idea of painting itself. There had been plenty of time to pursue her own ideas, and she had completed three new large oils for the exhibition, as well as finally finishing *The Ghosts of Allansfield*. She had gone to Florence and developed a passion for Ghirlandaio and Etruscan art; she had got a taste for black olives and espresso, Italian ice cream and grappa; she had met so many interesting people (the clientele for Rosa Serafini-Brown's art holidays was nothing if not eclectic), and had hardly given herself a moment to collect her thoughts until now, standing on this London balcony, looking at the Thames.

The thought that came into her mind was Hugh. She frowned and tried to dismiss it, but the idea would not go away. In her mind's eye she could see her image of him in *The Ghosts of Allansfield*. Irresistibly she turned and wandered back inside to stand in front of the picture. It was a futile gesture to rename it *Myth*, as if that could tame its significance. Suddenly the picture looked like nothing more than a jumbled doodle extracted from her subconscious. The wild garden in its lush detail, the ghostly figures of Gabriel and Hugh's ancestors drifting towards the rising figure of Athena in the centre and then, looking out towards the spectator, the beckoning figure of Pan. She had tried so hard to make him not look like Hugh, but he did all the same.

"Good old Pan," she heard Lionel saying behind her. "Now what is that bit of Milton? 'Universal Pan, Knit with the Graces, and the Hours in dance, Led on the eternal spring.' Impressive, eh?"

"Very," Kate managed to say.

"Let's go to lunch," he said.

"OK," said Kate, and then glanced down at her dirty white jeans. "Are we going anywhere respectable?"

"I thought we'd go to the Pont de la Tour," he said. "It's just down the road, in Butler's Wharf."

"Do you mind if I get changed?" said Kate.

"The bedroom's right through there," said Lionel.

The bedroom was as austerely white as

460

the rest of the flat, and just as impersonal, except for a framed photograph of Lionel's boyfriend in New York, sitting on the bedside table next to a jar of vitamins. She struggled to put together a reasonably smart outfit from the clothes in her holdall — her better clothes were mostly in the suitcase in the car — and she was not entirely satisfied with the result: her old plum-coloured velvet trousers and the beautiful hand-knitted jumper that Gabriel had given her when she moved into Allansfield. Putting it on made her remember that she would have to face him soon and deal with all that unfinished business.

But it was not just Gabriel whom she needed to see and talk to before she went to New York. She sat down on the edge of the bed to lace up her boots, and found herself staring at the London telephone directories, incongruously stacked in a pile on an elegant x-framed stool. Impulsively she reached out and took the A – K residential volume and began to look under E. There were more H. Erskines than she would have imagined — and she realised she did not even know if he had a second name. She had to consult the map of London she had bought on the ferry to track down that Spitalfields was in El, and that the Hugh Erskine she was looking for lived at 7 Bion Street. She was scribbling down the address and telephone number as Lionel tapped on the bedroom door.

"Kate, you ready yet? I'm getting seriously hungry."

"Yes, sure — sorry," said Kate, making for the door, stuffing the scrap of paper into her pocket. "I was just . . ." She stopped short as she looked at Lionel, standing on the threshold, representing all that the future might hold for her. She wondered suddenly why on earth she needed to bother herself about Hugh. Wasn't the thing best left untouched? Why did she feel she had to see him? She could not quite work it out.

Over lunch, in the airy chic of the Pont de la Tour, with a bottle of Sancerre to stimulate him, Lionel bombarded her with plans for her career, all of which she found easy to fall in with. Yet as they talked over the duck breasts with puy lentils of studios and possible patrons, she was conscious all the time that she had not made a complete enough mental break with the past. She wanted to leave with a clean slate, and that was why she must see Hugh, just to make certain that that business in the summer had been nothing more than a fling. For all the time she had been in Italy it had haunted her, his memory rising to her consciousness like a troublesome bubble disrupting the calm surface of her new life. Seeing him would settle the question once and for all.

After the blackcurrant sorbet and more espresso, Lionel asked, "When are you off to Scotland then?"

"Later today, I think," she said. "I told my mother I'd be in Edinburgh tomorrow night. And I have to get the pictures over to St Andrews pretty soon after. It's opening on the twelfth."

"So what will it be this afternoon? A trawl round the galleries? I'm off to the West End for a few appointments. There are some people I could introduce you to this afternoon, actually, who would be very useful."

"I can't. I have to see someone."

"Not another dealer?" said Lionel.

"Of course not," said Kate. "Private stuff, actually. A few little things to sort out before I make the big jump."

★ ★ ★

"Hugh, I really think you should get someone in to clean. This kitchen is . . ." Jane Cherrington looked doubtfully into the empty coffee mugs.

"Well, you can't expect hospital-level hygiene with three guys, Mum," said Hugh.

"You should make them clean their mess up," she said. "You are their landlord."

"It's my mess as much as theirs," said Hugh as he rinsed out the coffee pot. The kitchen at Bion Street was admittedly a wreck, for he had decided against a neat fitted kitchen in favour of a deliberate jumble of junk shop and skip furniture, which one day he intended to tidy up and paint some cheerful colour. It was another job to which he had not yet got around, and his two lodgers — a barrister and a session musician — had

464

with their irregular hours added their own collection of rubbish, mostly in the shape of take-away food cartons, wine bottles and discarded newspapers.

Jane shook her head. "If Andrew was living here you wouldn't let it get into such a state, I trust," she said. "This floor, Hugh . . . " The old pale-pink linoleum was certainly rather grubby.

"Let's go into the sitting room then," he said, steering her towards the door. "It is respectable in there."

"When are they coming, then?" said Jane, sitting down, as Hugh poured the coffee.

"About half-two, Lara said." Lara was bringing Andrew over for the afternoon. They had decided that once a week, Andrew ought to spend some time with both his parents together. Today he would have one of his grandmothers in attendance as well. It was pretend happy families, and Hugh scarcely felt very comfortable with it, but he supposed in the long run it would be reassuring for Andrew.

"Then she won't be here until three at least," said Jane with a sigh. "She's always late. Now, there's a bag in the hall, Hugh. I found a few things upstairs which Andrew might be big enough for soon."

He went and fetched the bag for her. It contained, rather as he had feared, the remnants of his own childhood — little Fair Isle jumpers and a Harris tweed coat with a velvet collar. Lara would be horrified by them. It was going to be an interesting afternoon. Standing with his elbow on the mantelshelf, he watched as his mother, consumed with tranquil nostalgia, sorted through them. It was curious, this new life of his — the way sometimes he was a responsible parent and son, and at other times he was definitely one of the lads, drinking perhaps rather more than he ought. He was aware that he could slip out of control here, although he was as yet still in control, and that if he stopped to think for too long about what his life was really about his anxieties would cease to be a quiet burden and become an obsession. There were too many plates spinning in the air, too many questions that still needed definite answers before he could really relax and enjoy life again. His father's treatment, Andrew's future — and of course Kate.

He turned to look at the ink and watercolour sketch above the mantelpiece. He had stolen it from Allansfield — Kate had left it in the day nursery as if it were a piece of scrap paper. It was too fine a piece for that, and he had had it framed and had hung it up in the sitting room in Bion Street. It showed the garden front of the house, caught in the violent, gloomy light that precedes a spring rainstorm.

His mother looked up and said, "Is that new?"

"Relatively," he said. She got up and came to look at it. "I suppose it is a very pretty house," she said.

"I thought you didn't like it," Hugh said.

"I never felt wanted there," she said, and squinted at the picture. "There's no signature on this. Who did it?"

"Kate," said Hugh.

"I suppose she didn't feel wanted either," said Jane after a moment. "Poor girl. She must have been so upset to find out about La Winthrop." She shook her head. "That business really does defy belief, doesn't it?"

"I'm not sure she knows about it," said Hugh.

"Why else would she leave? I mean, you wouldn't throw all that up without a very good reason."

"Like your reasons?"

"Well, I knew all about Henrietta. Every gory detail. To quote the Princess of Wales, 'There were three of us in the marriage'." Hugh frowned and she went on, "I know, I know, it isn't fair of me to say such things while your father's so ill, but . . . "

"But what?"

"I can't stop myself being angry with him."

"It's such a long time ago, Mum," Hugh said.

"Yes, but I did love him, and it hurt," it hurt terribly to realise that he simply didn't feel the same way about me any more. I suppose it was a blow to my pride, which I can't really forgive him for. But at least she wasn't there, stealing him from behind my back. The poor girl, I can't imagine how she must have felt."

"I don't think she knows," Hugh repeated. "I think that there were other things which made her leave him."

"Oh yes? You sound as if you know all about it," said his mother, sitting down again. She looked at him carefully and then again at Kate's sketch. "Did you get very friendly? I do remember you said you thought she was awfully pretty."

"Well, that means nothing," said Hugh quickly.

"Whatever you say," said Jane, reaching for her coffee cup.

The telephone in the hall began to ring, and Hugh was glad to go and answer it. It was Lara.

"I can't come," she said. "I've got a terrible headache. Come and fetch him. You can keep him tonight. He's really nasty today, but it's Terry's day off, you know."

"Sure, I'll come over straight away."

"Thanks, Hugh, you're my saviour — for once," she said, and put the phone down.

"Who was that?" said Jane.

"Lara," he said. "She's under the weather and it's Terry's day off. She

469

needs to be rescued from Andrew. I'm going to go and fetch him. Do you want to come?"

"No, I'll wait until you get back," she said. "In fact, I shall be a proper mother and clean up your kitchen for you. I don't want my grandson being poisoned by the floor. Do you have such a thing as a pair of rubber gloves, darling?"

27

BION STREET was a quiet backwater near to Spitalfields Church, a row of exquisite eighteenth-century brick houses in different states of distress. As Kate searched for number seven, she heard Indian movie music floating from one window, and admired a real urchin cat sitting on a sunny doorstep. There was a certain urban vibrancy in the air and it struck her as an intriguing place to live. It was a little how she imagined Greenwich Village was going to be.

Number seven was one of the restored houses, its woodwork painted a very correct and historical looking pea-green, but on the door, with its authentic brass door furniture, was a colourful number plaque that had obviously been made by Hugh. For a moment she hesitated, and then she rang the doorbell. It was probably all a wild goose chase. He would probably be at his workshop. She wondered why she had not bothered to look up that address as well.

"Yes?" The woman who opened the door to her gave Kate a start. She recognised her at once from the photograph in the library — it was Jane Cherrington, dressed in an immaculate and brightly coloured Tory-wife suit, as well as, rather surprisingly, a pair of canary-coloured rubber gloves.

"Hello. I wonder, is Hugh around?" Kate managed to say.

"Hugh, no, I'm afraid he isn't," she said, pulling off one of the gloves. She smiled. "Do I know you? Hugh has so many friends, I sometimes lose track . . . "

"No, no, you don't — but I do know you, from your photograph. I'm Kate Mackenzie, you see." She put out her hand tentatively. "You're Mrs Cherrington, aren't you?"

"Oh?" said Jane Cherrington. "Oh, er, yes — I am. Perhaps you'd better come in." She hastily peeled off the other glove. "Hugh will be back quite soon. He's gone to fetch his son, you know."

"Oh, well perhaps you could say I called . . . "

"Come and wait," said Jane. "I insist. We'll have tea."

"Well, if you're sure . . . "

"Absolutely," she said. "Do come in."

Kate followed Jane into the hall, which had been painted an exuberant Pompeian red above the dark oak wainscoting. There were sconces set in the wall, with candles set rather crookedly in them. The atmosphere was robustly Hogarthian.

"Just you wait in here, and I'll fetch us some tea," said Jane, showing her into the sitting room, a large panelled room at the front of the house, furnished somewhat sparsely with a few very solid-looking pieces of eighteenth-century furniture. On an oak settle, that looked like something from an old coaching inn, someone had put a little pile of neatly folded children's clothes. Did that mean that Andrew and Lara were still in occupation? Kate wondered. She looked around for other signs and found herself looking at her own sketch of Allansfield, very sensitively mounted and framed and hanging over the fire. How on earth had

Hugh got hold of that, and why had he hung it in his sitting room? She sat down, feeling an old fog filling her mind.

Jane returned a few minutes later with a tray of tea things. The cups and teapot were recognisably made by Hugh — she had seen another similar set in the kitchen cupboard at Allansfield.

Jane handed her a cup and sat down on the settle, smiling carefully at her. "You must have had such an awful time," she said.

"I'm sorry?"

"This business with Gabriel. I can imagine exactly what you've been through." Kate's confusion must have shown, for Jane said, "Oh, perhaps you don't know after all . . . oh dear."

Kate put down her tea cup on the table and said, "Is there something . . . What don't I know?"

"I think I've just been terribly indiscreet," said Jane. "You see, I assumed that was why you'd left Gabriel — because of Henrietta."

"Henrietta?"

Jane nodded rather portentously, prompting Kate to go on, "Henrietta's just a friend — she wasn't always, I know, but that's ancient history. Surely you don't think . . . no . . . "

Jane closed her eyes and sighed slightly. "We have been unlucky, you and I," she said. "Gabriel is a duplicitous person. I suspect he's been lying to you all along. Henrietta, you see, is — "

"Please, could you just tell me what has happened?"

"Well, she's moved in, hasn't she? You left and in she went, apparently." Jane shook her head. "And he never had the good manners to tell you?"

"Oh," said Kate. She had not meant to sound so surprised, but she could not help herself. "Are you sure?"

"Yes, of course. Hugh told me," she said. "She's been quite the angel of mercy, apparently, always being in the way at the hospital, I suspect, when Hugh wants to be with his father. Of course, Hugh hasn't said that in so many words, but really one can easily imagine what it's like — "

"Hospital?"

"Oh goodness, you don't know about that either, do you?" Kate had no words left, and Jane cheerfully filled the silence. "It's a dreadful thing, of course. Poor Hugh's been worried sick. It's a terrible thing to happen to anyone — cancer."

Kate closed her eyes for a moment, finding she was gripping the arms of the chair. "Cancer?" she managed to say. "Gabriel's got cancer? Oh my God . . . is he going to be OK?"

"I'm sorry," said Jane, getting up. "I really am so sorry. My husband does say I'm a terrible blabbermouth. I thought . . . Oh, but I don't think, do I? I am sorry, Kate. This is an awful thing for you to hear. Perhaps you'd like a little brandy or something?"

Kate clenched her fingers into a fist and pressed it to her mouth. She felt near to tears. "No, tea is fine, really," she said, mastering herself.

"I think you should have a brandy," said Jane, leaving the room.

Kate stared at the ceiling, choking back her tears, feeling a frightening cocktail of emotion rising up inside her. Was Henrietta the reason it had all fallen apart between her and Gabriel? Had Henrietta pulled him away from her,

476

made him seem so distant, so different? He had been different. Had she got the diagnosis wrong? Did she still love him after all — and was that why hearing that he was ill made her feel so frightened? All the certainties had crumbled in an instant. She found she was wiping away a tear as Jane returned with two glasses of brandy.

"I think you should have a jolly good cry," said Jane. "That's what I always tell my girls."

"I'll be all right in a minute."

"I know exactly what you're thinking," said Jane. "How could he do it? It does seem extraordinary, doesn't it? You're so young and pretty; why would he want Henrietta rather than you? She's older than him, you know. I found it very hard to accept. How much harder it must be for you."

Kate took a sip of the brandy and shook her head. With some effort, she began to organise her thoughts again. "I'm just surprised at the news, that's all. I left Gabriel because . . ."

"Because?" Jane prompted. Kate hesitated. What business of Jane's was it? And yet she decided that if she said it aloud it would help convince her again.

"I saw we had no future. I knew I wasn't sufficiently committed. I wanted a different sort of life."

"But you didn't feel committed because he wasn't," said Jane. "That's what happened to us. He might have stood up in St Giles' Cathedral on our wedding day and promised to love me for the rest of his life, but he was not telling the truth."

"He asked me to marry him, but I wouldn't," she said. "I couldn't. I didn't want him enough. It isn't the same, I don't think."

"Hugh did say that he thought you left for other reasons," said Jane, after a pause. "He obviously knows you quite well." She gave a slight smile, and then said, with a touch of suspicion in her voice, "This is a social call, I take it? Or were you thinking of using him as a go-between to settle things with his father? I should warn you, he's very partisan."

"I was just passing through; I thought I'd look him up," said Kate, as innocuously as she could.

478

"Did you?" said Jane. "That's very sweet of you."

"He's had a rough time," Kate said lamely.

"Yes," said Jane. "He's very bruised at the moment, and in what you might call a dangerous condition. I'm sure neither of us would like him to get hurt again, would we?" Jane thought for a moment and then added, "You know, he doesn't just look like his father, does he? They're quite alike in other ways."

"I'm sorry?" said Kate.

"I know he thinks a great deal of you," said Jane. "Perhaps it isn't my place to say this, but you should both be careful. I can't help thinking that you might have come here for some other reason than being merely friendly . . . "

"I came to tell Hugh I'm going to New York, actually," said Kate. "Does that put your mind at rest, Mrs Cherrington?" She got up from her seat. "And I really must get on now. I have to drive back to Edinburgh. Thank you for the tea."

★ ★ ★

Hugh got back to Bion Street, after a fraught drive across London, with Andrew in a particularly fractious mood. He found his mother sitting in a now clean and tidy kitchen, doing the crossword in last Sunday's *Observer*. As they came in, she stretched her arms to take Andrew.

"Hello, my lovely boy," she said, kissing him.

"He's been an absolute little rat," said Hugh, reaching into the fridge for a beer.

"Oh, I don't think so," said Jane, jigging a now angelic Andrew on her knee. Hugh growled at him, and Andrew giggled delightedly.

"I have no authority," Hugh said, and sat down at the kitchen table.

"Was the traffic awful?" she said. "You were quite a long time."

"Worse than awful," he said. "Anyway, thanks for doing all this, it looks almost unrecognisable."

"Well I shan't make a habit of it," she said, as Hugh flipped the lid off his beer bottle. "Oh, must you drink out of the bottle? And do I get a drink?"

"I was just about to do yours," said Hugh, getting up again, hoping that there was still some gin left.

"Jolly good," she said. "Actually, I had quite an interesting afternoon, your revolting kitchen apart. You had a visitor."

"Oh? Who?" he said, pouring out the requisite two fingers of gin.

"Kate Mackenzie," said Jane. Hugh turned to look at her, startled by the way she had said it. "Yes, isn't that interesting?"

"Is it?" he said, offhandedly, as he fetched the ice-cube tray out of the freezer.

"Perhaps you should tell me," said Jane. "I mean, I wonder why she came. She said she was just passing through, but you know I don't think it was just a social call."

"We got on well, that's all," he said, popping the ice out on to the draining board. "We have a lot in common — workwise, I mean."

"Really?" Jane said. "Are you sure, Hugh? I can't help thinking . . . "

"Well don't think, Mum, please," he

said, putting the glass of gin and the tonic bottle down in front of her.

"So, you do like her?" Jane said, releasing Andrew, who went running to the toy box in the corner of the kitchen.

"Mum, I don't want to discuss it," Hugh said firmly.

"Ah, I was right!" said Jane, and clapped her hands together in triumph. "Well, it's a jolly good thing she's going to New York. You shouldn't be getting involved with anyone just now, let alone your father's cast-offs."

"She's going to New York?"

"Mm, apparently," said Jane and looked at him. "Oh, Hugh . . . you haven't, have you?"

"Mum . . . "

"I don't think she's a good idea," said Jane. "I mean, she can't exactly be the world's most reliable person to go running off from Allansfield like that."

"You are so inconsistent," said Hugh. "Earlier today you thought Kate was a poor pitiable victim, and now — "

"Well, I hadn't met her then, and I hadn't realised why she'd left. She told me it was because she didn't feel committed enough to stay. She strikes me as a trifle fickle."

"You know nothing about her, Mother," said Hugh. "Absolutely nothing."

"I know she's very pretty and that you rather like her," said Jane. "I think that's quite enough for me to worry about. We don't want another Lara scenario, do we?"

"It's nothing like that. You're being so simplistic. Kate is nothing like Lara. Kate is . . . " He stopped, realising the passion in his voice had given far too much away. He reached out for his bottle of beer, shouting the rest of his sentence in his mind: Kate is intelligent, Kate is fun, Kate is an artist, Kate is passionate, Kate is, in short, everything I ever wanted in a woman. He took a deep breath and said, with more care, "Kate is an academic question. She's going to New York, OK, Mum? Subject closed."

"I hope so," said Jane, and looked at him hard for a minute. Hugh, with annoyance, realised she always knew when he was lying.

28

GABRIEL had been on the verge of falling asleep when the telephone rang. He was glad to be woken up. His body's refusal to function properly still irritated him profoundly, a state of affairs that four courses of combined chemotherapy, with all the attendant horrors, had only compounded. Falling asleep in the middle of the morning was such an annoying waste of time; he could bear it while he was in the clinic, when there was really nothing else to do, but here, at Allansfield, during his so-called recovery period, when he wanted to maintain at least a semblance of normal life, it was frustrating.

He reached out for the phone.

"Darling, it's me," said Henrietta. "How are you doing?"

"Trying to do a bit of paperwork actually."

"Same here," she said, "and failing."

"Same here," he said and heard her laugh.

"Do you think you are up to going tonight? You sound a little groggy."

"I always sound groggy now," said Gabriel. "And of course I'm up to it."

"But . . . "

"What an old woman you are sometimes, Henry," he said, smiling. "I think I know whether I can manage tonight. My brain hasn't rotted yet — or has it? You're probably the better judge of that."

"No, unfortunately not. You'd be easier to manage then, wouldn't you?"

"But you'd hate that. There'd be no pleasure in exercising your authority over a vegetable."

"John Hepburn might like it," she said. "After that last earful you gave him."

"You were as bad," he said. They had had quite a few scenes with the specialist, whose bedside manner and complete lack of humour had contrived to rub them both up the wrong way.

"He'll be charging us danger money next," she said. "Poor man."

"I've sent him a case of claret actually," said Gabriel.

"What? You creep," she laughed. "You darling, charming creep. Oh, I have to go — there's someone knocking at my door. I'll be back after lunch — and make sure you eat it, OK?"

"OK," he said, and put down the telephone. He heaved himself out of his chair and decided he would go for a prowl round the garden. He was supposed to be taking gentle exercise, after all.

It was one of those mild, damp, inviting autumn days, with the sun lying low across the landscape like a caressing hand. He went out on to the terrace through the glazed door and stood for a moment, crinkling up his eyes against the sun, wondering whether he needed to fetch a coat. He decided he would not. It was good to be cool for once. The tropical temperature at the clinic had only added another discomfort to an already long list.

He sighed, remembering it would be back to that routine next week; another dose of noxious chemicals being dripped into his bloodstream, doing, it seemed half the time, far more harm than good. And next week he would not have Henrietta there all the time to see him through the worst of it: no Henrietta to make the black jokes that made it bearable when he vomited yet again, or to read Jane Austen aloud to him when he was simply too tired to do anything but lie on his bed. It had taken some persuasion on his part to convince her that he would manage without her (especially as he was secretly not at all convinced of it himself), and that she must give her teaching priority now that the term had started again. She needed to be back at that particular helm. She was not made for nursemaiding him, and he hated to think that he had forced her into it, this endless, loving and fastidious care which she had given him, and for which he did not know how he could recompense her. He could only begin by insisting she worked.

He walked along the spectacular autumnal decay of the long herbaceous border and opened the gate to the wild garden, wondering what Kate's exhibition would be like. Disturbingly accomplished, he imagined. As he looked at the *Fallen Athena*, lying in her glade, with soggy golden leaves stuck to her grey granite robes, he knew he wanted to see her again and make a proper apology. He wanted to sort this wretched business out, as far as it could be sorted out, and he wanted simply to see her again. He had missed her. It was that simple.

It was not that he loved her the way he loved Henrietta. Nor did he feel any lingering passion for her youth and undeniable beauty. Those feelings had disappeared as quickly as they had come. His ego had given in to the terrible temptation of something so young and fresh, and it had tricked him into believing that he loved her in the way a man should love the woman he lived with. He had been drinking then from a drugged fountain of illusions. There had not been the right stuff there to make a partnership between them; he had not had that sort of love to give her — *that* had been locked up with Henrietta's name on it all those years. Yet he did feel for her strongly still, with a feeling that was stronger than friendship. Perhaps it was a more perfect form of friendship, a refinement of affection entirely independent of sexual feeling, that made him feel that Kate was still an indissoluble part of his life, as much as Henrietta was. He wanted to see her that night, and wanted her to forgive him, not just for the sake of a quiet conscience, but so that they could go on as friends.

★ ★ ★

As the day passed the weather turned bad, and St Andrews was caught in the grip of a violent autumn gale. The wind was like a fierce, unpredictable animal, constantly changing direction, leaping forward for a savage attack and then retreating into its lair for a few minutes, before jumping out again to bewilder from another unexpected angle. Now it was throwing the rain against the window of Kate's hotel room, as it charged in from the black shoreline in the distance. Kate stood, looking out at the dark turbulence. She had been in the act of drawing the curtains, but the strength of the maelstrom had caught her, and she pressed her palms to the window pane, enjoying the coolness of the glass after the almost tropical heat of the hotel room.

But you can stare as long as you like, she thought, and it still won't make any sense. She turned and looked critically at the room, which had been booked by and would be paid for by Lionel. It was one of those luxurious places that aimed at a so-called country-house style, with all the falseness that entailed. The room disturbed her. All those expensive details — the immense glazed chintz curtains that decorated both the bed and the windows with over-exuberant ruffles and bows; the solid reproduction furniture that did not quite succeed in convincing; the stilted arrangement of flowers on top of the vast television set; and the inevitable and absurd chocolate on the pillow — filled her with a sort of creeping despair. She felt like throwing up the window and howling. Instead she sat down on the bed and ate the complimentary chocolate.

There was a knock on the door.

"It's me, Kate," she heard Lionel saying.

"Oh, come in, it's open," said Kate.

Lionel, resplendent in a primrose damask waistcoat under his chalk-striped suit, came in.

"You should be dressed," he said. "You'll be late." Kate, who was still wearing her dressing gown, gave a slight grimace. "Are you nervous?"

"Why do I need to be there?" she said. "It's my pictures they're going to see, not me. It's not performance art."

"It's networking. The press will be there." He sat down in the armchair. "I've seen this before. You can call it what you like: shyness, false modesty, downright cowardice . . . "

"Oh, I know, I should relish the moment, shouldn't I? And normally I would, it's just there's — "

"You're not as bullish as you were in London, Kate," said Lionel. "Has something happened?"

"Nothing really . . . " said Kate. "I suppose I'm just being very unprofessional and letting my personal life get in the way of things."

"You want to talk about it?"

"Are you a therapist as well as a dealer?"

"Well, I don't mean to sound mercenary, but your state of mind is one of my professional concerns. I need you firing on all cylinders for my investment in you to pay off."

"Yes, of course you do. I'm sorry. I'll be ready soon."

"Do you want to talk about it first?"

"No, it's all right, really."

"OK, whatever you say," he said, going to the door. "Chop-chop then, Kate. It's showtime!"

Showtime, thought Kate, going into the bathroom. She took out the scarlet lipstick she had worn at the ball in June. She needed some more war-paint. Ever since Jane Cherrington had dropped that startling news into her lap, Kate felt like a child riding a bike without the stabilisers for the first time. Any certainty she had constructed for herself had suddenly gone. She would not have predicted that the news would have rocked her so. She ought to feel merely sympathetic that Gabriel was ill, not plain scared that he was going to die. She ought, quite rightly, to be extremely annoyed to discover that he had been playing some game behind her back with Henrietta, but that should not have made her doubt her own decisions. She had been so sure she had everything sorted out and was ready to move on with her life. It had been all fixed — except for Hugh of course — but in trying to get herself over that stumbling block she had simply uncovered all the rest.

With a bit of luck, she told herself as she got dressed, Gabriel would not be there tonight. He was probably too ill for such jaunts, although she had seen his name, along with Henrietta's, on Eleanor McCleod's guest list for the private view. Hugh's name had also been on the list, for some strange reason, but it was highly unlikely he would be there. At least she would not have to deal with that as well. Again, she found herself asking why she had gone to Bion Street. Of all the questions that were plaguing her, it was that one she had the least idea how to answer.

Hugh arrived in St Andrews and parked in North Street. He sat for a few minutes in the car, stunned with tiredness after the long drive to Scotland.

When the invitation to Kate's private view had arrived, he had filed it at once in the waste-paper basket in his bedroom at Bion Street. It had felt like a cruel joke, but he supposed Henrietta had added his name to the list without any malicious intentions. When, after his mother had left and he had taken Andrew upstairs to sleep, he had retrieved it, he had sat staring at the coloured reproduction of *Triptych*, wondering what to do. That she had come to see him was surely significant, but if she was going to New York, then what was the point of reading anything significant into it? But why had she come then? By the time Andrew had dropped off to sleep, he had decided he would go to the private view and ask her exactly why.

It had been too late to stop off at Allansfield — he would go there later — and so he dragged himself out of the car and dived into a pub for a beer and a sandwich, resisting the temptation to have a whisky for Dutch courage. He tried to rehearse what he wanted to say to her, but he was never entirely convinced by his arguments. He would just have to try and do his best. He knew what he wanted depended entirely on her. Clever advocacy was not going to make any difference if she felt nothing.

There was already quite a crowd at the private view, but neither Kate nor his father nor Henrietta was there yet. He was glad. He wanted a chance to take in her pictures first.

It was not a large exhibition space, and such a mass of her work hung quite closely together created a powerful effect. It was like walking into a highly decorated medieval chapel, with dazzling, saturated colour on all sides, burning as brightly under the artificial light as if the surfaces were covered with lustre glazes. It only needed a pattern of angels and clouds spiralling up and up towards a patch of blue sky to be painted on the ceiling to complete the illusion. Hugh was certain she would have been capable of such a magnificent piece of *trompe-l'oeil*, but glad as well she had not done it. This was overwhelming enough, with colour and form coming from all sides, attacking the eyes, like the trumpet bursts and soaring voices of Monteverdi.

It was not a chapel of course, but a distinctly pagan temple, he realised, as he looked more closely at what each scintillating image represented. Even Adam and Eve in *Eden* had shrugged off any biblical restraint, and stood, confident in their sexual potency, their flesh almost vibrating with life. He found he could hardly bear to look at Eve, it was so clearly a self portrait, and yet he stood there, transfixed by it, feeling any hope of curing his obsession crumbling away the longer he looked at it. It had been hopeless to think he could stop loving her. He managed to turn away at last, to find himself looking at the large canvas she had been working on so diligently in the studio. Then she had called it *The Ghosts of Allansfield*, but according to the catalogue it was now called *Myth*. It was as strange and as troubling as its new name implied; a green and grey composition, with rampant vegetation, full of furtive shadows that seemed more sinister than the various garden spirits who were running across the landscape towards the statue of the great breasted goddess who was heaving herself upright.

"Hugh!" He heard Henrietta's voice behind him. "What are you doing here?"

"I was invited," he said, turning to see her standing with his father. "How are you doing, Dad?"

"Fair to moderate," he said. "Good to see you, though," he added with a smile, and then caught sight of *Myth* over Hugh's shoulder. "Oh, good grief . . . " he murmured. He sat down and looked intently at it for some minutes.

"What an amazing picture this is," he said at last to Hugh. "She's quite surpassed herself with it. To have caught that atmosphere. I've felt it so often myself, but . . . there it all is . . . I can't say in black and white, can I?"

"In glorious Technicolor," said Henrietta.

Hugh turned away from the picture and watched as Henrietta began a tour of the room. She was wearing a rather dramatic long velvet coat the colour of an aubergine and matching trousers, her glasses perched half-way down her nose as ever, and speaking to the other guests. Her voice was rising above the hum of the crowd with its usual clarity.

"No, I'm afraid she's not here just yet, but I promise I'll introduce you the moment she gets here. I'm sure she'll be so interested to meet you."

His father must have heard her too, for he remarked to Hugh, with a smile, "There's some serious networking going on here. That's the critic from the *Financial Times*, I think."

"Great stuff."

"Reparation," said Gabriel. He shook his head slightly, and then returned his gaze to *Myth*. "This painting is quite extraordinary. It's as if she's always known us, that's she's always been one of us. This picture *is* Allansfield, isn't it?" he added, as he peered at the detail in the corner, where she had painted the Allansfield cats lying asleep in a patch of sunlight.

Hugh turned slightly and saw from the

corner of his eye that Kate had walked into the gallery.

★ ★ ★

For a moment, Kate stood on the threshold, a little astonished by the crowd in the gallery. It was hard to believe that so many people had come to look at her pictures.

"Listen to that buzz," said Lionel behind her.

"Great," she said, forcing herself to smile.

"In you go, then," he said, and gently put his hands on her shoulders, propelling her further into the room. She wondered what everyone was saying about the pictures. Was the hum of talk appreciative?

She glanced back at Lionel, who gave her a reassuring smile, and then she looked about again.

"I can't believe how many people there are," she said, and then realised how glad she was of the crowd. She knew that Henrietta and Gabriel were bound to be in there somewhere, but now she was hidden from them by a protective veil of human flesh.

"Ah, at last!" It was Eleanor McCleod.

Kate turned to her with a grin. "This is an amazing turn-out," she said.

"Henrietta's doing," said Eleanor. "It's a wonderful puff for the Centre, though. Now, I've the Principal of the university over yonder who wants to meet you."

"OK, then!" said Kate, feeling a sort of surging relief. At this rate she would be too busy to think about anything but her professional progress, and that was the way she wanted it to be.

But then, as Eleanor was taking her to meet the Principal of the university, the crowd readjusted itself and she saw Gabriel standing by *Myth*. For a moment, in fact, she actually thought it was not Gabriel she was seeing, he looked so different. She felt her insides knotting up. He had lost quite a bit of weight, and his hair seemed to have thinned out drastically. He looked about ten years older. He was dressed in a heavy tweed overcoat, with a thick roll-necked Aran sweater underneath, as if it were a night in the depths of winter. He was not looking at her, but at the picture, absorbed in it, looking with the same concentration as he had looked at her pictures in the Manzoni gallery.

And there, standing beside him, to her surprise, she saw Hugh. He was looking not at the picture but straight at her. She realised she had been deliberately blotting him out of her sight, as she had fixed her attention on Gabriel. Now their eyes met for a second and he looked quickly away, towards the picture. She had not seen his face long enough to read anything in its expression. All she could see now was a pair of Erskine profiles, very obviously a father and son, looking at her pictures about them: the profiles of two men who were so very different and yet so alike.

Then, Henrietta interposed herself between Hugh and Gabriel and threw her arm affectionately around Gabriel's shoulder. Kate had a powerful impression, as she looked from one to the other, that these two people had no secrets from one another, that they were not really, in fact, separate people at all, but two halves making up a whole. She had never loved Gabriel like that, she realised. She had been right to leave, and she felt a sense of extraordinary relief. She had not left because she had sensed his betrayal, but because she needed to leave for her own reasons. What she felt for Gabriel was profound affection, and it was that that had made her so afraid about his health. But it had not been love, she knew in that moment.

She looked back at Hugh then, and slowly he turned and returned her gaze, wearing almost exactly the same expression as her Pan. She felt her throat going dry as his eyes rested on her, and she felt her own desire crackling along her nerves like a flame on a fuse. She knew then why she had felt the need to go and see him in London.

"Now Principal, here she is," Professor McCleod was saying, and Kate swiftly had to gather her thoughts and turn to present a charming smile to him. "Kate, may I introduce . . . ?"

Kate hardly said a word, which scarcely mattered, for the Principal was cheerfully verbose. She found she was standing with a daft smile on her face as he talked at her, feeling at last an extraordinary sense of clarity in her mind. It was Hugh. It was Hugh, of course . . . That one nagging doubt was suddenly not a doubt but a glorious certainty. Why else had she not been able to forget him? Why else had his memory tugged always at her sleeve like an annoying child? Because she was in love with him.

The Principal had moved on and she was alone for a moment, relishing her discovery, when a voice behind her said, "Kate."

She turned and smiled. "Gabriel . . ."

"Hello there . . ." He was sitting down, and instinctively she sat down beside him. He stretched out his hands to greet her, smiling in that wonderful way that had first drawn her to him, so that his face crumpled up, showing all its crags and character. She took both his hands, but in a moment she was in his arms, holding him close, feeling his arms lock around her. Then they broke away, but he kept hold of her hand. "How's it going? Henrietta and Eleanor *are* making you work hard."

"Yes," she smiled. "I can't remember half their names."

"That doesn't matter. What matters is that they remember you."

"What matters is that they remember my pictures."

"Of course," he said, releasing her hand. He glanced around him, at the pictures. "And they will, I'm sure."

"How are you?" she asked tentatively. "I heard that — "

"Much better, thank you. And you?"

"You ask me that, after what you've been through? I've just been swanning around in Italy, haven't I?"

"Yes, but physical discomfort is not quite the same as emotional discomfort, is it? I think I caused you a lot of that, and — "

"There's no need to say anything," she said. "It wasn't working, that's all. You didn't do anything particularly heinous. You just love Henrietta, that's all . . . "

"But I gave you a right to expect — "

She shook her head. "Let's forget all that, please."

"All right," he said, with a slight smile. "If you like. Then may I dare ask you for lunch tomorrow?"

"Lunch? Sure," she said, getting up.

"I have to give you back the car, after all."

"You'll do no such thing," said Gabriel, getting up also. "About twelve, then? Hugh's here, you know." He glanced around. "Well, he was here . . ."

"I think," said Kate, getting up, "I had better go and find him."

29

WHY did they have to meet in such circumstances? Hugh had asked himself, as he had watched Kate shaking hands and smiling. Why could she not have been the one stranded in that house in the Dordogne instead of Lara? He tried to imagine what it might have been like to fall in love with her in a straightforward, uncomplicated way. He tried to picture himself being introduced to her at a party, shaking her hand and asking those banal but necessary questions that begin an acquaintance. How would the spark have been lit then? He wondered at what moment would he have decided he rather liked her? Would he have felt anything, in fact?

He knew he had asked this last question as a sort of test for himself. He knew without asking it that he would have been attracted to her in a deep, serious way that was not at all like the idle lusting he had felt for Lara on the one or two occasions he had met her before that holiday in France. The circumstances had nothing to do with it. He knew then, as he surreptitiously watched as she, with animated gestures, explained one of the pictures to someone, he would have fallen in love with her whatever the circumstances. He was in love with her then, after all. Three months away, and he felt nothing had changed. The feeling was as fresh as if it had only just occurred to him; it was, in fact, rather more intense and convincing than any of those previous feelings. The evidence of Kate in person, standing only ten or twelve feet away from him, was more than enough to demonstrate to him what he already knew. He could feel his heart pounding, his stomach churning and his nerves throbbing with a mixture of joy and despair. It was a horrible feeling, but he knew his state was incurable. He glanced at his father, who was talking to Bob, and wondered how he had managed all those years to survive, knowing that what he really loved was inaccessible. He wondered too how Gabriel had managed to forgive Henrietta for choosing her career rather than him; and then, seeing Kate again, hearing her laugh, he knew he could forgive her for anything. He knew he would have to learn to forgive her, because she was not going to stay with him. He was certain of it. The very air in the room seemed to reverberate with her triumph, and he knew he had no right even to ask her to stay with him when the whole world was there for her to take. He decided it would be better to get out of there and start studying resignation.

He got as far as the hallway and found himself dithering. Then the door to the gallery swung open, bringing with it the noise of animated chatter and Kate.

★ ★ ★

"Oh, I was just coming to look for you," Kate said, startled to come face to face with him so soon. He looked equally startled, like a rabbit caught in the headlights.

"Oh, right," he said. "Well, here I am."

"Yes," she said.

"Going well in there, is it?"

"Very well, I think, unless everyone's just being polite."

"I don't think so. It's good stuff."

"Thanks," she said, and then they both began to speak at once. "No, you first," Kate said.

"After you . . . "

"All right," she said, laughing nervously. "I was just going to say I was sorry I missed you the other day. What were you going to say?"

"Oh, that I hear you're off to New York." She nodded. "That's great. It's an amazing place. I went once with a friend, three or four years ago. You will love the Met, you know."

"I intend to live there," she said with a smile.

"They'll name a wing after you, probably," said Hugh, thrusting his hands into his pockets. "So, you're excited about that?"

"Of course."

"Good. Good." He glanced across at her. "I hear you met my mother."

"Certainly did."

"Well, her middle name is tactless,"

said Hugh. "Sorry about all that."

"It doesn't matter," said Kate, and then, suddenly exasperated, said, "Hugh, why are we talking like this? Don't you think we should talk properly? About what happened, about — "

"I don't quite see the point of that," he cut in crisply. With a nonchalance that was clearly false, he strolled away from her and looked down at the black and white chequer board of tiles on the floor.

"Hugh . . . " she began.

"Well, you are going to New York, aren't you?"

"It isn't Mars," she pointed out.

"Still," he said. "The thing is, you've got the world to conquer, haven't you? I mean, all those people in there — that's serious stuff, Kate. You are going to be someone."

"Hugh, what are you talking about?" she said, taking a step closer to him. He retreated slightly. "Are you saying what I think you're saying?"

"What I'm saying is: Go, do it!" And he gestured with his large white hands, as if he were trying to shoo away a troublesome goose.

"I will," she said. "Please don't worry about that. I don't need your blessing, do I? I mean, why would I?"

"Kate!" he exclaimed. "This is hard enough as it is. Will you just leave it?"

"No," she said. "Not until you tell me what's so hard. You didn't need to come all the way up here for this, did you? Why exactly are you here, Hugh, if it isn't because . . . "

"No," he said, shaking his head. "Look, Kate, I just want to do the right thing."

"Well, you might ask me first," she said. "I think that's pretty arrogant actually."

"It isn't supposed to be arrogant," he said. "I don't want to put you in a difficult position. Oh God, Kate, when I look at Dad and Henrietta, and what they went through, you know it strikes me as quite ridiculous that we should allow things to go that far and then have to stop because one of us — "

"You mean me," said Kate.

"Yes," he admitted. "I don't want to say anything that's going to get in the way of you doing what you have to do. Your work, Kate, it's wonderful, and you deserve all the glory you can get. I can't stand in the way of that, no matter what I feel."

"For someone who is trying not to say what he feels," said Kate, gently, "that was quite an admission."

"Well," he said, after a pause, "I do love you. There's no doubt about that, but I don't want to force you into anything."

"Oh Hugh, you . . . " Kate said, reaching out to stroke his cheek. She saw him close his eyes and shake slightly as her finger touched his chin. "You idiot. Why do you think I came to see you in Bion Street? Why?"

He opened his eyes and caught her hand in his. "Because every morning, like me, you've been waking up and thinking?" he said carefully.

"And thinking, yes . . . " she said, and stretched out to kiss him on the lips. "Thinking of us."

★ ★ ★

"I'm afraid I've eaten the complimentary chocolate," said Kate, unlocking the door to her hotel room.

"Well, in that case . . . " said Hugh, pretending to start off down the passageway. Kate switched on the light, and he gazed at the room. "Goodness . . . "

"I warned you it was pretty bizarre," said Kate. "Pseudo Allansfield."

"It's too warm for that," said Hugh, and went across to push up the sash window, promptly letting in a violent gust of cold air. "That's better. Still, it's a nice big bed . . . "

"Is that all you've been thinking about?" said Kate, with conscious archness.

"Well, just about . . . " he began. "No, it wasn't just sex. It was like you were in my bloodstream."

"Or an ineradicable stain?" said Kate. "That's what I kept thinking. No matter how many times it went through the wash, it was always there."

"Oh, that's charming, isn't it?" said Hugh, striding over to her and catching her in his arms. "A stain on your favourite shirt, eh?"

"A very nice stain," Kate said, giggling, and only pretending to resist. "A stain from a very good bottle of wine, that I wouldn't want to wash out ever."

"I'm glad to hear it," he said, and kissed her, and then manoeuvred so she fell back on to the bed with him on top of her. He looked down at her for a moment and then, shaking his head, he let go of her. He rolled on to his back beside her. "Oh God . . . "

"What is it?" said Kate.

"Nerves," he said, breathing hard.

"Oh," said Kate, sitting up again.

"I don't want to cock this one up, Kate," he said. "I've messed up before, remember, in a big way, and I can't bear the thought it might happen again. I don't want to hurt you. Can we be sure this will work? I mean . . . "

"No," said Kate. "To be honest, we can't. But we have to take a calculated risk."

"What do you mean?" said Hugh.

"Well," said Kate, getting up from the bed and walking across the room. "To me, this feels like when I'm starting a new picture. I have a rough idea where

I'd like to go, but there's always this fear that I won't get there, that something quite different will happen, that nothing will work out as I wanted it to. And often it doesn't, very often, but that doesn't mean to say it's a bad picture if it doesn't work out the way I wanted. Sometimes it's actually better, because you've let something more anarchic in, something from deep inside you that you didn't consciously want to express, something more authentic . . . " She smiled. "Am I making any sense?"

"I think so," said Hugh, but he looked pretty puzzled.

"Of course you're afraid of failing. So am I. We all are," she said, putting her hands on his shoulders.

"I suppose it's a national characteristic," said Hugh with a sigh. "We've all been trained not to be arrogant, and we'll only attempt what we feel we can reasonably achieve, in case we're accused of being over-ambitious."

"But that's the worst possible thing for anyone who's trying to do something creative, isn't it?" said Kate. "And being in love is creative, isn't it?" She pressed her forehead to his. "The thing is, I think," she went on, "that in my work I like to take risks. I'd hate anyone to think my work was safe — and I think I'm the same in life." She looked into his eyes for a moment and pushed him gently back on to the bed.

"You terrify me," he said.

"Good," she said, and kissed him. As she did, she found herself thinking of *Eden*, realising, perhaps consciously for the first time, that the picture was about the power of her own desires, the desires that hurt her and yet which found something in her that she would not have given up for the world. Yes, objectively it was wrong for Eve to eat the apple, to give in to the temptations of love — it had caused the exile from Eden, but whoever said that Eden was really paradise? What was paradise after all? Was it really paradise to be so in control of your life that there was no sharp edge of fear, of self-illuminating fear, left? She began to undo the buttons of his shirt, and to kiss the warm bare flesh of his chest.

"The trouble is, Hugh," she said softly,

"this isn't about thinking. We've both been thinking too much." Stretching out beside him, she laid her head on his chest and listened to the pounding of his heart. "Just don't think. Just let go . . . "

"Aah," he said, and he shook with laughter suddenly. "I know what you mean. At least, I think I do. I get this with my pots sometimes. If I'm trying to make a new shape, I find I think and think about it. I usually try sketching them out on paper and it never works. Never. Nothing comes — or what comes is lifeless, dead. But I get a lump of clay on that wheel, and get my hands on the clay and . . . it works. Is that what you mean?"

She laughed. "That's exactly what I mean!"

"Right!" he said, and rolled her on to her back, straddling her. He was bending towards her to kiss her, but she pushed him back a little.

"But I can't promise anything," she said. "I don't know what will happen . . . whether this will work or not."

"Neither do I," he said, looking down intensely at her. "But do you want to

517

know? What would there be to surprise us then? Eh, Kate?" And he pressed his cheek to hers and whispered, "Nothing, nothing at all!"

* * *

"Kate, are you asleep?" she heard him say.

"Not quite," she said.

"I was just wondering, have you ever wanted to go to India?"

"India? What made you think of India?"

"Just somewhere I've always wanted to go. I was just thinking, perhaps we could, one day."

"Sure — though we should wait until Andrew's a little older," said Kate. "That would be some place to take a child, eh?"

"Yes, much better than Disneyland," said Hugh, and shook with laughter. "Oh God, what an incredible thought — you, me and Andrew in India. I can't wait." His arms tightened around her. "You're sure you don't mind about Andrew?"

"If you don't mind me bombing off

for months at a time because of my work . . . "

"Well, it will be tough, but the reunions . . . "

"Ah yes," said Kate with relish.

"And then, when we're too old for all that, you might try a second stab of living at Allansfield?"

"I think I might be persuaded, eventually," said Kate. "Talking of which, we shall have to do some explaining there tomorrow."

"Oh, stuff that," Hugh said, kissing her on the back of her neck. "We don't need to explain anything. My mother will let them know, I'm sure of it."

30

"WELL, if you insist on knocking these towers down, Drew . . . " said Henrietta, as Andrew toppled a pile of bricks on to the hearth rug, "you cannot reasonably expect me to build them for you yet again."

"I think he does," said Gabriel. "Isn't that the point? You humour him once by rebuilding them and he expects a repeat performance, *ad nauseam*."

"How does anyone find the patience?" said Henrietta, as Andrew, picking up a large red brick, toddled off towards where Valerie Mackenzie was sitting. Solemnly he handed her the brick.

"Thank you very much, Andrew," said Valerie.

"Send him back to me in ten years' time," said Henrietta, watching as Valerie let Andrew climb up on to the sofa beside her. "No, make that fifteen — and I might be able to help him. You make a much better surrogate grandmother than I do."

"I've just had a bit more practice, that's all," said Valerie, as Andrew began cheerfully to punch one of the cushions. "And you are an irresistible wee thing, aren't you, Andrew?"

"It's the deadly Erskine charm, isn't it?" said Henrietta, sinking back on her heels and looking at the picturesque ruin of near-antique building bricks that Andrew had made on the rug in front of her. Nothing, she had noticed, ever got thrown away at Allansfield. When they had got out the Christmas decorations the day before, she had found packed in old dress boxes a wonderful accumulated glittering mess of at least fifty years' worth of Christmases. She had thought, as she looked at those fragile glass baubles and old scarlet candles (never quite burnt up and so economically put away for next year), how much her own parents would have approved of Allansfield. In certain respects it could not have been more different from the house in Massachusetts she had grown up in, but there was something there that was deeply comfortable and familiar. Moving into Allansfield, even in those early weeks, so fraught with complicated emotions, Henrietta had felt an immediate quietude and a sense of coming home, that not all the traumas of Gabriel's illness could destroy. And this, her first Christmas there, felt like the natural successor to the Christmases of her childhood. She had found herself wishing it might snow, and making (as much to her surprise as to Gabriel's) popcorn to thread into strings to decorate the tree as well as a truly disastrous batch of cookies. The disaster had gratified her at heart; she did not like to think she was too domestically competent.

Andrew had begun to babble in a good-natured way. He was as yet a child of few words, but the noises he was making sounded like a parody of language.

"That sounds distinctly Polish to me," remarked Gabriel. "Polish with a New Zealand accent." Terry, Andrew's nanny, had a most peculiar accent.

"What a dreadful thought," said Henrietta with mock horror. "Oh, what could be worse, Gabriel, an American accent perhaps?"

"I'm learning to live with that," said Gabriel.

"I got told off the other day for saying closet, would you believe?" said Henrietta to Valerie.

"Hardly," said Gabriel, getting up to put another couple of logs on to the fire. "All I said was, 'Oh, do you mean in the press?' — " He broke off, laughing, and said to Valerie, "Please excuse us."

Valerie managed to smile too. For a clearly rather conservative member of the Scottish middle classes, Henrietta considered Valerie was doing extraordinarily well given the peculiar circumstances, dandling her daughter's boyfriend's son on her knee, quite as if he were her own grandchild. Kate had acquired her generous spirit from somewhere, Henrietta supposed, and why not from her mother? They had been diffident about inviting Valerie to spend Christmas at Allansfield, although it had been Gabriel's idea, warmly endorsed by a fax from Kate. She had been in New York since mid-September and would be going back directly after New Year, this time with Hugh in tow, as Lara was off to Poland for a month to show Andrew to her relatives. So Hugh had Andrew for Christmas, but had relinquished his fatherly responsibilities today to go and fetch Kate from the airport. Gabriel, Henrietta and Valerie were doing their best, but Henrietta for her part was sure they would all be glad when the calmly competent Terry got back from her day off in Edinburgh. Gabriel was still not quite up to rushing around after boisterous small children.

The worst of his illness was, however, over. The treatments had finished, and they seemed to have been effective. There would be a few more exhaustive tests in the New Year, before, hopefully, he was at last declared as clear of the wretched thing as he could ever be. Then, when Henrietta had completed her final duties as a Lennox visiting fellow, they planned to go on a long lazy holiday in the spring, to Italy, just as they had promised themselves all those years ago. Henrietta had just discovered it was possible to rent an apartment in the Browning's Casa Guidi in Florence and had, hidden in a drawer upstairs, a nice old edition of *Aurora Leigh* for Gabriel's

Christmas stocking. She would convert him to the Brownings yet. After that they had no settled plans, but Henrietta had already had a letter from the dean of the English faculty at Harvard asking her which courses she wanted to teach next fall. It was a subject she had not yet raised with Gabriel, because she was as yet unsure how she wished him to answer. It was something she would have to deal with soon, she thought, watching as Gabriel relieved Valerie of the now restless Andrew and carried him over to the piano, but quite how she would deal with it she did not know. There was a side of her that never wanted to leave Allansfield again, but she had to go back at some point, for legal reasons as much as anything — her work permit would expire. Now that it seemed they had their future back — while the doctors' discreetly phrased warnings had been in force they had not allowed themselves to think beyond the middle of the following year — they had to decide how they would live it. Asking Gabriel to leave Allansfield and come with her to Boston seemed churlish after all he had been through. They needed some elegant compromise, but Henrietta could not find it yet. Perhaps over the next few days, she consoled herself, the answer would come to her. In the meantime, there was this extraordinary family Christmas to be got on with.

* * *

Kate distinguished herself by falling asleep in the car on the drive back to Allansfield. Hugh decided it was his fault for taking his father's ridiculously comfortable Range Rover instead of his own car. With the heating full on, and the seat reclined, Kate, with jet-lag, had really no other choice than to drift off. The drive from Glasgow airport was not an exciting one at the best of times, and on a wintry afternoon, with the light fading, he felt slightly drowsy himself. But the sight of Kate, her head falling back on the headrest, her mouth slightly open, kept him awake. She had had her hair cut — a short, rather radical crop that made her look even more sleek and animal-like while making her features seem more determined and crisp.

He decided he would get her to sit for a terracotta bust. He had not done any of that sort of modelling since he was a student, but it struck him as an interesting thing to try out. He had been experimenting with all sorts of techniques lately. Even in her absence, he had felt charged by creative enthusiasm. They had taken to faxing drawings to each other rather than attempting to write letters, which had improved his lacklustre draftsmanship no end. Not that he could ever match Kate's exuberant sketches. She had recorded the New York art scene mercilessly, and he was not sure he would be able to keep a straight face in January when he met the originals of her devastating caricatures. She reserved her cruellest lampoons for herself, however, presenting herself as an exaggeratedly skinny figure, dressed always in a black suit and sun glasses, who spoke broad Scots out of balloons and craved Earl Grey tea and Branston pickle.

He rolled over the first cattle grid

at the entrance to the estate and she woke up.

"Have I been asleep?"

"Since Glasgow."

"Oh, sorry," she said, and then yawned. "It must have been all those freebies on the plane." She peered through the windscreen. "Is that snow coming on?"

"Mm . . . it's been raining a bit — yes, you're right, it's turning into snow."

"I thought I'd got away from snow," said Kate.

"You can't be blasé about snow, well not at Allansfield at Christmas," said Hugh. "If this settles, it will look wonderful."

"And I shall rush out and do half a dozen ersatz Sisleys," said Kate.

"I'm not letting you out of my bed, let alone the house," said Hugh. "We've got a lot to catch up on."

"Oh, did I not tell you?" she said flippantly. "Sex is desperately out of fashion in New York."

"Well, this is not New York," he said, and pulled up in front of the house. "Ah, your mother's got here, I see," he added, seeing Kate's mother's car.

"Poor Mum, she must be squirming. This is all so . . . " Kate laughed. "Actually, it's probably much easier for her to take Gabriel as my pseudo father-in-law than ever it was . . . "

She did not continue because Hugh had leant over to kiss her.

"Do we need to go in?" he said, breaking away from her for a moment. "We could just steal over to the cottage and pretend we got stuck in some traffic. I mean, we won't have any peace otherwise. I'm sure it wouldn't be thought of as too bad manners. We haven't seen each other for three months, after all . . . "

Kate laughed and said, laying her hand on his thigh, "Well, if you feel sure that Andrew's being adequately looked after . . . "

"Your mother did all right with you," though Henrietta and Dad, well . . . "

"Henrietta — I can't imagine how she's coping with Andrew," said Kate.

"Well, let's leave her to get some real experience, shall we?" said Hugh, reaching for the ignition key.

"Too late," said Kate with a giggle, as the front door to the house opened. "No peace for the wicked." Then she leant over and whispered in his ear, "Don't worry, Hugh, the thing about jet-lag is that when we finally get to bed my body won't think it's time for bed at all, will it? So perhaps you'd better conserve a little energy yourself — for later."

"Perhaps it's a good thing you've been in New York," said Hugh. "I'm not sure I could cope with you on a day-to-day basis."

★ ★ ★

Gabriel came into their bedroom and found Henrietta brushing out her hair. She had completely transformed the room, something Gabriel had never quite had the courage to do. He had left it very much as his parents had arranged it, with a Georgian sofa table in the window acting as a dressing table for his mother. Henrietta had turned this into a desk, and moved the mirror on to the marble-topped chest of drawers at the side of the room, where it joined a clutter of exotic bottles. Her almost childish weakness for sweet-smelling potions was enchanting to him. She had brought another armchair into the room, and had had sent over from her house in Vermont a large, faded rug made up of plaits of coloured wool, a very handsome old quilt decorated with pineapples and roses, which apparently her grandmother had stitched for her wedding bed, and a small carved wooden loon which she kept on the bedside table. These very North American objects made him feel slightly guilty. They were the sentimental keepsakes of an exile, and every time he saw them he found himself wondering how homesick she actually was. Kate had bought her a bottle of duty-free Bourbon, and she had been in ecstasy about it. It was time to sort that little matter out.

He sat down and watched her pinning up her hair. She had changed for dinner, because they were celebrating Kate's return, and had put on a very dashing tartan silk dress that he had not seen before.

"What do you think of that?" she said, turning to him. "Do I not look like a bona-fide member of the Scottish gentry? The mistress of Allansfield?"

He saw then that she had put on his great-grandmother's drop pearl earrings and choker. He had given her the family jewel case, but she had not before worn any of the pieces.

"Quite," he said, getting up and kissing her on the cheek. "If that's what you want to look like."

"What do you mean?" she said.

"You don't have to," he said. "Look like that, I mean. It does suit you. but it isn't you entirely, is it, Henry?"

"Start again, Gabriel, you've lost me," she said.

"And you're being deliberately obtuse," he said. "What I mean is, what about Dr Winthrop of Harvard? I did happen to notice there was a letter the other day . . . "

"You did, did you? I hope you didn't steam it open and read it."

"No, I just saw the postmark, and it reminded me of what I never quite forget — that you do have a job back there. They'll be expecting you back at some point or other. I'm sure the department is reeling at the loss of you."

"God, no," she said. "Glad to see

532

me go, they were. I have a talent for getting people's backs up, you know that."

Gabriel shook his head and took her hands in his. "Look, what I'm trying to say is, I don't want you to feel that you have to give that up because of me, because of all this."

"Are you saying what I think you are saying?" she said. "You want me to go back to Harvard — you don't want me to quit my job."

"Of course I don't. What I think we should do is go back together."

"You'll give this up? What about the garden, Gabriel?"

"You do have long vacations, I take it? We'll come back then."

"Yes, of course. Oh Gabriel, I can't believe you've just said that. I've been trying to think what to do. I would quit for you, quite gladly, you know."

"Not entirely gladly. You love teaching, don't you? And it is your home, and you have friends and family there. I can't make you give that up."

"I would," she said.

He shook his head. "I shan't let you.

Besides, it is about time I saw something of the world. I've been so damned insular. New England would be a challenge for me. I'll have to find something to do over there, that's all."

"Write a gardening book," said Henrietta, and then laughed. "I can't believe you just suggested that. Oh Gabriel, I do love you so much." She kissed him and then said, "Oh, but there is one little problem. Residency. You'll need a sponsor, a green card, all that stuff. It would probably be easier . . . " She hesitated, smiling slyly, and then, pressing her forehead to his, said, "if we got married."

"Oh, then I could be your faculty wife," he said. "Wouldn't that be fun?" Their arms intertwined, they shook with laughter for a moment. "I'm glad you raised the subject actually, Henry," said Gabriel. "You see, there's something I've been meaning to give you, but I never had the chance." And he took from his pocket the battered ring box containing the small diamond and sapphire ring that his father had grudgingly allowed him to take as an engagement ring for Henrietta.

"This, you see, has had your name on it for nearly thirty years."

★ ★ ★

Before dinner they all sat in the drawing room, drinking old oloroso sherry out of eighteenth-century glasses. Hugh had made up the fire and lit dozens of candles, but he had not drawn the curtains, and through the large windows the dazzling white snow light flooded in, brilliant despite the darkness. Kate stood in the window embrasure, watching the snow falling, drinking in the rich scent of melting wax and wood-smoke.

"You owe me five pounds, Gabriel," Henrietta said. "It was Pope."

"Show me," Gabriel said. Kate turned to see Henrietta handing over a book of quotations to him.

"Five pounds, please."

He glanced at it and gave a slight growl. "Put it on my slate, Henry," he said.

"You're going to run up terrible debts," said Henrietta, taking the book back from him.

"Or I shall stop gambling," said Gabriel.

Hugh laughed. Kate watched him. He was sitting with both the cats jostling for attention on his lap. He was wearing a collarless white shirt and in the candlelight he looked like a figure from a Caravaggio painting. She looked beyond him at the pale walls with the elaborate plasterwork frames, and found herself frowning.

"What are you thinking?" Hugh asked.

"I was thinking these walls need something more on them," said Kate.

"You're right," said Gabriel.

"A mural," said Hugh. "A mural by Kate Mackenzie."

"Oh yes," said Henrietta.

"Kate?" said Hugh.

She strolled into the body of the room and squinted at the wall. There were a few small landscapes hanging there that could easily be moved elsewhere. With those gone, she would be left with three large panels, enticingly blank, to be filled up, little by little, with whatever her imagination could dredge up. It would be difficult — the plasterwork had been designed by Philip Winterfield and could not be trivialised, and the act of balancing form and colour in such a space was certainly a challenge . . .

"It'll take some time," she said.

"Paint a bit every time you come back," said Hugh. "It'll make you keep coming back as well."

"Ha, do you think I'm so flighty?"

"Well, to quote my mother . . . " he began, but Gabriel cut in.

"No, Hugh, please spare us."

"But Hugh," said Kate's mother, "I thought your mum had calmed down a bit."

"She enjoys griping," said Hugh. "She's not as civilised as you are."

"Well, I don't quite see the point of making endless trouble about it," said Valerie. "You are grown-ups with your own minds, aren't you?"

Kate glanced at her mother. She was sitting in one of the bergère chairs, looking more at home with Allansfield than anyone might have expected — but then who could resist the charm of the place? Kate sat down herself on the sofa, and stretched out her hand to Hugh, who took it and lifted it to his lips. He looked down at her intently as he kissed her hand, his eyes shining with affection. Behind him Henrietta began another round of the quotations game that she and Gabriel always seemed to play in their spare moments.

"All right, how about this?"

There is sweet music here that softer
   falls
Than petals from blown roses on
   the grass,
Or night-dews on still waters between
   walls
Of shadowy granite, in a gleaming
   pass;
Music that gentlier on the spirit
   lies,
Than tired eyelids upon tired eyes.

Henrietta sighed when she had finished the quote. "Any offers, ladies and gentlemen?"

"Tennyson," said Hugh and Gabriel almost in unison.

"Oh, I give up!" exclaimed Henrietta, snapping shut the book of quotations.

"You damnable, damnable Erskines! Aren't they infuriating, Kate?"

"Absolutely," said Kate, grinning at Hugh. "But it seems they're unavoidable." She shrugged, and pulled Hugh down on to the sofa beside her, adding, "Yes, a fact of life."

THE END

TO FIGHT THE WILD
Rod Ansell and Rachel Percy

Lost in uncharted Australian bush, Rod Ansell survived by hunting and trapping wild animals, improvising shelter and using all the bushman's skills he knew.

COROMANDEL
Pat Barr

India in the 1830s is a hot, uncomfortable place, where the East India Company still rules. Amelia and her new husband find themselves caught up in the animosities which seethe between the old order and the new.

THE SMALL PARTY
Lillian Beckwith

A frightening journey to safety begins for Ruth and her small party as their island is caught up in the dangers of armed insurrection.

NURSE ALICE IN LOVE
Theresa Charles

Accepting the post of nurse to little Fernie Sherrod, Alice Everton could not guess at the romance, suspense and danger which lay ahead at the Sherrod's isolated estate.

POIROT INVESTIGATES
Agatha Christie

Two things bind these eleven stories together — the brilliance and uncanny skill of the diminutive Belgian detective, and the stupidity of his Watson-like partner, Captain Hastings.

LET LOOSE THE TIGERS
Josephine Cox

Queenie promised to find the long-lost son of the frail, elderly murderess, Hannah Jason. But her enquiries threatened to unlock the cage where crucial secrets had long been held captive.

TIGER TIGER
Frank Ryan

A young man involved in drugs is found murdered. This is the first event which will draw Detective Inspector Sandy Woodings into a whirlpool of murder and deceit.

CAROLINE MINUSCULE
Andrew Taylor

Caroline Minuscule, a medieval script, is the first clue to the whereabouts of a cache of diamonds. The search becomes a deadly kind of fairy story in which several murders have an other-worldly quality.

LONG CHAIN OF DEATH
Sarah Wolf

During the Second World War four American teenagers from the same town join the Army together. Forty-two years later, the son of one of the soldiers realises that someone is systematically wiping out the families of the four men.

THE LISTERDALE MYSTERY
Agatha Christie

Twelve short stories ranging from the light-hearted to the macabre, diverse mysteries ingeniously and plausibly contrived and convincingly unravelled.

TO BE LOVED
Lynne Collins

Andrew married the woman he had always loved despite the knowledge that Sarah married him for reasons of her own. So much heartache could have been avoided if only he had known how vital it was to be loved.

ACCUSED NURSE
Jane Converse

Paula found herself accused of a crime which could cost her her job, her nurse's reputation, and even the man she loved, unless the truth came to light.

THE PLEASURES OF AGE
Robert Morley

The author, British stage and screen star, now eighty, is enjoying the pleasures of age. He has drawn on his experiences to write this witty, entertaining and informative book.

THE VINEGAR SEED
Maureen Peters

The first book in a trilogy which follows the exploits of two sisters who leave Ireland in 1861 to seek their fortune in England.

A VERY PAROCHIAL MURDER
John Wainwright

A mugging in the genteel seaside town turned to murder when the victim died. Then the body of a young tearaway is washed ashore and Detective Inspector Lyle is determined that a second killing will not go unpunished.

DEATH ON A HOT SUMMER NIGHT
Anne Infante

Micky Douglas is either accident-prone or someone is trying to kill him. He finds himself caught in a desperate race to save his ex-wife and others from a ruthless gang.

HOLD DOWN A SHADOW
Geoffrey Jenkins

Maluti Rider, with the help of four of the world's most wanted men, is determined to destroy the Katse Dam and release a killer flood.

THAT NICE MISS SMITH
Nigel Morland

A reconstruction and reassessment of the trial in 1857 of Madeleine Smith, who was acquitted by a verdict of Not Proven of poisoning her lover, Emile L'Angelier.

SEASONS OF MY LIFE
Hannah Hauxwell
and Barry Cockcroft

The story of Hannah Hauxwell's struggle to survive on a desolate farm in the Yorkshire Dales with little money, no electricity and no running water.

TAKING OVER
Shirley Lowe and Angela Ince

A witty insight into what happens when women take over in the boardroom and their husbands take over chores, children and chickenpox.

AFTER MIDNIGHT STORIES,
The Fourth Book Of

A collection of sixteen of the best of today's ghost stories, all different in style and approach but all combining to give the reader that special midnight shiver.

DEATH TRAIN
Robert Byrne

The tale of a freight train out of control and leaking a paralytic nerve gas that turns America's West into a scene of chemical catastrophe in which whole towns are rendered helpless.

THE ADVENTURE
OF THE
CHRISTMAS PUDDING
Agatha Christie

In the introduction to this short story collection the author wrote "This book of Christmas fare may be described as 'The Chef's Selection'. I am the Chef!"

RETURN TO BALANDRA
Grace Driver

Returning to her Caribbean island home, Suzanne looks forward to being with her parents again, but most of all she longs to see Wim van Branden, a coffee planter she has known all her life.

SKINWALKERS
Tony Hillerman

The peace of the land between the sacred mountains is shattered by three murders. Is a 'skinwalker', one who has rejected the harmony of the Navajo way, the murderer?

A PARTICULAR PLACE
Mary Hocking

How is Michael Hoath, newly arrived vicar of St. Hilary's, to meet the demands of his flock and his strained marriage? Further complications follow when he falls hopelessly in love with a married parishioner.

A MATTER OF MISCHIEF
Evelyn Hood

A saga of the weaving folk in 18th century Scotland. Physician Gavin Knox was desperately seeking a cure for the pox that ravaged the slums of Glasgow and Paisley, but his adored wife, Margaret, stood in the way.

DEAD SPIT
Janet Edmonds

Government vet Linus Rintoul attempts to solve a mystery which plunges him into the esoteric world of pedigree dogs, murder and terrorism, and Crufts Dog Show proves to be far more exciting than he had bargained for . . .

A BARROW IN THE BROADWAY
Pamela Evans

Adopted by the Gordillo family, Rosie Goodson watched their business grow from a street barrow to a chain of supermarkets. But passion, bitterness and her unhappy marriage aliented her from them.

THE GOLD AND THE DROSS
Eleanor Farnes

Lorna found it hard to make ends meet for herself and her mother and then by chance she met two men — one a famous author and one a rich banker. But could she really expect to be happy with either man?

THE SONG OF THE PINES
Christina Green

Taken to a Greek island as substitute for David Nicholas's secretary, Annie quickly falls prey to the island's charms and to the charms of both Marcus, the Greek, and David himself.

GOODBYE DOCTOR GARLAND
Marjorie Harte

The story of a woman doctor who gave too much to her profession and almost lost her personal happiness.

DIGBY
Pamela Hill

Welcomed at courts throughout Europe, Kenelm Digby was the particular favourite of the Queen of France, who wanted him to be her lover, but the beautiful Venetia was the mainspring of his life.

PREJUDICED WITNESS
Dilys Gater

Fleur Rowley finds when she leaves London for her 'author's retreat' in the wilds of North Wales that she is drawn, in spite of herself, into an old tragedy.

GENTLE TYRANT
Lucy Gillen

Working as Ross McAdam's secretary, Laura couldn't imagine why his bitchy ex-wife should see her as a rival.

DEAR CAPRICE
Juliet Gray

Clifford Fortune married Caprice but his brother, Luke, knew the marriage was a mistake. He could allow himself to love Caprice blindly but that would be betraying his own brother.

IN PALE BATTALIONS
Robert Goddard

Leonora Galloway has waited all her life to learn the truth about her father, slain on the Somme before she was born, the truth about the death of her mother and the mystery of an unsolved wartime murder.

A DREAM FOR TOMORROW
Grace Goodwin

In her new position as resident nurse at Coombe Magna, Karen Stevens has to bear the emnity of the beautiful Lisa, secretary to the doctor-on-call.

AFTER EMMA
Sheila Hocken

Following the author's previous auto-biographies — EMMA & I, and EMMA & Co., she relates more of the hilarious (and sometimes despairing) antics of her guide dogs.

LEAVE IT TO THE HANGMAN
Bill Knox

Dope, dynamite, guns, currency — whatever it was John Kilburn and his son Pat had known how to get it in or out of England, if the price was right. But their luck changed when one of them killed a cop.

A VIOLENT END
Emma Page

To Chief Inspector Kelsey there was no shortage of suspects when Karen Boland was murdered, and that was before he discovered that she stood to inherit substantially at twenty-one.

SILENCE IN HANOVER CLOSE
Anne Perry

In 1884 Robert York is found brutally murdered at his home in Hanover Close. When, three years later, Inspector Pitt is asked to investigate, the murder remains unsolved.

A RARE BENEDICTINE
Ellis Peters

Three vintage tales of medieval intrigue and treachery featuring the author's monastic sleuth Brother Cadfael.

POIROT'S EARLY CASES
Agatha Christie

In this collection of eighteen stories, Hercule Poirot begins his celebrated career in crime.

THE SILVER LINK
— THE SILKEN LIE
Lynn Granger

Elspeth is determined to preserve her Scottish heritage and the Elliot name, but running Everanlea, a large hill farm, presents problems.